HUNTING THE GREAT CAT

Like snakes they advanced, writhing softly through the brush, until at last Thunder Moon was gripped in the small of the back by a deadly chill. He jerked his head over his shoulder and saw behind him two phosphorescent disks of light, huge as lanterns in the dusk beneath the shadow of the trees. He knew that the hunted had turned hunter. He touched the leg of the boy who was crawling in front of him with the flying tips of his fingers, and made the sign: "Danger is behind us." Then he gripped his rifle.

The brush confined him on either side, and he felt that before he could swing the gun through the crackling leaves, the monster would spring. So, he drew from either hip holster a long-barreled Colt, and cast up through the boughs above him a single glance to the moon-flooded brightness of the sky. Then he turned and planted a bullet straight between the eyes of the beast.

The answer was a roar that made his nerves leap. The giant shadow lurched forward at him. He fell, firing as he dropped, and as he twisted on his side a striped belly drove above him. Into it he sent a forty-four caliber slug, and got to his knees again.

The thought of Standing Antelope was in his mind, but now he saw that the boy was safe at one side of the path. The great tiger had leaped blindly and cleared the bodies of both its enemies. Now it stood in the midst of a patch of stout brush such as that through which Standing Antelope and Thunder Moon had been forcing their way. It seemed like a vast cat, gone mad with rage because a mouse had escaped it, and at the slashing strokes of its forepaws the brush was uprooted, beaten aside, knocked flat.

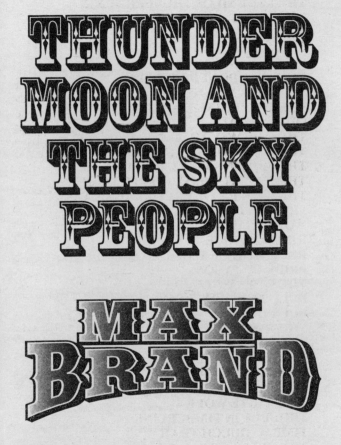

THUNDER MOON AND THE SKY PEOPLE

MAX BRAND

LEISURE BOOKS NEW YORK CITY

A LEISURE BOOK®

January 2000

Published by special arrangement with Golden West Literary Agency.

Dorchester Publishing Co., Inc.
276 Fifth Avenue
New York, NY 10001

The present text is based on the author's original typescript and this book appears now in paperback for the first time as the author wrote it. Published in hardcover by University of Nebraska Press. Acknowledgment is made to Condé Nast Publications, Inc., for their cooperation.

ISBN 0-8439-4673-3

CONTENTS

THUNDER MOON AND THE SKY PEOPLE

FAREWELL, THUNDER MOON

THUNDER MOON AND THE SKY PEOPLE

Chapter One

An Early Ride

The big man at the window, as though fascinated by the flood of light within the room, remained for a long time staring. Finally he turned, and instantly he grappled with the smaller shadow behind him.

"It is I!" whispered the Cheyenne hastily. "It is Standing Antelope. Take your hand from my throat, Thunder Moon!"

He was free, and the two slipped silently through the garden, through the hedges, and back into the adjoining woods where they had left their four horses.

"I, also, have seen," said the boy.

"What?" asked the other.

"I have seen the reason that brought you from the Suhtai and made you travel all these moons into the land of the white men. I have seen his face!"

"You have seen him? Then who is he, Standing Antelope?"

"If he were younger, he would be your brother. But he is too old for that. This is the reason that your skin is pale, Thunder Moon. This is the reason that your ways are not the ways of the Cheyennes. The man who sits in that lodge is your father and you have come this distance to find him."

There was a rattling of hoofs on the hard surface of a bridle path through the woods nearby, and suddenly one of the horses neighed loudly. The riders paused and one of them said loudly, in the English tongue which was only beginning to have meaning to the ear of Thunder Moon, "The horses have broken the pasture fence again. George, go in there and have a look and tell me what you find."

"Yes sir," answered a thicker, huskier voice.

Saddle leather creaked as the servant dismounted; and then there was the noise of the man forcing his way through the brush.

Thunder Moon and his companion, however, already were on the backs of their horses; and the pack animals were taken on the lead. Standing Antelope went first, for he had eyes which, among the Suhtai, were said to see in the dark like a cat's. Softly he wove among the tree trunks but, in spite of all his care, the animals made some noise and there was a sudden hail behind them: "Who's there? Stop!" Then the voice shouted loudly: "Mister Sutton, I see a man on a horse there. There's something wrong!"

"Thieves, George, by heavens!" cried the other. "Stop them! Fire on them with your pistol!"

"Ride!" said Thunder Moon to the boy ahead of him.

At the same instant a gun cracked behind them and a pistol ball hummed above their heads; while a moment later they heard the crashing of brush as "Mister Sutton" jumped his horse in from the roadway.

By this time Standing Antelope had put his pony to full gallop. It was no easy thing to ride with speed through the crowded trees of that copse but, flattening themselves along the necks of their horses, they swept onward at a smart pace. To the rear they heard shouting voices. Then the noise of one horse in pursuit. In a few minutes, as they hurdled low fences and plunged across cultivated fields and through strips of woods, the sounds died out.

On a low hilltop they drew rein. They could hear nothing at first, except the panting of their horses. Then they made out a dim noise of voices from the direction of the great house, and presently there was the cry of dogs.

"I have heard it!" said Thunder Moon in excitement. "The white man hunts with dogs. And now they are coming for us. Ride on, Standing Antelope."

They rode until they came to a sheer slope, at the bottom of which was a considerable stream. It did not stop them; swimming their horses through, they drifted the animals for some time down the shallows on the farther side, then climbed out and up the opposite bank. There they wrung the water from their clothes and listened.

Dawn was beginning as they heard the music of the dog pack swell over the woodland and swing toward them, until the cry of the hounds echoed loud and full over the water.

"If it is your father who lives in the great lodge," said Standing Antelope, "let us go to him. He will give us shelter in his tribe."

"How can I tell that he is my father?" replied Thunder Moon. "Two bulls may have the same look, and yet they

13

may come from different herds. I hardly can speak in his tongue; how could I call him my father? Besides," he added more sternly, "I do not come even to a father and ask for help. The men of the Suhtai are free. They do not cringe like coyotes."

The boy answered a little grimly: "If you are a Suhtai, he is not your father. If he is your father, then you are white and not free. For all white men are slaves. They are slaves to their law at least, as we learned in the wagon train. For their law can whip them, starve them, tie them with rope, or hang them by the neck so that the body and the spirit die together. If you are a Suhtai, you should not be here. If you are a white man and still wish to be free, then go back with me to the Suhtai and live as one of us and remember these people only as one remembers a dream after waking. This is good council, even if I am not a great warrior."

"Peace!" said Thunder Moon. "You speak with a knife in every word. I shall do the thing that comes to me."

They waited, and heard the noise of the hunt break over the river and stream up to them, through the trees. Then they rode through the copse until they came to a winding roadway. On its firm footing the horses flew. A dust cloud swirled up behind them in the morning light; and Thunder Moon laughed with pleasure.

He did not laugh for long, however. For, looking back down the roadway, he saw that a dozen men were riding hard in pursuit, and gaining fast. He had no doubt that his stallion could leave the pursuit safely behind. Instantly he doubted the ability of the Indian ponies to withstand such a challenge and over such a course as this. Even in the distance he could see that the pursuing riders were mounted on animals like his own fine horse. They did not move with a bobbing gallop, like Indian ponies at full speed, but with a long and swinging rhythm they slipped over the ground.

"Full speed!" he called to Standing Antelope.

The boy, with a shout of determination, gave the whip to his pony and the pack animals. They did not need two minutes to see how the matter was coming. Tired by a long journey, with many weeks of labor behind them, the ponies were failing fast. Besides, they had behind them horses of some matchless breed which filled the hearts of the two with wonder and with admiration. Thunder Moon made up his mind at once.

"There a way turns on the right, Standing Antelope," he said. "When we come to it, take that turning. Take the two spare horses with you, and when the time comes I promise you that all those riders shall follow me."

The boy was too well trained to dispute the word of an older warrior. He cast one desperate glance behind him at the danger cloud which was rolling up on them so rapidly.

"I shall lead them away," called Thunder Moon, "and then come back to you and find you. Keep to broken country. The short legs of your ponies cannot match the long legs of those horses behind us. What horses they are! But now they shall see what Sailing Hawk can do."

By a mere pressure of his knees he reduced the pace of the stallion so that he fell well behind; and, turning in the saddle, he drew his rifle from its long holster beneath his right leg. He balanced it in his hand, and finally twitched the butt of it to his shoulder and fired. He smiled grimly, seeing two of the pursuers duck low on the necks of their mounts; for he knew that the ball he sent, though he missed them purposely, must have hummed quite close to their ears.

He waited, then, to see them check their pace, for so any Indian of the plains would have done against such

15

accurate long-range practice as this. They thrust ahead after him more violently than before, as though they were striving to close the gap before he could load again. He who could load and fire almost as rapidly as another Suhtai could whip arrows out of a quiver and onto the string. To prove to the pursuit his skill and the danger of pressing him too closely, he loaded like lightning and discharged a second ball. This time he took a still closer aim, and again the two leaders winced as the ball cut the air between them. Still they kept on.

It turned the heart of Thunder Moon cold with wonder. These were not the tactics of the plains. Then, in a burst of anger, he prepared for a third shot, which should find a target. Not a man—for these men had not harmed him—but a horse was to be his mark. When he took within the sights the reaching, lean, beautiful head of one of the horses, his heart failed him. To shoot such an animal was almost worse than to drive a bullet through the body of a rider.

He glanced ahead. Young Standing Antelope, with his two lead horses, had disappeared down the turn to the right. This was the time, then, to show the pursuit what Sailing Hawk could do. Leaning back a little in the saddle, Thunder Moon called on the stallion, and there was instant response. From hand canter to racing gallop the big chestnut leaped at a single bound.

For a mile at least that dizzy pace was maintained, and then Thunder Moon looked back to see if the forms of his pursuers were in sight. The result was a shock. They were still in sight and if they had lost ground, it was a negligible amount. Their speed still seemed to increase and there were more than the original half dozen riders now. Others seemed to have come in from some side road, and fully fifteen horsemen were pressing behind him.

Keen for the hunt, he heard them shout to one another, their voices tingling faintly through the crisp morning air. It dawned suddenly upon Thunder Moon that this might be his last day of riding.

Chapter Two

Overtaken

As he steadied the stallion for the race, Thunder Moon tried to understand what was happening. Hitherto, when Indians on the plains challenged him, he had been able to draw away from them with ridiculous ease, in spite of his weight in the saddle. Now his bulk was doubtless greater than that of his pursuers, and doubtless the edge of the stallion's speed had been taken by the long, long journey through all weathers and footings. Still it seemed strange that in all the world horses could be found that would keep up with him like this.

The hunt was drawing out behind him, in a string of riders. So much the speed of Sailing Hawk was accomplishing. There was no vast distance between the leader and the last of the group. They were fresh, terribly fresh, the lot of them. Sailing Hawk ran well, and well he would run until he died. In the meantime his strength was going. It was not the beginning but the end of a long day for him.

So Thunder Moon decided to try the effect of cross-country work, and sent the stallion at a neighboring fence. Nobly the big chestnut cleared it, and rushed up a gradual slope beyond toward a copse.

Before he disappeared into the woods, Thunder Moon glanced back and saw the first flight of the hunt drive at the same fence. He smiled, waiting to see the disaster. To his amazement, every one of the horses took the obstacle in their stride, not flinging high in the air like Sailing Hawk, but skimming low, with a certain accustomed air, as though jumping were an old matter in their lives. Certainly it was not so with the stallion, accustomed as he was to the open ranges of the plains. The heart of Thunder Moon sank again.

However, he sent the stallion through the woods, and coming out on the farther side he saw beneath him a stretch of low ground, the surface of which was rosy with the morning light. It was marshland, he could see. Every step of it was glistening with water, and he was forced to turn his horse along the edge of the boggy ground.

A moment later, the hunt poured through the woods. He heard them shout with triumph which had a meaning in it, for Sailing Hawk began to flounder heavily. He had gone almost knee-deep in wet soil.

That was the end. Back to the dry ground he had to turn the stallion and, so turning, he was going straight into the midst of his enemies. There was no need of the rifle here. He thrust it deep in the holster and snatched out the two revolvers which hung at the bow of his saddle. The sway of his body would guide Sailing Hawk as well as reins; each hand was free for a gun, and unless all his long years of training with those difficult weapons had been wasted, there might be a death in every bullet.

Yet it would be hard to fire point-blank upon those men. There was hardly one of them who had not unlimbered rifle or pistol or revolver in turn; but they came toward him now with cheerful shouts, laughing, like careless children at the end of a race for fun. So he held his fire and waited.

"He's going to fight it out, the nervy devil!" called someone. "Don't shoot, boys. We'll talk some sense into his head, or try to. Jack, you're right. That's one of your horses that he's on."

They were in evening clothes, all these youths—though such a term had not entered Thunder Moon's vocabulary—and yet they were such born horsemen that they seemed as much at home in the saddle as if they had been in a ballroom. Clean faced, clear eyed, eager as hounds, they gathered around Thunder Moon, keeping a proper distance from his poised guns.

In the meantime, the man referred to as "Jack" came to the front and eyed Sailing Hawk with a proprietary air.

"Now, my man," he said, "you're caught, and you're caught barehanded. But you've given us a fine hunt. Only how the devil did you manage to make Cyrus take that jump in such spread-eagle style? Get down, give up your guns, and go along with us. You'll get nothing worse than justice, and maybe something better."

"By all means better, Jack," broke in one of the group. "I never knew your Cyrus had such foot. He beat us all."

"My mare was only warming to her work," protested another.

"But you weigh fifty pounds less than that man-mountain."

They chaffed one another gaily.

"Get down," repeated Jack. "Get down, man, when I tell you to. You don't think you can stave off the lot of us, do you?"

19

The English tongue came roughly and slowly to the mind and the lips of Thunder Moon.

"My friend," he said, "you are the chief of this band?"

The other opened his eyes a little more widely.

"Hello!" he said. "This is something special. Am I the chief, he wants to know. Who are you, stranger?"

"I come from the Suhtai," said Thunder Moon gravely.

"Who the devil are the Suhtai? Where do they breed?"

Thunder Moon opened his eyes in turn, for it had not occurred to him that there might be men who did not even know the name of that famous tribe.

"Wherever you come from," said the other, "you've stolen my horse Cyrus. Get off his back, and after that we'll talk."

"You say a thing which is not true," said Thunder Moon sternly. "This horse is not yours."

"Watch him," said Jack to his companions. "He has a grand face for this sort of work. Doesn't move a muscle while he gets out a thing like that. I don't know my own horses, I suppose?" he continued with a chuckle, facing his captive again.

"If he is your horse," said Thunder Moon, "speak to him, and he will come to you."

There was a general shout at this.

"That's right, Jack. Talk to him. Make your horse answer back."

"Hold on," replied Jack. "Maybe the fellow's a halfwit. Let's go easy with him."

He controlled his expression and asked more calmly: "If he is your horse, then he'll come when you call, I suppose?"

"He will, of course," said Thunder Moon.

There was a chorus of whistles.

"Let's see a proof of that."

One brief syllable of guttural Cheyenne was spoken, and Sailing Hawk dropped to his knees. No trick was more necessary or valuable on the prairies, where a warrior might wish to use his pony as a breast-work in case of a fierce attack. There was a general shout of admiration and amazement from the spectators.

"This *is* something special, Sutton!" said one of the young men.

"Special," said Jack Sutton, "but it doesn't change matters. I suppose no one doubts that that's a Sutton chestnut?"

"He looks the part," said a companion, "but, after all, you can't tell what horses may be in other parts of the world. Certainly that's not a Sutton saddle."

"We'll talk over the details later on," said Jack Sutton. "Now, my man, just jump off the horse at once, will you? Throw down your guns."

Thunder Moon made no reply.

"Because if you don't," said Sutton, "we'll have to make you, you know."

"The Suhtai," said Thunder Moon quietly, "die before they give up their guns and their horses. If you fight, some of you must die. In each gun there are six voices."

"Can you believe it?" asked Sutton with growing irritation. "The fool really seems to think he can bluff us out. Now, my friend the horse thief, I'll give you till I count ten before I take you off that horse."

"Friend," answered Thunder Moon, "come one pace nearer to me, and your spirit goes to the Sky People."

It seemed as though Jack Sutton were about to make that step forward, when one of his friends caught him by the arm and jerked him back.

"The beggar means to do it," he exclaimed, "and by the look of him I think that he'd shoot straight."

"Are fifteen of us to stand here stopped by one brazen-faced blackguard?" asked young Sutton in a rising fury.

"Come, Jack," said another. "You're the hope of your house. Don't throw yourself away. Besides, we don't want to murder this nervy rascal. More than that, though, you haven't proved that this is your horse. If he is, he's developed a taste for strange languages. Let me try to handle the case, will you?"

He stepped forward.

"Now my friend," he said, "you see that we have the numbers. And, of course, we can't afford to be outdone by one man. However, we don't want to keep your back against the wall, and we don't want to murder you. Come with us to the colonel's house and let him hear the story. You make good your claim to the horse and the colonel will never give you a shady deal. You know Colonel Sutton, of course? And of course, you can trust him to do what's right?"

Most of this speech was rather beyond the understanding of Thunder Moon. All that was clear to him was that this speaker was apparently acting as peacemaker; and vaguely he gathered that someone called Colonel Sutton was to be the judge. Colonel was a title like chief among the whites. He knew that also.

So he said: "Let us go to the chief. Some of you may ride beside me to see that I do not run away. But no one rides behind me."

"All fair, all square," said the other. "Satisfactory, Jack?"

"I'd rather have the thing settled here," said Sutton. "Looks as though there weren't enough of us to do justice."

"Enough to do murder, Jack, old fellow; but you spell justice a different way, I take it. Come along, boys, and we'll hear the end of this."

Chapter Three

It's a Wise Father

With panting horses, with laughing voices, the party went down the long dusty road.

"That was a run," one said.

"What a burst!"

"Better than fox hunting! The beggar nearly nicked me twice."

"And if he isn't a thief, why did he shoot?"

On the whole, never was there better humor shown by Cheyennes returning from a lucky buffalo hunt than was exhibited now by these fellows who rode so gaily around Thunder Moon. He regarded them not, for his dignity forbade; but all the time, with careful eye, he watched the men who rode on either side of him. Yet, to his surprise, though he had sent two balls so near them, they treated him with perfect good humor. They rode until they came close behind the great house which he had sat down to watch in the middle of the night. Then they turned in, and paused in the arch of the driveway just in front of the mansion.

Since it seemed impossible to get Thunder Moon off his horse, as a compromise they sent into the building for Colonel Sutton. He came at once, his wife beside him.

The sun was just up, the air was cool and brisk, and the roses which twined up the face of the dwelling were

23

showering their fragrance on the breeze. Thunder Moon looked up to the pair standing on the verandah of the house, between the tall, thin, white pillars which framed its entrance. The man, whom they called colonel, was big, powerful of shoulder, grim of expression, and his hair looked silver in that rosy light; by his side, the woman seemed wonderfully thin and delicate. He supported her on his arm, and she seemed frightened, as she looked down on this array of wild young men on their prancing horses. The ball had lasted late at Sutton House and, when the last farewells were said and breakfast finished, they had come to this bright hour of sunrise.

"You'll have to be judge as well as colonel, sir," said young Jack Sutton, standing on the steps beneath his parents. "We've caught a fellow who's a horse thief, as I live. And if that isn't Cyrus that he's riding, any one may have me."

The colonel came forward to the edge of the porch.

"The blaze of Cyrus is not so short and wide as that," he said almost instantly. "That isn't one of our horses, Jack. But for all the world, he's one of the strain. That dark chestnut isn't a frequent color. Young man, where did you get that horse?"

The question was clear enough to Thunder Moon, and yet he could make no answer. For a strange new emotion swelled in his throat and stifled him, and he could not take his eyes from the face of the colonel or from that of the little white-haired woman beside him.

"There were two of them in the woods yonder," explained Jack Sutton. "George and I guessed them out and they ran for it. Two men and four horses, and two of the nags with big packs. You'd better look to the silver, mother. This rascal here, when we took after him, opened fire on us. No man shoots to kill unless he has a guilty conscience. That stands for common sense, I suppose."

Thunder Moon was stirred to answer, and he said: "I did not shoot to kill."

"Come, come!" broke in another youngster, though still good humoredly. "Two balls whistled within an inch of my ears. What would you call that?"

"Very interesting," said the colonel. "Very interesting. Come up here, young man, and let me have a talk with you about yourself, and what brought you loitering in the woods, yonder, long after midnight."

"He won't dismount," broke in Sutton. "Sticks to Cyrus as though he were glued there."

His words were instantly disproved, for Thunder Moon leaped from the back of his horse and, pausing only to sweep his buffalo robe about him, advanced with stately stride toward the porch. Sailing Hawk came close in his rear, and when his master mounted the steps the stallion went up behind him.

There was a little murmur of wonder. The colonel could not help smiling, and his eyes shone. This was a companionship between man and beast such as he loved to see. Not for nothing had he spent the better part of his life and his talents in the rearing of Thoroughbreds.

The man from the plains and the colonel stood face to face. There was not a fraction of an inch of difference between them in height; there was no difference in the bulk of their shoulders, which made even the magnificent dimensions of young Jack seem paltry by comparison.

"Now, sir," said the colonel, "let's have an understanding. In the first place, I don't really suspect you. Because a fellow who can train a horse as you've trained that one can't be a sneak thief or a burglar. Where did you get that stallion?"

Thunder Moon, slowly, stretched forth his hand to the west. His blazing eyes did not leave the face of Sutton for a moment.

"West, eh?" said the colonel. "Well, I didn't know that they raised such animals farther west than my estate. How far west, my friend?"

It was difficult for Thunder Moon to speak, so much was his mind loaded with many reflections. Then he said, slowly, as he had made his gesture: "Far west . . . beyond the rivers . . . in the land of the Cheyennes."

There was a faint cry—a moan—and the colonel's wife drooped and swayed.

The colonel was swift to turn to her, and his son was still swifter, but the gliding step of Thunder Moon was swiftest of all. He passed between them and caught her in his arms, and held her lightly.

"Now, by heaven!" cried Jack Sutton, vastly alarmed, and reached for his pocket pistol. He did not draw it, however.

For the stranger, standing tall and solemn before them, had altered most wonderfully—a light appeared to break from his eyes and his breast heaved.

"She is not sick," he said quietly. "But the woman is fallen in darkness. She will see again, later on."

"She's overtaxed herself with this infernal ball!" cried the colonel, pale with fear. "Confound me if I'll have dance music in this house again. These waltzes are fit for a madhouse; besides, they're indecent. Martha, do you hear me? Are you better, my dear?"

There was no answer. Mrs. Sutton lay limp, and her head would have fallen back had it not been for the supporting arm of Thunder Moon.

"Give her to me!" exclaimed the colonel.

A dark, gloomy glance was all that answered him, and Thunder Moon stepped past him into the house.

The high rooms soared above him. Beneath his feet was a soft carpeting that mysteriously muffled the fall of his feet—and yet it was not turf. He carried the unconscious woman to a couch, laid her there and kneeled by her side.

"I won't have him touch her," said Jack Sutton furiously. "I won't have it! Why, the common rascal . . . the scoundrel of a thief!"

"Be still, Jack," said his father. "Don't be ridiculous. He treats her as though she were precious. There's something not common about this man."

"Hello!" cried Jack. "What's in that flask? Are we going to have her poisoned? What's in that leather pouch?"

Thunder Moon turned his head toward the younger man and answered: "Water . . . brother!"

There was something in the intonation of his voice, and something in the dark glance of his eyes, that made Jack Sutton catch his breath and look to his father as though for advice.

At the taste of the cold water, the colonel's wife stirred, moaned a little, opened her eyes, and stared wildly up to the stern, dark face above her.

"Randolf!" breathed Mrs. Sutton.

At that, the colonel moved between her and Thunder Moon.

"What is it?" he asked. "What is it, Martha? Did something upset you? What's wrong?"

"I can't think. I don't dare to think! I'm going mad, Randolf."

"Ruth," said Jack, to a girl who now ran into the room, "see what you can do. Something's wrong with mother . . . and I think it's that rascally horse thief fellow who's done it."

"Who?" cried the girl.

27

She turned and saw Thunder Moon, wrapped again in his robe, his arms folded beneath it, his bowed head turned toward the woman on the couch.

"Ah!" gasped Ruth Sutton, and she clung close to her brother.

"Good Lord!" exclaimed Jack, irritated rather than sympathetic. "He's not a ghost. He's a man, you know. He's not a ghost."

"Are you sure?" stammered Ruth. "Are you sure that he's not a ghost?"

Jack Sutton had stood enough. He strode up to Thunder Moon.

"Sir," he said, "whatever happens, I'm afraid that you're a scoundrel. But before you're one minute older, I'll have your name, and who you are, and where you've come from, and all the rest of it."

"Brother," said the tall man, and again there was a strange intonation of the word, "on the plains in the West the Suhtai know me, and they have given me a name."

"Suhtai, again. And who the devil are the Suhtai?"

"Are you better Martha?" asked the colonel. "Steady, now. Has this fellow upset you at all? Is it he? I know the Suhtai. And so do some of our troopers, worse luck. They're a tribe of the Cheyennes, Jack."

"God bless me!" Jack cried, and moved a pace away. "I thought there was something odd about him. Are you an Indian, then?"

"What I am," said Thunder Moon, raising his head, "I cannot tell. And as for my name, I have come a great journey; I have traveled for more than one moon, to come at last to this place to learn what my name might be."

"Why, the fellow has no wits, Indian or white," said

28

Jack Sutton. "He says that he's come here to find out what his name may be."

"I knew it!" cried the colonel's wife.

"I knew it! I knew it!" cried Ruth, pointing with a rigid arm.

What the colonel's wife knew, they could not discover instantly, for at that moment she fainted dead away, and the colonel, much alarmed, called for help.

Jack Sutton was too excited to be of assistance, but he took his sister by both arms.

"I almost think there's some foolish plot between you and mother," he said. "I really almost think there is. What the devil is it that you and she know that has to do with this fellow, that neither of you has ever seen before?"

"Oh, you're blind! You're utterly blind!" cried Ruth. "Both of you are blind. Look at him again."

"I see him. What of it? What of it?"

"Dad," Ruth exclaimed, running to her father and clinging to his arm as he helped his wife back to the couch.

"Let me alone. Your mother's dying, Ruth, I think."

"She's not . . . joy doesn't kill. Dad, won't you look at him? Won't you see?"

"See what, child? Damn it, Ruth, what's in your mind? What is this mystery?"

"Don't you understand? He says that he's come back here to find his name. . . ."

"That's nonsense."

"But it isn't. I know what his name is."

"The devil you do. What is it, then?"

"It's William Sutton, and he's your own son. Don't you see? He's come back. He's come back to you!"

29

Chapter Four

Where's the Proof

Whatever the emotion of the others, when the excited Ruth Sutton made this startling announcement, no one felt more keenly than her brother Jack, though his sentiment may have differed from the rest. For as the eldest child, the only son, he had naturally expected to come into the majority of his father's great fortune. Though perhaps Jack was no worse than the next man, this announcement thrust him literally to the heart. Whatever his first thought might have been, certainly his first movement was to touch the pocket pistol which he carried with him always, like most of the gay lads of that time. Perhaps he recalled a picture seen a little earlier that morning, when this same danger to his hopes then stood with the marsh behind him and fifteen armed men before. One shot would have done a great work, at that lucky time. Now the time was past.

There was no opportunity for the others to observe the expression on the face of Jack, for they were all too busily engaged on the subject of this suspected horse thief.

The poor colonel, utterly taken aback, caught at his wife and drew her to him, and stared for a moment at Thunder Moon as though he were looking at a leveled gun rather than at a lost son. Ruth Sutton recoiled from this great man of the prairies. Her keen eyes had seen a resemblance, but the mark of the wilderness was visibly on him, and she was frightened.

Only Mrs. Sutton, weakest of all a moment before, went unafraid to the strange visitor. She drew herself out of the arms of the colonel and, going to Thunder Moon, she took those terrible hands which Pawnee and Comanche and stalwart Crow knew and feared. She drew close to him, peering keenly into his eyes.

"You are William!" she cried softly. "Ah . . . you are my dear boy come back to us. Only tell me. Will you tell me?"

"My heart is sad," said Thunder Moon, and he fought back an impulse to take her in his arms. "My heart is sad. All that I know is what an old man of the Suhtai told me. He sent me here. But of myself I know nothing."

"You see, Father," broke in the matter-of-fact voice of Jack, "we'd better go a bit slowly. God knows no one wants him to be the true Sutton more than I do. But we have to have more proof than the sketchy resemblance of two faces. We have to have something better than that. You see . . . he isn't a bit sure himself."

"How could he be sure? He was an infant when he was stolen!" exclaimed the colonel, who was turning from deadly white to violent crimson.

"As for the word of some lying Indian . . . some old chatterer. . . ."

"I tell you, Jack, you mustn't speak that way!" cried Mrs. Sutton. "Isn't there a call of blood to blood? I felt it when I first saw him. Randolf, do something. Let me be sure."

The colonel hesitated, looked about wildly, and finally said: "Let's try to be calm. Let's make no mistake. It would be too horrible to think that we had him back again and then find it was only a fraud. You understand?

31

Let's try to work out the testimony. Somebody tell someone to give those young fools outdoors some mint juleps . . . or anything that will keep them quiet. We have to think this out. We have to feel our way to the truth."

"Here! Here's the truth!" Mrs. Sutton said.

She snapped open a little pendant at her throat and showed a miniature which was painted on the inside, showing her husband as he had been when he was a young man. The colonel looked at it gravely and long; then he raised his eyes as though afraid of what he must see. The result was a start of amazement and joy.

"By heaven!" cried the colonel, "he's most like! He's certainly most like. Jack, examine this. William, if you are he, forgive us for going slowly now . . . but once you've been admitted to our hearts . . . then there'll be no uprooting you."

"I speak little English; talk slow," said Thunder Moon, knitting his brows with the effort of listening.

"Poor boy!" breathed Mrs. Sutton. "My poor, darling, honest boy. Oh, I believe you."

"Damn it, Martha! Will you be still?" cried her husband. "Are you going to make a baby of him before we're sure that the thing is settled?"

"If he's not Indian," said Jack, "I'd like to know where he got that color of skin. He's dark enough to be a red man . . . or a smoky mulatto, I'd say. Could the sun do that?"

Thunder Moon turned his head and looked calmly, judicially, toward the youth.

"You'll have trouble on your hands in a moment, Jack," said the colonel. "He doesn't like that way you have of putting things, you can see."

"My dear sir," said the boy, "I don't want to stand between a brother and the light. But I'm simply trying to make us all use our common sense. That's only fair and right, I take it. What do you say to that, Ruth?"

She, pale, tense, eager, raised a hand as though to brush the question away from her; all her soul was busied in devouring this stranger-brother with her glance.

Thunder Moon said in his deep voice—a soft voice, but one which filled the room with a slight tremor—'I understand. My face is dark. You want to know why. You ask the sun. He will tell you."

Then, letting his robe fall from his shoulders, he stripped off his shirt of antelope skin with a single gesture. Brightly and beautifully beaded was that shirt so that it glistened like a parti-colored piece of chain-mail in his hand, but there were no eyes just now for the fine shirt for which Big Hard Face had paid five good horses, five horses ready for the war trail, a strong knife, and a painted horn. Instead, there was a general gasp, as every glance fastened upon the body of Thunder Moon, naked to the waist.

If he had broken any conventions, he was totally unconscious of it. He raised an arm along which the interlacing muscles slipped and stirred with an uncanny life of their own, and he pointed to his body.

"See," he said, "that my skin is not all dark. This is paler. Yet I see that it is not as pale as yours."

With that last honest admission, he waved his hand toward them as though inviting their closer inspection.

The colonel, indeed, had taken a quick stride toward him, with an exclamation of admiration; but little Mrs. Sutton seemed overwhelmed by this revelation. Ruth clasped her hands together, and Jack moved back a little and became rigid, as though he were responding to a challenge with proud defiance.

"It isn't all a question of color," said Jack firmly. "Of course, if he's an impostor, he wouldn't be such a fool as to come unless his skin were actually white. But the thing to decide on is the testimony. I don't know. It's rather queer, though. Taking a fellow on the strength of his face. Such things have been tried before. Clever devils! Use a striking family resemblance to worm their way into a million or so. Cheap at twice the price, you know."

"Would an impostor be ignorant of the English language, Jack?" asked the colonel sharply.

"Ah, sir," and Jack smiled, "of course he'll *say* that he is a Cheyenne. Why . . . that's not hard to say. Just be reasonable, please. You know that I could learn a bit of Indian ways, pick up a few of their words, and then say that I had passed most of my life on the prairies. Why not? Then I wouldn't have to answer a lot of embarrassing questions as to where I'd spent my days. Isn't that clear?"

It was, after all, a telling point. Some of the enthusiasm faded from the gentle eyes of Mrs. Sutton, and she looked anxiously to her husband.

He saw the appeal in her glance.

"I know, Martha!" he said. "I'm doing my best. But I'm not a prophet, and I can't look through the secrets of twenty years as if they were glass, you know. Look here, my young friend, tell us how we can be sure that you have spent all of this time with the Cheyennes?"

"I cannot understand," said Thunder Moon simply.

"I thought he wouldn't," sneered Jack.

"I say," repeated the colonel more loudly, making a vital effort to be clear, "will you tell us how we can know that you really spent these years with the Cheyennes?"

"And by the way," said Jack, "if you can talk just as well, you might put on your clothes, you know."

Thunder Moon with one gesture, as he had removed

the shirt, donned it again. He swept the robe around his shoulders.

"Young man," he said sternly to Jack, "what coups have you counted and what scalps have you taken that you raise your voice and that you talk when chiefs are here?"

Even Jack blinked a little at this, but recovering himself instantly, he said coldly: "That's well done. Clever, by gad! Worthy of the stage, and a big stage. But we want some good, and sound, actual proof that you've been with the Cheyennes all this time."

The color had been growing slowly in the face of Thunder Moon and now it became a dangerously dark crimson; and his eyes glittered as he stared at Jack.

"Do not ask me; do not ask my friends," he said at last. "Ask the enemies of my people. Ask Sioux, ask Comanches, ask Pawnees, ask Crows. They know my face. They have seen it in the battle. No man has asked: where is Thunder Moon in the battle? No, for they have seen me. So ask them and bring them here. They will tell you if I am a Suhtai."

There was a stunned silence after this remark so filled with conviction and disdain.

Jack, who in a way was playing desperately high for stakes that were worth winning, now broke in: "After all, my friend, you can't come over us as easily as that. Of course, we're a thousand miles or so from the hunting grounds of the Sioux and the rest of 'em, whatever you called 'em. Facts, however, are facts. And it seems to me that you should be able to give us some proofs . . . some plain proofs . . . that you've been with the Cheyennes all this time under the name of Thunder Moon, or whatever you may be called, or say you are called."

"Steady, Jack," said the colonel. "By gad, he looks a bit dangerous, just now."

Chapter Five

Recognition

Now the excitement of Thunder Moon had been growing with great rapidity, for he felt the constant check of the questioning and sardonic Jack. It came in such a manner, too, that he was half maddened by it. Since he was a youngster and first distinguished himself in feats of arms among the Suhtai, his name had been known far and wide, not in his own tribe only but all through the Cheyenne nation and among the neighboring tribes. Now his very identity was questioned—not so much as the son of this stern-faced Colonel Sutton but as Thunder Moon himself.

He could endure it no longer. The passion that was rising in him must find some outlet and, since he could not act, he must speak. Since he must speak, it had to be of himself. It was a theme on which he was not much practiced, for when the other braves at the end of the warpath danced the scalp dance and told of their exploits or when the coup stick was passed around, Thunder Moon was nearly always silent. Something in his nature had prevented him from joining in these self-acclaiming outbursts. Now he began to speak. He drew back a little until he stood close to the wall. He did not dance, as a pure-blooded Cheyenne would have done, but as passion and fury and exultation mastered him, his voice became a sort of chanting rhythm, and his whole body swayed in unison. Much of what he said came in Cheyenne; sometimes he used what English words he had absorbed into his vocabulary; but in some manner, as a very intense speaker usually can do, he made his audience realize what he was saying.

"I do not talk of common warriors. I only speak of chiefs who have counted five coups, and taken scalps. Make medicine and call down their spirits. Let them tell you what I am.

"I am Thunder Moon, of the Suhtai.

"The eagle feathers flowed behind the head of Little Wolf, and the bravest Pawnees were around him. The hearts of the Suhtai were sick, seeing those heroes charge. But a young warrior went out to meet that charge. He called to the Sky People and they gave him great strength; they turned the bullets and the spear points. Like a snake through the grass he wove through the men of the Pawnees. He came to Little Wolf. 'Pawnee, your spear I headed with burned wood; its point crumbles on my shield. My lance is in your heart.'

"And all the Suhtai shouted: 'Thunder Moon!'

"Three hundred warriors followed Waiting Horse. Among the Comanches he was the strongest man; scalps dried continually in the smoke of his teepee, and with scalps all his clothes were fringed. He did not go upon the warpath alone; but I, alone, met him. The eagle stood still in the wind and the buzzards circled above us, watching. 'Waiting Horse, your medicine is weak. The Sky People fly with my bullet and send it into your brains. You lie on the plain with a broken forehead and your spirit slips out and flies on the wind.' 'It is Thunder Moon!' cry the Comanches.

"Now in his lodge a great Pawnee was very sad. His brothers and his two uncles were dead, and when he asked his heart who had killed them his heart answered:

'Thunder Moon!' He made great medicine. He asked the greatest medicine men of the Pawnees to help him, and they gave him strength to go out and harry the Suhtai.

" 'Ah-hai! What is wrong with the horses of the Suhtai? Why do they throw up their heads and gallop away? The cunning Pawnee wolves are among them.' Fast they ride, but faster rides Thunder Moon. 'Turn back, Three Spotted Elks. Turn back and avenge your three dead kinsmen. Their spirits are crying to you in that strong wind. They are giving you power.'

"He is a brave man. He has heard their voices and turned back from among the flying horses. Now, Sky People, how shall I kill this man? I offer him to you as a sacrifice.

" 'Kill him only with your knife, Thunder Moon.'

"So let it be! His arrows stick in my shield. His arrows hiss at my ear. He has thrown away his bow and seized his strong war club, stained with blood. Your war club is strong, Three Spotted Elks, but my hand is stronger. My knife is in your throat. Sky People, accept his blood; this is my sacrifice.

"Behold, now, the Comanche camp sleeps. All the lodges are white under the moon. All the new lodges are shining and bright. There is a shadow among them. Beware, Comanches, for it is Thunder Moon. He steals from lodge to lodge. He comes to the medicine teepee and there sits Yellow Man grinning, the great spirit, the metal wizard. I take him up and carry him away. With his medicine he calls his people to follow me. Your medicine is weak, Yellow Man. I throw you into the deep water. I carry only your arm away with me so that the Sky People may laugh when they see you with only one arm. I ride away, and with me I carry the fortunes of the Comanches.

"But who are these men whose hair flows to their waist or waves in the wind behind them as they ride? They are Crows, tall and noble of aspect. But none is so tall and none is so noble as Gray Thunder. The ground shakes before him and the waters stand still and shrink to let him pass.

" 'Now, my brothers, let us charge the Suhtai, for I see a great man among them. It is Thunder Moon, and he has killed many of our people. Charge beside me, my blood brothers.'

"Noble warriors, brave Crows from the mountains, my heart swells to see you. Come swiftly. I am waiting. I shall not run away. In my hands are guns having six voices apiece. Now they speak to you. What, do you fall down when you hear them? Three men fall, and the rest are daunted, but not Gray Thunder.

"Sky People, save him for my hands! With my hands I shall kill him. My bare hands must destroy him. Ha, Gray Thunder, your bullet has missed me. Your rifle as a club is lighter than a piece of rotted wood. I pluck it from you. Now, my hand against your hand. Ask mercy, and you shall live to die by the hands of the Suhtai women. He will not ask mercy. He bites like a wolf at my wrists. But now it is over. He is dead. Come back, you Crows, and bury your dead chief. Why do you run away so fast? He is dead, and his scalp will be taken, and his soul will vanish in the wind.

"Such things I have done. Hear me, you people! My name is not something which has to be asked after on the plains. All the tribes know it. Sky People, give these white men a sign that I do not lie. Sky People, if my medicine is strong, hear me! If ever I have sacrificed to you guns and strong lances and painted robes and beaded suits, send them a sign!"

To this strange narration, half story and half mad

chant, the Suttons had listened with great eyes, silent, crushed with wonder and with fear. Now, as the speaker raised his voice in a shout, there was a tremendous answer from without: a horse neighed like many trumpets blowing together; hoofs clattered on the wooden steps; the porch quivered; and through the window was thrust the head of Sailing Hawk, searching for the master whose voice he had heard.

Thunder Moon laughed with joyous triumph.

"Sky People, I thank you!" he cried. "This is the sign. Now will you believe me?"

Believe him? They were almost too frightened to disbelieve.

Mrs. Sutton and Ruth drew closer to each other, but the colonel listened with shining eyes.

Before he could speak, however, it seemed as though the Sky People, to whom Thunder Moon appealed, had sent a more visible sign and one more easily understood. For up the driveway came young Standing Antelope, his hands tied behind him, his feet bound in his stirrups, and a smear of blood on one side of his head. With him were the half dozen men who had captured him—not spruce young gentlemen like those who had hunted Thunder Moon, but rough, brown-faced men in rude clothes.

"Here's number two," said Jack, willing to break the trance which had fallen on all in the room. "Here's the second of 'em. There are the three horses. Now may we get at something. It's Tom Colfax who's brought them in."

They could hear Tom speaking to the scattered group of men in front of the house.

"Here's a rank Cheyenne, gentlemen. Dog-gone me if he ain't. I was starting out with the rest of the boys here and our guns for a hunt when we seen this fellow jump a fence, but his pony wouldn't clear it. He came down with a slam. And we picked him up. I been enough years on the plains to talk some Cheyenne. And I gathered from his lingo that he might have a friend over here. Anybody know what he means?"

They led Tom Colfax in. He stood at the door, hat in hand.

"Colonel Sutton, sir, the Cheyennes always was the wildest and far-ridingest red devils on the plains, but I never thought that they'd come raiding as far as this."

The colonel went to him in haste.

"You know the Cheyennes, Tom?"

"I've traded with 'em. I know a parcel of them, of course. This boy opened up when he heard me talk his own lingo, and he says that he's the son of Three Bears. I know Three Bears. An upstanding Indian as I ever seen."

"Look!" said the colonel, and he took Tom by the arm and turned him a little. "Do you know this man?"

He pointed to Thunder Moon, who still stood near the wall. The effect upon Tom Colfax was amazing. He started back with an oath and at the same instant drew a great, old-fashioned horse pistol.

"Know him?" he gasped. "Know him?"

"I mean what I say, man," the colonel said. "This is more important than it may seem. Do you know the name of this man?"

"Know him?" echoed Tom. "I never seen him except once, and in the distance, but every man on the prairies knows him or knows about him. Why, Colonel, this is him that's strung his war trails from the Rio Grande to Canada. If I ain't a half-wit and lost my eyes, this is the right bower and the best bet and the long arm of the Suhtai and the whole dog-gone Cheyenne nation!"

"His name!" said the colonel. "What's his name, man?"

"Ain't I told you enough to place his name? His name is Thunder Moon. What else would it be? And if I was you, Colonel, I'd have the militia out and bury this Suhtai under ten feet of solid rock. Otherwise you'll be waking up one of these nights . . . you and about twenty more . . . to find that you're all spirits singin' on your way to heaven. This is a bad boy, sir, and he makes all his marks in blood!"

Chapter Six

William, Big Indian

Mrs. Sutton had heard and seen more than her nerves could stand, and she broke into hysterical weeping at this point. The colonel bade his daughter take her mother from the room. Then he left Jack with Thunder Moon, and he took Tom Colfax into his private study.

"Tom," he said, "this is a serious moment."

"Sir," said Tom, "I got eyes and ears enough to understand that. But I feel kind of in a dream . . . after seeing that red devil in your house!"

"But is he red?"

"Is he red?" asked Tom, more bewildered than ever. "Why . . . well, he's a half-breed, maybe. He *does* look a little pale."

"If you know him, do you know his father?"

"The longest hand you ever seen in a trade. Of course I know Big Hard Face."

"Big Hard Face?"

42

"Their way of saying December."

"Do you know the mother of this boy, then?"

"Her? No, I don't."

"Did you ever hear of her?"

"Matter of fact, Big Hard Face don't live with a squaw."

"Then how does he come to have a son?"

"The ways of an Indian ain't our ways with women and children, Colonel Sutton. Maybe he just picked up the boy some place. Maybe he adopted him."

The colonel caught his breath.

"That's all you know?"

"No, it ain't half. I can tell you about Thunder Moon all day. Why, they've had articles about him in the papers. He's the only Cheyenne that don't count silly coups and that don't take scalps, and. . . ."

"What of his honesty?"

"The Suhtai are an honest lot. And Thunder Moon's word is better than gold."

"He wouldn't lie?"

"I don't say he wouldn't. But the last yarn I heard about him was that his worst enemy among the Pawnees trusted Thunder Moon enough to come right into the Suhtai camp. But I can tell you how he's raised hell from Mexico to. . . ."

The colonel lifted a rather unsteady hand.

"I think that I've heard enough about that already. As a matter of fact, Tom, it begins to appear that this man, this wild Cheyenne, is really the child who was stolen from my house more than twenty years ago."

Tom Colfax opened his mouth and eyes.

"Does he say that?" he asked.

"He does."

"If it's a lie," said Tom slowly, "it's the queerest lie that I ever heard tell of. They ain't a match to it any

43

place. For what would bring a Suhtai a thousand miles, pretty near, to claim you for a father? Why should he pick you out?"

"You'd believe him? You know Indian nature, Tom."

"Leastways," observed Tom dryly, "it wasn't *money* that I got out of my stay on the plains."

"Go with me and let him tell the story simply to us. Do you think that you could spot a lying Indian?"

"I dunno. But I could make a fine try."

They went back to Thunder Moon, and found him with folded arms standing against the wall just where they had left him, while Jack, a very nervous lad, fidgeted in a chair.

"Thunder Moon," said the colonel, "I want you to tell us, clearly, just what the old man of the Suhtai told you."

Thunder Moon answered: "He had no squaw. He had no child. He was no longer a boy. So he went off to do some great thing before he died. He rode a great distance. No great thing came to him to be done. He came to the land of the white men. He rode among their lands. Then he came to a great house, and near the house he saw better horses than he ever had seen before. He saw that the great thing he was led to do was to take some of those horses. So he took the best. He waited until dark in the woods near the house. There he saw a woman come out and leave a child under a tree. He thought he would go and take the scalp. The scalp of a white man is good to have."

"Good heavens," breathed the colonel.

"But when he went to the child, it held up its hands to him and laughed. His heart became soft. He carried the boy away and raised him in his lodge. That is the story as it was told to me."

"Colfax," called the colonel sharply.

"Sir," said Tom Colfax, "if this here man is lying, I'm a fool that knows nothing."

The colonel drew a breath. "I have gone slowly," he said to Thunder Moon. "Even now, perhaps, we have no testimony that would stand in a court. But you ride a horse that may well have descended from my stock. You have a distinct resemblance to me. Your skin is white. You have been raised as an Indian. More than that, there is something in my heart that speaks to you, William! Come with me, and we'll find your mother."

"It's settled?" asked Jack, springing up.

"Certainly it's settled, my boy. Do you object to my decision?"

"I don't know," Jack Sutton said slowly. "It may not be sound reasoning. But . . . if you've made up your mind, that settles everything. William, I've held back and made things rather hard for you. Will you shake hands to show that you forgive me?"

Thunder Moon paused, and said in his grave way: "In the lodge of Big Hard Face he was called my father, and White Crow was a mother to me; but I never have had a brother. Our blood is the same. Let our hearts be the same, too."

He took the hand of Jack with a strong pressure.

They went up to the room of Mrs. Sutton. The colonel rapped, and the door instantly was thrown open by Ruth.

She shrank at the sight of the tall warrior.

"Ruth my dear," said the colonel, "unless God has blinded me terribly, this is no Cheyenne Indian. He is a Sutton, the heir of Sutton Hall, and your own brother."

"Mother!" Ruth cried. "It's true. I was right. I was right!"

She took Thunder Moon's hand.

"Come quickly! I've put mother to bed and she

45

mustn't get up. Come quickly. Oh, Father, what a day for us! William, my dear big Indian!"

She drew him along, laughing up at him, to the door of a big room. Inside, Thunder Moon saw a large bed, and a small feminine form half rising from it, and the sunlight streaming through the window, glittering on her white hair.

"Do you mean it, Ruth?" Then, seeing Thunder Moon, the mother cried: "My dear boy!" and her arms went out to him.

The colonel would have entered behind his son; but his daughter, with a finer tact, held up her hand and warned him back.

As she closed the door, softly, they saw Thunder Moon moving across the floor with a long, slow step— the Indian's peculiar stride, the toes touching the ground first, and the footfall making no noise whatever.

Then, as the door closed, they heard Mrs. Sutton crying: "My darling. My poor baby!"

Ruth began to laugh, a little wildly. "Did you hear?" she said. " 'Baby' . . . to a monster like that. 'Baby' to that terrible man-slayer."

Father and daughter went to the window together, their arms around one another, and their throats so choked that they could not speak. Looking down to the back terrace, behind the house, they saw Jack walking slowly up and down, his hands clasped behind him and his head bowed low.

"Poor Jack," said the colonel. "He's taking it very hard, indeed."

Ruth said nothing. She merely watched with an anxious eye, and shook her head a little.

Chapter Seven

A New World

Why should sorrow be beautiful or beauty sad? Thunder Moon in the bedchamber of his mother went through such an agony of joy and of love and of yearning that the muscles of his throat swelled and ached. Though not ten intelligent words were spoken at that interview, the soul of the Cheyenne was reborn the soul of a white man, as it had been in the beginning.

At last he sat by her bed and held her hand, and she looked up to him with love; possessing him, reading in his face as in an endless book, sometimes with tears in her eyes, cherishing him, and sometimes holding her breath and trembling a little as she contemplated his power of self-control. From the steady mask of his face, it seemed that nothing had touched him in the slightest degree in this interview; but she saw that he could not meet her eyes steadily, and by that she guessed that his stern nature was troubled to the bottom.

"William," she said.

There was no response.

"Thunder Moon!"

He looked quickly at her.

"Are you happy?"

"Yes."

"Are you sad?"

"Yes."

47

"Why are you sad, my dear?"

"Because I have found my people, and lost my people."

"They never really were yours."

"My tongue is their tongue; and part of my heart is their heart."

"I understand. But when you have our speech, then it will be different. There will be many new things for you to learn. You will have a great deal of patience, dear?"

"Yes."

"Now I have kept you long enough. Go to your father. He is a stern man, William. But you will find that there is a great deal of love and tenderness under his sternness. Also . . . your brother is young; and is still younger than he seems. Will you remember that?"

"Yes."

"You may have to forgive him very often."

"I understand," said the warrior. "He has been the only son of a great chief. The lodge and the medicine pipes and all the horses have been his to look forward to."

A faint, sad smile crossed the face of Mrs. Sutton. "A little time will make everything right," she said. "I trust in time and . . . in the goodness of men. Now go to your father, dear. But come back to me often. I have not drawn your picture in my mind. Not completely. It will take me years of looking to make up for lost time. Good bye, dear."

When Thunder Moon left his mother's room he found that the wild news had gone forth in every direction, and the Sutton ball was being continued through the day as a sort of impromptu reception. Already half of the young blades of the neighborhood had taken part in the chase, and the news of what they had captured had been spread. Newcomers began to arrive; farmers on plodding horses; dashing boys of any age; sedate landholders and plantation workers. Just as Thunder Moon came out into the upper hall, there was a screech of wheels turning sharply on the graveled road in front of the house, and Ruth Sutton went to her new brother and drew him to the window so that he could look down.

"You see how many people are happy because you've come home at last?" she asked, and she pointed down to the growing crowd.

Three four-in-hands had just torn up the driveway, one after the other, and the filmy clouds of dust which they had raised were just blowing away in snatches under the cuffing hand of the wind. Those vehicles were loaded with people, and Thunder Moon stared at them with wonder. They looked a different kind of being from those he had been accustomed to. They seemed more delicately made, more slender, and even their voices had a fragile sound in his ear.

Suddenly he stretched forth his long arm.

"What do you see, my boy?" asked the colonel.

"I see," said Thunder Moon, "the woman who should be my squaw."

Ah, fickle-hearted Thunder Moon. What of the Omissis girl with the braided hair like red metal? What of her? Has her memory been dismissed so quickly?

"Hello!" the colonel said. "That *is* rapid work."

He was not altogether pleased, and he cast a worried glance at Ruth, as though a woman should know best how such an affair as this should be managed, and how serious this symptom might be. Ruth, laughing silently behind her brother's back, shook her head as a token that his was not such a dangerous affair, after all.

"Which one, William, dear?" she asked.

"That one . . . that one!" he said. "That one with the face like a flower."

"Oh! It's pretty little Jacqueline Manners. Of course it would be she. She *is* a darling, Father, isn't she?"

"Is it she?" asked the colonel, beginning to smile in turn. "That one with the flowers in her hat?"

Thunder Moon looked at him with eyes of wonder. "No, it is that one . . . she gets down from the wagon now."

"Heavens!" said Ruth Sutton, "it's Charlotte."

Thunder Moon stepped back from the window with a black brow. "She is the squaw of another man, then?" he asked.

"You haven't wasted your time with the Cheyennes," said Ruth. "That's Charlotte Keene. Every young man in the state has asked her to consider him."

At this news Thunder Moon shrugged his shoulders, as much as to say that a battle not already lost still might be fought out. Then he was taken to his room, for the colonel and his daughter had to go down to receive these thronging guests.

First of all, a rapid fire of orders was given to several grinning, delighted Negroes. They went scampering here and there, bringing in several suits of the colonel's clothes. There was only one request from the warrior, and that was that he might have young Standing Antelope brought to him. While the garments were being laid out by the servants, Standing Antelope entered, and his eyes flashed with joy when he saw his friend before him.

"I thought that they were talking and jabbering and getting ready to turn me over to the squaws for torture," said Standing Antelope, "and I thought that they were bringing me just now to the place where I was to die."

"And what of me, Standing Antelope?"

"I listened to hear your death song, but I thought that the wind might have blown the sound of it away from my ears. But behold, brother, our hands are free.

Through the hole in that wall we may escape and climb down to the ground. There are fast horses everywhere. Never have I seen so many so fine. And with two knife thrusts we can make these two black men silent."

"Do not touch them, Standing Antelope. Touch no one in this house; every one is under my protection."

"Ha?" cried the boy.

"This place is my lodge," said Thunder Moon. "It is given to me to live in."

"It is very well," replied the boy. "I understand. The great chief understands that you are a part of his family."

"Yes, and so does his squaw, who was my mother."

"That is good," said the boy without any enthusiasm, "and how great a sacrifice will this chief and his squaws and his warriors make to Tarawa because he has led you back to them?"

"I cannot tell," said Thunder Moon, troubled. "All these people laugh and talk much like children in the street of the Suhtai town, but I have not heard them speak a great deal of the spirits. There is not much religion in them, and I have seen no making of medicine, and I have heard no promises of sacrifice. However, you and I must take care of that, for otherwise the Sky People will be very angry."

"You and I?" said the boy. "Ah, Thunder Moon, you have come home to your teepee, and you have your people around you. They seem to me very strange. And though I hope that you may be happy with them, I must go back to our nation."

"Peace!" said the older warrior. "You are young and you cannot think for yourself. But I have seen many fine squaws and you shall pick out one for yourself, and I shall buy her with many horses. Then, if you must go back one day to our people, you may travel with a woman and with the horses I shall give to you, and many guns, and when you come back to the Suhtai you will be a great and a rich man, and you will tell Big Hard Face and White Crow how to follow the trail in order to come to me."

This conciliatory speech the boy listened to, only half convinced, but the overwhelming authority of Thunder Moon kept him from answering immediately. He said, pointing suddenly, "Thunder Moon!"

"Aye, brother?"

"The medicine of these people is very terrible and wonderful. Look! There is a pool of water standing on one edge."

For, at this moment, one of the Negroes had uncurtained a tall mirror that stood at one end of the room. Both the wanderers stared at this apparition with horror. Thunder Moon looked suddenly at the ceiling. "Sky People," he said, "if you are angry with me, do not send this miracle as a sign. If you are angry because I am changing my tongue and my dress, I shall give them up. I shall return to the Suhtai. No, Standing Antelope. I think it is not a bad sign." So saying, he began to advance, though slowly and with much trepidation, while the boy shrank close to the window, ready for flight at the first sign of danger. Thunder Moon at last stretched out his hand and touched the cool surface of the glass. "Now I know!" he cried, straightening himself. "It is like the little mirrors that the traders sell; it is like those, made large."

At this there was a convulsive burst of laughter from the two Negroes. It died in a shriek of fear, for Standing Antelope, recovering from his terror the instant that he learned the true nature of the miracle, seized one of the valets by his woolly head and at the same time presented a knife at his throat.

Chapter Eight

A Warrior in Captivity

'Black dog!" said the young warrior. "Do you laugh at two warriors of the Suhtai?"

"Don't touch him! Take away your knife," said Thunder Moon, not displeased at this touch of discipline, however. "Does he not belong to my father? The anger of a chief is very great if one of his warriors is touched by the knife of a stranger."

"Warrior?" snarled the young Suhtai, in great contempt, as he released his captive. "Warrior? A creature like this?" He thrust home his knife in its sheath with a snapping sound as the hilt rapped the leather. "What warriors are these, brother?"

Thunder Moon considered. "We are in a strange country, friend," he said. "Their ways are not our ways, and their speech is not our speech. They are hard to understand. They are even as hard to understand as the tight clothes which they wear. However, when in a Comanche lodge, eat like a Comanche."

"It is a proverb and a true saying," admitted Standing Antelope with a grimace. "However, it would have done me a great pleasure to see a little of the blood under that black skin. Look at them now. They are very frightened. We could laugh now if we wished."

"Do not laugh at a coward," reproved Thunder Moon. "The curse of Tarawa already is upon them. Now I must

53

put on these robes. What medicine is in them, do you think?"

A bath had been prepared by the servants and Thunder Moon sat in the tub and for the first time in his life scrubbed himself with soap. Burnished and glowing from a rub with a rough towel, he came out to Standing Antelope. "I am a lighter man," he said. "My heart is better. There is no harm in this medicine, Standing Antelope."

"For my part," said the boy, "I cannot see why men should sit still in a bowl when they might swim in a river. Besides, this is hot water and steam baths are good, as the medicine men say, but hot water always is bad."

"With the Comanches, be a Comanche," repeated Thunder Moon. "Have no fear, Standing Antelope. But what has become of the black men? Have you frightened them away?"

"I only looked at them once or twice," grinned the boy," 'and they backed away through that door."

"You are a young wolf among the village dogs," chuckled Thunder Moon. "How am I to arrange these medicine clothes?"

He got them on, in some fashion. They were not a bad fit, for Colonel Sutton was a big man, famous for his strength; yet his coat was very tight upon his new-found son. Up to the neck, Thunder Moon was a civilized white man; but he knew nothing of the manipulation of a cravat. His great brown throat rose like a column, and over his shoulders flowed a tide of wild black hair. His toilet was not completed by these labors, however, for, feeling that something still was lacking, he made a little paint with the materials which he carried on his belt and decorated his face in a becoming manner. Then he reviewed himself in the mirror with much gravity.

"How do I appear, Standing Antelope?" he asked.

"Above the shoulders, like a great warrior of the Suhtai," said the boy instantly. "But the rest. . . ." He made a gesture to indicate his displeasure and disdain. "You are neither a white man nor an Indian," he said. "You will see. They will laugh at you."

Thunder Moon looked again, anxiously, but he could not see in what manner he was ridiculous. Therefore, he picked up his robe and flung it over his shoulders, and from a packet which was a part of his equipment, he selected a few of his best eagle feathers and arranged them in his hair—an effect which materially increased his height. When he had finished thus arraying himself, he turned his attention to his young companion, but Standing Antelope, finding that the day was warm, was neatly and efficiently clad in a breech-clout, with his robe flung over one shoulder. Thunder Moon regarded him with attention.

"I never have seen a white man dressed as you are dressed now, Standing Antelope, except the squaw man High Creek, who married the daughter of Lame Eagle. What will they say when they see you?"

"What will the braves of the Suhtai say when they know how Thunder Moon has changed himself!" cried the boy indignantly. "Besides, what is wrong with me? Except that I need a little paint?"

So saying, he borrowed some from Thunder Moon, daubed himself over each eye and turned himself instantly into a hideous mask.

"That is much better," said Thunder Moon approvingly. "Now I think we can go out and let them see us."

"Oh, my Father," cried the boy, "you who have harried the Comanches in their far southland, and made the

Crows tremble, and the Pawnees to run like dogs, do you have a care in your mind, and do you wonder how these white strangers may look on you, and what they will say?"

Thunder Moon finished combing his long, black locks and tying again the band which circled his forehead to keep the hair from falling across his face. He had no adequate answer for the boy, so he merely replied: "There are many things which you are too young to understand, my son. Give me my war belt, and then go down before me."

Standing Antelope handed to his companion the belt which supported the two heavy Colts and the hunting knife of Thunder Moon. This the warrior fastened about his hips and gave the finishing touch to his costume.

With Standing Antelope leading the way, they left the room and crossed the hall. They were about to go downstairs, when they encountered two Negresses, housemaids, who screamed at the sight of them—then turned and fled.

"Ha," murmured Thunder Moon. "All these black people have the souls of birds, my son. They run and tremble at a clapping of hands."

"I could not tell," replied Standing Antelope, "but it seemed to me that they screamed more from laughter than from fear."

"Laughter?" said Thunder Moon, coming to an abrupt halt and staring at his companion. "Laughter? At me?"

The idea startled and enraged him so much that he folded himself in his robe and strode on down the stairs in silent indignation. A moment later he was in the midst of a sensation. All the lower rooms of the house were now filled with eager-eyed, whispering friends and neighbors, all come to congratulate the colonel upon this miraculous recovery of a lost son; and even Mrs. Sutton, recovering rapidly from her weakness, had come down to be among her kind friends.

Into that audience walked Standing Antelope, garbed chiefly in the clothes which God had given him at birth, and with a beautifully made buffalo robe, flung lightly over one shoulder, because the day was warm. Standing Antelope was very young and he did not respect these strangers; otherwise he would have stalked in as Thunder Moon did behind him with his robe gathered carefully around him. People were stunned, and, though they managed to keep their faces, it was only by looking down at the floor.

It was not an old district, as has been said, but it had been settled by very old families, moving here from more easterly parts of the South. There was a lesser proportion of small landholders in the region than in most parts of the country. When the new lands were opened to safe settlement, purchasers had come and bought in great blocks, notably as Colonel Sutton had done so many years before, so that this was a region of big estates rather than of many farms.

Those who bought had come from the cream of an older society, and they brought into their new environment the manners with which they had been raised. Therefore, Thunder Moon could walk in on them with the hideous mask of a Suhtai and dressed in the clothes of Colonel Sutton without provoking a smile from the men or an exclamation from the ladies. There was an interchange of glances, but that was all, while Thunder Moon looked gravely around him, then raised his right hand solemnly and gave them all: "How!" One or two, not quite ignorant of Indians and Indian ways, at least by hearsay, returned the greeting, but the rest were silent.

Mrs. Sutton, amazed, though she had tried to prepare

her guests for something strange, was unable to stir, but the colonel rose valiantly to the situation. He took his new-found son in tow and escorted him around the rooms. The introductions were not altogether without result.

"Mister Kilpatrick is a very old friend of mine, William."

"And of yours, too, my dear boy," said old Kilpatrick. "Remember me, William?"

"If you are my friend," said Thunder Moon in a grave, loud voice, which reached to every corner of the room, "tell me if all these women have some big medicine? Why do they sit, while the braves stand?"

At this blow, the colonel flinched a little; and the murmur of conversation ceased for an instant, but was immediately resumed. "Here are Mister and Missus Stanley Graham, our neighbors, William."

"How," said Thunder Moon; and then adopted the white man's etiquette by seizing the hand of Mr. Stanley Graham and nearly crushing its bones in his terrible grip.

"Is this your squaw?" asked Thunder Moon, as the face of young Graham went white with pain.

"Yes," said Stanley Graham politely.

"Tell her to bring me water, friend," said Thunder Moon. "I am thirsty, for the clothes of a white man are hot to wear."

"One moment," said the colonel, biting his lip. "A servant. . . . "

"I'm very happy to get a glass of water," said Mrs. Stanley Graham, and went off with the pleasantest of smiles, and returned with the water.

Thunder Moon took it at a draught. "Thank you," he said to Stanley Graham.

"I think," observed old Mr. Kilpatrick, "that the weaker sex is about to be put in its right place."

Chapter Nine

Two Points of View

A moment later Standing Antelope, who was following his leader through these mazes, spoke abruptly to his companion, and Thunder Moon translated to his father: "What is wrong with the legs of Standing Antelope? Why do the braves and the squaws stare at them?"

There was a stifled burst of laughter and Thunder Moon turned a dangerous eye to locate the noise. The laughter ceased.

"There is nothing wrong," declared the colonel in much haste. "All is well, my son."

He carried Thunder Moon farther into the crowd. Faces began to blur in the eyes of Thunder Moon. He was a stranger in a strange land, and yet all these people spoke to him with the utmost cordiality. Sometimes, at his replies, there were little compressions of the lips, and sometimes there were slight changes of color, but on the whole he noticed nothing very wrong. Those who are not accustomed to diamonds think them little better than bits of glass.

It did not occur to Thunder Moon as strange that the party began to break up suddenly, and that people began to hurry away. So Indians came and went at a feast. There was only one ominous form to him. That was his brother, Jack, who was always somewhere in the background, with a white face which wore a continual faint sneer, or a smile which was like a sneer. Then there was his sister, Ruth, who seemed half amused and half pained. It was easy for him to speak to her. As the last of the guests moved away, he crooked his finger. Obediently, she came to him.

"Are the strangers all gone?" he asked.

"Yes."

He sat down cross-legged on the edge of the carpet. He produced his pipe and filled it.

"Bring me a coal," he commanded.

Readily, she brought what he wanted. He blew a puff of smoke toward the floor, and another toward the ceiling.

"Peace to this lodge," said Thunder Moon, "and peace to all the people in it. May their robes never rot with mold and may the buffalo never fail them in hunting season. Now, sister, tell me what came of the woman with the flower face?"

"Of Charlotte Keene?"

"You called her that. The name is hard to say."

"She was here with the others. Didn't you meet her?"

"Sometimes many clouds hide the mountains," observed Thunder Moon gloomily. "Where is the colonel chief?"

"Do you mean . . . our Father?"

"Yes."

"I'll call him for you."

Thunder Moon leaped to his feet and touched her shoulder with his iron hand. "Girl," he said, "is it proper for a great chief to be called to his son; or for a mother to be called to her daughter? Go, and I follow you."

So Ruth led the way, and did not smile; and soft-footed Standing Antelope followed to where the colonel and his wife sat in the library, in close and anxious consultation. Thunder Moon, in the doorway, paused.

"How!" he said.

"How!" said the colonel gravely.

"Oh, my Father, is this teepee filled or is it free for me to come in to you?"

"Come in, William. Come in."

Thunder Moon strode in. "Send away the women!" he said.

"You had better go for a moment," said the colonel. "And you, Ruth. These ways will have to be endured for a time. Then we'll begin to make a few alterations."

Mrs. Sutton and her daughter left; but Thunder Moon, turning a little, followed the form of his mother with a smile. She, looking back at the doorway, saw the smile. All was well between them.

The door closed. Thunder Moon had sent Standing Antelope away; he was alone with his father.

"There is no shadow on the mind of my father?" asked Thunder Moon, with a keen glance.

"No!" The colonel hesitated, but he found the word at last.

"Shall we smoke together?" asked Thunder Moon.

"Yes, if you will. Sit on this chair, my boy, not on the floor."

"I am not an old man," said Thunder Moon, "and my legs are still strong enough to support me. However," he added with instant and instinctive courtesy, "you do sit on the chair, my Father. You have fought in many battles. How many coups the colonel chief has counted and how many scalps he has taken. But he has been wounded, and he has had the spear head of the enemy in his flesh. Therefore, sit on the chair, my Father. It will be easier for you."

"Have I been wounded? Who has told you that?" asked the colonel, turning curious.

"My eye is not the eye of Standing Antelope," said

Max Brand

Thunder Moon, "and it is true that the Suhtai have called me a blind man. Yet I can see what is put in my hand . . . or a cloud in the sky . . . or the rising sun. Therefore, my Father, I could see that your left leg was more tired than the right."

The colonel started. Many and many a year ago a bullet had torn through that unlucky left leg, but he had thought that all traces of a limp had disappeared from his gait long since.

"When the knife," went on Thunder Moon, "cuts in the soft flesh of the throat, it is a danger."

"Could you see that scar? My boy, you're a hawk."

"And the right side of my father is weak. Perhaps he was struck there, also?"

"By heavens," said the colonel, "your mother has been telling you about these things."

"My mother?" said Thunder Moon, surprised. "We did not talk."

"No?"

"Except with our eyes and with our hearts," said Thunder Moon gently. "What are words? They cannot speak of love."

The colonel looked intently at his older son. In another this would be a speech something more than flowery, but the grave honesty of Thunder Moon could not be doubted. He simply was translating as well as he knew how from his old dialect into his new one. "She did not tell you that I was wounded in the right side? How do you guess it then? Do you look through cloth, my boy?"

"The old pine is still strong," said Thunder Moon. "It will not fall during the lifetime of a man. Yet it has begun to lean. It is not standing on a mountainside, and yet it is leaning to the right. Why does it lean, my Father?"

62

"You mean that I incline a little to the right?" said the colonel, straightening his shoulders. "I don't think so, William."

"When you stand," said Thunder Moon, smiling.

"Blind?" said the colonel. "You are a mind reader. Well, sit on the floor if you insist. Will you have some of this tobacco?"

"No, Father, but shall we smoke your pipe or mine? This tobacco of mine is a good medicine. It is a dream tobacco. Old Flying Crow had a dream, and the head of a buffalo rose above water and told him where to get the bark to mix with this tobacco. He gave me some, because I had helped his son in a battle."

"Let us smoke your tobacco then," said the colonel, interested. "But why should we have only one pipe, my lad? I'm fond of this old black pipe of mine."

"How does wisdom come except with time?" asked Thunder Moon. "Lo, I am young. The years have not carried me very far down the stream, and it may be that your pipe is better. But a long stem makes a cool smoke," he went on, fitting the stem into the pipe bowl. "Also, this is a gift of the Sky People. Low Cloud made this pipe in the old days. The Crows took it from him when they killed and scalped him. Then Sleeping Wolf, the Pawnee, took the scalp of the Crow who had it, and with that scalp he took the pipe of Low Cloud. Then the Sky People gave Sleeping Wolf into my hands. As he died, he told me the story of the scalps and the pipe. I found the body of Low Cloud, two days dead. I fitted the scalp back on his head. I raised him on a platform. I put weapons beside him and killed a horse beneath him. So his spirit rode off to hunt the buffalo over the blue fields of the sky. His pipe has been good medicine to me ever since."

The colonel was silent for a moment. He had loved

63

war and battle all his days, and yet this calm reference to a triple killing as a mere part of a story about a pipe made his blood run cold.

"All this is well," he said, "so we'll smoke your pipe, my boy. This old one of mine? Why, I've never done a thing for it except to cut out the cake once in a while, and polish it up a bit. It hasn't a bit of meaning except that I've smoked it these many years."

"It is not really medicine, then?" asked Thunder Moon, opening his eyes.

"Not a whit."

Thunder Moon blushed for his father, and he said hastily: "However, many a strong and rich man will use a cheap thing. But let us smoke this pipe of mine."

He lighted it with a flint and steel, showering sparks on a bit of dry tinder. Then he blew the customary puffs to the earth spirits and the Sky People, and passed the pipe reverently to his father, holding it by both hands, the pipe stem horizontal.

"That is the way to hold it," said Thunder Moon. "The Pawnee taught me before he died."

"Was he your friend?" asked the colonel, trying not to make a wry face as the horrible taste of tobacco entered his mouth. "Was he your friend before he died, my boy?"

"He was my friend," said Thunder Moon gravely. "His scalp was safe on his head. His spirit could fly to Tarawa and give thanks. I took no scalps."

"You took no scalps?" asked the colonel, brightening a great deal.

"A dead man cannot lift his knife to fight," said Thunder Moon. "And who can scalp the living?" After this simple and satisfactory explanation, he went on smoothly enough. "Now I shall tell you why I have

64

come to speak to you this morning. Are you ready to hear me?"

"Yes."

"In your keeping there are many horses, my Father. You have harried your enemies and wisely stolen their horses. Many a brave walks to the hunt because the colonel chief has stolen his horses and his mules. I have seen them on your lands."

"Bought and raised," broke in the colonel, growing a little hot of face. "I hope that not one of them has been stolen."

At this Thunder Moon opened his eyes a little. Again he blushed for his father and said hastily: "Well let it be so. I have heard before of men who love a bought horse as well as one that is nobly stolen from an enemy."

"*Nobly* stolen?" gasped the colonel.

"What is nobler?" asked Thunder Moon. "What is better than to ride, and make an enemy walk? Well, but the truth is that you have many horses and many mules?"

"That is very true. I am mighty glad to say that I have many of them."

"In my own land and among my own people," said Thunder Moon, "I, also, have many ponies. They are of the best Comanche breed, small and strong and tireless. Now give me ten of your horses, and I shall give you in return as many of my ponies as you wish to have in payment when I can send for them."

"You want ten horses?" asked the colonel. "You shall have as big a riding string as you want, dear lad, as a matter of course. But I'm curious. Why do you want ten horses?"

Thunder Moon stirred a little, and impassive as he kept his face, he could not prevent a slight shadow from crossing it. "I understand," he said, "my father is about to ride on the warpath. He has need of all of his horses to mount his young men when he goes to take scalps. I am sorry that I asked. Forget that I have begged ten horses from you."

"Good God!" exclaimed the colonel. "Am I refusing you the first request you've ever made to me? No, no William. A hundred horses if you want them. Take a hundred. I only asked . . . why, lad, there's no harm in a question is there?"

"A hundred?" said Thunder Moon, smiling. "This is very well. I do not think that I shall need so many. But you are kind. The Sky People have brought me to a good lodge and to a kind father. I, Thunder Moon, call them to hear my words. I shall not forget this kindness."

Here there was a loud clamor outside at the rear of the house, and then a frightened voice calling at the door of the library: "Mass' Colonel! Murder! Murder! Come quick!"

The colonel rushed from the room with Thunder Moon behind him and, running out the rear door, they had sight of the cause of the disturbance. Perched in a fork of a tall tree was a very frightened Negro, and on the ground beneath him stood Standing Antelope, with a rifle at the ready in his hands.

Chapter Ten

Red Men and White

"That young red devil will get himself hanged!" exclaimed the colonel. "Don't let him shoot, William."

"Friend!" Standing Antelope was calling in ringing Cheyenne, "come down from the tree. I shall give you a running start of fifty paces toward the forest. If I tag you with a bullet before you get into shelter, then the game is mine; but if you get away, then you may laugh at me again."

"Brother," said Thunder Moon, "is this well?"

"Look!" the angry boy said. "That black man laughed at me and pointed at my legs. When I told him that that was wrong, he pointed his gun at me and shouted. So I only took the gun away from him, and he ran up that tree like a wild cat. Is a Suhtai brave to be laughed at by every fool?"

"Give me the gun," said Thunder Moon and, taking it, he went on: "Do we know, Standing Antelope, all that goes through the mind of a Comanche or a Pawnee?"

"No," said the boy, "nor do we care."

"But they are raised as we are raised," said Thunder Moon, "and they live to do the same work on the warpath. But if we cannot know them, how can we know these people with white skins? They laugh a great deal and mean very little. Their tongues will start wagging at every little thing that happens. A leaf cannot fall without bringing a word from them. But every time a dead leaf rustles and they laugh at it, are you going to kill a man?"

"What is more fair?" the boy asked. "He had a gun. I took it from him, and counted a coup upon him while he was still alive. For this I shall sing my song and dance my dance among the Suhtai. But afterward why should I not kill him, yes, and scalp him, too? All this is according to the law of the Suhtai. Is he of my tribe? Or is he my brother raised in my father's lodge?"

"You speak like a good Suhtai," said Thunder Moon, "but now we are not among the Cheyennes, and if you killed the man, they would call it murder, as if a Suhtai brave should kill his wife or his father."

The boy shuddered. "That is something to hear, but not to understand," he said. "Is it true?"

"It is true."

Thunder Moon turned to the colonel: "Let me talk for a while with my friend."

"Do it," said the colonel. "We can't have such things around my plantation, William. It simply won't do. Every slave on the place will run away from me if I let such a wild cat loose to run around and claw them."

"They laughed and pointed at him," said Thunder Moon. "That is not fair. If they were on the plains, Standing Antelope would have taken many of their scalps before this time. Let them treat him like a man and he will treat them like brothers."

"Arrange it with him as you please," said the colonel, "but if he is to stay here for any length of time, it would be a very good idea to dress him as the other people are dressed in this part of the world . . . and to cut his hair as well."

He added the last hint with an involuntary glance at the flowing locks of his son.

"To cut his hair?" exclaimed Thunder Moon. "How could he go back to his people with short hair? They would call him a Pawnee and the little boys would follow him and point their fingers."

The colonel sighed. "Tell him to be more quiet, then," he insisted. "When he's in doubt, tell him to come and ask you what to do. When you're ready to speak to me again William, I shall be in the library. I am working there today."

"Only tell me," said Thunder Moon, "where I can find the lodge of the chief who is the father of the young girl, Charlotte Keene?"

The colonel glanced sharply at his son, and then he smiled a little.

"I think that you'll want to call there before long," he said. "Well, when the time comes, we'll take you over, or have the Keenes in for dinner. No finer people in the world than the Keenes, my lad, and I'm glad that you have an eye for them. They live five miles down the road. It's the white house with the long front and the columns in front . . . very like mine. You couldn't miss it."

The colonel went back into the house and Thunder Moon said to the boy, whose head was still hanging with sullen anger: "Go with me, Standing Antelope, and show me if you have forgotten how to catch a horse."

"My feet still carry me," and the youngster smiled, "and I am not blind. Let us go, Thunder Moon."

At the fence of the broad pastures, they looked over the horse herd and Thunder Moon, sitting on the topmost rail, checked over the ones which he wished to select. "There is no reason," he said, "why a man should spend the finest horses in a herd to make a purchase. A horse is a horse. Take the young mare, yonder, to begin with. Ah, Standing Antelope, what horses these are. No wonder that the heart of Big Hard Face swelled in his breast when he looked on these chestnuts. How many dozens of generations have men lived and worked to breed such animals?"

"They are the gift of Tarawa," said Standing Antelope, coming back and leading the mare which had been selected first. "They are the gift of the Sky People, because it is plain that no men could breed such horses as these. The great chief, your father, must have very strong medicine."

"He has," said Thunder Moon, proud of his family for almost the first time since his return to the home of his race. "It is not hard to catch these ponies, Standing Antelope."

"Look!" the boy said. "They come to the hands like dogs. They have fine eyes. And see how they step, touching the grass with their toes as they walk. And see how the muscles work in their shoulders. Ha-hai, Thunder Moon, if they did not belong to the father of a friend of mine, I should slip down to this field some black night and in the morning . . . well, they would be eating grass in another place."

Thunder Moon smiled in broadest sympathy. "Young wolf!" he said, "follow another herd. This is not the place to fatten your hollow ribs. Now get that tall gelding which looks a little weak in the flanks, and the colt which is low in the croup, also. . . ."

So the ten were selected and gathered in a group, and Thunder Moon mounted his war horse, the great Sailing Hawk, and rode off, with Standing Antelope on his own pony. They went straight down the highway until they came before the long, low facade of the Keene mansion. They turned into the driveway, and Thunder Moon tethered the horses to the hitching rack which stood at one side. That done, he and Standing Antelope swung into

70

the saddle and galloped back—not directly back to Sutton House, but through the country by a winding way that carried then carelessly and freely here and there. For they needed to talk to one another. They had not been long in the house of the white man, but already they were feeling the galling bondage of civilization.

Chapter Eleven

Ten Horses for a Lady

In the meantime, a string of beautiful chestnuts, sleek and bright in the sunshine, was being conducted back to Sutton house by the Keene servants, and Judge Keene himself, mightily perturbed, hurried on ahead, riding his fastest mount. When he came to Sutton House, he asked to see his neighbor at once, and was brought into the presence of the colonel, on whose face there was a mingling of brightness and of shadow.

"I'm glad to have one moment alone with you, my dear Randolf," said the judge. "I've wanted to have a chance to congratulate you again, quietly, personally, on the great joy that has come to you today. God knows, Randolf, that no man ever less deserved that such a tragedy should come to him as came to you twenty years ago. No man deserves more to have the effects of it undone. And here your boy is back among us."

"Thank you, thank you," muttered the colonel. "But I hardly know how long he'll stay."

"What?"

"I mean it. He's like a wild tiger. He starts away at everything or shows his claws. I only pray that he doesn't murder someone . . . he or the little devil of a Cheyenne that's with him."

The judge rubbed his chin. "I understand you," he said.

"I suppose," said the colonel, coloring a little, "that the entire countryside is still laughing over this morning's affair?"

"Laughing?" the judge cried hotly, "laughing at such a thing as the return of my dear Sutton's first-born son? By heavens, Randolf, I'd horsewhip the rascal who dared to laugh at such a thing in my presence."

"Would you? I think that you would. But everyone in this neighborhood is not a Keene."

"No, sir," answered the hot-headed judge, "nor would we want to include every Tom, Dick, and Harry in our family, I hope."

"You always must eat a bit of fire," exclaimed the colonel. "Well, God bless you, Dick. You do me good. At the same time, it was a shocking thing, rather, to see him come down the stairs . . . civilized up to the neck . . . and wild Indian above."

"Shocking? Not at all."

"But I thought that perhaps there was an ironical little prophecy in it . . . that we would be able to civilize him in manners and speech and dress, but that probably we'd never be able to change his heart and his mind. I couldn't help feeling that there might be something of a symbol in the picture he made as he came down the stairs . . . with that hideously painted face and the . . . well, Dick, it nearly stopped my heart."

"You're wrong," the judge said. "You're wrong. Of course, every man is a little oversensitive about the appearance of his family. But every man and woman in your house this morning must have known that there was a Sutton heart in the wild man who came down those stairs."

"But, my friend, to remark about the women sitting . . ."

"Tush! Do you expect an Indian to sit up and spout Shakespeare? Give the lad a little time. Remember, he is Indian by education. And what a presence he has, Randolf. What a stature of a man. If I had a son, I would want one like that."

"What, with horrible paint on his face?"

"What the devil is paint, Randolf? What has that to do with the mind of a man? He needs to learn other ways, that's all. All you need to do is work on the surface. He's already a man and a leader of men."

"I might try to send him off to school," suggested the colonel. "He's a bit old for school, but . . . there's the place that that cousin of yours runs. . . ."

"As a matter of fact," the judge put in hastily, "that school has some very sacred traditions which it clings to. And . . . and. . . ."

"Don't say another word. I understand perfectly. And every other school worth sending him to would have the same."

"Besides, Randolf, there would be something absurd in sending a great chief, a famous warrior, to sit with school boys. You'd better try a tutor."

"I'll try a tutor," decided the colonel, "and I'll be the tutor myself, by heaven. What better have I to do in the world than to see that my son has the proper chance in life?"

Here the judge was compelled to turn his head and to clear his throat with violence. He put in: "By the way, Colonel, there's another matter that brought me over here. It's only some practical joke among the grooms, I suppose, but I thought it was serious enough to be reported to you at once. You don't want your grooms to take liberties with your Thoroughbreds, I imagine?"

"Certainly not! What have the black rascals been doing?"

"Which ones were up to mischief, I don't know. But a while ago we walked out and found a string of ten of your chestnuts tethered to the rack in front of the house."

The colonel sat down suddenly, and with violence.

"Ten, did you say?"

"Ten."

The colonel passed his hand across his brow. His eyes had become a trifle wild. "Heavens!" he said.

"What's wrong? It's not so serious as all that, I hope?" exclaimed the judge.

"I . . . Dick . . . before anything more happens along this line, I think that I'd better tell you my suspicion."

"Go on, my dear fellow."

"The fact is, that this morning when the people were arriving, William looked out the window and saw only one face, really."

"Well."

"You can imagine what face would stand out in any crowd. It was your girl, Charlotte."

"Charlotte!"

"Yes. Charlotte. "A face like a flower,'" he said, and he was quite right. Later on he asked me for a gift of ten horses . . . would give no reason for his request, simply wanted them. I suppose that you begin to see the connection?"

"The connection between Charlotte and ten horses? No, sir, I confess that I don't understand what you may mean."

"Simply this. I hate to say it. It makes me blush, old fellow. But the fact is . . . as I've heard it . . . that when the Indians on the plains decide on a girl they want for a wife, they simply lead out a string of their horses . . . one horse for an ordinary squaw who may have been married before; two horses for a fine young girl; five horses for a beauty . . . and . . . you understand now, I hope?"

The judge's face was purple.

"Extraordinary!" he said.

"Extraordinary, of course," agreed the colonel. "But in a case like this, with a man just from the plains . . . twenty years as an Indian makes an Indian, in a way. . . . That ought to be clear enough, my dear Dick."

The judge made a turn up and down the room. He cleared his throat. He had turned from purple to a fiery red.

"There's something to be said . . . ," he began, and stuck.

"For what?" the colonel said, very good-humored.

"For a natural sense of delicacy and decency where women are concerned," said the judge.

"Ha?" said the colonel.

"A certain fineness of perception. . . ."

"Dick, you're rather running on a bit, it seems to me."

"Am I? Am I? Colonel, I want you to remember that we've mentioned my only child . . . my dear Charlotte."

"It seems that we have," said the colonel, becoming a trifle dry.

"In connection with . . . er. . . ."

"In connection," the colonel took up the sentence and went on, more dryly than before, "with my oldest son and heir."

"Hm-m," said the judge. He added stiffly: "I don't quite follow you in this, Dick. Do you suggest that you are making a formal proposal of marriage on behalf of your son?"

"I?" said the colonel, raising his bushy brows. "By no means. By no means."

"Ah."

"Marriage among all the plains Indians is rather an informal matter," said the colonel.

"Really?"

"Yes. As I understand it, a man gets a wife almost as casually as he gets a horse. And, of course, I don't imagine that William's ideas about marriage differ much from those of the people he's been raised among."

"A very unusual idea," said the judge. "I can hardly imagine that any son of mine . . . that is to say. . . ."

The colonel rose. "Perhaps you'd better not hunt for the word, judge," he said.

"No?"

"Perhaps I understand you well enough as it is."

The judge was silent. When the thunder clouds are piled high in the sky, though there may not be either rain or lightning, at least the thunder must rumble, here and there.

"By Jupiter!" exclaimed the judge. "A price of ten horses for my daughter's hand. My Charlotte."

"I attempted," the colonel said, growing stiffer still, "to explain away an embarrassing moment for both of us. It seems that you don't follow me. I can only assure you that I never shall be a party to any attempt to inveigle your daughter into exchanging your house for mine."

"Colonel Sutton, you use decided language."

"Judge Keene, you suggested the terms to me."

The judge was silent. For a moment the friends stared at one another.

"I think," the judge said softly, at length, "that the ten horses have, by this time, been returned to your paddock."

"Sir, you have shown the most neighborly . . . thoughtfulness. I thank you."

"Don't mention such a small matter, sir. Good morning."

"Good morning, Judge Keene."

The judge bowed, turned upon his heel, and left the house.

He was not a tall man, and he was a trifle inclined to pudginess, but even from his back, one could have told that he was a Keene. There was a crispness about his step that belonged to no other family in that neighborhood. The very last people in the world that could stand laughter were ever the Keenes.

Precisely, rapidly, the judge went down the front steps. He approached his horse. He mounted and thanked the Negro who held the stirrup for him.

The Colonel, from behind a curtained window, watched all of this proceeding, and he marked how his old friend raised his eyes and glanced quickly and searchingly over the face of Sutton House, very much in the manner of one who wishes to take away a clear mental picture of a thing he never may see again. Then the judge rode off.

The colonel went slowly back to his library and there sat down and pondered. On the whole, the humor for work had deserted him. He wanted to be alone and turn matters in his mind.

Certainly the gifts of heaven are not all sweet. Already he was beginning to pay a price for the return of his son. He had been made ridiculous in the eyes of the neighborhood. He could endure that. Now it had cost him the friendship of a very old and dear friend. The heart of the colonel began to sink.

Chapter Twelve

A Lady Who Likes Horses

As for the judge, his irritation increased all the way home. No very honest anger sustained him, and for that reason his temper became worse and worse, for he could not help telling himself that the colonel must have meant no insult to him. After all, the alliance which had been proposed had been with the eldest son of the most honorable family in the neighborhood. If that eldest son appeared to be more Indian than white man, the appearance was doubtless rather seeming than actual. So the judge got to his house in a white-hot temper, much more out of patience with himself than with his oldest friend.

Straightway, he did what a sulky person usually does. He began to burn his bridges behind him and thereby made the possibility of reconciliation with the colonel more impossible than ever. He sent for his daughter, and Charlotte came to him. He heard her singing through the big echoing halls of Keene House. She came in wearing a riding habit with a long, trailing skirt such as the ladies of that prim day affected, a foolishly small hat perched on her head, and a riding crop in her hand. It makes an odd picture to describe, but in it Charlotte was not the least strange. Some women make all fashions their own, and she was of that type.

The judge looked upon her with a dull eye, for he was seeing not only his daughter but all his dreams of what a woman should be, and in nothing did he find her lacking.

"Charlotte," he said, "I have broken with Colonel Sutton."

He waited to let these terrible tidings take effect.

Charlotte merely said: "You silly dear."

"You don't understand," explained her father. "I have severed our old relations with Colonel Sutton."

"How long have we known the Suttons?" she asked.

"Since you were born, my dear."

"But before that there were Suttons and Keenes, I take it?"

"Naturally."

"And they've always been friends. They were neighbors in Virginia. They were neighbors in England in the musty old days, weren't they?"

"Naturally," said the judge, and he blinked a little as he saw the direction his girl was taking.

"So I don't see how you and the colonel can break off such a friendship in one moment, Father."

"I'll show you the reason," said the judge. He gathered his evidence in his mind. It was not quite as black as he wanted it to be, and therefore he fell back upon artificial stimulus and brought his brows together darkly. "What is my greatest treasure in this world?" he asked.

"Keene House, of course," said Charlotte.

"And what in Keene House?"

"That faded old picture of General Sir Charles Keene."

"Nonsense. Not a faded picture at all. It is you, Charlotte."

"Thank you, dear," she said, and kissed him on the forehead.

Now that she was closer, she remained there, and smoothed back the gray-sprinkled hair.

"Now, Charlotte," he said, wishing for the sake of his anger that she were farther away from him, "do you know what the colonel has had the audacity to suggest to me?"

"Well, dear?"

"That I give you in marriage to a wild Indian . . . a Cheyenne . . . a blood thirsty. . . ."

"To William," said the girl.

Her father paused and stared at her. The name came pat enough from her lips. "You may call him William. His real name is an infernal Indian jumble that means Thunder Moon."

"That's delicious, don't you think?" she said.

"Good grief, Charlotte, how can you take it so lightly? A man who has worn war paint and really taken scalps."

"But he didn't. He wouldn't take scalps. That was the white instinct cropping up and overcoming barbarian teachings."

"He's done everything else. Worshipped idols, no doubt. Stolen up on enemies. Stabbed men in the back while they slept. . . ."

"Not a bit," said the girl. "The Cheyennes thought he was a fool because he insisted on giving his enemies fair warning."

"How do you know so much about him?" her father asked.

"Simply that I've talked with Tom Colfax. Tom knows all about him. He can talk for hours about Thunder Moon. I've heard. . . ."

"The fact is," said her father stiffly, "that at this time I'm not particularly interested in what you've heard about that young man. We've both seen him, and I'll trust the evidence of my eyes rather than the gossip of an ignorant . . ."

"I never saw a finer man," interrupted the girl.

"Ha!"

"Have you?"

"The long hair of a savage."

"Or a Samson."

"The painted face of a savage."

"The paint may be rubbed away."

"Charlotte, you insist on being contrary. Admit that when you saw him come downstairs you were shocked and frightened."

"Of course, I was frightened. That's why he's so wonderful. But how silly of the colonel to want to marry him off at once. Besides, he's not the sort of man who would marry at his father's bidding. Or is that Indian manners?"

"I show you a nightmare, and you smile at it!" exclaimed the judge. "I show you a wild red Indian. . . ."

"Whose name is William Sutton, who has white skin, and who is heir of Sutton House. Go on, Father."

"Bah!" snapped her father. He glared at her. Then he played his trump card. "You talk about his savagery without realizing what it is!" he said. "I'm going to show you. Do you remember the ten horses which were brought here today?"

"Of course. How beautiful they looked, standing together there. I wish we could get some of the Sutton strain, Father."

"Damn the Sutton strain!" said her irascible father. "Will you listen to me, or will you not?"

"Of course, I'll listen."

"I tell you, then, that those ten horses were brought here by Thunder Moon . . . to buy him a wife."

"Oh!" the girl cried, and caught her riding crop in both strong hands.

"Yes, sir. Brought over here to buy you with, Charlotte."

"Then he wants me of his own will."

"The young brute looked out of the window of Sutton House and saw you . . . and said something about a flower-face . . . and swore that you must be his wife. Straightway, he takes ten horses and ties them at our door."

She hesitated. "Well," she said at last, "Bob Sherman sent me flowers one day and perfume the next, and the third day he asked me to marry him."

"Do you think the cases are parallel?" shouted her father, losing his temper.

"Fundamentally about the same," she said.

"Gracious, Charlotte!" cried the judge, "I believe that you want to marry this barbarian from the prairies."

She puckered her forehead. "The idea is rather attractive," she said.

"Charlotte."

"Well?"

"What do you know about him? This stranger . . . this wild. . . . "

"I know that he's a hero . . . a brave and strong man . . . a glorious rider . . . a wonderful fighter . . . and . . . and. . . ."

"What else, if you know these things?"

"That he's kind to his horse."

"Charlotte, I think you are mad."

"Not a bit!" she said. "Let him tie ten horses at the door of any other girl around here and see if her head doesn't swim."

"I hope not," said the judge. "I have a higher respect," he went on bitterly, "for our young women, raised with such care and nurtured so delicately. I could not attribute such thoughts to them."

She was not insulted. She merely smiled at her father. "We look very fine," she said. "We're not cut on such

broad, strong lines as men. But never think that we're
so delicate, dear. Because we're not, and besides . . . ah."
She broke off and pointed through the window. The
judge looked and saw two riders sweeping like the wind
up the driveway of his house, and one of them was
Thunder Moon.

Chapter Thirteen

The Gift of Tarawa

Never had such a person appeared at the door of Keene
House. Gone were the clothes in which Thunder Moon
had startled the neighbors that morning. Now he was
clad in one style only, and that was the style in which
he had been raised for twenty years.

Over his head towered lofty eagle feathers, which
hung in a double row down his back and to his heels,
well-nigh. Around his forehead was a narrow band of
doeskin, set with a complicated pattern of colored beads
worked by the masterly hands of White Crow herself.
The rest of his outfit was not the product of Cheyenne
craft. He had drawn upon half the tribes of the plains to
gain his wardrobe, and he had paid for it by heroic dar-
ing, and not in gold. His beaded shirt, heavy as mail,
was the product of Mandan art in another age; from the
Mandans it had passed into Sioux hands, and was at last
taken from the body of a Sioux chief who had fallen in
battle under the bullets of Thunder Moon. His trousers,
of softest leather, intricately fringed, were decorated

with beadwork of another kind, laboriously sewn on by Crow women; and lost when one of their warriors lost his life in war. His moccasins were of Pawnee craftsmanship; the buffalo robe came from the mountain-loving Blackfeet; and the snakeskin sheath of his knife had been fashioned in the hot southland by Mexican artificers, stolen by the wild Comanches, and plundered from them in turn by this warrior of the Suhtai. Upon his left arm he carried that dream shield which, as he thought, had so often brought him safely through the dangers of battle. Some few deep scars were upon its face, showing where bullet had glanced or lance had fallen from the front of the thickened buffalo hide. The shield wore its mysterious paint; but the face of Thunder Moon was without that adornment.

The Negro who opened the front door to this apparition grinned at first, feeling that there must be a game behind such a festival appearance. Then he almost fainted as he realized that this was not a sham or a mask. The next moment, the judge himself confronted the tall young man.

The right hand of Thunder Moon was ceremoniously raised. From the wrist dangled the long canine tooth of a grizzly bear, slain valorously in single combat, a prize not less in the eyes of an Indian than the scalp of a chief. "How!" said Thunder Moon.

"How!" said the judge, answering dignity with dignity, in spite of his irritation. "Will you come in . . . William?"

Thunder Moon pointed to the sky. "I have to speak a great word," he said. "In your lodge that word might be lost, for the eye of the judge chief will look on many things which are big medicine and which are his already, and so he will not regard the medicine which I offer him. But there is a place where we may stand and talk."

He pointed to the lawn in front of the house.

"Very well! Very well!" said the judge, and he walked uneasily down the steps behind the tall visitor.

He felt that he made a very poor second to such a lofty fellow. He was all the more annoyed by this consideration because he knew that from some window nearby his daughter must be spying upon them with a curious eye. He would have liked to tell himself that she was above such childish eavesdropping, but in his heart of hearts he knew that she was not. The judge knew not whether to sigh or to swear.

Upon the plot of grass, Thunder Moon took his stand. Nearby Standing Antelope sat upon his pony, the butt of his war lance resting on the ground, his hand grasping it near the head, both man and horse apparently turned to stone. Only, from time to time, a touch of wind fluttered the single feather which adorned his hair.

The great stallion, Sailing Hawk, followed his master upon the lawn, and the judge was about to make a pettish remark as he saw the hoofs digging into his favorite bit of grass, but he felt in this situation an element of almost tragic dignity and importance which kept him from speaking of smaller things.

Thunder Moon struck instantly into the main current of his message. "You are my father's friend," he said, "therefore you are my friend. My father is your friend, and therefore I am your friend. This must be true. The blood of man is not as cheap as the blood of buffaloes in the spring hunting, and such friendships do not come and go lightly."

The judge could have said something very much to the point about this matter, but he restrained the desire to speak, and listened, merely nodding a little in polite assent.

"This day," said Thunder Moon, "I looked out from

the lodge of my father and I saw the woman who lives in your teepee. I was troubled. In my home I have no woman. I never have looked after them. But we are in the hands of Tarawa. He guides us where he will, and what he wishes, he puts into our minds to do and to speak. I felt him touch me when I saw the maiden. He touched my heart and put words on my tongue. I said to my father, "There is the squaw of Thunder Moon."' After that, I took ten horses and I brought them to the lodge of my father's friend. For I said to myself that sometimes between friends a woman is given out of mere friendship, but never such a woman as this maiden. I left the horses at the lodge of my father's friend. I hoped that he would accept them, and that he would come again leading the maiden and leave her at the entrance to my father's teepee.

"But I was a fool, and a great fool, for I did not understand that what is greatly desired by the heart must be paid for from the heart. He who desires glory must risk his life for it. He who desires love must pay for it with sorrow. For a long time, I did not know what to do. That which we love is like a part of the flesh. We cannot think of doing without it. So I did not know what to do, but at last I had a great thought. It made me very sad, but also I saw that it must be accomplished before I could have the maiden. My friend, behold."

Thunder Moon stepped back a little and threw out his hand with a gesture of much dignity, pointing to the stallion. Sailing Hawk, unmindful of the solemn occasion in which he had been included, playfully pricked his ears, and nibbled fearlessly at the hand of his master.

Now the judge looked more earnestly at the stallion. Hitherto, he had been wishing only one thing, which was that the strong voice of this young warrior might be lowered so that it would not carry to the ears of a dozen listening, spying slaves; most of all, so that it would not reach to the girl who, somewhere, surely was listening and drinking it all in. Would she smile at the ridiculous scene?

The judge was not so sure of that, for the scene was not really absurd. It was more; it became almost sublime. With all his heart he wished that something would happen to interrupt. What devil had prompted this reclaimed Suhtai to act his play upon such an open stage? A sense of courtesy chained the judge. Much, he felt, was due to his own dignity, but still more was due to the conventions in which he had been raised.

He regarded the stallion now, more intently. The animal was, in truth, the most glorious bit of horseflesh that the judge—an expert in such matters—ever had looked upon. He himself had bought beautiful horses, and he had raised them. But never before had he seen such as animal as this. Moreover, there was performance behind the big horse. It was well proved that, after a long, long journey, under the crushing bulk of his master, he had met the challenge of the swiftest coursers in that neighborhood, and held them at least even, or better than even. So the judge looked and looked again, and for a moment he forgot the foolish situation in which he stood; he forgot his anger at the colonel; he forgot the watching girl who was drinking in all these happenings.

"What a king of horses!" cried the judge. "What a grand fellow he is."

"In all his life, he never has failed me," said Thunder Moon solemnly. "When his mother foaled him, I, Thunder Moon, riding the plains and watching, saw the colt and knew that he was great. It was known by the white star in his forehead and by the bigness of his bone and the goodness of his legs. From his back to his belly there was also room for a good heart and strong lungs.

87

"I helped the colt to its feet the first time that it stood. I helped it up. Since I was the nearest to it, it came nibbling at me. The mother was very angry, but I led her son to her, and watched him feed, while I rubbed her between the eyes and said to her: "Little fool. Great fool. Hereafter, you will know me better. Let your son know me better, also. The Sky People witness me, whether he grows big or small, straight or crooked, I shall be a friend to him, as I have been a friend to you.""

"Now this foal grew into a colt and, when the herd galloped, he ran in the lead, until the old mares threw their heels at him. From a colt he grew into a horse. He was so filled with fire that when he was only two years old he met the great stallion in the herd and beat him, and he became the king of the herd from that day. I watched him. When he was three, Big Hard Face said: "Let him be ridden."" But I watched and waited. I said that no man should ride him save me. I watched him, and when his fourth year was almost ended, one day I saw the herd running at full speed, and all the fastest stallions and the swiftest mares were working with their heads stretched straight before them and their tails whipped straight behind by the wind of their going. But in front of them ran this great horse. His tail was arched, and his head was high, and he looked carelessly from side to side as he galloped, and yet for all their straining they could not gain upon him. It seemed that the wind blew him forward.

"Have you seen a hawk with broad, still wings sail swiftly, even against the wind? So it was with him, and at that moment I shouted with all my might. He ran on as though he did not hear me, but I knew him, and I would not call again. Yet I began to grow a little angry, and to fear that he had become too proud from running unmastered so many years. However, all was well. He presently threw up his head, and came heading back for me. Then he ran indeed. He flattened his ears upon his neck. The herd could not stay with him. He leaped away from them. They disappeared in his dust. So he rushed up to me. He stopped and put down his head and began to pretend to crop the grass carelessly, but all the time he was watching me from the corner of his eye to make sure that I had noticed his greatness.

"Truly, I was not blind. I stretched up my hand to Tarawa, and gave him thanks for the horse and the friend he had sent to me."

Chapter Fourteen

Sailing Hawk

When Thunder Moon had said this, he made a pause and gathered himself in great composure for a moment, for his eye had begun to shine wildly. Even though he commanded himself with some difficulty, he could not wholly master his enthusiasm as he went on:

"Since that day, I have hovered over all the prairies like a sailing hawk dropping from the sky on a victim, and then sweeping away again out of sight when pursuit was attempted. I have been like a swift hawk or an eagle falling from above when prey attempted to escape from me. When the Pawnee line charged upon us, on the back of Sailing Hawk I have been like a lance flung through them. Their arrows flew behind me; where they aimed, already I was not. To strike me with their spears was

like striking at the wind, so swiftly Sailing Hawk bore
me among them. The warriors have praised me many
times when the glory should have been to Sailing Hawk.
For with a sound of the voice or a pressure of the knee
he can be made to swerve, to turn, to halt, to leap onward again. With him beneath you, you think your way
through danger. Where you would be, there you already
are in an instant. I have said many things, oh, my friend,
though I know that he who praises his horse is praising
himself. But look on him yourself, and you will see that
all I have said is true."

The judge stared enviously and hungrily upon the stallion. As has been said, he was a round man, built to fill
a most comfortable chair, and his weight staggered the
beam of the scales to an amazing figure. When the rest
of his neighbors, and even the ponderous Colonel Sutton, floated across the fences on their Thoroughbreds,
the poor judge was forced to labor in the rear upon some
stiff-shouldered nag whose hot blood had grown cold.
As a rule, therefore, he broke down more fences than he
cleared, and he could not help knowing that he was more
or less a joke in the hunt.

Now, when he looked on the tall horse from the prairies, he saw none of the stirring battle scenes such as
Thunder Moon had been describing, for he had no desire
to hunt down personal enemies, and he himself had no
foes with whom the law could not deal adequately. What
was far more important to him was a dazzling mental
image of his stalwart form blown forward against the
wind and leading the hunt at a terrific pace, with a good
double wrap taken upon the pulling jaw of the stallion.
To the judge it seemed, at the moment, that there was
nothing in the world comparable with the beauty of this
thought. He turned to Thunder Moon with a sigh.

The young man went on: "You have heard and you

have seen, and I see that you believe what I have said. Now, oh, my friend, I give you this great horse. I separate myself from him. I thrust his spirit away from me. . . ." He was slightly interrupted in the midst of a dignified gesture, for the stallion caught at his beaded sleeve and held it mischievously in his teeth. "I give him to you," said Thunder Moon, increasing the volume of his voice as it became suddenly a little husky. "I give him to you," he went on, his arm under the head of the big horse, "and in exchange, I ask you to remember that if your daughter comes to my lodge, she does not come to be the common squaw of a common warrior. The fleshing knife need not strain her hands, and the back of my woman shall not bend under heavy loads. I go, my friend. Take my horse and this thought into your heart and consider well."

He laid the reins in the hand of the petrified judge, looked once full into the eyes of the horse and then turned and hurried away. Behind him, as he walked down the drive, Standing Antelope turned his pony and followed his chief respectfully.

"Wait!" called the judge. His voice did not carry far. "Wait!" cried the judge again, but this time Thunder Moon had turned the curve of the driveway, and a rising breeze drowned the call.

Mr. Keene looked helplessly around him, and now he saw in a lower window of the house the grave face of his daughter. She came outside and said: "It seems to be settled, Father."

"Settled? What is settled?" asked the judge, growing crimson.

"The exchange seems to be made," the girl said.

"Hang it!" exclaimed the judge. "What exchange do you mean?"

"I don't think you've done badly," said Charlotte.

91

"After all, I was bound to marry before very long. And, ordinarily, you wouldn't have such a horse as that to fill my place in the house . . . in the stable . . . or at the hunt, you know."

"Charlotte," declared her father, "the fool of an Indian. . . ."

"Indian?"

"He is. An infernal wild, red Indian. My dear, what am I to do? Tom! George!"

Two Negroes instantly appeared.

"You infernal scoundrels," called the hot-headed judge, "have you been eavesdropping?"

They had heard him call, and that was all that brought them. They rolled the whites of their eyes as they declared it.

"Take this horse," said the judge, "and get him back to the Sutton place as fast as you can. George, jump on his back and take him over. You can walk back across the fields. Hurry!"

"Yes, suh!"

Into the saddle went George. The stallion did not seem to move violently; but though George was an expert rider, out of the saddle he sailed far more gracefully than he had swung into place. Out of the saddle he went and reached the lawn in a sitting posture with an audible thud.

"You ride like a fool," said the judge. "You, there, Tom, you worthless Negro, you. Get into the saddle and ride that horse home."

Tom settled his tattered hat on his head and setting his teeth, cautiously got into place. The same swift, soft move of the stallion followed. Daylight showed beneath Tom, but he kept his stirrups. Not for long, however. There followed something like the snapping of a whip, with a sixteen-hand chestnut playing the part of the curling lash, and Tom rose into the air with a screech like a skyrocket and landed with a louder yell.

The judge looked on in amazement. These two Negroes rode as well as any men in the district, white or black. "How did it happen?" he gasped.

"Big medicine," suggested his daughter.

"I would have been murdered!" breathed the judge. "That last fall . . . it would have broken my back. Tom, if you can walk, you and George take the head of that ugly brute and lead him back." He turned his back resolutely on the stallion and stamped into the house with Charlotte at his side. "You were in here listening?" he asked savagely.

"Of course," Charlotte said, smiling.

"A lady . . . ," began the judge hotly.

"Is always human," Charlotte said.

"It is much better," said the judge, "to admit one's errors frankly. Charlotte, to eavesdrop. . . ."

"After all," she said, "when one is being sold. . . ."

"Charlotte. The ignorant bland-faced ruffian."

"I thought he was a glorious figure!" she said.

"Glorious, child? Glorious? A man who is fool enough to think that I would exchange my daughter for a horse and. . . ."

"Not a horse," interrupted Charlotte, shaking her head. "Not just a horse. He was offering you a part of his greatness. He was offering you half his glory. And, besides, I've an idea that he loves that horse about as well as most men love their wives. And . . . why shouldn't there be some exchange?"

"Do you think I want a horse to help me take scalps?"

"Look at it from Thunder Moon's viewpoint, not the viewpoint of a Keene or a Sutton."

"Charlotte," cried the judge, "I think that you want me to marry you to that man."

93

"I don't know," she said, "but certainly it's true that I've never seen a man before that I could think of marrying so easily."

The judge recoiled in horror. "Little fool!" he shouted. "Go to your room. Go to your room at once."

Charlotte went. Even before she was upstairs, she was singing most cheerfully, and the judge, agape, listened to that cheerful voice as to a voice of doom.

Chapter Fifteen

What Is Greatness

Now it was that events began to group around the families of Keene and Sutton. Trouble had been gathering head for some time and now had reached such a point that it was time for danger to be stirring. It began, indeed, almost at once. Trouble stepped first into the shoes of a woman—no other than Charlotte Keene. For when she went singing into her chamber, as her father had commanded, she did not linger there very long.

She stood at the window and looked out at the trees and above their tops at a cloud which was blowing up the sky; and something about the solitary beauty of that cloud, filled with shadow and with liquid radiance as it swept through the blue fields of heaven, made her think of Thunder Moon, who no more would rove the prairies. Now he plodded homeward, but his head was high, and in his heart there was the hope of an exchange which was worth his war horse. She smiled a little.

Suddenly she wanted to be out and away. Anywhere she told herself, rather than in this house and its shadows. Her father had told her to go to her room; not necessarily to stay there. With such shallow sophistry she defended herself, and walked out of her room, and through the empty guest suite, and so down the side stairs and out. She might have walked, but she was dressed for riding, and she still held her riding crop. Moreover, fate put a grizzle-headed old Negro in her path almost at once.

"Go get Sir Toby for me, Uncle Jerry," she said. "And hurry. Hurry!"

She watched him shuffle on ahead, pretending to hurry, but never actually getting out of a walk. However, presently Sir Toby was captured and saddled. Charlotte mounted and shook her riding crop at Uncle Jerry and a pair of the stable boys.

"Don't dare to tell Father that I've gone away and taken the back path. Don't any one dare."

"There ain't nothin' but your own conscience gunna report on you, honey," said Uncle Jerry.

Away went Miss Charlie over the fields toward the house of Colonel Sutton. Why need she have ridden that way? She would have told you that it was the direction of the setting sun, and that she was merely riding toward the light.

In the meantime, big Thunder Moon and his young companion had passed down the road. They had not gone far when Standing Antelope slipped from the back of his pony and offered the place to his chief.

"No," said Thunder Moon, smiling. "My heart is now so high that there is only one horse in the world that I would ride."

"And where is that horse?" asked the youth darkly.

"Let him stay where he is," said the warrior, making

95

an effort to control himself. "You are young, Standing Antelope, and therefore you cannot understand what I have done."

"Can I not?" asked the boy. "But nevertheless, I can understand the value of the horse, and I know that he is worth the hundred horses which run in the herd of my father. A hundred good ponies are in that herd, and each of them is worthy of carrying a brave into battle. But my father gladly would give them all for the sake of one Sailing Hawk. For there is no price on glory and on honor."

"It is true," Thunder Moon said, "but now hear me when I tell you that if I had a herd of a hundred, and each of the hundred was as great as Sailing Hawk, I would part from them all to make up the price of the woman I have seen."

Standing Antelope said not a word. He began to strain to keep pace with his long-legged companion, and it was only by chance that he glanced behind him.

He cried out at once. "Look. Look. This is the work of Tarawa. He has blinded the man so that he thinks even Sailing Hawk is not a sufficient price for his daughter. And here comes the stallion back to us, oh, Thunder Moon."

The latter, amazed, turned and saw that the boy had spoken the truth, for in the distance he could see two men leading the great horse. They came a little nearer, and now the Indian could see Sailing Hawk rear. The two Negroes were snatched from their feet and dropped again to the road, while the stallion galloped to his master.

Around Thunder Moon he played more like a dog than the king of a herd, but Standing Antelope said bitterly: "Go back to the stable of the stranger, Sailing Hawk. Go back to the white men. You are not wanted here. Many a time you have saved this master, but now he has thrown you away, and will a great warrior pick up the worn moccasin which another has thrown away and left in the dust of the trail? Go away, Sailing Hawk. Never come back again. You are worthless here."

Thunder Moon, however, laid his arm across the neck of the stallion and stood for a moment in deep thought. At length he said gloomily: "What does it mean, Standing Antelope?"

"It means," said the boy, "that you cannot please a blind man with a great light. This man does not want glory. It is too dangerous to own it. He knows that fame as a warrior always must be fought for, and that a great reputation must continually be kept bright. What does he care for glory? What care have the rest of these white men? What coups have we heard them count? Did they count coup on me when I was taken, or on you when you were taken? No. And because this man does not love honor, how could he love Sailing Hawk? A horse to him is not a means of coming up with an enemy. Let enemies keep as far from him as possible and he will be best pleased. Let them keep far away, for if they come too near he will not shelter himself with his strength and his speed, but he will rear between him and his foe the great wall of this thing called the law."

The bitterness and the contempt of Standing Antelope fairly bubbled over as he spoke, and Thunder Moon listened with a good deal of sympathy. "However," he said, "one cannot learn Pawnee in one day, and in one day we cannot expect to understand the white men. They are much greater."

"In what way?" asked Standing Antelope. "How are they greater? We have seen some great villages filled with them. They have black men to do their work for them while they lie in chairs and on couches and become

97

soft and fat and lazy and useless as a horse with a broken leg. What is their greatness?"

"The lodges which they build!" said Thunder Moon. "Is there not greater work and more medicine in the making of one of these houses than in all the teepees of the Cheyenne nation?"

"Ah," answered his companion readily, "a house that shelters a man with no heart is a house which is worse than useless, because it has been built for nothing. Consider the house of a swarm of bees. It is small, but far more wonderful than even the house of the white man. Will you say that bees are greater than Indians, then?"

By this comparison, Thunder Moon was struck to silence. After a time he drew his hunting knife, and with a careless flick of his hand he turned the heavy blade into a streak of light that struck four inches deep in the side of a poplar near by. Then, walking on, he took the knife by the handle and drew it out again, saying as he did so: "Who brought the Indian the knife?"

"Knives of bone and rock also may be used," said Standing Antelope sullenly.

"Who gave us powder and lead, and guns to use them?"

"The arrow will kill a man and also it will kill a buffalo."

"But tell me, Standing Antelope, what do we know about the white man? Have we seen him go out to fight in companies?"

"I have more than once looked for scalps in his lodge, and I have found none."

"We have not been long in this land," answered Thunder Moon. "But remember that I myself am a white man."

"Your skin. Your skin alone is white," said the boy, in the greatest excitement. "But Tarawa has made your heart as the heart of a Cheyenne. And, so long as you may live, you cannot change yourself and make yourself white. You may give all your life to these people, but in the end still you will not be able to understand why any woman should be worth more than Sailing Hawk. Come! Go with me. Let us leave them. Let us hurry back to our people, oh, my brother."

So said Standing Antelope, but he spoke in vain. Thunder Moon had raised a hand to silence his companion, and had begun to stare straight ahead. Standing Antelope, staring also, saw a woman galloping across the nearby meadow toward the setting sun.

Chapter Sixteen

The Sky People Speak

As if the stallion indeed were a hawk, starting suddenly a-slant through the air at sight of prey, so Thunder Moon on Sailing Hawk rushed down the road, with the pony of Standing Antelope laboring helplessly in the rear. As Charlotte Keene jumped her horse over the hedge which rimmed the road, the great stallion drew up beside her.

She, drawing rein, played to perfection the part of one surprised, except that her color was perhaps of an unusual richness. Yet she was more than a little frightened, also. Even when many friends stood around, the presence of this wild man from the prairies seemed not altogether without danger, and now as he lifted his hand and greeted her with a deep-voiced "How!" she was half of a mind to wheel her horse about and flee. She felt that if she did, she might be followed; and though her own mount was the fastest horse in the stable of her father, yet she guessed that it could not escape for a moment from the flight of Sailing Hawk.

Like the difference between the life of red man and white was the difference between Sir Toby and Sailing Hawk as they touched noses. Sir Toby, with thin mane and thinner tail, with his skin carefully polished by long grooming, was like some formally dressed gentleman. Sailing Hawk's luxurious tail and mane were braided and inwrought with feathers worthy to appear in the headdress of a great chief of chiefs. The Indian saddle appeared clumsy on his back; as for bridle, he had hardly more than a halter, with thin reins of rawhide. At his breast was the rawhide loop through which an Indian thrust his left arm when he disappeared over the side of his horse and opened fire with bow or gun beneath the neck of his running charger.

Charlotte did not miss any of these contrasts. What the eye did not note, the sense was vaguely aware of. Sir Toby was reaching out his nose curiously and sniffing at the other horse; Sailing Hawk was a dark-red statue. Like a lifeless thing his master sat upon his back, except that his keen, wild eyes were burning.

"What a lucky thing that we've met!" she said. "I was going over to see your father. Now we can ride together. Are you going to send Sailing Hawk to the races? Or does he need some schooling over the jumps? I don't suppose that you've had much chance to jump him on the plains, and that's a pity, of course."

Thunder Moon did not know how the conversation had been made casual, and how the tension of their meeting had been relieved. His stallion was quickly walking down the road, and he was looking down at the top of Miss Charlotte Keene's hat, and now and again he had a glimpse of her bright face as she tilted her head to look up at him. It was distracting. Thunder Moon became more and more silent.

"But he could be schooled," she went on. "He has the legs and the stamina for it, and I suppose that he has the head for it, too. And what a glorious thing if you should win the cup the very first year of your return. Your brother Jack has a perfect seat and a lovely pair of hands. He could handle Sailing Hawk. Unless Sailing Hawk bucks every one off. Did you teach him to do that?"

"I?" said Thunder Moon in surprise, "I never have seen him buck. He never was ridden by another man."

"What? Never?"

"Never."

"When he was out in the pasture, didn't some of the young men slip out and put a saddle on him to try his pace across the flat?"

Thunder Moon smiled faintly at her. "No," he said.

"But what could keep them from doing it?"

"He is a medicine horse," said Thunder Moon gravely.

"Medicine? What is a medicine horse?"

"I do not know the words in your language. Only, it is true that the Sky People are in certain things. They give them power. And those things are medicine. Here is a medicine gun." He touched the butt of a Colt.

"Why is it medicine?" she asked.

"It cannot miss a man."

"A man," she exclaimed. "Have you fired it at men?"

He did not stare. But one quick glance of wonder flashed at her. "At five men," he said.

"Good heavens!" said the girl. "Has that revolver murdered five men?"

"Ah, no!" said Thunder Moon, "only one it killed. That was a Comanche. But in battle, it knocked down four Crows; and the young men who ride behind me in battle, they counted the coups and finished the fallen men, and took the scalps."

Charlotte was utterly silenced, though she was a girl to whom words came easily enough.

He could not help misinterpreting that silence. "When I first got this gun, I prayed for a long time to the Sky People to make it a medicine gun. I had a painted robe. An old man had worked for five years painting it. I sacrificed that robe to the Sky People, and they accepted the sacrifice and made this a medicine gun which cannot miss."

A bird flitted above the road.

"Try the pistol on that!" she cried, pointing.

Thunder Moon shook his head, replying: "A medicine gun is a sacred thing. It can only be used in battle, and with men or a grizzly bear. For other things, it would have no more power than a puff of wind."

"Do you really believe that?"

"Yes."

She was silent again, fumbling blindly across the great void which lay between her and the mind of this man. She began to see that he had not been living a thousand miles away, but a thousand ages, and in another world.

Then he said: "Daughter of the judge chief, hear me."

"I hear you," she said.

"Every man has a secret heart. What is the secret of your father? What is it that he values? I have offered him a great thing. He would not take it. But what is there in the world more wonderful and valuable than a perfect horse? If a horse cannot touch the heart of your father, what will he want? I have prayed to the Sky People. I thought that they told me with a clear voice to give Sailing Hawk. But I was wrong, and I did not understand. Therefore, you tell me. It is not right that a man should ask a woman what price her father puts upon her, but I must ask you."

Charlotte Keene grew brightest pink. Then she made herself look her companion fairly in the eye. "Women are not bought and sold among us," she said.

"Ha?" he cried. "Are they given away?"

"Yes . . . I suppose that they are. Not, by their fathers, but by themselves."

Thunder Moon cried softly: "This is very wonderful. If I am a father, do I raise a daughter and teach her how to prepare hides and do bead work, and then give her away for nothing to labor for her husband?"

"That is the way with our fathers," she said. "All that our fathers ask is a kind and good husband for their daughters. But the daughters give themselves away."

A great brown hand seized the reins of her horse. Sailing Hawk swung suddenly closer; and the nerves of the young girl were put under a terrible strain as Thunder Moon leaned above her. "Then give yourself to me!" he said. "It is good to be the wife of a chief. I have many horses on the plains. Also, my father is not poor, I have many robes and much beadwork. Your hands are soft and the fleshing knife has not made your fingers hard and strong. Well, I shall take a second wife and she shall do all the work for both of us. Tell me, then, that you will go with me to my lodge."

It was not the first time that Charlotte Keene had been asked personally in marriage. Smooth-spoken men of the world, and young neighbors who had grown up with her, and suddenly smitten men of every sort had told her, stammering or with much eloquence, that they loved her and wanted her for a wife. Never before had she listened to such a speech as this. She looked up to the bronzed, powerful face of Thunder Moon and, to her own amazement, she knew not how to answer. For she felt that with

103

a single word or the lightest gesture she could thrust him away from her forever; but she felt as though that were the very last thing in the world that she wanted. So, seeking desperately for words, she finally said:

"You are a great chief, Thunder Moon. I know that on the plains all the nations know you and fear you. But here you are William Sutton. Don't you see that that makes a difference? I like you. I think you are brave and strong. It makes me happy that you want me. But I do not know you. You are not a Cheyenne Indian; but still you are hardly a white man. How can I know you? And if I don't know you either as an Indian or a white man, how can I ever answer you?"

"I understand," he said at once. "Women make a foolish noise with their tongue. But I understand you. You are not like the others. I must be a white man. I shall become one. Only tell me, what I must do? What sacrifice do I make? To what spirits do I offer it?"

Charlotte answered simply: "There is no sacrifice to make. Your father is a good man, to whom everyone looks up. Watch him and simply make yourself like him. See that your clothes are like his clothes, and your . . . your hair no longer than his."

At this, Thunder Moon took a great handful of his long locks and held them out before his face to regard them strangely. "I should be then like a woman who mourns," he said.

It was nearing sunset. The western sky was dark with clouds as Thunder Moon, with a stroke of his hunting knife, severed a dark mass of his hair, and held it up streaming in his hand. "Sky People," he said in Cheyenne tongue, "if this is wrong, give me a sign; if it is a right thing to do, give me a sign also."

So he rode on, with his hand still raised above his

head. Gradually the red of the fallen sun streamed up through a cleft in the clouds and strained them with gold, and filled them with crimson. Thunder Moon had received his sign.

Chapter Seventeen

An Earth Man Advises

It had been the firm intention of Charlotte Keene to continue her ride to the house of Colonel Sutton, for she wanted to talk to him for five minutes and tell him how sorry she was that, on her account, her father had allowed trouble and ill-feeling to come between the two families. She fell into a sudden nervous panic now, having given her advice to the big white-Indian. Whether or not he intended to do as she said, he had made such a strange figure, holding up that tuft of shorn hair to the wind and the sky and calling upon the spirits, that she was fairly shocked. The growing dimness of the light, the shadows which swarmed so thickly through the trees, and the low flight of the homing birds, all combined to make her ill at ease. She managed to flash a smile at Thunder Moon.

"I'm going back," she said. "I didn't realize that it was so late." She swung Sir Toby straight to the side and at the nearest fence. Once her back was turned, she had a dreadful feeling that she was being followed, but she dared not make sure until the horse had winged across the second fence. Then she glanced over her shoulder and was struck dizzy by fear to see that Sailing Hawk was, indeed, on the nearer side of the first hedge. There his rider had pulled him up. His first wild impulse to follow her had been checked. It left her white—and laughing—as she rode on to Keene House.

She was rather sure that never before had she known a man, and she was also sure that she was barely approaching the outside limits of a knowledge of this one. Many a trail would have to be broken across the dark continent of his soul before she could say that she understood.

A moment later, she was really shocked with terror when a shadowy horseman broke out of the woods at her right; but she recovered with a gasp when she saw it was Harrison Traynor, tall, slender, and grimly handsome. He came up beside her, whip and reins in one dexterous hand; and, in spite of the wild twistings of his horse, he made the most graceful of bows to her.

"Hello, Harry," she said.

"Hello, Charlie. You came across those fields as if you were being hunted."

He did not glance behind as he spoke, but she knew that he had in mind the distant figures of Thunder Moon and Standing Antelope, now disappearing down the road.

She laughed at him, laughing with relief and a sort of hysterical exultation: "I've had the wildest time . . . like bearding a lion, or being in an ogre's cave, or something like that."

"Rather a nice giant, then," suggested Traynor.

"I've been a missionary, Harry."

"It's Thunder Moon . . . William Sutton, I suppose we should call him."

"I'm civilizing him."

He shook a finger at her and his lips smiled, though

his eyes remained grave. "Barbarism is more catching than civilization," he said. "You'd better be careful, Charlie."

"What are you heading for now?"

"You ought to know. He has a lot of dash. He's been something in the way of a scalp-taker, or whatever it is that makes a man distinguished on the plains. And then, he's strange. That's the great distinction. Before you know it, you may be dreaming about that flying long hair of his."

He knew her very well, and she knew him. She looked firmly at him, at first, rather tempted to take offense; yet she merely said: "I'll show you how wrong you are. I've been encouraging him to cut off his hair."

"Will he do it?"

"He chopped off a handful right away and asked the Sky People if they would send him a sign. He did it in the most tremendous way, Harry. You've no idea."

"I have, though. Suppose," mused Mr. Traynor, "that he were a sham, after all."

"What an idea."

"Well, think it over. Someone sees the rich Colonel Sutton, whose eldest son was stolen many years ago. Then in the West he comes across an Indian, or a half-breed, who looks a vast lot like the colonel. He coaches him for the part of the stolen son. And, granting a little touch of genius to the actor, that would account for everything that we have heard or seen of Thunder Moon since he came to this part of the world."

Miss Keene tried to think of some arguments, but all she could find to say was: "He couldn't fool a mother's instinct so thoroughly."

She was sorry that she had made such a lame remark and she blushed angrily. Traynor did not take advantage

107

of the opening, but smiled a little, as though in sympathy.

"Of course, one wants the romantic side to triumph," he said, "and the hero ought to win in the last act. However . . . just considering the mathematics of the probable. . . . there's hardly a chance in ten million that an Indian horse thief would carry a squalling baby so many hundreds of miles across the plains, as it's claimed the Suhtai chief did. That's the first improbability. The rest are stretched nearly as far."

"But how do you explain," began the girl, "the quality of the horse and the color of that chestnut and. . . ."

"I don't explain," interrupted Harrison Traynor, "I haven't anything to gain by unseating Thunder . . . I mean, William Sutton. Besides, he ought to amuse us all for a few years. Unless you tame him too quickly, Charlie.

"You're a cruel fellow," she told him. "I know that you're gibing at me. You're beginning to make me angry, in fact."

"No," he said, "I know that I annoy some people. But I wouldn't dare try to annoy you."

"That needs a little explaining," said Charlotte.

"I have a sharp tongue, my dear, but it isn't half as sharp as yours. I heard of the remark you made to Missus Taliaferro about me."

"I don't remember."

"You do, though. You said to her," he went on remorselessly: " "Harrison Traynor doesn't like to ride; but he knows that he does it well. That's why he's in the saddle so much." "

Charlotte bit her lip.

"I'm not wanting to bother you with personalities. But as a matter of fact," he went on, "I don't dislike you for remarks that make me wince."

"I don't understand you," she broke out. "You're not a country squire, and you could be at Washington or abroad . . . in diplomatic service or some such thing. But you stay here, growing more and more metropolitan and European and all that . . . and rather despising the audience that you perform for. I don't understand you, really."

"There you are again," he replied. "Some men pray to be understood, but they don't mean their prayer. How well you understand me. You're quite right. I'm a self-conscious fellow. You know it, and that's why I'm afraid of you."

She stopped her horse. They had come to a little rise of ground and looked down to a narrow run of water with a broken fence where the cattle went to drink; beyond was a wide meadow, with big trees scattered over it, and all was filmed over and bathed by the sunset mist and sunset color.

"What are you thinking of?" he asked her.

"Of how well you ride."

"Yes?"

"And that you never seem to be going anywhere."

He waited, and she went on: "If you were just seasoned with some of the quality of William Sutton."

"Skill in manslaughter, Charlie?"

"No. But there's a touch of the child in him. He's so extremely earnest and simple. And he stands before life like a child before a mystery. But you. . . ."

"Well?"

"You're just the reverse. You've seen through everything, and you are the sphinx with your hands folded, smiling at life as it passes by. I never heard of men more opposite."

As though the idea angered her, her whip flicked on the wet flank of Sir Toby and made him gallop down the slope. Traynor took the water-jump beside her and she looked across at him as they hung in mid-air, looked across and smiled in admiration of his perfect balance. He had a wild young horse beneath him, and he made the unschooled tyro perform like her own veteran hunter. She pulled up Sir Toby, and they jogged softly through the meadow beyond. A belated string of cows, driven in for milking, were fast disappearing in the distance with a jangle of bells.

"You think things out extraordinarily well," said Traynor. "Let me do a little thinking for you, in turn."

"Please do!" she said eagerly. "I want a clever head to help me think just now."

"Well, Charlie, this wild fellow has tipped you just a bit off balance."

"Ah? Do you think that? What have I said?"

"Our thoughts have an aroma, or they're like a shadow that falls before us. I think I've guessed right, however. Have I?"

"I don't know," said the girl.

He saw that she was thinking frankly, speaking her thoughts aloud. "I came over to tell you about hearing of the remark you'd made to Missus Taliaferro, and how it convinced me, more than ever, that we ought to be married. I'll change that, and simply ask you not to marry William Sutton, alias Thunder Moon. Not till you're sure he's honest."

"What test shall I use?" she said, giving him no other answer.

"Well, watch him closely, and you'll see how quickly he'll shed the red skin and put on the white. And if he changes too quickly, make up your mind that he's a faker, my dear. There's Keene House and the pasture gate is open. Good bye, Charlie. I'm going home."

Chapter Eighteen

Liberal Education

As he had learned to concentrate on the war trail and the hunt, so Thunder Moon flung himself into the task of becoming a civilized white man. He took the model which had been suggested to him—his own father. He worked through his difficulties with his gentle and patient mother. From her he learned those little intricacies of deportment which the well-bred pick up by degrees and hardly know how they have learned them, gradually drawing in the precepts by force of example rather than by actual study. She was a gifted teacher. Thunder Moon went forward so rapidly in his work that he himself was amazed.

The dancing teacher came, and with gritted teeth and face burning under the sardonic smile of the little man, Thunder Moon went through his paces, and learned to bow, to enter a room, to shake hands, to go through the steps of the various dances; but when he was ready to do murder and take scalps, he had some slight recompense, for his sister, Ruth, would come down, and his mother would play the piano, while he and Ruth waltzed up and down the long drawing-room. Sometimes, he would stop suddenly, shuddering with horror, and the blood rushed hotly to his head. He, Thunder Moon, the great warrior, the famous brave, who had headed the great war dances so many times—he was now dancing with a woman in his arms.

However, all these things were necessary. As he told himself, the girl, Charlotte, had been right. Either he must be totally a white man, or he must be totally red. Very odd it was, that the two best pieces of advice that had been given to him had come from the lips of girls. Red Wind had made him see that he never could be a true Cheyenne. Now here was Charlotte Keene who had thrust him into this arduous apprenticeship.

Thunder Moon's appearance was vastly changed, now. The cropping of the long hair made his head appear smaller, his shoulders broader, and his height greater. Moreover, the weeks of confinement indoors had removed from his face and hands some of the layers of brown varnish which the sun had baked into him on the plains. His clothes were properly tailored to his form. He would have passed anywhere not only as a white man, but as a white gentleman.

There was only an occasional touch of strangeness about him. He carried himself with a dignity which was not to be seen in the young men of the neighborhood. He had the air of one who has handled affairs of gravest importance. On the other hand, now and again his eyes flashed fire.

"You are going too fast with him," said Mrs. Sutton to her husband. "You should not let him study so hard. All day long he's busy. Writing, reading, arithmetic, dancing, geography, spelling, history . . . and now even Latin. Good heavens, Randolf dear, you're going much too fast with him."

"He has to learn!" said the colonel. "I tell you, Martha, that every moment that young man is with us he's a danger to the community until he's had a chance to adjust himself and learn what law and society mean.

That's why I'm rushing him ahead. Because, if I can get him a little farther on, law will be more than a name to him. It will be an instinct."

"Danger in what way?" asked his anxious wife.

"I haven't told what happened yesterday. I'll tell you now to show you the need for pushing his education ahead with energy. We went to town, as you remember, and after we'd dismounted, young Marston came around a corner, half drunk and wholly vicious. He shouldered William, cursed him, and William simply walked on. Marston followed us. I told William to pay no attention and I thought he would obey, but all at once he whirled and leaped at Marston like a tiger. The sound of his fist striking Marston's face was like the clapping of hands together.

"And even before I could come up, he was throttling young Marston on the ground with one hand and drawing a hunting knife with the other. By good fortune, I got to him in time. I spoke. I had to speak twice, and then he looked up to me with such a terrible glance, Martha, that it waked me out of my sleep last night, dreaming about it over again. When he seemed to understand me, he was quiet at once, stood up and put away his knife, but not before some of the men who were running up had seen the flash of it. We got Marston into a house. His face seemed to be literally beaten in; I've never seen such effects from a blow of the fist."

The colonel paused, and his wife, white and sick, compressed her lips and said nothing.

"I tried to reason with William, and explained to him that a gentleman must not do such things, that he must rely upon the law in most instances, and that in others his riding whip will have to do. Or, in extreme cases, he may call out the other man to a duel. I tried to explain all this; he listened and nodded, but there was not much understanding in his eyes. However, I never can tell whether my words have taken root. He slips his mask over his face, and I'm talking to a blank wall."

Said Mrs. Sutton: "Marston is of a good family, Randolf, he'll call William out for this."

"No man in the country will commit suicide by challenging William," said the colonel dryly. "But that's not the point. I can explain a little better by telling you that as we left town we met John Exeter and he took me aside and told me that I really must teach my son not to draw a knife on a stunned and helpless man." The colonel bit his lip and added: "I had to swallow that. But if I had not been with William yesterday . . . he would be in jail for murder today. Or . . . what if he had resisted arrest? Lord knows how many murders would be charged against him by this time."

Mrs. Sutton was overwhelmed and thereafter made no opposition to the rigorous régime which the colonel had imposed upon his eldest son. So Thunder Moon's education forged rapidly ahead. The crowded weeks went by, and his progress was bewilderingly fast. He seldom left the house. Books which had been a labor became a pleasure.

Who could tell that the old devil often was up in him? He masked himself carefully. There had been only that one exhibition of violence which young Lawrence Marston suffered. For the rest, it was Standing Antelope alone who was permitted to see the craving for the past freedom.

Standing Antelope was himself eager to be off to the Suhtai once more, but a sense of loyalty restrained him. Moreover, he was learning a great deal. He could speak English of sorts. He had a thousand curious details to report to the red men when he returned to them. He could range through the woods, with an excellent rifle or shotgun, and with all the ammunition that he cared to burn up. More than that, however, he was devoted to the great cause of winning his leader from the whites and taking him back, someday, to the Cheyennes.

He was waiting with truly Indian patience for a good opening. One evening the two friends walked their horses up a winding saddle path through the trees. The summer day was turning cool. The shadows floated over them and the sun was well down in the west. They had dismounted, Standing Antelope leading his pony, while Sailing Hawk followed like a dog behind his master. The book which Thunder Moon carried gave the boy his opening.

"Among our people," he said, "the old men and the women paint on the robes the stories of the great things which other warriors have done. A painted robe is good for the sake of wearing as well as for the story it tells, but what good is in that book, except for what its words say? And can words keep a man warm in winter when the north wind is blowing?"

Thunder Moon admitted that they could not. "These are not stories, however," he explained. "They are songs."

"And what good is a song," said the boy, "which is not sung aloud? It goes into the mind of a man and stays there. What good is that? But a song among the Cheyennes may send all the warriors on the trail or start them shouting to celebrate some old victory. All white men are shadows and they live like ghosts before they are dead."

Chapter Nineteen

The Result

As the boy delivered this gloomy speech, they came to a winding country lane, up which a team of mules drew a heavy cart, dragging it with much labor through the deep, dust-choked ruts. Beside them walked a Negro slave, his blacksnake whip in his hand, his eyes rolling with anger as he lashed the poor straining mules before him.

At sight of the Indian boy and Thunder Moon, he winced a little and hurried on with more blows of the whip.

"Look!" said Standing Antelope, taking advantage of this spectacle. "They are all like that . . . all who live here. Some are called free and others are bought and sold, but all of them are slaves. Some are in harness and others are not, but all are drawing burdens. The mules are laboring, and the driver is laboring also. His burden is not strapped upon his back, but it is piled upon his mind, and it never can slip away. You are making yourself like them, Thunder Moon. You are changing yourself and your face and your soul. Between your eyes there is a deep mark of trouble. Is it true?"

"The mark is there," admitted Thunder Moon slowly. "It is also true that these men carry burdens . . . like the mules they harness to their carts."

"And what is their purpose in living?" asked the boy.

"Tell me as you see it," said Thunder Moon.

"All their days," said Standing Antelope, "they labor to raise grain in their fields or horses in their pastures, or else they heap up money with which they can buy all they need. Otherwise, they do nothing."

"In what way is an Indian's life better?" Thunder Moon asked.

"Ask your own heart, which already has answered your question," exclaimed the boy.

"You tell me."

"Gladly, then. The Indian trusts to chance and his own skill and the medicine he makes to bring him on the trail of the buffalo herds and, when he has found them, he rushes among them on his tireless horse. The crowding herd is dangerous. The horns are sharp and the bulls are strong. With blood and with danger and with life, the Cheyennes buy their food, oh, Thunder Moon."

"It is true," admitted the warrior, his brow darkening.

"The Indian does not raise horses like a coward. He lets his horse herd increase if it will. But when he wants more, he rides out and steals from his enemies, and again he risks his life to gain what he needs. Is not that glorious?"

"It is," admitted Thunder Moon again, with a sigh.

"And every day in the city of the Suhtai there are stories of the great deeds of other times, or else there are plans made for the next trip on the warpath. Is not that true, also? Every day is important. Every day, something is done."

"Yes, that is true, also."

"But here," went on Standing Antelope, "the men, like women, live in order to talk about the crops, the horses they are raising, and the lodges they are building. And when, oh, my brother, when do they win honor on the warpath?"

117

Thunder Moon was silent, and his brow was dark indeed. "They do not need to fight," he said. "Their tribe is so great that they have no enemies. And they are kept from quarreling with one another by the law."

"I have heard much talk of the law," said the boy, "but I cannot tell what it is."

"The law," said Thunder Moon, striving to work out the problem as he spoke, "is something which has no substance and no body. It belongs to every man and every man belongs to it."

"That," said Standing Antelope, "sounds like talk by Spotted Bull when he is trying to put many words together just to bewilder the braves and make them think that his medicine is big."

"Law is medicine," Thunder Moon said.

"Who makes it, then? What man?"

"No man. It has been made before."

"It is dead medicine, I suppose. Being old, it must be stale."

"No, it never dies. It never can grow old. And all the white men belong to it. They are children, and it is the father."

"Ha?" said the boy.

"It is true. If I strike another man, I have not hurt him, but I have hurt the law. He cannot do anything to me. But the law will punish me."

"It is true, then," said the boy, "that all white men are like mules in harness, and what they pull is the law. They do not live for glory or honor; glory and honor may be bought only by danger. Alas, oh, Thunder Moon, you are selling yourself and buying an empty load of law to pile in your lodge. Is that to live?"

"All that you say," replied the warrior, "I say also, in my heart. And yet there is something more, I hope. What it is, I cannot tell. But I think that it is the work of the minds that they live by and that they live for. We work with our hands. But the work of our hands is forgotten, and only a few are remembered by the old men of the tribe, and their true faces are not preserved but only faint shadows of them go down. Who was your grandfather? Who was his father? What were their deeds? Where did they hunt and what scalps did they take?"

Standing Antelope was silent.

"Our lives are like our lodges, which must be made new many times in one man's life. But the white man builds forever. In my house my great-grandson shall live. He takes from the past and he gives to the future; and in his house, which stands forever, he puts the thoughts and the lives of the great men of the past in the books which stand against his walls."

"The white man's life," said the boy, "is spent in a chair. Is that life? It is only a dream."

"The buffalo," said Thunder Moon, "travels more days' marches than any Cheyenne. Is his life greater than a man's?"

This knotty question silenced Standing Antelope for a time. As they wandered slowly up the bridle path, they heard the sound of hoofs before them, and into their thoughtful silence rode Charlotte Keene and Harrison Traynor, his sharp, intellectual face turned continually to the girl beside him. The breast of Thunder Moon swelled instantly with jealous anger. The malicious voice of Standing Antelope drove a veritable knife into his breast.

"And there is the white man's way again," said Standing Antelope. "Your squaw has ridden out with another man, and she has not asked your permission to go." For he knew all that passed in the mind of his older companion, and he could not resist this opportunity to deliver a thrust. The pair checked their horses, as the man and

119

girl came nearer. "How!" said Standing Antelope gruffly, and raised his hand.

"Good evening," said Thunder Moon, and, removing his hat, he bowed.

"Good heavens!" said Charlotte Keene. "Good heavens, Harry, it's William Sutton."

Traynor did not answer. He merely smiled, and somehow Thunder Moon could guess that that smile was a comment upon a conversation which had passed between the man and the girl before this day and of which he, Thunder Moon, had been the subject. His jealousy increased to a raging fire.

Charlotte, however, pressed closer at once. She stretched out her hand, and Thunder Moon took it with a politely limp touch of his fingers. "I didn't recognize you," she said, "but I'm *so* glad we've met. I've been wanting to come over. Or to ask you and all the Suttons over. But Father is as obstinate as he can be."

Thunder Moon stood a little more stiffly. "Of course, I offended him," he said. "And I must come to apologize, if he will receive me. What I did before, of course, I did because I did not know what was correct."

"Of course!" said Charlotte. She bit her lip and glanced at Traynor, but he with a pleasant smile regarded the glistening sunlight which slipped through the branches of the trees. He would give her no help in this conversation. The silence continued. Charlotte moved restlessly in the saddle. "If *you* will come over . . . ," she began, with forced cordiality.

As she paused a little, Thunder Moon filled in: "I shall write a note to Judge Keene and ask for his permission."

She was turning colder and colder. Thunder Moon wondered. Before, there had seemed no barrier between them, though he was an Indian and now he was surely in all appearance a white man. He was sure that he had made no slip in manners, in language.

"We'll expect to see you before long. Good bye, Mister Sutton."

"Good bye, Miss Keene."

He bowed to her again. It was very easy to do. Some lessons had been so thorough that now he was performing instinctively.

Miss Charlotte Keene rode furiously, swept over a tall fence, dashed across two meadows, and recklessly jumped a hedge and ditch beyond before she allowed her Thoroughbred to pull up. She looked beside her. There was the cool, calm face of Harrison Traynor, with the faint smile in his eyes, but not on his lips.

"You're pleased, of course!" she said.

"I?"

"Don't be a hypocrite, Harry. You know you're pleased."

"About my prophecy, you mean? Well, it does seem odd that a man could have turned into a real Sutton in such a short time. One wouldn't guess that he'd been raised since infancy among the Suhtai."

Charlotte Keene sighed. "What do I care about the Suhtai and the rest of the Indians?" she demanded. "All I know is that if he was an actor playing a part, he played it delightfully. And now if he's being his natural self . . . well, I think that he's given himself very dull lines. Heavens, Harrison, what an awful bore." She clipped her horse with her whip again.

Traynor allowed her to pull a length or two ahead, because he was willing to be unobserved until his smile should have disappeared. For his part, in leaving Mr. William Sutton, alias Thunder Moon, he had received a glance so startlingly direct and filled with ominous lightning that he was still quivering, but so long as the girl had not seen, all was well with his game.

Chapter Twenty

One Battle Ended

The rift between the families of Sutton and Keene continued, simply because the heads of the families refused to take a step toward a reconciliation. Since her second meeting with William Sutton, whose Indian alias seemed quite unworthy of remembrance, Charlotte Keene was less worried by the alienation. Handsome Harrison Traynor filled her days and most of her evenings with his attentions, and, for his part, he was perfectly well contented with the progress of affairs. In the household of the Suttons there was happiness for everyone save young Jack. Traynor saw him at a coursing match one day, and touched his shoulder.

"You're out of sorts, lately," he suggested.

The youngster looked keenly up at him. "Can you guess why?" he quickly asked.

"I can more than guess."

They were old acquaintances and, besides, the bitterness of Jack's heart required a confidant. "It's not the idea of the split inheritance," he said. "It's the blindness of everyone, not seeing that it's all a sham."

"It's always easy to believe what one wants to believe," agreed Traynor. "But I'll tell you, Jack, a wolf looks like a dog until it shows its teeth."

"What do you mean by that?"

Traynor already was moving off. Jack stared earnestly

after him. It was not difficult to put that suggestion into a plainer form: the way to make the so-called William Sutton reveal his true nature was to stir him up with a violent stimulus. Advice easy to give, perhaps, but who would want to scratch such a tartar? However, the idea ate deeply into the memory of the younger man, and he lodged it in his heart for the future.

In the meantime, a most unexpected stimulus was injected into the lives of all concerned by the arrival of Adler and Kahn's Greatest Circus on Earth. They sent vast red bills ahead and splashed the countryside with streaks of crimson advertising their hordes of dangerous jungle beasts and their dazzling air acts. They were only to be in town for a single day, and for that day the entire countryside turned out to be thrilled.

There was not much thrill to be found in the performance, however. There was one splendid young tiger, with huge, supple shoulders, which looked mighty enough to rip out the bars of its gilded cage, but the rest of the beasts were a mangy lot. There was a motheaten lion minus its teeth, a sleepy bear which ambled through some stupid tricks, a few acrobats in dingy white, and the very popcorn and the pink lemonade were stale. Even the children pronounced it a poor show and dozed in their seats. The evening performance was attended by the merest handful.

Before midnight, however, the show of Adler and Kahn had given the countryside a thrill and a start. The big tiger did exactly what had seemed so impossible. He ripped out two bars of his cage, battered aside two others with blows that would have done credit to a grizzly, and then squeezed his way out and paid a visit to the bear's cage. Half a dozen frightened, shouting attendants fired blank cartridges into the face of the jungle monster, but they could not keep it from sweeping open the cage and

123

going in after the snarling bear. It emerged quickly, leaving a dead carcass behind, and now it left the circus and loped softly away into the nearby woods.

An alarm was sent out. The community armed itself. Excited searchers went out in bands. The tiger had melted away in the shadows among the trees, and not a trace of it was found. Rumor declared that in the earlier days this beast had been an East Indian man-eater. At any rate, it seemed marvelously artful in covering up its tracks, and for a whole day there was no slightest report of it.

Then a fine three-year-old Thoroughbred was found with a broken neck in a corner of the Harmon pastures, and the body had been partly devoured. The trackers followed the prints of huge feet away from the spot, but they led to a creek, and in the waters of the creek the trail was lost. In vain the hunters watched around the carcass. The tiger did not visit it again. The following day but one, Judge Keene lost a beautiful young mare, slaughtered by the savage destroyer.

Panic seized the horsebreeders. They had in their midst an enemy with a special taste for horseflesh, and they shuddered with fear. A price was laid on the tiger's head. Five days later the price was doubled, so that it stood at two thousand dollars, for three more animals had gone down before this crafty jungle devil. One was a common mule. Two were high-priced hunters.

People ventured out in the evening only in large parties, and there was a general panic at every stir of shadows even during the broadest daylight. Every midnight creak in every plantation house was felt to be caused by the stalking foot of the tiger.

Standing Antelope came to Thunder Moon and, squatting on his heels, he made a great print upon the ground. "That is the foot of the striped one," he said. "I shall find him, oh, brother, and we will kill him, and take the price. It is the value of forty ponies. And I am not a rich man."

Thunder Moon smiled and shook his head. He felt that he was pledged to more serious work; but in the middle of the night he wakened, and the bright moon was shining in his face. He got up and entered the adjoining chamber where the boy slept.

Standing Antelope was already up, bringing a hunting knife to a fine edge, and with a rifle laid out before him. He glanced keenly at his leader. "I have been waiting a long time," he said, "but now let us go."

Thunder Moon, rather sheepishly, went with him out of the house and into the woods. Just at the verge of the moon and the shadow, they lighted a pipe and smoked, with puffs to the Sky People and puffs to the earth spirits, alternately. Then Standing Antelope took up a handful of dust and pebbles and blew the dust away. He closed his hand and faced to the north, the east, the south, and the west. Then he opened his hand and counted five little stones.

"It is luck and medicine, brother," he said. "Four days I have followed the sign of this great one. This is the fifth day. Four times I rode behind you in the other times, and the fifth time you noticed me and took me with you and made me a man. Hai, Thunder Moon. We shall kill before the morning." He turned and began to run across the country.

Mile after mile they put behind them until they came to a group of wrecked buildings, the site of a deserted farm house. There Standing Antelope paused, and said: "Look at the great trees, brother, that go up against the sky and the moon. All underneath them is thick, thick brush."

"Good!" gasped Thunder Moon. "Is he in there?"

The boy smiled at him. "You are fat, oh, my friend," he said. "You are fat and your wind is not good, if a little walk as we have taken steals it away from you."

The long arm of Thunder Moon reached for him, but with cat-like speed he avoided it. "Did you follow the tiger here?" asked Thunder Moon.

"I have followed it for four days, and each of the four tracks disappeared. And each time the tracks pointed in this direction from different quarters of the horizon. He could come by that stone ledge and lose his tracks. Or he could jump from one fallen log to another, there. You will see. Something will happen before long."

They followed the line of the logs which the boy had pointed out, and at the end of the last one, where the ground was soft, Standing Antelope lifted a little patch of fallen leaves. He made a quick signal, and Thunder Moon peered over his shoulder. There, plainly visible in the moonlight, was a great round print of a foot. They spoke no more, except with signs.

"This was not here this morning," said the boy. "Surely he is inside."

Like snakes they advanced, writhing softly through the brush, until at last Thunder Moon was gripped in the small of the back by a deadly chill. He jerked his head over his shoulder and saw behind him two phosphorescent disks of light, huge as lanterns in the dusk beneath the shadow of the trees. He knew that the hunted had turned hunter. He touched the leg of the boy who was crawling in front of him with the flying tips of his fingers, and made the sign: "Danger is behind us." Then he gripped his rifle.

The brush confined him on either side, and he felt that before he could swing the gun through the crackling leaves, the monster would spring. So, he drew from either hip holster a long-barreled Colt, and cast up through

126

the boughs above him a single glance to the moon-flooded brightness of the sky. Then he turned and planted a bullet straight between the eyes of the beast.

The answer was a roar that made his nerves leap. The giant shadow lurched forward at him. He fell, firing as he dropped, and as he twisted on his side a striped belly drove above him. Into it he sent a forty-four caliber slug, and got to his knees again.

The thought of Standing Antelope was in his mind, but now he saw that the boy was safe at one side of the path. The great tiger had leaped blindly and cleared the bodies of both its enemies. Now it stood in the midst of a patch of stout brush such as that through which Standing Antelope and Thunder Moon had been forcing their way. It seemed like a vast cat, gone mad with rage because a mouse had escaped it, and at the slashing strokes of its forepaws the brush was uprooted, beaten aside, knocked flat.

Something more than rage had blinded it, Thunder Moon could guess. Standing Antelope's rifle spat fire. The tiger stood like a soldier at attention. Then, with a quick shot from the gun which he had just picked up, Thunder Moon drove a bullet behind the shoulder of the monster and through its heart. So that battle ended.

Chapter Twenty-one

Big Game and Small

The moonlight was failing as they began to skin the tiger. The dawn was gray in the east when the pelt finally was stripped from the body. Still much had to be done to clean the hide and, by the time the preparation was complete, all the sky was rosy with the day. They had carried the pelt outside the brush for better light, and here they were observed at a distance by one of Paul Leicester's slaves, who went to report to his master. Leicester, riding over the meadow, came on the final stage of the work, and saw William Sutton, stripped to the waist, laboring with a will. It was Leicester who looked on the scene of the combat, and saw where the fight had taken place, where the hunters had been hunted, where the tiger had battered down the brush, and where it had fallen. It was he, also, who had a pair of horses brought for the victors so that they could ride home with their pelt.

There had been what seemed to them an equitable division of the spoil. The reward for the killing was to go to Standing Antelope, as was the twenty knife-like claws of the great cat which, their points blunted, already were strung as a necklace to ornament the boy's neck. Like a young savage he went, rejoicing in the blood-stains which covered his body, his hands, and his clothes. William Sutton, stepping out of the role of

Thunder Moon, was properly clad when he mounted the borrowed horse and tied behind his saddle the share of the loot which went to him—the head and pelt of the tiger.

Already he knew what he wanted to do with it, and he went straight as an arrow across the countryside to the house of Judge Keene. It was still early morning, but the judge and his daughter were at breakfast under a pergola in the garden when Thunder Moon rode up.

He raised his hat, dismounted, and bowed to them again. Judge Keene came hastily toward him. He was only waiting for some such chance as this to show that he regretted the words which he had spoken in heat on the subject of this young man and his novel courtship. He took the hand of William Sutton with much warmth.

"You're up early, William," he said. "I'm delighted to see you." And isn't that the Austrian horse of Mister Leicester. Isn't that Fregoli? Hello, though. What have you been hunting?"

He saw the roll of fur which bulked behind the saddle and a moment later Charlotte screamed with excitement, for Thunder Moon had taken down the pelt, and the huge, grinning, head of the tiger appeared. At the feet of the girl Thunder Moon laid down the spoil. He unrolled it, and the pelt glimmered like black-striped velvet. Though the hide was empty, the great fangs seemed locked with power and malice upon the stout stick which Thunder Moon had placed between the jaws.

"This is for you," he said. "If you will take it, I shall leave it here."

She stared into the terrible mask of the jungle beast. "How can I take it?" she asked.

"Why not?" broke in her father. "It's a most magnificent present. Sit down here, my lad. Ask your wild young friend to come here, too. I want to hear all about it. By heaven, there's still blood on that youngster. Did you fight hand to hand? Sit down, William."

Thunder Moon glanced toward the sun and marked its height. "In a few moments," he said, "my mother will ask for me, and she will be frightened if I am not there. I must go back at once." He stepped to his horse and gathered the reins. Then he turned toward Charlotte for a last word. "I'm glad that you'll keep the skin," he said. Leaping into the saddle, he bowed to them over the horn with bared head, and presently his horse was scattering the gravel down the driveway, and Standing Antelope was galloping in the van.

The judge could hardly finish his breakfast. He jumped up from the table again and again to look at the trophy. Suddenly he said: "Charlie, the scoundrel really loves you."

Charlotte did not answer. She leaned over and felt the hide. "It still seems warm with life!" she said.

So a double sensation was given. There was the killing of the tiger to talk about, and more than that, there was the presentation of the pelt to young Charlotte Keene.

"If he hadn't done it quite so soon . . . in a few days . . . but to take it there straightway . . . why, my dear, it was almost as though he had been hunting the tiger for the sake of Charlotte Keene."

So said the colonel to his wife, and she answered: "Well, and perhaps he was."

"But we don't publish our affairs of the heart for the attention of the entire world."

"Let him go his own way," said Mrs. Sutton. "It will turn out right in the end."

"Let me have another month with him," said the colonel fervently, "and I think it will. Let me have another month to train him, and then I think he'll understand what law means, and real self-control."

Now, while the colonel was making this prayer aloud, young Traynor rode through the woodland with Charlotte Keene. He was saying to her: "This fellow William Sutton . . . or Thunder Moon . . . or whatever his right name may be. . . ."

"We'll call him William Sutton," suggested Charlotte coldly.

"I thought he was quite sidetracked," Traynor said, "but he seems to be one of the sort who never fires single guns. Silence or a broadside, from him."

"You're speaking very frankly."

"Of course I am. What could be franker? I'm afraid of how he may get on with you with these odd presents, given at odd moments."

"There's something devilish about your frankness," said the girl. "It always makes it harder to guess what you're really thinking."

"Like Iago, you mean? But tell me, my dear, when a fellow gallops out of the heart of the morning, so to speak, and lays a handsome tiger skin at your feet, doesn't it open your soul to him a bit?"

"You may be as frank as you please," she said, "I'd rather talk about the weather."

"Yes," said Traynor, "he's gaining ground with you, I see. One can feel his cleverness. He won't stay in the field for steady maneuvers, but he lays ambushes, makes night attacks, and carries forward in five minutes further than others go in years of effort."

"Do you think he's simply crafty?"

"Of course he is. Plenty of brains, he has. He's not so sure of his rhetoric, you see. Won't trust himself entirely to words. So he sets up a tiger skin to speak for

131

him with all its stripes. And, by Jove, it seems to have worked most successfully."

"I think," she said, "that he's simply filled with impulse."

Mr. Traynor laughed gaily. "You wouldn't be so charming, my dear," he declared, "if there was not so much of the child in you. It's delightful to see the way you trust people. Mere impulse? In a fellow clever enough to play such a role as he's carrying off and. . . ."

Charlotte Keene checked her horse.

"I shouldn't have said that. I really apologize to him and to you. My tongue simply stammered it out, confound it!" he said.

"It wasn't fair!" she said.

"Of course it wasn't. It was like hitting from behind, and I never do that. I'm eternally sorry, Charlie."

Such a silence came between them that a squirrel which had been hiding behind a little shrub ventured out a step or two, turning its bright little eyes here and there, hungering bravely to cross the road.

"You're angry, Charlotte," Traynor said softly, at last.

"I am," she confessed. "I think I'd better ride on alone and get rid of my temper."

"Do just as you think best," he answered.

"Then I'll turn back. Good morning, Harry."

"Good morning, Charlie."

He raised his hat to her and kept it off, watching her around the turn of the road.

Chapter Twenty-two

Listeners

"I am no more to him than a schoolmaster to a pupil," said Colonel Sutton gloomily. "If there is any emotion in him, I have failed to see it. And what does he do when he sits with you here in the evenings? Does he speak at all?"

The family was on the small side verandah of the house, facing the rose garden.

Mrs. Sutton touched her husband's arm. "I'm not worried," she said. "He cannot show himself to you as he does to me. Something prevents him. But come tonight and sit just inside the window, so that you can listen. I don't know. Sometimes he says nothing at all. Sometimes he says such things as no one else can say."

Ruth asked softly: "May I be there, too?"

"I want you to," said the mother. "And you, Jack. It will be a shorter way of coming to know your big brother than any other I can think of."

Jack stood up and shook his head. "It's too much like eavesdropping!" he declared.

It was after dinner, and William Sutton had not yet come down to the porch. When he appeared, a little later, the father and the others excused themselves. Mrs. Sutton settled to her needlepoint close to the hooded lamp. Thunder Moon, when the rest were gone, stretched himself on the porch floor, with his hands behind his head, so that he could stare up into the star-strewn vault of the sky. For many minutes nothing was said. There was some sound which was inaudible to the listeners inside the window in the dark.

"What was that?" asked Mrs. Sutton.

"A night hawk."

Another silence.

"Who taught you the calls of the birds, William?"

"Big Hard Face taught me. Mostly when we went away to hunt eagles."

"To hunt eagles?"

"Yes. For their feathers. They are a good medicine, you know."

He still used some words out of his old Indian vocabulary, even when he was calmest. When he was excited, they came forth in troops.

"But how can they be hunted?"

"It is best to go with a very wise and patient man. One learns to be patient. Big Hard Face used to say that was the better part of wisdom."

"Was he a patient man?"

"He *is* a patient man," replied Thunder Moon, quietly correcting the tense. "For many years he wanted to make me a great warrior and thought that I was a coward. I could not stand pain."

"But I have seen . . . why, William, of course you can stand pain."

"No, I cannot. Even to think of it makes me sick. When Snake-that-Talks was young, someone dared him to pick a coal out of a fire, and hold it to light his father's pipe. There is a way of handling a live coal so that it will not burn. He did not know how. It stuck to his skin. The smoke went up from his flesh while he held the coal to light his father's pipe, but he would not make a sign. Afterwards, when the burn healed, his fingers were stiff for more than a year. And there were many other young men among the Suhtai who despised fear, but I never was like that."

"I am glad you were not!" Mrs. Sutton said. "Such absolute folly. Such ridiculous pride in self-torture. I am glad that you were not so foolish, dear boy."

Thunder Moon was silent for a moment, watching the waving branch of a climbing vine, like a dark arm against the stars. "Ha!" he said, softly, at last. "That is the way with mothers. I have listened to the women among the Suhtai, and even when many spoke at once, I always could tell when a mother spoke to a child. I listened and came to know. I had no mother."

"You had," said she very gently. "For during all the time when you were away, my thought was flying after you. My heart cried for you. Somehow, I know, my prayers brought you back."

"It is true that you pray," remarked Thunder Moon after a pause, "but you pray upon your knees, and not standing. Even the men kneel, as I saw when I went with you to the church. Does the God to whom you pray hold a whip? Why do you kneel, and why are all your faces sad?"

"Sad, my dear?"

"When I pray to the Sky People, I stand straight. I hold a dream shield in my left hand and in my right I hold my spear. If I were weak and fell on my knees, they would laugh at me and they never would hear my words."

"Has your father told you nothing about our God, William?"

"I have heard a little about hell and heaven," William said, carelessly. "Also, among the Suhtai, Spotted Bull used to talk a great deal about Tarawa. But every man must learn for himself. The Sky People have taken me into the camp of my enemy and brought me out again with their medicine bags in my hand. Twice they have done this. When I was a boy, they lightened my feet so that I could win the races. In return, I have given them good payment of buffalo robes, and buffaloes, and weapons. Once I sacrificed three new rifles to the Sky People. And that same day I found the trail for which my war party was hunting. But your people never give anything. You only ask."

Mrs. Sutton answered quietly: "Some day you will learn more about these things. I'm not wise enough to tell you. Only this . . . that our God owns everything and has everything. There is nothing that we can give Him except our love."

"I cannot understand," said Thunder Moon. "Much asking and little giving makes few friends, Big Hard Face used to say. But some other day I may understand. Now I have another thing to say to you. My brother and my sister do not love me. How shall I win their love?"

"You are very busy with your studies. When you have more time, then you will be able to talk with them."

"I shall find what they wish and learn how to give it to them," he replied. Then he sat up.

"That owl is very near," said Mrs. Sutton, listening also.

"Yes, it is near."

"Are you going to bed, dear?"

"Yes." He kissed her good night, and disappeared into the house.

He tapped at the door of Standing Antelope. There was no answer. He opened the door and saw that the room was empty. As though that made him hasten, he slipped out the window, peered keenly among the shadows of the garden beneath, and then climbed swiftly down the side of the house.

Chapter Twenty-three

The Owl Hoots

Halfway down the side of the house, Thunder Moon clutched a drain pipe and hung by one hand, listening, for the long, soft hoot of an owl again drifted through the air. The next instant he was on the ground and, heading back through the shrubbery, he worked swiftly around toward the point from which the call had seemed to drift.

A shadow stepped from behind a tree trunk. Thunder Moon swerved as if from a pointed gun, but the quiet voice of Standing Antelope said: "I shall watch for you and wait here, brother. Let me be your eyes."

Striding forward, Thunder Moon stepped into a little open space among the trees and saw before him a shadowy outline, and the starlight glinted faintly upon two copper-red braids of hair. "Red Wind!" he said.

"How!" answered the calm voice of the girl.

"Red Wind," he repeated, gasping out the words in Cheyenne. "How have you come here? Who brought you here?"

"Someone who rode this trail before."

"Someone who rode this trail before? But no other person ever came here from the Cheyennes except . . . ah, do you mean Big Hard Face? Is he here with you? Did the old man bring you?"

"White Crow is dead," the girl said. "The teepee of

137

Big Hard Face is empty and sad. I could not fill it. So he came away to find you."

"Bring me to him, then. Where is he? What could have made him come into such danger, Red Wind?"

"He has many things to say," she answered, "and it is not fitting that a woman should speak the mind of a war chief! This way, Thunder Moon!"

Full of excitement, he hurried with great strides, and the girl began to run to keep up and show him the proper direction, only murmuring to him: "Thunder Moon, your feet fall on the ground like a stick on the face of a drum. Everyone will hear in the great lodge. They will all come out and look for you! Hush! Hush! Go softly."

Suddenly he saw a tall form hooded in a great robe. "My Father!" cried Thunder Moon.

"How!" said the old chief, and raised his hand.

Thunder Moon rushed in under the saluting hand and clasped the old warrior in his arms. It was no trembling, time-worn skeleton that he took in his grasp, for the years had fallen thickly upon the head of the chief but they had neither bowed his shoulders nor made his step infirm. He had grown slower, heavier, but he was as majestic as ever in demeanor and in presence. The arms with which he embraced his foster son were like the arms of a bear. "Come in with me," said Thunder Moon, as they separated a little. "I want to have light so that I can see you, my Father."

"Would you take me into the lodge of the strangers?" asked the chief.

"It is my lodge also," Thunder Moon said, "and if. . . ."

A gruff exclamation of anger stopped him. "Your lodge stands among the Suhtai," said the chief with emotion. "How can a man have lodges among two people? Your place is back on the plains where the Suhtai wait for you. How many warriors ride behind your white father into battle?"

Thunder Moon replied: "He does not ride to battle, and there are no warriors behind him. Only friends. Things are not with the white man as they are with the Indians, Father."

"Ha!" cried the chief. "This is good. What has kept you so long then, among people where there is no glory to be gained? What has kept you here, Thunder Moon? Honor and fame call you back to the plains. The Suhtai await you. Listen to me while I tell you a true thing. They let you live among them and gave you only a little praise. Now that you have gone, the Pawnees and the Comanches know of your going. The great chief, Falling Stone, hangs on the edge of our sky and rides down and strikes us like a bolt from Tarawa's hand. The Pawnees charge and have no fear of the Suhtai, because they know that Thunder Moon is not among us. Lame Eagle is dead. Snake-that-Talks is dead, also. The leaders of the Suhtai look at one another and no man wishes to take the warpath. We have no strong medicine left. The Comanches are coming up from the south, and they sweep away our horses by hundreds. Before long, the Suhtai will have to walk on the plains. Dogs will pull their travois. All the Indians of the plains will laugh at them. They will be beggars. They will have to creep up to the buffalo by stealth. They no longer will be able to ride among them like warriors and hunters."

"Be silent for a moment!" broke in William Sutton. "You fill my heart with trouble and misery, Father. Let me think and draw my breath again."

Red Wind, as though she read his mind, stepped close and drew about his shoulders her own robe, made of the lightest skins, delicately prepared and dressed. He pulled it like a hood over his head, and covered his face in the age-old sign of grief and suffering.

Big Hard Face seemed touched by this, and he went on in a gentler voice: "Now that our enemies scorn us, the Suhtai are beginning to talk to one another and they say: 'It was not like this in the days when Thunder Moon was among us. When he led out our young men, they came back with scalps and they counted many coups. He was himself like a strong war party, able to dash into the camps of our enemies and fill them with terror. He was like a fire upon the fields. All the nations fled before him.' "

The imagery of the chief had taken wings. But Thunder Moon said suddenly: "Still there is the wizard and medicine man, Spotted Bull, who hates me and turns the hearts of the people from me."

"Spotted Bull is like a young man who has never counted a coup," said the chief. "A few old women still listen to him but the men have turned away from him, for they know that it was he who drove you from us."

"He did not drive me!" said Thunder Moon. "And ten like him could not have driven me. Tell me. Is it true that the chiefs and the young warriors speak of me and wish me back among them?"

"Ha?" cried Big Hard Face. "Is it strange that their prayers for your return have not walked even this far through the air to you. Come back, for you will be made the chief of all the Suhtai. Come back, and by lifting them from misery to greatness you will make yourself great also. At the last council of the Cheyennes, the other tribes shrugged their shoulders at the Suhtai, and the Omissis chief, Walking Horse, even the father of this wretched girl, offered to take us among his people and add our teepees to his."

"Ha?" cried Thunder Moon. And his strong fingers,

in the darkness, found the haft of the hunting knife which was always somewhere in his clothes.

"It is true, and the young men of the Suhtai listened and are disturbed and they said that perhaps it would be wise for them to join the Omissis, and so they could escape from the Pawnees and from the terrible Comanche riders."

"You spoke, however," said Thunder Moon.

"I spoke," admitted the old chief, "and I restored their hearts to them for a little. But they will change again."

"Ah, my brave and wise Father!" said the youth. "How much I honor you. I shall go out with you and find my people again and, when I come, let the Comanches and the Pawnees make their prayers to Tarawa, and let them offer up their sacrifices, for I shall take them with a vengeance that our grandchildren shall speak of. I shall carry off their horses and leave their dead without scalps. I shall make the Pawnees howl like wolves. Do you hear me, my Father?"

"I hear you!" said the old man, his voice trembling with joy. "I hear you, and I bless you. Tell me that it is a promise and a true thing that shall happen, Thunder Moon."

"I tell you," began Thunder Moon, when the soft voice of the girl broke in upon him: "Do not promise. Our people are red men, and your face is white. Live here among the men of your own blood. You must not leave them. What right have we to ask for your life."

The riding whip of Big Hard Face hung by a noose from his wrist. He raised it with a groan of fury and lashed the girl heavily with it. She did not stir. It was as though she had not felt the stroke.

"Stay here," she said, "and send the old man away. He has a name; but he is no more kin to you than the dog that howls there in the darkness."

Chapter Twenty-four

A Dog Barks

Somewhere in the night, a dog was calling mournfully for a moon which had not yet risen. Thunder Moon was too amazed by this speech to speak a word. His foster father stood with arm and whip suspended, ready to give the second stroke but held back by some inexplicable force. At length he dropped his hand and said bitterly:

"I know, now, why this woman followed me, and trailed after me for two days before she came up to me on the plains. I know now why she cared for me as a daughter cares for a father since the time when White Crow died. It was because out of her malice, she wished to be with me when I spoke to my son, and then she would destroy whatever I said. For that is the curse that she brought to the Suhtai . . . she has lived only to send Thunder Moon away from us, and now she will prevent him from ever returning."

Thunder Moon stepped close to the girl and stood above her in the darkness. "Why is it that you have hated me so?" he asked her. "What is the harm that I have done to you? When have I struck you or reviled you? I brought you back when you would have gone away with a Pawnee wolf from our teepee. Otherwise, I have not injured you. But now you hate me terribly. You would lay down your life, I think, to keep me from going back to the Suhtai."

"You will not go back," the girl said. "They are not your people. Even when you lived among them, you were not one of them. And now, if you went back, you would see that they eat raw entrails of freshly killed game. They would be horrible to you. No, you will not go back."

"Why do I not strike her dead?" asked Big Hard Face, panting with emotion. "Why do I stand and listen to her, as if my hand were numb? But I do not need to strike her to silence her. I need only say to you that I, a chief among the Suhtai, raised you as my son. I taught you the law of the tribe. I gave you food and shelter. I gave you horses and arms. I enabled you to go out on the warpath. If my flesh is not in you, my spirit is in you, and the spirit is greater than the flesh. You have heard her speak, Thunder Moon, and you can see that there is nothing but evil in her. Now tell her to go. I think she would obey you."

For answer, Thunder Moon whistled softly. Standing Antelope bounded up to them, his foot making hardly a sound among the dead leaves which covered the ground.

"Give me a light," said Thunder Moon in English. The boy, with a flint and steel and tinder, struck a light, kindled a bit of fir branch in the flame, and stood up with the snapping fire in his hand.

This Thunder Moon took and, raising it above his head, he stood close to the girl and looked down at her. The olive skin was as much lighter than that of the Indian women as it was darker, say, than the complexion of Charlotte Keene. The twisted, massive braids of her red hair fell like flowing copper over her breast, and the dark, changeless, inscrutable eyes regarded him.

"So, so!" said Thunder Moon, stepping back from her. "I have seen your eyes even in my dreams since I left the Suhtai. All evil things have a life of their own, and

143

so you have a life, Red Wind. Never since I was a boy have I feared anything as I have feared you and, now that you have come to me again, I know that there will be great trouble and danger before me. Why do you haunt me like a spirit which has lost its scalp in the battle? No Cheyenne ever has died under my hand. You cannot say that brother or father or lover was killed by me. Why do you haunt me and hate me, Red Wind?"

"It is of no use to speak with her," said Big Hard Face. "Let her go. There is nothing but evil in her. You were about to give me a promise that you would return with me to your people . . . to our people, Thunder Moon. Let me hear you speak it now."

"I have heard you," said Thunder Moon. "Someday, of course, I shall return to the Suhtai, but it is true that my skin is white, and now the great lodge is my lodge, and I have a place in it. Let me at least stay until I know a little more of them."

"No good journey can be made when the face is turned in the wrong direction," replied the chief. "It is the voice of the girl which has changed you. Leave me, Thunder Moon. There is no joy in my heart. You have given me nothing but pain. Go and leave me alone with my sorrow."

He turned his back resolutely on his foster son and strode away, but so blindly that he would have crashed against a tree, had not Red Wind, with instant care, drawn him to one side. She sprang back to Thunder Moon.

"Go back!" she said. "I shall come to you again. Now, go back, for there is nothing more that you can do to-night."

He turned gloomily, and went toward the house. A dozen times he paused, and a dozen times he was about to return to the spot where he had left the old man. Each time he remembered the words of the girl, and the strange surety with which she had spoken. Whatever was the strength of Big Hard Face, or whatever was his own might, Thunder Moon could not help feeling that in this girl there was an uncanny influence stronger than either. He acknowledged it, and he wondered greatly.

In the meantime, moving as if in a trance, he came toward the house. The night was warm and still. He did not want to go to his room so be went out on the stretch of lawn before the house and paced up and down until a stealthy form moved behind him. He did not stop to think that he was not out on the plains. He whirled and leaped like a tiger, and instantly a muscular body writhed in his grasp. He found the throat with one hand; with the other he drew his knife—and then a gasping voice reached him. He relaxed his grip at once and stepped back.

"Why are you here, Jack?" he asked. "And why did you sneak up on me like that?"

"Good Lord," Jack Sutton cried, "it's Thunder Moon . . . William, I mean. What a pair of hands you have. I thought my throat would be torn out. Ah-h-h!" He drew a long breath, and then he added with a shudder: "I'm still half alive, at least. Confound it, you've spoiled my cravat, I think. You might look before you leap, it seems to me."

"I'm sorry," answered William Sutton. "But you slipped up behind me . . . you shouldn't have done that."

"How the devil was I to know that it was you?" asked the irritated youngster. "I saw a shadow out here on the lawn . . . everyone had gone to bed . . . you'd gone to bed first of all. How was I to know that it wasn't a thief sneaking up on the house?"

He flung away into the night and disappeared.

Chapter Twenty-five

A Maiden Speaks

The estate of Colonel Sutton was so far-flung and his interests were so many that he himself had only a vague idea of all that was going on over his domain. He felt that while it was due to the property to show it a respectful attention and interest, it was due to himself not to be troubled by details. What details there were. There were lumbering and lath-making at one mill and shingle-making at another. There were wheat-raising and the growing of barley and oats and corn. The chief crop was tobacco, and to tobacco the colonel gave some attention, a matter about which he had intimate knowledge. The other crops interested him very little.

Thunder Moon said as they rode through the estates: "This tobacco is very much. It will fill many pipes. All the Comanches and the Sioux and the Cheyennes could fill their pipes from that one field. But still, those trees are very many, and the creeks turn the wheels of the mills, and the wheat grows thick and tall. There must be a great profit from those things, my Father."

The colonel responded: "The rest are nothing. Look at the book of profit and loss. Curly thinks I ought to sell out everything except the tobacco land, and I'd do it, except that the fellow who wants to buy is a Yankee. I can't have a Yankee for a neighbor. However, it's a temptation to sell to this one. He offers a great price.

146

For the timber alone he would pay . . . well, enough to make your head swim."

"Why should he offer so much?" William asked.

"Because the Yankees know how to make money."

"What profit do you make from the lumber each year?" William pursued.

"What cash return? I don't know. I leave those things to Samson. Samson handles the books. He could tell you, I suppose."

Samson was a mulatto who had been made a free man a dozen years before because of a long and faithful service. He was a big fellow with a pleasant manner and a smile that never stopped, and the real management of the great estate was in his hands.

"Next to you," said William, "Samson is the chief of all these lands and the people who live on them?"

"Chief? Well, he has many responsibilities. Takes a vast load off my shoulders. Don't you like Samson? Pleasant fellow!"

"Among the Suhtai," answered William, "they do not choose a war chief because he is kind, but because he can get scalps for the young men who follow him. I do not think that Samson would be made a chief among the Suhtai."

The colonel made a wry face at this comment. "Don't mix your standards of judgment," he said. "Remember that what's true for the Suhtai on the warpath is not true for white men living in peace."

To all this William listened intently, but he reserved judgment. It seemed to him that some lessons learned among the Cheyennes would be useful among the white men, particularly that rule which declared that the war chief who wished for success must make sure that every one of his followers was well equipped.

In the meantime, he wanted very much to speak to

his father about the two visitors who had come to him from the plains; but the last speech had, in a sense, made it impossible for him to talk of what was nearest to his heart. A man who held that the white man and the Indian were different humans could not be expected to sympathize with Big Hard Face and Red Wind.

This conversation had taken place during a recess of the morning's work, and after it the work began again. Labor, labor, labor! Thunder Moon's head was bowed, his brain staggered as it approached new problems of infinite smallness. Of what real use was *any* of this book learning? Did it teach one to strike harder, stand straighter, hit the mark more squarely, ride, tell the truth, be faithful to friends and terrible to enemies?

Revolting for the thousandth time, he started up from his table in the little summer house and strode impatiently to the window. All embowered in rich greens, the landscape fell away before him. Through the vistas of the mighty trees he could see the distant fields and the laborers moving through them. He shuddered with sympathy as he watched them.

"It is true," said a voice. "It is a smaller horizon than that of the plains."

It did not startle him; it was no more, hardly, than an echo of his thoughts. Then he remembered that he had not spoken and he stared wildly around him. He saw nothing, at first, but then, not three steps away, hardly screened by the showering tendrils or by the copper-bright blossoms of the big, climbing vine, stood Red Wind. His face darkened as he looked at her.

"Where is the old man?" he asked.

"He did not sleep all the night. But now he is sleeping."

"Why are you here where everyone can see you?"

"No one will see me. The people here are blind; even

Thunder Moon does not see very clearly." Only in her eyes a faint smile appeared. He rested a hand against the side of the trellis and looked calmly, thoroughly at her. "No," he said, "a thousand men could look at you and never see the truth about you."

"What truth, Thunder Moon?"

"I, in my life," he said, feeling the familiar Cheyenne speech like a charm upon his tongue, "I, in my life, have not sat all my days in a lodge and looked at old women painting images of the world. I have ridden out and beheld many things. Is it not true?"

"Men say among the Suhtai," the girl said, "that Thunder Moon has ridden from the great south river to the northern snow. However, a blind man could ride forever and see very little."

"Peace!" he said, stamping with anger. "I say, that I have seen many things, splendid rivers, and noble mountains, and glorious horses, and young and old people of the white men and the red, but never have I seen so much beauty as there is gathered together and made into Red Wind. She is like a thing molded of fire; and the image of her is burned into my mind. Behold, I have not seen you for many moons, and much has flowed into my eyes since we parted, and yet at all times I could not close my eyes upon the face of Red Wind. By day and by night the thought of your beauty has blown through me. What I see of you is good. It fills the heart, and the heart overflows, and words of praise are on the tongue of him who looks. But the mind sees you more clearly than the eyes. Now, that vine falls over you with grace and with beautiful blossoms, but there is more grace and there is more beauty in you; and yet with my mind I know you. Among the Omissis you were a shadow of trouble and to the Suhtai you have brought disgrace and ruin, and you have sent me away into a

149

distant country. And what man in the world can speak good of you? Do not call me blind, Red Wind? For I see you and know you."

"However," said the girl calmly, "the bad horse suffers from the whip, and I have suffered also." She drew aside her robe at the throat, and he saw the livid streak left by the whip stroke which Big Hard Face had given her the night before. "Big Hard Face," she said, "is a kind man. When he strikes, he used only a whip, and after a while the mark of the whip is healed and goes away; but other men strike heavily with words, and the marks that they make never are healed and they never go away. Do not blame your father too much. I have almost forgotten that he struck me."

Thunder Moon gritted his teeth. "You say that I am cruel and wicked," he said. "Then come into this small lodge and sit down with me. I shall talk to you. Tell me about my wickedness. I shall listen."

Chapter Twenty-six

In the Garden

There was no chance for Thunder Moon to receive an answer to this, for hoofs spattered sharply up the driveway, and two riders came to a stop not far away, where Mrs. Sutton was busy with her trowel in the garden.

"Dear Missus Sutton," called the voice of Charlotte Keene, "how lazy you make me feel. And what a beautiful garden you have made here."

"I openly potter around, child," said Mrs. Sutton. "We have such an industrious member of the family now, you know, that he shames the rest of us into some sort of labor."

"That's William, I suppose. Have you heard about the present he gave me?"

"Oh, the skin of the tiger, you mean? He gave all the reward to the Indian boy."

"He has no business sense, dear Missus Sutton. But he couldn't give away the glory of such a killing, could he? Where is he now?"

"In the summer house, there. In this fine warm weather he prefers it to indoors."

"May I speak with him?"

"Please do."

The hoofbeats crashed closer. Through the lattice work Thunder Moon saw Charlotte swing to the ground, and now she was standing before him at the little arched entrance over which the climbing vines streamed and showered color and fragrance beyond telling. She came to him smiling and took his hand.

"Are you too busy to see me for one moment? Thank you. May I come in then? What a lovely place for work."

Somehow he hoped that she would not look through the other window and see Red Wind standing among the shadows. In the distance he heard the quiet voice of that young aristocrat, Harrison Traynor, speaking to Mrs. Sutton in the garden.

"You have it decorated, too, I see," said the girl. "*What* a lance. Like a knight of the old days, isn't it?"

"What is a knight?" asked Thunder Moon.

"Ah, your father will tell you. But . . . a real bow and real arrows. Don't tell me that you've actually used them . . . not with your own hands."

151

"I have."

"But can you hit anything with them? Will they really go straight and pierce through?"

For answer, he slipped the bow from the wall, saying: "I never could handle a bow as the rest of the tribe manage it. But, still you can see how rapidly they work . . . at short range they're very good. You see?"

With a swift and easy motion he drew the bow, an arrow on the string. Strong were the Cheyennes, and strongest of all were the Suhtai, but no hand, save that of Thunder Moon, could wield this mighty war bow. The twang of the cord was like the stroke of a finger upon the harp. There the arrow quivered in the heart of a sapling twenty yards away.

She ran to look. The keen steel point had pricked through on the farther side. Though the tree was young and slender and the wood was soft with youth, yet Charlotte could not help a shudder when she thought of how that arrow would have driven through human flesh. She touched the shaft; it still was quivering in its lodgment. Then she came back to Thunder Moon.

"Well," she said, "of course you make everything possible. But if every Indian can shoot as well as this, why aren't the white men wiped out of the plains country?"

"I'll tell you," he answered. "Every Indian shouts as he fights. The white man shouts afterward. The Indian fights so that he may tell about it afterward, but the white man is willing to die in the battle. That is the great difference, and that is why the white men grow stronger and stronger."

"You say it sadly, William."

"It is a vast country," he said for answer. "And there should be room for every one in it. But the white man is a king, and so is the Cheyenne. They cannot live beside one another."

He fell into gloomy thought, in the spell of these reflections. Charlotte had an opportunity to turn her clear, bright eyes from one thing to another in the room, and finally to the fatal book of geography over which he had been poring. She smiled at him, then, partly in amusement, and partly in pity.

"I'm giving a dance tonight. Not a real ball. Can you come, William?"

"The Suhtai do not dance like the white men, who go around and around with a woman in their arms," he answered.

"You may dance as you please," she said. "But there are a great many young people in our neighborhood who want to know you better. Say that you'll come."

He thought of Big Hard Face in the woods nearby, of Red Wind, of all the trouble that lay before him, and of the many decisions which he would have to make.

"I cannot come," he said.

"Is it your father?" she asked, tilting her head a little. "Is he still very angry with my father?"

"My father?" he answered, with a start. "Which father?"

Charlotte stared. "Which father?" she asked in bewilderment. "Oh . . . but if your foster father is here also. . . ."

"I don't . . . ," he paused.

Among the Cheyennes social lies were not in favor, so he checked himself in the midst of a denial. He glowered at her, and she drew back a little toward the door, almost as though she were afraid.

"Everyone said that you wouldn't come," she declared. "Of course, you wouldn't have to dance, unless you wished to. You could sit and talk. My father would talk to you. And I'll talk, too, if you let me, and if I'm able. I wish you'd think it over."

He began to smile a little.

"You're relenting, I think," she said, and her smile was much broader than his.

"Why do you talk like a child?" he asked her suddenly.

"I?" the girl cried.

"Yes. You make your eyes open wide, but your heart is not so open. You speak very simply, too, like a child; and yet I am sure that you are much wiser than I am, and that you know a great many things which I do not know. Why do you talk to me like a child, when you are *not* a child?"

She bit her lip. It was the first time since early girlhood that anyone had spoken to her in so blunt and frank a fashion. Her color grew high. She was about to make a quick and keen retort, but she checked herself and said: "I suppose I *do* play a part and that I'm not always entirely honest. But, really, that's what we're expected to do, you know. However, I see that you want me to go...."

He stepped a little closer and did a thing which no other young man would have dreamed of doing. He laid a hand upon her shoulder in order to detain her. The other hand he put on top of her head, and bent her head gently back, so that she was forced to meet his eyes. Why she did not exclaim angrily at this familiarity, she herself could not have told. Yet there was something about his manner and his air which was not in the least rude.

"Do you think it would be well for me to come?" he asked her.

"Only if you wish to."

"If I come, it would not be to see the others, but only to see you. Because of all the people I have met here, there is no other who puzzles me so much as you do.

154

And of all the people in the world, only one has seemed stranger to me." He released her. "I shall come," he said.

"I am glad of that," answered Charlotte, much sobered. "Who was the other strange person, William?"

"An Omissis girl who came like a curse to the Suhtai," he said. "She lived in my teepee and brought the curse into my life also."

Miss Keene grew very white. "She was your squaw, your wife, William?"

"She? No, I would not take her with that curse on her. Besides, she would not have taken me. She hated me."

"But you were a great and rich chief."

"No chief was great or rich enough for her. The rivers that run from the mountains to the sea are filled with wisdom, but they are not so wise as she. They are beautiful, but not so beautiful as she. Nothing in the world, I think, is so beautiful as she."

"Ah?" said the girl coldly.

"Nor so evil," he finished.

"It makes an attractive portrait," she replied. "What was her name?"

He stopped at the door and picked up a bit of dust. "May her name be forgotten and may she disappear like this dust!" he said, and he blew it into the air, where it hung in a thin mist, and then dissolved.

"That seems like magic," she said, and laughed a little shakily. "You will come, then? Please do. Good day, William."

She got to her horse and rode from the place.

"You were hardly civil to Missus Sutton when you said good bye," remarked her companion, Harrison Traynor, "and you look like a thunder cloud just now. Nothing went wrong with your talk with William, I trust?"

"I'm not going to bother with him," she exclaimed.

"He's simply too different to understand. He . . . he makes my head spin. Do you know, I think that his foster father . . . the Indian one . . . has come out of the plains. Think of that. But . . . he talked to me as if I were a little fool, Harry. And he actually made me feel like one."

Harrison Traynor said not a word. The least syllable might break the train of thought, and he wanted her to utter her thoughts aloud.

"He put his hand on my head and looked into my eyes and said that I shouldn't try to talk like a child. Am I such an affected fool? Heavens, it makes me furious when I remember. What unutterable impertinence."

Again he was wisely silent; and very grave was Harrison Traynor then.

"I've half a mind to go back and tell him that I can do without him at the dance tonight."

Traynor checked his horse. "Shall we turn back?" he said.

"Of course not!" she said. "I can't be so rude as that. But, oh, Harry, what a man among men he is. There's no other like him, is there? Did you see him drive that arrow through the tree? The point came through on the farther side. It would have gone clear through a man, I think."

"No doubt."

"He told me about a fascinating and beautiful Indian girl, too. Do you think that Indian girls ever are truly beautiful?"

To have resolved that question, she should have looked not to her companion but back to the summer house, where, at that moment, Thunder Moon turned from the door and saw Red Wind standing at the opposite latticed window.

"You have stayed to listen to me, then?" he asked.

156

She smiled at him and glided away. "Come back Red Wind. I have something more to say and to hear." When he strode to the window, she was gone, and instinct told him that he could not overtake her or find her. Afterward, he puzzled for a long time above his book, but he found that the letters were dancing before his eyes.

Chapter Twenty-seven

The Constable at Work

Mr. Traynor was a polite man, but also he could be astonishingly direct. He was when he saw young Jack Sutton later on that same day.

"No one seems to see through him," exclaimed Jack peevishly. "It's as plain as day that the fellow is a sham and a farce, but no one seems to be able to make it out. Not even," he added with a touch of keener malice, "not even Charlie Keene. She's come over to ask him to her dance tonight, you know."

"You're right." Traynor nodded. "You have me there. Or rather, Thunder Moon has me. It seems to me, old fellow, that something should be done about him before long. And I have, in fact, the idea of how we can work it."

"Good!" said Jack Sutton, a glint in his eyes. "What shall we do, then?"

"Nothing. But make *him* do something."

"I can't guess my way through that puzzle. Be a little more explicit."

"Well, Jack, we both know that the fellow is a ruffian at heart, eh?"

"Naturally."

"And the great idea is to make him act like a ruffian, too."

"But how to do that?"

"I had the key to the situation today, I think. From a hint that was dropped, I believe that the father of Thunder Moon . . . the Cheyenne father . . . is hanging around in this vicinity. Well, the last time he was here, some horses were stolen. And lately Patterson missed that good bay mare of his. One might put two and two together."

"It was three weeks ago that Patterson lost his mare."

"That makes no difference. It isn't the matter of a horse that's important to us. It's the chance to get Thunder Moon into trouble."

"Get his father into trouble, you mean?"

"My dear fellow, you don't follow me at a great distance. Consider this: they've put the fighting talents of young Larry Marston into service by making him constable, and he's doing the work for the fun of it. But we all know that he hates William Sutton, so-called, and would do anything to take a knock at him. Now, then, go to Marston and let him know that a vagabond Indian is hanging around the Sutton place . . . and isn't it likely that he'll find the man and lock him up?"

"So far, so good. William will be annoyed."

"Is that all? My boy, he'll be so annoyed that he's apt to rip that jail apart in order to get the red man out."

"Hello! I hadn't thought of that. And if he does, why there's an excuse for Marston to raise a posse to help him capture the escaped criminal. And then Thunder Moon intervenes to protect his father . . . and then there's grand trouble . . . and perhaps Father is tired of

the disgrace of the thing and cuts Thunder Moon off . . .
or comes to his senses and sees that the man is a mere
pretender."

"Jack, you argue like a sleuth. The next thing is to
carry the message to Larry. Will you do it?"

"As fast as a horse can take me to him."

"Not too fast, though. It's just a casual thing thrown
out . . . an old vagabond Indian has been seen near your
house, you've heard. Let Larry think out the rest for
himself. At any rate, he's as keen as mustard to make
every arrest that looks dangerous, and I suppose that
arresting a Cheyenne chief ought to appeal to him."

Those were the instructions under which Jack rode to
find Larry Marston, and he found him, luckily in the
very act of galloping from his home. Young Mr. Marston had become a new man since he had taken over the
office of constable. However wild his antecedents had
been, he now proved that excitement and not mere trouble was what he wanted. The slaves dared not run away
since this new power was in the field. The ruffians dared
not group in their familiar gangs. The solitary criminals,
who drifted across the country looking for bank safes to
crack and houses to rob, rapidly began to desert this hot
region. Larry Marston had been considered a black
sheep, not many weeks before. Now, he was an honored
and most valued member of the community.

He frowned a little as young Jack Sutton came up to
him. For the marks of William Sutton's fist still were on
the face of Marston, and there they would remain until
his death-day. His nose had been crushed a little at the
bridge, and there was a ragged red scar running up one
side of his upper lip. So he scowled a little as one of
the hostile family came up to him.

"Well met, Larry," said Jack Sutton cheerfully. "Are
you hot on a trail?"

"I'm riding over to Everett. Old fool there has got a jug of moonshine and locked himself into his house, threatens to blow off the head of anyone who comes near him."

"That's an ugly job for you," said the boy. "Why don't you wait for him to sleep the jag off?"

"He has a wife, you know, and it's really not right that he should be allowed to keep her out in the cold, is it? Besides, he's defied the law, and we can't stand for that for a minute."

The business-like tone of Marston made Jack Sutton smile a little. "Best luck, old fellow," he said. He began to turn his horse. "Hold on!" he cried as an afterthought. "If you happen to come by our way, you might have a look through the woods for an old vagabond Indian who's hanging about there."

"What? An Indian?" Marston brightened with keen interest. "You don't mean it, Jack. A red man . . . in this part of the country?"

"It's not the first time that they've come this far from the plains . . . according to history," said Jack. "Horse stealing, I suppose. You know Patterson lost his fine mare not long ago."

"Of course, I remember all about it. Let Everett sleep off his jag. No use making blood flow for the sake of a fool like that. I'm coming back with you, Jack."

Back he turned, bubbling over with questions—and looking to his rifle as he went. He wanted to know when the Indian had been seen, and where, and how he looked, and how old he was, and how he was mounted—or was he on foot? To all of this, Jack returned vague answers. If Marston found an oldish Indian, it would be sure to be the right man. Once the fellow was safe in jail, then it would be time to ask many questions. Marston agreed. Straightway he cached his horse in the woods, and he started out on foot through the late afternoon to comb the place for the suspect.

There was no keener hunter in all the district. From the days of his boyhood, by himself or with his dog, he had worked every inch of the country. With Indian woodcraft, he knew how to stalk with speed and with silence, and he knew how to cast through a countryside with scientific precision. All his art was brought into play on this occasion, and it mattered not that the evening came and thickened the woods with shadows. Now he could not read the trail, but he could hunt with his keen eyes for other shadows moving among the trees, and with his keener ears he could listen for every unusual sound.

Once, coming close to Sutton House, he saw the big carriage rolling off beneath the stars with Jack and Ruth and William Sutton in it. He heard the gay laughter of the girl, and could make out distinctly the wide, strong shoulders of William. The sight of them made him touch his bruised, scarred face, and he gritted his teeth in revengeful anger. Someday, fate willing, he would make the fellow pay for that. Yet how it would be managed he could not tell. Strength of hand and skill with weapons were his chief attributes, but he knew that in neither quality could he stand for an instant before this newly reclaimed hero of the plains.

So he stood among the shadows and stared, and saw the carriage wheel away, heard it crunching the gravel out of sight among the trees, heard the big, wrought-iron gates scream on their hinges as the lodge-keeper opened them wide, and then he was left alone with his gloomy imaginings of the future. No, not quite alone. Presently there was a stir not far from him—hardly to be heard but rather to be guessed at. Out of the woods stepped a tall man in a blanket up to his neck. His head was distinguished by long, flowing hair such as Thunder Moon had worn, and, in silhouette, the watcher could perceive several long feathers at the crown of the man's head.

This, undoubtedly, was either a masquerader or an Indian, and what masquerader would show himself like this, at the verge of the silent woods? The young constable was about to steal up from behind, gun in hand, to make his challenge, when he saw a second form come out of the darkness, and then a woman's voice addressed the first comer in a language which Marston never had heard before. His heart jumped. If a woman were here— why, it was as though an entire Indian tribe had slipped through the settlements and come to this rich and cultivated section of the country. Fear thrilled the constable, and then keen eagerness for the work which he saw before him.

He heard the man answer in gruff, unintelligible words, and the girl went swiftly away among the trees. So skillfully did she step that after one or two slight sounds, there was no further trace of her. The mere whisper of the wind had been enough to efface all trace of the noise she had made. He listened again; then he stepped out behind the statuesque giant. Not William Sutton himself was wider of shoulder than this man. Again the heart of the constable failed him a little, but he went on, as a brave man does, fearing shame more than danger. When he was very close: "Who are you, friend?" he said in a firm voice.

The answer would have surprised most men, but Marston was nerved for almost anything. He swerved to avoid the knife-thrust that was aimed at his throat, and with a sidelong blow of his rifle barrel, he felled the giant. Kneeling above him, he bound the hands of the unconscious man. Then he felt for the place where his blow had fallen, and found that no blood was flowing.

After that, he waited for consciousness to return. He knew that a shout would bring slaves from the Sutton place to help him, but he scorned making any appeal. In the meantime, he watched the woods behind him with a scrupulous eye. A dozen times he felt that he saw forms drifting to the edge of the trees, stealthily preparing to spring out at him, and a dozen times he told himself that he was mistaken, and steadied his nerves by gripping the rifle harder. There is nothing like the touch of steel to bring the mind to focus. But no danger leaped at him from the wood. The fallen man. stirred, at last, and groaned faintly; but, as consciousness returned, it was easy to make him stand erect, and then to walk forward, impelled by the muzzle of a rifle pressed against the small of his back.

They came to Marston's horse, which he mounted, and so he rode on into the town, and the big man still walked with a long, soft tread before him. The first lamplight from a window on the outskirts of the village glinted on him, and Larry Marston felt his heart bound. This victim was older than he had expected; but, also, there was an air of surpassing greatness about him and Marston felt very much like some Titan who dared to grasp the thunderbolt of Jove and found it obedient to his hand. Just before them was the jail.

Chapter Twenty-eight

The Owl Hoots Again

It was Thunder Moon's formal entrance into society, and the rumor that he was to be at Charlotte Keene's dance made every other invited guest certain to be present. He was unused to many of the ways of the white man, but he was familiar enough with the peculiar hum of voices which arose when he entered the Keene house. That same hum, less subdued, he had heard many times before, as when he entered the lodge where the wise men of the Suhtai held council, or when he stood in the center of the circle at the scalp dance. There was a little pressing toward him, but Judge Keene captured him the moment he appeared and carried him off to his library.

"You're not interested in dancing, William," he said, confidentially. "And I had to chat with you for a moment. I want to bury the hatchet. Naturally, I'm referring to the first visit you paid me. On that day, frankly, I played the fool. It takes a wise man to look through surfaces to the inner man. I was not wise. Now, William, I want to tell you that I've changed my mind. Because you killed a tiger? Not at all. But because you've shown conclusively that you're going to become a respected member of our society. You've changed yourself profoundly, most profoundly, and in a few short weeks."

He scanned William Sutton from head to foot; certainly nothing was wrong with the costume of that youth. The soberness of his clothes merely added emphasis to the dignity of his demeanor. The judge continued: "You came to me, on that first day, to tell me that you wanted to ask for . . . er . . . in fact . . . that you looked rather kindly upon my girl but, since that time, of course, you've seen a great many of the beauties of this county and no doubt you've changed your mind."

It would have required a duller wit than that of William to fail to understand the drift of the judge, and he said quietly: "I have seen many other faces. They are like pictures which stay in the eye for a moment and then are rubbed out by a little time. I haven't seen another woman like your daughter."

"Well said!" exclaimed the judge heartily. "And I hope, my lad, that no matter how long you live among us, you won't lose the outland flavor which you have in your speech. Now, William, I shall come straight to the point, for I'm a man who hates circumlocution. You saw Charlotte on the first day and wanted her. What she feels about the matter I really don't know and, even if I did, I wouldn't be free to speak about it. The girl has a mind of her own and she's only too apt to use it. But from my viewpoint, I don't know of another young man in the community who would suit me better as a son."

He held out his hand. William grasped it firmly and, leaning forward a little, looked deeply into the eyes of the judge. "No matter what she says when I speak to her," he declared, "tonight we have become friends. And my father will be happy."

"Of course he will," said the judge. "Randolf and I have been as close as brothers all our lives, and we'll be close again. I was an ass, that was all. I've half a mind to ride over to see him now, but first I want to know what Charlotte says to you. Find a chance to slip out into some quiet corner with her and tell her what's in your heart. And the best of good luck to you, William. By heaven, I think you'll have it. Now run along. Strike while the iron is hot."

William Sutton stepped from the library and into a swirl of light, of music, of color. Kind eyes smiled at him and welcomed him. It was as though every one wished to enter into conversation with him. This homage filled him with delight. He heard the murmur of compliment and light laughter, as though pleasure overflowed in these people at the sight of him.

"The tiger was a half-wit to tackle such a man."

The heart of William Sutton swelled in him, and he felt, for the first time since coming to the new world, that he was a part and portion of these people. They were his, and he was theirs. The universe in which they lived, so petty once in comparison with the war and the hunt on the distant plains, now seemed a universe indeed, not bounded by physical horizons but stretching dimly on the endless plane of thought. As for the dry labor to which he was confined, it no longer seemed dull or pointless, but rather it was the alphabet through which he would eventually become conversant with the vital spirit of this strange life. As the immensity of all these new dimensions crowded in upon his brain, so he felt a mental strength waken in him and expand to meet the new necessity. It was not vanity. In the midst of that murmuring applause and under the light of those kindly eyes he felt the humility of the worker, ready to assume the burden of his task.

Yet something was lacking, something was out of joint. He stood in a corner, watching gravely the whirl and the gaiety of the dance, and the sound of the violins pierced his mind like arrows pointed with sweet pain. The circles of the dance dissolved into confusion as the music ceased, and the floors were filled with couples moving toward the chairs or toward the lighted coolness of the garden beyond. Charlotte came by him with a red-faced youth.

"Run along, Jimmy," she said to him. "There's Mary waiting for you, and I have to talk to William Sutton."

Jimmy grinned affably at William and nodded as he vanished.

"Do you like it?" said Charlotte.

"It is a pleasant thing to see, but not to take part in," said William. "I am used to people who are happy and celebrate because they have done something real. But here the people are going through motions and imitating happiness in order to be happy. But I think these are jumbled words which make little meaning."

"Not the sort of things that usually are said at dances," she said, looking up to him and frowning a little. "You seem to be an extraordinarily serious person."

"Is that a fault?"

"No. But, come out in the garden and let the night wind blow the taste of the dance out of your mind."

They went into the garden. The great bare face of the night pressed close down above them and subdued the voices of the girls and boys; even the fountain in the farthest corner dared no more than a whisper, and the wind lifted its falling spray and shook it out like silver hair. They paused beside it. As they watched, the music began again inside. The crowd swept back into the house. From indoors they heard only a throb and rhythm of music, and the night noises began to grow audible, the rattle of leaves, and the booming chorus of the bull-frogs around the pool in the next meadow.

"Now you are thinking of what?" Charlotte asked.

"This wind comes from the west. It has blown over the lodges of the Crows; over the teepees of the Suhtai, over the Father of Waters, and it comes to us here. I breathe of it and try to smell the wood smoke from our fires; but a man is less than a coyote and cannot read the wind with his nose."

She began to laugh a little, though her eyes were still grave. "You still want to be there," she suggested.

"A frog goes by land and water both," answered William. "He lives in the water, and yet he is not a fish. I have been taken out of the water. I never could be happy in the old life again, but still I want to get back in the pool. I am used to it. Sometimes I crave for unseasoned meat and air in a teepee, choked with wood smoke, and the harsh songs of the young men at night. I shall always turn back to those things, even when I am an old man among the whites. That is a weakness."

"No, that is a strength, I should say. You have two ways of being happy. Other people only have one."

"But a man cannot divide his body or his spirit into halves and live in two lives at once."

Charlotte was silent. "No," she said at last. "One has to make a choice. If I were you, I'd hardly know what to choose. I've never known anything else, but still I'm frightfully bored with life here more than half the time. Perhaps that's because we're never satisfied with what we are. We want to step around the corner. But around the corner there are other people just as restless."

"Horses, guns, men, women are real," he said. "We fill our hearts with such things on the plains. Well, there are horses, guns, men, and women here. But they are not real. The horses do not give you speed to escape from an enemy, or to catch him. They simply help you to follow a fox. The guns do not save your life or kill your foe. They simply make a noise and drop a bird or squirrel. They do not even give you food. The men live in chairs. The women do not make the teepees or take care of their children. Even the shadows of the dead

Thunder Moon and the Sky People

Cheyennes chasing the shadows of the buffalo through the sky live more, really. But still, there is something else in this land and among you white people. I first guessed at it when I leaned out of a window at Sutton House and looked down into your face."

He turned as he spoke, and looked down in her face again. Her eyes grew larger to receive his glance. The talk had taken this personal turn so quickly that she caught her breath.

"Ah," he murmured. "Whenever I look at you, I see the thing again. It makes me want to take you and possess you. It makes me want to come close to you. I wanted you for my squaw when I first saw you, but even then I knew that if I had you even in my teepee something of you would not be mine. Still I would be trying to capture you. I might be a hundred marches away from you, and yet closer than when I stand beside you near this water. Do you understand?"

She did not answer, still receiving his glance.

"Hai!" cried William Sutton softly, like a hunter on the plain. "Stand farther away from me. My arms open to receive you. I have a song in the hollow of my throat. I want to tell you . . . well, that I shall kill many buffalo for you if you let me take you to my teepee. You see, I forget that you do not live on buffalo meat. Let us go back to the house. There is nothing that I can say to you."

He turned away in obedience to his own suggestion, but the girl did not stir and, stepping back to her, he saw that she was smiling.

"Are you laughing at me?" he asked.

"Not altogether."

"You had better come back into the house with me."

"I can't," she said. "I wouldn't dare to show my face to them all."

"You wouldn't?"

"No. I'm frightfully red."

He touched her face. "Yes," he said, "your face is hot. You tremble. Are you afraid?"

"Heavens!" cried Charlotte. "You will drive me mad."

"Are you angry?"

"I am so excited, William, that I'm almost fainting. My heart is beating like ten hammers. I can't possibly go inside."

He paused. "I almost think," he said, "that you want me to talk to you some more."

"I thank heaven," said the girl, "that you see that much."

She made a little gesture as she said it, and he caught the hand deftly and none too gently in mid-air.

"Charlotte!" he said, hoarsely.

She began to laugh brokenly, and William was drawing her closer and closer when the steady soft hoot of an owl sounded from the nearest woods. He dropped her hand as though at a spoken order.

Chapter Twenty-nine

Captive

"There is danger?" asked the girl, with a gasp, not of fear but from the strain of recovering suddenly from her emotion.

"Go inside," William Sutton said. "There is always danger," he added bitterly. "No, not danger to my life, perhaps." He waved her toward the house.

She started in instinctive obedience. Half way to the door, she turned and glanced back, but he was still waiting, tall, stern, passive. Realizing somehow that a crisis was upon him which was a crisis for her also, she hurried on to the house and closed the door behind her hastily, almost like one who has escaped from pursuit.

William, as he saw the door close, turned from the garden, leaped the hedge with a single bound and, upon the farther side, touched by a faint glimmer of the light from the house, he saw Red Wind and the gleam of her hair.

"I did not mean to drive you away from your squaw," said the Omissis girl quietly. "Only, I came with something to tell you."

"It is something evil," he answered sternly. "You never have come to me with good of any kind."

"It is neither good nor evil to you," replied Red Wind. "When Thunder Moon was a Suhtai, the lives and the happiness of the Suhtai were life and happiness to him, also. But now he is changed. What happens to them is nothing. They are like a dream. And he is awake."

"It is Standing Antelope!" exclaimed Thunder Moon. "He has stepped into some trouble. Tell me, Red Wind. He has struck a knife into someone. That is it . . . and nothing can tame him."

"It is not Standing Antelope," she answered, and he saw that she smiled faintly. "It is Big Hard Face."

"He is sick?"

"He is worse than sick."

"He is dead. Sorrow and trouble have broken his heart."

"No, he is worse than dead."

William was silent. He waited for the great blow to fall.

"To be shamed and captured is worse than to die," said Red Wind. "He has been taken. I followed as fast as I could. It was hard to follow without being seen, but I saw him closed into a house and I saw armed men come to watch at the entrance. They have taken him, and he never will come back to us. I went to Standing Antelope. He said that you were here. So I left Standing Antelope putting on his war paint, and I came on alone to tell you. I am sorry that I troubled you. Go back to your squaw and forget the Suhtai. Alas, they never can forget you."

Thunder Moon laughed softly. "That is a small thing," he said. "My father has great power. I shall say a word to him, and he will set Big Hard Face free."

The girl shook her head.

"You will see," he said. "Go back toward the Sutton House. I come at once."

In the Keene stables he borrowed a horse easily enough and, sweeping down the driveway, with no pause to make excuses to his host, he drove the poor animal at frantic speed up the highway until the lofty trees that clustered around his father's house were visible. He was out of the saddle and on the front steps with a single movement, and then into the high, hushed hallway, where a Negress in white uniform shrank with frightened eyes from before him.

"Where is the master?"

She seemed too disturbed to answer. She ran before him and stopped at the library door. William tapped softly at the door and waited until the deep, familiar voice bade him enter. So he went inside the room, and saw two pools of lamplight, where his mother sat with her needlepoint, and where his father sat, pouring over the white pages of a book.

"Now what's up, William?" asked the colonel.

"What's happened to bring you back so soon?"

"My foster father has come back from the Suhtai," William said, "to find me. And he has been taken and closed into the jail in the town. Will you set him free?"

The colonel and his wife started up, she with a faint cry.

"Be at ease, Martha," said her husband. "There'll be no trouble about this. You go along to bed . . . it's time for you to sleep. William and I shall handle this little matter, eh?"

He led her to the door, but she broke from him and ran to her tall son. Clinging to him and peering up into his face, she begged: "Nothing will happen to you, dear? *You* will do nothing rash? You'll trust everything to your father?"

The colonel answered cheerfully: "Good gad, my dear, what else would he do, and who's the person to handle this other than I? Of course, I'll look into everything and, if Big Hard Face has done no wrong, of course I'll have him set free."

He drew his wife from William and ushered her up the stairs. He was back at once. Not a word was said while he swung into an overcoat and ordered a rig. But as he drove his high-stepper toward the town, he said to his son: "Did you know that Big Hard Face was back?"

"Yes."

"When?"

"Yesterday."

That was all. The silence of the colonel was eloquent to William. He could feel the criticism which it implied—the lack of perfect confidence in his parents which had led him to keep back the fact of the Suhtai's arrival. For some reason the sense of opposition in his father caused in him a swift revolt. He set his teeth, and looked down at the hands of the colonel as they held the

173

reins tight upon the trotting horse. The trees shot back behind them on either side, and the road spun inward, as though upon a reel.

The lights of the town loomed up before them, and presently they were within the fencing rows of houses, within the mingled sounds of many voices, lost upon the colonel but audible to those wilderness-trained ears of William Sutton. The little city seemed to him the very face of civilization, huddled, confused, filled with significance at which he could guess rather than intimately understand. No outlying guards rode post around that swarm of people. All their wealth of horses, cattle, sheep, of garnered grain, and of houses, and all the treasure within the houses was open to the hand of violence to strike and take where and what it pleased. The mysterious spirit of the law had extended its arm around the place and kept it secure. Yes, and now that that same spirit of the law had taken within its grasp the wandering chief of the Suhtai—what then?

The jail loomed on the left, squat, dark, with little windows like many eyes in ranges, regular and level. Within it lived the very spirit of the law itself. They drew rein, they dismounted, and went up the steps of the building, William last, after tethering the horses, the colonel in the lead. William, looking at the squared shoulders of his father, felt that surely there was no force, even in the law itself, to withstand the dignity and the power of this man.

The colonel rapped at the door. A heavy sound came back, and he could guess at the strength of the solid slabs of wood which made the door. With the silence of oiled hinges, with the slowness which testified to its weight, the door swung open. Out to William came the thick, strange air of confinement, like the air of a cave, but without the fresh earth-scent. Before them stood the jailer.

"Good evening, Colonel Sutton," he said, touching his hat.

In his other hand he held a sawed-off shotgun, ready for instant use. William knew that weapon. At close range, three rifles and a half a dozen revolvers could not make up the sum of its deadliness. Then he looked into the face of the jailer, calm, square, lined, with the dull eyes of a fighting man. Such were the ideal warriors upon the warpath; such were the enemies most to be dreaded.

"You have a man here," said the colonel, "an Indian. I want to know what charge he's held on."

"Mister Marston just brought him in," said the jailer. "Horse stealing is the charge, I think. That's the usual Indian thing, ain't it? Will you step in, sir?"

The colonel passed in, and William entered guardedly behind him. He did not like the place. Neither its odor nor the solemn sense of strength which it exuded like a human being. He became all eyes and, though looking only before him, he saw every detail of the interior as he walked.

They were shown into a little office where Marston was sitting. He rose to meet them with no air of surprise, so that William guessed he had expected this visit. The colonel repeated his question.

"You know that we've been missing horses in the neighborhood, sir."

"I didn't know that."

"No? There was the Patterson mare."

"That was weeks ago."

"Of course, these fellows steal and then send their spoil west by their confederates. As a matter of fact, you've suffered at their hands yourself, Colonel Sutton, I believe."

"A good many years ago, Marston. May we see this man?"

"Certainly. You have some reason to be interested in his case, I suppose?"

The colonel looked at William, and the latter said slowly: "He was my foster father among the Suhtai."

He half expected to see the face of Marston harden and his eyes glitter, and he was not disappointed. Quite by accident, the young constable had been able to strike a blow at the man he most feared and hated, and it was plain from his expression that he relished the accident.

"Certainly you may see him then," said Marston, politely. "Just come this way. Of course, I'm very sorry. Very!"

He led the way with a lantern. There was no other light in the place, and as he swung it the shadows of the bars of the cells striped the ceiling and the walls in crazy patterns.

There was no other person in the jail except one old vagabond, lying face downward on his cot. He reared on one arm and blinked at them. They came to the cell where Big Hard Face sat Indian fashion on the floor. He rose to greet them and raised one hand above his head.

"How!" he said.

A little silence came over the group. There was such a world of uncivilized dignity about the chief that they could find no words to answer at the moment. Then William said in Cheyenne: "We have come to help you out of this place, Father. This man declares that you have stolen a horse."

"He says a thing which is not true," said the Indian.

"Big Hard Face," translated William, "says that he stole no horse. He has been in this neighborhood only two days. How could he have taken the mare?"

"I'm glad to hear it," said the constable. "But of course I can't set him free . . . not on his bare assertion. We'll have to have some proofs."

"My dear Marston," replied the colonel, "the burden is put on the state in maintaining that the man it suspects is guilty. Isn't that the law?"

"We have to have special ways of handling the Indians," said Marston. "You surely realize that. If he didn't come to steal horses, why did he come?"

"To persuade me to come back to the Cheyennes," William said.

"Ah, yes," murmured Marston. "We'll pan the whole thing out at the trial. I wish the man all the luck in the world, of course."

His eyes were grim, and it was plain that he would not relax his grip on this prisoner if he could help it.

Chapter Thirty

A Thunderclap

The colonel, in the meantime, took stock of the situation in silence, looking once or twice at the captive, but giving more of his attention to his son. William seemed profoundly troubled and, gripping one of the bars, he frowned in at the Cheyenne as though about to tear a way open through the steel and take the chief away with him.

He could see that Marston had marked the same instinct in his enemy and he could make out, furthermore, that the young constable was not unpleased. Why, could be understood without too much difficulty. A long revenge was what Marston wanted, and any attempt at violence on the part of William would give him his opening.

"Marston," said the colonel at last, "even if Patterson may prefer and prove a claim against this man, I'll stand good for the price of the lost mare if need be. Turn the Cheyenne loose, like a good fellow, will you?"

The constable flushed a little. Colonel Sutton was a great man in the community, and it would not be the wisest political move to win his hostility. However, his heart was set. He took refuge behind a legality. "It's my job to bring in the suspects," he said. "It isn't my part to turn them loose again. You must know that, sir."

The colonel made no further effort. "You see, William," he said, "that nothing can be done. Just tell your friend that we'll do what we can for him, have a lawyer to defend him, of course . . . and that everything doubtless will turn out all right."

The deep voice of William, strangely musical now that it was burdened with the language of the far plains, translated obediently.

The chief was greatly moved, though he wore his usual mask of indifference. "Tell him," he said to William, "that I had no reason to expect kindness from him. I have raised my hand against him. But behold, Thunder Moon, you are armed. The enemy is only one. You and your father are two. Strike him down! He wears the key which opens this door. Take me away now, because otherwise you never will free me with words and with money."

"Let me be alone with him for a moment," said William to his father and Marston. "You can let the jailer watch to see that I pass nothing to him through the bars," he added scornfully.

Marston flushed as he withdrew to his office with the colonel, but nevertheless he took the suggested precaution and placed the jailer on guard at a little distance from the occupied cell.

"I cannot shoot him down," explained William, when he could speak freely without danger that his meaning might be guessed by the gestures of the prisoner, or by his own. "Here in the land of the white men, weapons are not used except to kill cattle or birds. It is the law that holds you, Father, and the law cannot be broken."

"Is it medicine?" asked the chief solemnly. "One man came and stole up behind me and struck me down, yet I am not on the warpath. I have done no harm to these people. They lie about me and say that I have stolen horses. But I came not for horses but for you. If they have medicine, you have medicine, too. You have a greater medicine than their law. Pray to the Sky People. They will tell you what to do for me."

"Farewell," the foster son said sadly. "I shall come again in the morning. Perhaps there will be someway. My father is a great chief. Through him I shall work."

"Farewell, my son," said the old Suhtai. "But beware of a gift from the hand of an enemy."

William, moving away, from the corner of his eye saw the chief draw a blanket over his head. He went to the office. The heavy door which closed it against the interior of the jail had been left accidentally a trifle ajar and, as he came closer, he heard a phrase of the voice of his father which made his heart stop.

". . . but what I really want is to see this Cheyenne jailed the rest of his days."

William halted, aghast. The warning of Big Hard Face was yet in his ear, and now he heard this.

"I hardly follow that," said Marston.

"My lad," said the colonel, "there's no doubt that the Suhtai deserves something worse than a cell. If he had justice for his murders, probably he'd hang at once. I don't want that. But so long as he's in jail, I have assurance that my son will not be turning his heart west. He's still restless. This civilization of ours is a heavy load on his shoulders. I know, Marston, that you have no reason to like him. But in this case you and I can work together, and afterwards perhaps I can show you that my help in this county is not worthless."

"Colonel Sutton," said Marston, "nothing possibly could please me more than to feel that I had won your confidence. If I can do it in this way, which lies right in line with my legal duties, of course, I simply welcome the work. In the meantime, you'll let William think that you're really working for the freedom of Big Hard Face?"

"Naturally. We'll keep the little secret, you and I. You might let the judge know beforehand how I stand on the matter. I'll have a lawyer hired. Perhaps young Trowbridge. But you can let the judge know that I'm against the cause I am ostensibly representing."

"Certainly!" Marston chuckled. "Nothing could be simpler. Judge Whittaker has a sense of humor, as everyone knows."

A sense of humor? William set his teeth and controlled himself sternly, and then he entered the office. There was no purpose in letting the pair know that he had overheard them.

He and the colonel left at once and started back for the house. On the way, his father was most amiable, and talkative beyond his wont. He talked kindly of Big Hard Face, spoke of the magnificent presence of that worthy, and hoped that the time would come when he could see the chief in his house. All the time, as he listened, the heart of William swelled big against this hypocrisy. If love for him occasioned it, and if nothing but care for his welfare was behind this duplicity on the part of his father, nevertheless he could not forgive the sin. He made himself answer. He forced himself to tell stories about the greatness of Big Hard Face and his deeds upon the plains; but all the time he was telling himself that there was no trust to be put in anything now, except in the strength of his own hand—and perhaps in the cunning of Standing Antelope.

When they reached the house, therefore, and he had gone to his room, he was not surprised to find Standing Antelope waiting for him, hideous with paint, and busily at work cleaning a rifle. He gave Thunder Moon merely a glance. "I knew that you would fail," he said.

William went to the window and leaned out into the night. It was very late now. No voice rose and no lights shone from the huts of the Negroes from beyond the trees. All of the house was still. He had come to a turning point, he knew and, once having put his foot on this trail, how could he tell how he might withdraw it peaceably? He was about to raise his hand against the whites; and such a raising of the hand never was forgotten and never was forgiven, as he understood. It was not against a mere human. It was against the figure of the law, and in the deathless memory of the law the act would be enshrined and held vividly until penance had been done. So William thought, staring into the night.

He closed his eyes and drew before his mind the pictures of all who slept in that house. Jack and Ruth still were at the ball, quite unconscious of what was happening here. His mother slept, and perhaps she dreamed of him, happily, unaware of any rift in their quiet family life. There was his strong-minded father, too, now fall-

181

ing asleep in the smiling consciousness that he had hoodwinked his troublesome son. William set his teeth.

There were other things, however, to hold him to this place. Now that he was thinking of leaving it, the house itself appeared to him a thing worthy of love, almost like a human being. All the broad acres of the estate had a meaning to him—not the meaning of wealth alone, but a sense of unity and the rich pride of a small kingdom obedient to the master as to a king. That estate would, in time, pass into his hands. What was a chieftainship among the Suhtai compared with the overlordship here? The Suhtai could put their swift volleys of warriors in motion across the prairies, strike down the buffalo, and set up their white teepees in the spring. Under the first war chief there were other chiefs, each with a personal following. The medicine man, in many matters, was actually the head of the tribe. The authority of the head chief, in many respects, was limited to the extent of his own lodge.

How different on this place! Fenced with wilderness here, the river there, and on the other two sides bordered by wide roads, the estate held within its bosom great woods where the axe never had fallen, springs leaped from the ground in the scarcely explored depths of the forest shadows, swift creeks ran chattering across the meadows, and the broad acres were sowed with many crops. How vast were the barns and sheds to contain the harvest, how many the houses of the slaves who tilled the fields, and each of those houses far richer in all things than the stateliest lodge of the richest man among the Suhtai.

These were things to think of more than once before deserting them. William sighed as he looked out on the dark of the night. The stars were out, but gave only enough light in the central heavens to indicate the great masses of cloud which were rolling across their faces.

"Bring me," William said, "bring me the dream shield and the lance."

Instantly they were placed in his hands. He stepped out onto the little balcony outside his chamber. There he raised shield and spear to the dark face of the heavens. The Christian teaching of his kind mother was blotted from his mind in this tense emergency.

"Sky People, wonder workers, keepers of the medicine of the spirits of the air and earth," said Thunder Moon, "you have heard my voice on the prairies and given me a sign. If you can hear me and see me now that I stand in the land of the white man, give me a sign here, also. If I may stay here and let Big Hard Face die of a broken heart in the jail, be silent. I shall know that your silence, like death, concerns him. But if I am to raise my hand and strike for him, and then flee away from my father and my mother, my sister and my brother, and from all of this life around me, let me hear you, or show me a sign."

He stretched his hands high above his head laden with the long lance and the dream shield. For a long space he waited, and he heard behind him the superstitious groan of the boy, Standing Antelope, as the latter read the silence of the Sky People as an eloquent sign. Then, ripping boldly across the face of the sky, a bolt of lightning split the clouds and dropped jagged to the earth.

There was a faint, choked cry of joy from the boy. Almost instantly, a vast double roll of thunder shook the very house. The sign had been given in no uncertain form.

Chapter Thirty-one

Raiders

When William came back into the room, pale, his eyes fixed and staring as one who has been looking into the face of a deity, young Standing Antelope drew back from him, thoroughly frightened. His opinion of his celebrated companion had passed under some shadow of late months when he saw him taking so swiftly to the ways of the whites, but now he changed his mind violently, for a man to whom the upper spirits shouted in strong thunder and upon whom they looked with flashing lightnings was a dealer in medicine so dreadful and so strong that the boy was overwhelmed. Never again would he entertain unworthy doubts.

He had brought out the Indian clothes which Thunder Moon wore when he first came to the house of his father and had laid them upon a chair. Now, since he could not speak, he hardly dared to point toward this costume. Thunder Moon, with flashing eyes, went to it and picked it up. In another minute he began to tear off his clothing, saying to Standing Antelope that it was time to get the horses. The youngster was through the window and away in a moment.

The warrior now dressed in the fringed and beaded suit of softest deerskin. Moccasins were upon his feet. About his waist he belted two heavy revolvers; in his hand he took his rifle, and over his shoulders he slung the dream shield. Even with all this accouterment, he was able to descend deftly and swiftly to the ground. On the verge of the trees he found the boy waiting. There, too, was Sailing Hawk, whinnying softly with delight as though he felt in this midnight excursion a promise of some more of those wild rides which they had enjoyed together upon the prairies. Thunder Moon, rapt in his grim determination, hardly noticed that Standing Antelope had taken for his own use the favorite charger of Colonel Sutton himself. A thing which the stern master of Sutton House never could forgive. The led horse for Big Hard Face was a chosen beauty.

Now they were in the saddle and away. Going softly beneath the trees, they cut out across the meadows, gained the roadway, and then fairly flew toward the town. The rush of the horses and the keen cutting of the wind against Thunder Moon's face raised his heart to a fierce exultation such as he had not felt before during all these weeks. He wanted to shout and, from the corner of his eye he could see Standing Antelope swaying in his saddle, laughing like a mad creature.

They drew rein as the lights of the town glimmered, twinkled, and grew into long, bright rays before them. Quietly they rode into the village. There were no voices now. All was still, but there seemed to be a lurking danger in the silence. For no Indian town was like this at night. There never was a time among the Suhtai when dogs were not fighting and barking and snarling, when infants were not crying in the teepees, and when horses were not tramping or neighing. So it was through a strange silence that they went, and Standing Antelope instinctively allowed his mount to draw closer to the side of Sailing Hawk, and his keen glances went eagerly to this side and to that, prying beneath the hedges, seeking in the shadowy doorways.

"The law never sleeps," Thunder Moon had been told by his father, and that they saw no danger before them was no real reason why they should think all was safe. Restless as two wolves, the pair came before the jail. Close under the shadow of the jail wall they halted, the grass muffling the tread of the horses and there, in a whisper, Thunder Moon told his young companion to hold the bridles and wait for him.

A groan answered him. With all his heart, Standing Antelope yearned to have a part in this expedition, but he dared not protest against the orders of a leader at such a moment as this. He gritted his teeth and remained behind. Thunder Moon, rapidly adjusting a mask over his face, spoke quietly to his companion.

"Keep their heads turned toward the mouth of that street which leads north," he said. "We must not let a soul suspect that it is William Sutton who takes part in this rescue. Arrange the feathers so that they stand up in your hair. Now I wish that my long hair could be replaced by a wig. But, wrapped in this buffalo robe, I must seem an Indian if I can."

He went straightway to the front door of the jail and knocked. Had he known it, the instant reply was suspicious.

"Who's there?"

"A friend!" William said, his voice going husky.

"Friend? What name?"

Purposely, William made his answer a blur.

"Wait a minute."

There was a noise of a bolt turning, and then a little iron shutter a foot square was opened near the side of the main door and a ray of light darted out against the masked face of William. His long arm drove through the aperture; his hand fastened on a throat; and, as he jerked the victim to the small port, he saw the fear-distorted face of the jailer.

"Give me the keys," said William sternly, pressing a gun against the man's head. "Give me the keys to the door and to the cell. Point them out in your bunch."

In a choked voice, for the grip that held him was cutting off his breath, the jailer answered as he obediently held up the keys: "Give me air. For God's sake don't murder me. The biggest one for the door . . . this new one for the cell of the Indian."

How did he know so instantly which cell was to be opened? Thunder Moon did not pause to think of this. His mind was too thoroughly filled with the work which lay before him. He merely murmured: "If you give an alarm and call for help, I'll shoot you down when I come inside the jail. If you stand fast and make no sound, I'll reward you."

The jailer nodded. He was past speech now and, as William's iron grip relaxed, the poor fellow staggered back, gasping heavily. The big key fitted the jail door, the lock turned smoothly back, and the next instant William stepped inside the building. There was not a sound. The jailer had sunk into the shadows. William walked lightly down the central aisle until he came to the cell where Big Hard Face sat in the darkness.

"Father, are you there?" he asked in Cheyenne.

There was a moment's pause. His heart stopped with fear lest the old man had been removed. But then the deep, quiet voice of Big Hard Face made answer: "You have come, oh, my son, and all is well."

The next instant he fitted the key into the lock and turned it. It was only a slight, grating sound that the key made, but it seemed to be a signal which was instantly answered, as from three different portions of the big cell room three lanterns were that instant unhooded, and their well-focused shafts of light struck full upon the cell, Big Hard Face, and Thunder Moon.

"Thank God for the mask!" thought Thunder Moon.

The very first cry was: "William Sutton, in the name of the law I call on you to surrender."

They knew! And how? He was acting too swiftly to allow much thought, and he cast the door wide and let Big Hard Face rush out into the aisle.

"Shoot!" shouted someone—and William thought it was the voice of the jailer. "You've let them get together already."

Thunder Moon had placed his rifle in the hands of his foster father. A heavy Colt lay in each of his. As the warning rang, a gun belched with a terrible roar, not like the metal clang of an exploding rifle, and then they heard the clattering of a charge of buckshot as it scattered among the steel bars of the cells, striking out sparks of fire. That charge was aimed not at the old chief, but at Thunder Moon, and he heard the keen hum of the shot around him. Something stung his leg, but it was only a scratch. For the rest, perhaps the bars of the cells saved him. Imperious chance intervened on his behalf, and he was unscathed. But not relieved from all danger, for as he heard the unlucky marksman cursing, two rifles spat at him with tongues of flame.

"Shoot to kill! Shoot to kill!" shouted the voice of Marston. "The two devils are together, and they're both armed now."

Though he had laid the trap with consummate skill, he had forgotten one most important item, which was the light of the lanterns, shining through the bars from different angles. They filled the room with a bewildering madness of shadows, and through those shadows two men were running, by no means an easy target, in spite of the close range.

"Straight ahead . . . the door is open!" cried Thunder Moon, and as his foster father rushed ahead of him, he snapped a shot to the right and shot to the left at the shadows which crouched near the lanterns. Either an intervening bar or carelessness made the first shot miss; but the second was answered by a wild burst of cursing and he knew that he had struck his mark. He knew it, and his heart failed him, and he set his teeth. All that he had done hitherto might be condemned by skillful lawyers, but nothing in the world, his father so often had said, could make up for the shooting of a fellow man. The law, now, would follow him like a relentless bloodhound to his death. However, if the man were not dead he. . . .

In that hope, he sped on with his foster father. Again the rifles crashed behind them—two of them. The door was close before them. Ah! A wheeling shadow swung across the open gap, and the door shut with a heavy slam in their faces.

"Drop! Drop!" commanded Big Hard Face, instantly and coolly. "Drop and let us kill these devils and take their scalps. Afterward, we shall find a way out of the place. They are only two to two, now."

Well for them was it that they had dropped to the floor at the suggestion of the old chief, for the straight-focused fire of two well-aimed rifles was now turned toward them. They heard the thud of bullets striking against the iron plates upon the inside of the door. Little shreds of lead fell upon them.

The odds still were not two to two, however. Yonder lay one fellow groaning and moaning and cursing, quite out of the battle, but making more noise than a fatally hurt person should be able to do. Marston and some other fellow, with a supply of weapons at hand, were keeping up a steady fire. Now from the side the jailer opened with a revolver. He it was who had mustered his resolution to fling the door shut in their faces.

Knee-high, Thunder Moon aimed his shot. There was a gasp, and the jailer was down. Big Hard Face, moving sideways across the floor, came to a pause and fired, the heavy report of the rifle was half drowned and then prolonged by the shout of a hurt man.

"Are you done, Mike?" cried Marston's voice, in agony of fear.

"I'm a dead man, Larry," said the other. "Make terms with Sutton or he'll murder you too and. . . ." The voice trailed away.

"Will you surrender, Marston?" called Thunder Moon. "Will you surrender?"

"You've got the odds against me," said Marston. "I'll surrender, then, and . . . no, damn you, I'll fight on to the finish. I have you now, and I'll hang you for tonight's work."

There was a reason for this change in his speech, for loud and heavily, at this moment, a hand had beaten against the door of the jail, and the sound of many voices could be heard calling from the street.

Chapter Thirty-two

Whither?

'Shoot low! Shoot low!" whispered Thunder Moon to Big Hard Face. "No, shoot no more. He has stopped firing. . . ."

"Kill him," said Big Hard Face through his teeth.

"Now I praise Tarawa. I shall die fighting, and leave the dead men heaped around me. There shall be something for you to say when you reach the Suhtai and sing to them of how your father died. For now you have killed the whites in their own land, and they cannot forgive you. They will hunt you back to your people, my people, the Cheyennes."

"It is true," Thunder Moon admitted, "but we shall fight our way out together. How shall we leave this place, oh, my Father? Listen! The people are gathering in the street. Soon there will be hundreds of them with guns. And the coward, Standing Antelope, fired no gun and made no stand against them to keep me protected, or warned at least of the danger."

"That boy is brave and wise," said the old chief. "You will find that good comes of him. Now I see a way, I think. See, they press against the door and beat on it."

For many voices were raised on the outside calling: "Marston! Marston! Open the door. What's happening?"

The loud voice of Marston answered with a shout: "Murder has happened! Three men are down in here, dropped by William Sutton and his Indian father. Break in the rear door because that is the weakest."

"Throw open this door," whispered the chief to his foster son, "and then we shall rush out through them."

"We shall rush through them," agreed Thunder Moon. "The Sky People sent me to you tonight, and they would not send me to my death."

"But first, let us kill the dog who barks at our heels in this room."

"He has hidden among the shadows and waits. Let him live. We have spilled enough white blood, and the white law never forgets."

"Let your way be my way, then," said the chief. "Here! I have the handle of this door."

He had been fumbling in the darkness, for under the deadly fire of Thunder Moon and Big Hard Face the jailers had extinguished the lanterns. Now, with a strong pull, the chief flung the heavy door open, and half a dozen men who were beating against it and shouting on the outside, lurched in with cries of alarm. Beyond, on the narrow platform, clustered on the steps of the jail, and scattered in the street, were fully fifty armed men. In all the adjoining houses lamps were being lighted, casting yellow, glowing streams into the street so that all these figures were faintly illuminated.

"The gun-butt," said Thunder Moon, "and save the bullet for the last crisis! Charge them, Father!"

As he spoke, he beat the heavy barrel of his revolver into the face of a big man who lurched toward him, arms outspread. The man went down, and as Thunder Moon fired rapidly into the air the others fell back with shouts of fear and confusion. Guns were raised but, before bullets could be fired, the two had swept on through the crowd and a shot was more apt to strike a fellow townsman than one of the fugitives.

Those behind were hindered by their own numbers. Those ahead had something to do to guard themselves and escape from the rush of danger for, as Big Hard Face strode forward, the rifle circled with crushing force in his hands, and the revolvers of Thunder Moon spat fire in the faces of the crowd. How could they mark that the bullets were not aimed at them, but just above their heads?

It was a lost battle, however, and Thunder Moon knew it, and groaned as he set his teeth. These fellows were not like red men of the plains, who could be startled into flight by the surprise attack of a bold handful. They gave back a little, to be sure, but they came again, and their numbers were beginning to mass together.

"Ah hai!" cried Big Hard Face. "We have come to the last battle, oh, my son. Stand with me, and guard my back as I shall guard yours. Let us pile the dead around us before we die. Stand with me, Thunder Moon. A few great deeds, and then the end."

It seemed, indeed, that the last moment had come. A knife flicked the shoulder of Thunder Moon. He barely swayed away from the stroke of a clubbed shotgun. Then, piercingly sweet in the ears of the two, the terrible and familiar war yell of a Cheyenne rang up and down the street. As the startled whites gave back a little, there was heard the volleying beat of many hoofs, and again the screaming, wailing, battle cry of the Suhtai, pitched high, stabbing at the eardrums and curdling the blood.

Four tall horses were rushing into the crowd, and the townsmen gave back with a shout of fear and astonishment. It seemed as though a whole tribe were pouring to the attack. Through an opened avenue in the press Thunder Moon made out the familiar front of Sailing Hawk sweeping toward him, and then he recognized the furious voice of Standing Antelope as that young brave fired a revolver blindly to either side and came on, screaming like a demon. There was a second rider. As the horses came to them Thunder Moon recognized by the light which glimmered on the copper braids of hair, sleek as metal, Red Wind.

"Brave girl!" cried Big Hard Face, leaping to his saddle.

"Little brother, well done!" called Thunder Moon to Standing Antelope, and all four turned their horses into the mouth of the nearest street, which opened before them a black gulf of refuge from their danger.

Guns were roaring behind them, but roaring vainly, for the street bent sharply to the right, and in another instant the Indians were flying safely through the night.

The last lights of the town shot past, and the open country received them.

"Ah hai!" shouted the chief. "Four Suhtai strike through four hundred. This is a night for singing. This is a night the tribe shall remember. But do not ride out your horses, my children. Slowly and softly. The race will be long. The white devils will rise up against us. They will hunt us with horses. Dogs will show them the way that we have gone, and we and our horses shall need much strength."

They heeded his caution, and drew back to a soft trot. They left the road, and went into a pasture, so that they would not leave behind them a stain of dust in the air to direct their immediate pursuers. Now that the grass muffled the tread of the horses, they could talk. How the picture of the stern and self-composed Indian would have vanished had that group been seen and heard by many witnesses, and how Big Hard Face laughed and boasted.

"They shut me behind iron," he cried. "There was around me more iron than goes to the making of a thousand guns. Thunder Moon came and struck the iron, and it turned to rotten wood. He took me by the hand, and I stood up. The white men shot at us. We killed them to the right and to the left. The head man was left. Like a frightened prairie dog in its hole, he dared not speak or move. We threw open the doors. We walked out through hundreds of warriors. We struck at their faces and they were blinded by our might and by our valor. And then a boy and a woman rushed at them and made them flee, screaming. But the boy and the woman were Cheyennes. And a Cheyenne woman has more courage than the bravest men of other tribes. Look on her, Thunder Moon."

"Look on her!" said Standing Antelope. "Yes, you

have said that she has made bad medicine. But she came to me and warned me that there was danger gathering in the town and that the people were awake in their houses though they showed no lights. She came to me riding a fine horse and so, when the crowd poured out and the shooting began inside the jail, I would have charged at their faces, shooting to kill, but she was wise and told me that I should go away and wait to help you as you left the jail. I saw that she was wise and I followed her."

He paused. The girl, who had ridden with downward head, now turned a little and glanced at Thunder Moon. One glance, and that was all.

"I have been a fool," said Big Hard Face. "I have not seen what was in her. Tarawa sent her to us as a blessing. For her sake, I shall offer up five painted buffalo robes when I return to the Suhtai. She shall have honor among the warriors and even the oldest women and the wives of the chiefs shall stand up and wait on her. On all things she was made to be the squaw of Thunder Moon. Take her hand. Ask her if she will belong to you and cook in your teepee and flesh the hides and cure them for your sake and be the mother of your children."

"Hush! Hush!" the girl said. "You talk and talk." She galloped her horse ahead.

"Go after her, Thunder Moon!" the chief said. "Go after her. She rides just fast enough to be overtaken. Ah hai! Go! Go!"

Thunder Moon did not go. He was too filled with wonder at the state of his own mind. For after all these months during which he had felt that the red men were divorced from his thoughts and his life forever, at a touch all the old glamour came back to him.

It had not been life. It had been like sleep. Only two faces looked in on his heart—his mother and Charlotte

195

Keene. Though Charlotte was beautiful, she had no beauty such as the wild loveliness of this Omissis girl. Though she was graceful, she had no grace such as that of Red Wind. If there were a delicate mystery and the sense of a soul surrounding her, nevertheless there was no such bewildering strangeness as that which surrounded the Cheyenne maiden. What friend had he won in all his stay among the whites equal to the friendship of Standing Antelope? Ay, and what was the love of his stern, thoughtful, busy father compared with the devotion which had drawn Big Hard Face out of the plains and across the long marches to his side?

He began to breathe deeply. He listened to Standing Antelope and his foster father laughing gaily together, as though they had struck upon some capital jest, and a lump rose in his throat. Whether it was joy or sorrow he could hardly tell. As he looked at the stars above him, he knew that they were traveling the *West*, the *West*, the *West*; and the goal of their travels was the safety and the peril of the open plains. Suddenly he was hungry for it. He wanted again the smell of the lodge fires, and the noise of the dogs and the children in the village, and the chanting of one of the old criers, inviting to a feast. He wanted again the rush and the dust of the buffalo hunt, and the long and terrible marches along the warpath.

Westward then. Now, at a rousing gallop, they swept down a slope and came upon Red Wind, who was giving her horse water in the brook which glimmered in the heart of the little valley. She raised her hand, and they halted around her.

"There is no pursuit," murmured Standing Antelope. "Listen! There is no sound of the hoofs of horses behind us. We are safe. The white men are fools, as I have told you a thousand times, Thunder Moon."

"You are a child," said the girl gravely. "We are all in danger, except Thunder Moon. There is no easy way for us, except through Thunder Moon. He could make our peace and let us go. But then he would have to stay behind us."

"The evil spirit comes into you again, Red Wind," said the old chief in a fury. "You speak with no wit."

"Look!" said the girl. "Up that valley lies the house of your father. Are you willing to leave it behind you?"

"I have killed," said Thunder Moon. "I cannot turn back now."

"The white men have ways of dodging the white man's law," said the girl with perfect surety. "Do not let fear drive you. Go look at your father's house. We shall wait for you here. For a little while there is no danger to us if we stay."

Chapter Thirty-three

Bloodhounds

The pursuers, however, were not men to give up without an effort. There was not a saddled horse in the street to follow the flight and, by the time the mounts were ready, the swift galloping of the four had put them well beyond the reach of immediate detection. They might have followed any one of a whole great network of trails, roads, and bridle paths which was flung down over the face of that country. Other citizens in similar circumstances might have settled back and cursed the stupidity or the negligence of the officers of the law who had been detailed to guard the jail. But the men of this town were of better stuff. They paused to inspect the interior of the jail, and there they found Larry Marston busily tying up the wounds of his three companions. One was shot deep through the shoulder; two others had wounds in the legs which would not have kept them from handling guns if they were heroes. Heroes they were not, and they had had enough of Marston's little party.

He himself was grimly set on revenge; his words were few; his face was set; and a glare was in his eyes. Calmly, in a hard, rapid voice, he told his fellow townsmen what to do. The four had escaped from them. All of them had been seen, and having been seen they might be trailed. There was the Indian chief; there was the Indian boy, Standing Antelope, now a wildly familiar figure at Sutton House; and there was William Sutton upon whom the eyes of the entire county had been fixed for so long. In addition, there was the mysterious figure with the dress of a man and the face and braided hair of a woman. She, too, should not be hard to find. To find them, let not the townsfolk worry about spotting particular trails, but remember that they could often strike a target by firing rather blindly with scatter shot. So Marston bade them mount their horses and ride furiously, urged on by the consciousness that if they allowed this jail break to be consummated without catching the guilty, the whole community would become a laughing stock to every other village and every other town throughout the state.

In the meantime, let them go coursing through every road and every path near the town and ride on and on until the morning brightened. Wherever a house stood near, let them rouse the sleeping people with shouts and with a fury of excitement and tell them what had happened and describe the fugitives. So, by the time that morning light came, the entire circle around the town would be aroused and, after that, it could hardly be that the pursuit would miss the trail. However, should this broadcasting method fail, Marston had another thing to do as a final resource, and let all his fellow citizens trust that he never would give up this work, no matter what days or weeks or years were required. William Sutton had broken open the jail which was in his charge. William Sutton had managed it with incredible skill and audacity in spite of the fact that a special committee had been arranged to lie in wait for just such a raid. Now Marston would have blood for blood in repayment.

The villagers heard these bits of advice and promise which were something more than advice and something less than commands. They hurried to do as they were bidden. And so it was that the hasty, earnest riders of the town rushed away through the countryside. Wherever they reached the cottage of a slave, they beat on his door until he came, trembling. To him they shouted the word. Let all eyes be tensed with suspicion. There was a liberal reward for the finding of the criminals. Enough to buy the freedom of a whole family of slaves.

Wherever they came to a great house, two or three would strike at the door until the proprietor came down, or flung up a window, usually gun in hand, to find out what the uproar meant. Then they gave him the word, and sped on toward the next plantation. It was true that, the farther out they rode from the town, the fewer were the houses, whether of masters or of slaves, or of solitary small landowners and hunters. When the morning came, they themselves would be lying in a great ring, ready to take up the trail should any rumor of its direction come to them, ready also to spread the news of the trail-finding

199

through their entire far-flung band. Once a clue was picked up, the whole force of the township instantly could be flung in that direction. Altogether, it was a skillfully organized effort. Even a novice could have seen that the work would by no means be easy, for they were pursuing Indians, instinctively wise in all matters of war and concealment, and in addition most nobly mounted. All they needed to do, then, was to fling straight out on their courses, and it would be most hard to overtake them.

Marston was not prepared to trust everything merely to the numbers of his followers or to the eagerness with which they would go about their work. Several times he had had to chase runaway Negroes, and he had hunted them, on every occasion, with a pack of sturdy bloodhounds. They belonged to one of the oldest settlers in the district, a queer, solitary fellow named Kingston. Men were apt to say that Kingston kept the hounds not for the trail of deer or other four-footed game but for the pleasure which it gave him to hunt men. Whenever there was call for them to chase the fugitive Blacks, not only would Kingston give them readily, but also he himself was sure to ride in the hunt. To him Marston rode now, accompanied by seven of the best fighting men in the town. They were not of the upper class. They were square-jawed warriors, every one, men used to the handling of guns, and too familiar with the shooting of big game to hesitate a great deal in pointing their weapons even at human targets. He had selected them by degrees, and every one of them he had used before and recompensed out of his private purse. For the constableship to Marston was not a political plum, but a luxury and game. Now, well-mounted, keen for their work, armed to the teeth, they followed their leader down the road to the house of Mr. Kingston.

They did not have to complete their journey, for half way to the place they encountered the pack, brought forward by Kingston himself and handled by three mounted Negroes. A dozen great beasts, tugging at the leashes which secured them to the horses, they lurched down the road, keen to be at some important trail. Kingston came rapidly on through the darkness.

"Is that you, Marston?"

"It's I, Mister Kingston. How did you happen to turn out your pack tonight?"

"I had word from someone passing the place. I heard that young Sutton has finally kicked over the traces. Well, I've been expecting it. I've been expecting it."

He spoke with sort of exultation in his tone. He turned back with Marston toward the jail.

"This may be bitter work for the dogs," said Marston, as they cantered on. "We have four people to follow and though one of them is a woman she seems to be an Amazon. I don't think that, if we come up with the quarry, all of your dogs will be alive to tell the tale tomorrow."

"I've hunted the boar and the deer," said Mr. Kingston savagely. "And I've hunted desperate fugitives and never regretted a dog or two lost along the way. Why should I begrudge a few of my best now that we have something worthwhile on foot? And tell me. If we get at William Sutton, do you think he'll shoot . . . at men?"

The constable laughed harshly. "It's a point on which I don't think. I don't have to," he said, "because I know. I've seen something of him, as you know. And if he's not a natural killer, then I'll admit that I've learned nothing about human nature from my work as a constable. He'll shoot to kill and, furthermore, he will kill. We're going to pay, on this trail. We're going to pay, both in dogs and in men. Are you unwilling to keep on the trail Mister Kingston?"

Mr. Kingston laughed in turn, a crooning brooding laughter. "We have only one life to live," he said. "Sport has been the greatest thing for me, and yet I've never had a chance at real sport before this evening. Is it likely that I'll turn back? Four of 'em . . . and one a woman. Why, my dear young friend, this is going to be something to remember . . . or to die for."

Marston did not answer. Words were failing him somewhat, as he looked for the first time into the nature of his companion and found him with the soul of a sleuth hound. It turned his own blood a little cold. After all, this was the sort of spirit which he could use to the best advantage for such work as lay ahead of them.

They got back to the jail, and the pack was brought inside the building. First they were taken to the cell where the Indian had been confined. After that, they were shown and allowed to smell and mouth the buffalo robe which Big Hard Face had been wearing, which had been left behind when he fled from the jail and attacked the waiting mob outside. It was as good a clue as possibly could have been given to them. Next they were pooled at the spot where many signs of horses showed where the four mounts had been brought up in the street so that Big Hard Face and William Sutton could escape.

The scent of man and beast now was in the nostrils of the pack, and they gave tongue in a mellow thunder the instant they were loosed. Straight down the side street they drove, close together, letting one high-shouldered veteran take the lead in person and in tongue. Behind them rode the constable and his men in company with Kingston. Altogether there were twelve souls, though no doubt the expedition would be reinforced by others who would flock to the music of the dogs as they headed across the country.

"We've started late," Marston said, "but I think this trail will lead to something."

"It will lead to blood," replied Kingston, fiercely prophetic. "I feel it, man, I feel it."

Chapter Thirty-four

Whips and Spurs

While these things were happening in the town, William Sutton had left his companions and galloped up the way toward the house of his father. Under the trees nearby, he left Sailing Hawk. Then he climbed up to the top of the front porch and from that point came under the window of the room in which his parents slept. He slipped in through the window and began to cross the floor stealthily. A dim, white form rose from the farther bed.

"Who is there?" said a ghostly whisper.

He whispered back: "William!"

Instantly he saw his mother rise, saw her throw on her dressing-gown and step into her slippers. He delayed no longer in the room, but went softly into the little library adjoining. There she joined him, her slippers whispering on the deep pile of the carpet. She came straight to him and reached up her hands to his shoulders.

"What has happened, William? What have you done?"

"I've taken my foster father from the jail."

"Ah!" she murmured. Then she added faintly: "I knew that it would happen. I dreamed of it. I told your father; but he wouldn't believe."

"I couldn't trust the thing to my father," said William sternly. "If I had been able to leave it in his hands, I should have done so."

"And now, William? What will you do? At least, you weren't recognized? They won't be able to trail you?"

"Yes, I was recognized."

She moaned with fear and with grief. "It will make a great trouble," she said, "but your father will be able to handle the thing, I know. He'll see that no harm comes to you from it. I'll go and wake him now. Wait here until I've told him for the first time. If he's very angry, you'll control your own temper, dear?"

"There's no use calling him," he said. "He can't help me in this. I would have left everything in his hands, but I overheard him plotting with Marston to keep Big Hard Face in the jail forever. I overheard him betraying my foster father and in that way betraying me as well. But matters have gone too far for his help. *No* one can help me now."

"What do you mean? And what have you done, in the name of mercy?"

"There are dead men lying in the jail, Mother." She clung to him, swaying and stunned by the blow. "I'm going back to the plains," he said. "After all, I never was meant to be a success in this part of the world. Sooner or later I should have made a break, and, therefore, it's as well that I should make the break now. There are only two things that make my heart ache."

"William, wait a moment. I can't hear you. I don't understand. You are going back to the plains?"

"I'll find a way to come to you again, now and then," he said, with great emotion in his voice. "I'll find some way of doing it . . . once every year, say. I'll try to come back to you, and perhaps I can come back to Charlotte Keene. Mother, this same night I've told her that I loved her. I think she was about to say that she loved me, too, but just then the messenger came and I was called away. You see, it is all the work of the Sky People. They don't want me here, and therefore they are driving me away."

"There are no Sky People, William. There is only the kind and patient God who. . . ."

"Mother, keep your own gods, and let me have mine. This same night I called them for a sign, and they gave it to me."

"The wind is up. The rain will be coming soon," she said. "It's turning into a wild night. I shall die of grief and of fear if you go out into it, my dear, my poor boy."

"Shall I wait here, then? Listen?"

He drew her to the window. The gale blew fairly from the town and, as it whistled around the corner of the building, they could hear something more than the mere spirit of the storm in the sound, for there was a booming voice, and then a chorus of voices, far away, but seeming to run up on them with an amazing speed.

"Do you hear?"

"The bloodhounds!" she said. She added hysterically: "Go quickly. And how shall I send word to you after this? How shall I let you know when it is possible for you to come back to us?"

"I'll find some safe messenger to send to you if I cannot come myself. But it will never be safe for me to come back openly. Tell Charlotte Keene that I shall never forget her. The lodge where she lives is my heart. But we are drawn into different trails. I must go back to the plains, and she must stay here and work out her own way through the lives of the whites. She will marry. God keep the man she marries out of my path. I feel very

205

sick, mother. I have two hearts. And both of them are broken with sorrow. Good bye!"

She was sobbing so that she could speak no more. He kissed her forehead and left as he had come, through the window and then down a column to the ground below. There he did not hesitate, but with one upward glance at the dark square of the window above him and the white, slender form of the woman in it, he hurried back to the spot at which he had left the stallion.

He found Sailing Hawk extremely nervous, alternately throwing up his head and sniffing at the ground, very much as he often had acted when on the debatable ground of a warpath in the old days upon the plains. As Thunder Moon swung into the saddle, he heard the cause of the disturbance of the big horse.

Far on the horizon was a cry of dogs, the unmistakable chorus of a pack, not like the wild calling of a band of wolves in winter running down a blood trail, but filled with the same deathless terror and malice. It seemed safely distant but, as the wind fell a moment later and atmospheric conditions altered, the full chime of the chorus beat suddenly and fully upon his ear. He realized that the pack was rapidly closing in upon the trail.

What trail they followed, he did not need to ask. He was perfectly familiar with the dogs which Kingston was in the habit of donating to the constable and the officers of the law in that vicinity. Therefore he set his teeth, but not in any ecstasy of fear. Rather, he was grimly determined to make those who rode behind him realize that now they were not on the trail of some frightened and desperate slave.

He rode rapidly back to the place where the three Indians waited for him, and as he came to them he saw that they, too, had heard the calling of the dogs and had understood it perfectly. Standing Antelope had warned them of its significance. Now the boy called anxiously to Thunder Moon: "How do we ride? Where shall we go to dodge them? They are coming fast, and they never tire."

They held serious conference upon the matter. Should they ride straight down one of the main roads and trust to the speed and the wind of their horses? Or, should they attempt to take half-known byways and cross water many times in order to delay the hounds behind them as much as possible?

There were other possibilities, also, such as frequently taking a course across some of the farm yards which might lie more or less in their way where the strong odors of many animals might kill their scent. But this Standing Antelope was against. He had been behind this same pack of hounds when they ran down a fugitive who had tried that very precaution, and they had captured the man and, indeed, nearly torn him to pieces, before the posse of the constable arrived on the scene and rescued the victim. They continued their grave debate, all speaking in turn except the girl, who looked first at one and then at the other. At length Big Hard Face was addressed by his foster son.

"Father," he said, "on the plains you have been a hundred times upon the trail. These hounds are very swift and their noses are sure, but I think that they are not so sure and not so swift as Pawnees in pursuit. Now tell us what we must do, and we shall attempt it."

"Each man," said Big Hard Face, "is only wise in his own country and among his own people. The wise man in his own lodge is a fool in the teepee of the stranger. This land is strange to me. I am used to the broad plains and to the way of the plainsmen. Therefore my advice may be very wrong, but I should ride by the broadest and swiftest way and put a march between us and the enemy swiftly. Let it be, however, as my son wills it."

"One march," Thunder Moon said, "cannot take us away from our enemies. We have killed white men, therefore the white law follows us. It lies behind us and before us. It will follow us into the prairies. However, what use have we for secret ways in a strange country? Even Standing Antelope is not so familiar with it as are the white men. Father, let us ride straight and fast and trust to the legs of our horses."

He ended, and straightway they headed for the nearest road, and then bore west along it at a brisk gallop. Presently Big Hard Face called for a slower speed.

"We are not children in the saddle, Thunder Moon and I," he said, "and therefore we must save the strength of our horses, as wise men save water when they cross the desert." He drew his own mount down to a trot, and the rest imitated the example, reining in their horses. They made less noise now and, taking the grassy edges of the highway, where the softer ground was better for the hoofs of the horses, they passed along with practically no sound. Like four shadows they drifted across the countryside. Then the moon rose and began to silver the tops of the trees in the woodland before them.

"There may be traps and traps before us," said Standing Antelope. "Phaugh! This country chokes me. If ever I come back to the prairies where the sky is a full half-circle above our heads, I never shall leave it again."

"The shadows that may conceal our enemies from us may conceal us from our enemies," said Red Wind. "Have a great heart, Standing Antelope, and we shall win through."

"Woman," said the boy, "you forget that you speak to a Suhtai warrior. Be silent until I ask you for words."

"Let her talk," broke in the old chief. "Has she not fought for us tonight better than any brave? Let her talk.

Get Four Books Totally
F R E E* –
A Value between
$16 and $20

Tear here and mail your FREE* book card today!

PLEASE RUSH
MY FOUR FREE*
BOOKS TO ME
RIGHT AWAY!

LeisureWestern Book Club
P.O. Box 6613
Edison, NJ 08818-6613

AFFIX
STAMP
HERE

I myself have said evil of her. But now I look upon her as a daughter. Take heed how you regard her and handle her with your words."

"Look!" cried Standing Antelope. "The woods. The woods. Turn to the side; whips and spurs."

They heeded his warning and scattered to either side, their horses bounding under the lash. At the same time a full dozen rifles rang from the ambush and the bullets sang among them. The treacherous moonlight, and the timely warning of Standing Antelope, however, had made that volley bite only empty air.

Chapter Thirty-five

An Interrupted Dance

To understand how that volley happened to be fired into the faces of the fugitives, we must go back a little to a time when Charlotte Keene's ball was at is height. No one could be there and be unhappy. Charlotte herself went around like one in a delighted dream. Harrison Traynor, pale and grim of face, guessed at the cause of her absentmindedness. He determined to ask the question point-blank and, therefore, he drew her to a corner when he could and said:

"Perhaps you don't know it, Charlotte, but William Sutton isn't here. He's disappeared quite mysteriously. Hasn't been here for the last two hours, I take it."

"What makes you say this, Harry?" she asked.

"Someone was inquiring for him. That's all."

"Has there been any trouble?"

"No," said Traynor, "not that I know of. He's learned his lessons fairly well, it appears, and he knows how to keep his claws masked behind the velvet. He never lets people see the danger in him lately."

"You always have an ugly manner when you speak of him," the girl said coldly. "You shouldn't, Harry, it isn't becoming."

"Of course it isn't," he admitted, with a disarming smile. "Only . . . you're the hostess, you know, and you really ought to keep an eye on a tiger after you've invited him to a party."

"He was called away from the house," she replied, "but I don't think there's any trouble, really."

"You knew he was gone, then?"

"Yes."

"Ah?"

"Why are you so pointed about it, Harry?"

"You've been going about with a mysterious look most of the evening. I don't suppose that his disappearance has had anything to do with it?"

She hesitated.

"I think it has," said Traynor.

"Well?"

"You don't have to tell me anything that's an important secret, Charlie," he continued, "but I have a right to know when it has become actual folly for me to bother you with my attentions. Now, I have an idea that this William Sutton has edged me out. Well, more power to him, if that's the case. But at the same time, it appears to me that I should be informed. Just tell me when the door has definitely been closed in my face."

"What's made you so serious?" she asked gravely.

"Because," he said, "you look to me tonight exactly like a person who has been made giddy with good news.

And I guess that the good news has something to do with what you and Sutton have decided. Perhaps it's connected with his disappearance from the house this evening. I don't ask any details. I only want you to tell me when I must consider myself simply . . . your best friend."

"It's true," she said suddenly. "You have a right to know. And you've guessed. It isn't for general circulation, you must understand, but. . . ."

"I'll never repeat until you yourself tell me that I may. Ten thousand hearty congratulations, Charlie."

He shook hands warmly with her. Afterward he managed to get out into the garden, and there he leaned against a corner of the wall and closed his eyes. He felt rather sick and helpless, for he had fought a long fight for this girl. He was not rich, and she was. He was well placed in their social circle, but not a whit better than the daughter of Judge Keene. From all viewpoints it was a match most to be desired. Beyond this, it was undoubtedly true that he loved Charlie for her own sake. He felt it now as he never had felt it before. For five minutes he remained there, breathing deep. Even after that interval, before he trusted himself to return to the house, he practiced a smile and rubbed the color into his cheeks. Then he came back with apparent cheerfulness, and had no sooner entered the room than there was a disturbance and general confusion in the front of the house and immediately thereafter young Luke Masterson came striding into the ballroom.

"Gentlemen!" he said. "I beg your pardon, Miss Keene, but will you ask the ladies to excuse the gentlemen for one minute. I have important news for them."

"What is the news? You can tell it before all of us," said Charlotte Keene.

Harrison Traynor, tall and erect, came beside her.

211

"Certainly," he said, "let's have the excitement, Luke. Talk out, old fellow."

"There's excitement enough!" exclaimed Masterson. "The jail's been broken into by William Sutton. Three men are lying dead inside the place now. Sutton has escaped with the Cheyenne Indian who was arrested this evening by the constable. I've come to get you men on your horses. Will you come along with me?"

Dead silence followed this stunning bit of news. All heads turned toward Jack Sutton and his sister, and they themselves stood like statues.

Charlotte Keene held Traynor's arm to steady herself, but her voice was clear and firm enough as she called: "You've made a mistake, Luke Masterson. William Sutton never would shoot to kill."

"By heavens, Miss Keene, I had the word from the constable himself. He said that three men were either dead or dying inside the jail when he started on the trail."

For that was the message with which wily young Marston had sent his emissaries through the countryside. Afterward, when it turned out that no one had been killed, he could easily say that he thought the wounds all were fatal. He knew that it made a vast difference. A mere case of jail-breaking was one thing—and, considering the motives which William Sutton had for his action, he was apt to meet with a good deal of sympathy—but, on the other hand, if it were felt that he had committed murder, then every man in the community would be willing to ride hard and shoot straight to avenge the deed.

As for truth, that could take care of itself. What Marston wanted was to look into the dead face of William Sutton before the morning came, and thereby wipe from his mind and his conscience the sense of a wrong suffered and a blow endured perforce. Moreover, he felt that unless he stirred the heart of the community deeply the young men, brave though they might be, would be most unapt to press hard on so deadly and desperate a fighter as William Sutton. Give them murder as a spur, and they would charge like cavalry into the teeth of overwhelming danger.

There was little chance that the information which had been sent out by his messengers would be questioned, for there was no time for the true report to follow on its heels. And so it happened at the house of Judge Keene that the voice of his daughter was the only one raised in doubt. Among the rest went a gloomy and deadly murmur.

"This comes of trying to domicile a wild man among civilized people. Colonel Sutton should be held to strict account for this."

If the men were stern, the women were no less determined. Murder! Moreover, Thunder Moon had been too busy with his studies, and his manner was too coldly reserved, to make him many friends. When he ceased being a freak, he almost ceased being interesting.

"What's the murder of three men to a cold-blooded devil who thinks nothing of taking a boy along and trailing a man-eater into a forest at night? Nothing's beyond him."

Such was the first reaction toward the news which was brought to this house by Masterson. The constable's call for volunteers brought a notable response, for every man who was able to ride a horse rushed for his mount. Those who had not come in the saddle were furnished with horses from the judge's stable. He himself, pale and troubled, was met by his daughter, who caught one of his hands in hers.

"Father," she said fiercely, "you sent William to speak to me tonight."

"And he did?"

"Yes."

"And you?"

"I told him that I loved him."

"Wipe it out of your mind, Charlie. A murderer . . . a jail brawl . . . three men dead . . . good heavens, how unspeakable. My daughter and such a man?"

"Father," she urged eagerly, "ride with the rest, just to keep them from shooting at the critical moment. Ride with them and try to keep them back. I'm going myself. He's got to be saved. I don't care what he's done."

"Charlotte!" cried her father, "I explicitly forbid you to do anything so mad. I. . . ."

She slipped from him. He ran after her, but she slammed the door behind her and turned the lock. By the time he had gone around through the hall, she was lost to sight, and he knew that she would be mounted and off with the hunt before he could prevent. So, grinding his teeth and groaning, the judge rushed in turn to get a mount at his stables, and there he found a press of hot-blooded youths, cursing William Sutton, and swearing that they would do their part to take vengeance on him for his crime.

Charlotte was nowhere in sight. No one could give him word of her. That was not strange, for the stables were like madhouses this evening, with men calling for saddles and bridles, and then having to help themselves and find what they could. Every instant, in little groups of three and four, the riders pushed away into the dark of the night, past the pathetic figure of Ruth Sutton, who stood beyond the gate imploring each wild-riding band to wait until the next day had given them surer word of what had happened and what guilt belonged to her older brother. She was unregarded. The judge himself paid no attention to her, and dashed through the gate with a rifle in his hands. Whatever the others had to spur them on, he had before him the high goal of preventing for his daughter a most unfortunate, mad love affair.

Chapter Thirty-six

A Lost Trick

First man from the house, on that night, and first to reach the stables was Harrison Traynor. He had paused only to take the hand of Charlotte Keene and say to her, with his heart apparently in his voice: "I've said that I was your best friend, and tonight I'm going to try to give you a proof of it."

"Dear Harry! God bless you!" she cried.

He went away, smiling grimly. He only paused at the gun room in the back of the house. He was familiar with it and with its contents, and he was able to select, even in the dim light of one small lamp, a fine new rifle, and a quantity of ammunition. He took a Navy revolver of the newest stamp as well. With this equipment, he hurried for the stables, cursing the fortune that had made him leave his riding horse behind him on this night of all nights in his life. However, he was the very first in the stables, and he could take his pick.

He did not have to ask. A big-headed roan had taken his eye long before. It was not a clean-bred one, but it had plenty of hot blood. It was just a trifle over in the knees and went lame for the first ten minutes of a ride. But there never was a gamer horse, a better winded runner, or a better head for cross-country running, where horse brains truly tell. He snatched a saddle from the saddleroom, and rushed for his prize. He had hardly started work when the pale face of Jack Sutton gleamed under the lantern light, running for a horse in a neighboring box. Fast though the hands of Traynor worked, Jack was a little faster, and they led their horses from the barn together. Quickly and softly, in spite of the turmoil which was beginning all through the stables, Harrison Traynor developed a little dialogue with his companion on the way to the open.

"Now, Jack," he said, "you have your opportunity. You can help to polish off the existence of this impostor tonight."

"*I?*" cried Jack. "I'm going to help him if I can."

"Help him? Good heavens, my dear Jack, you don't mean that."

"What else can I do? What else will people expect me to do?"

"They'll expect you to stand up for law and order, no matter who may have broken the law. A murderer is a murderer, Jack."

"I'd be outlawed from every decent house."

"You talk like a fool, Jack. Everyone would understand."

Eagerly Traynor pressed his point. There was not a cooler head, not a steadier hand, not a deadlier shot in the county than Jack Sutton, unless it were Traynor himself. And he wanted the services of the marksman, wanted them most terribly. Better one sure rifleman than a hundred bunglers. Better and more to be trusted in this keen hunt which, fate willing, would end the life of William Sutton, and the love affair of Charlie Keene.

"I couldn't aim a gun at him," said Jack.

"Tell me this, old fellow. Is he really your brother, or is he an impostor?"

"Lord knows, not I."

"You do know. What's your instinct in the matter?"

"I admit that I can't call him a brother with any feeling."

"Of course you can't, and the intuition always is right. Trust instinct, Jack."

The boy turned suddenly, fiercely, on Traynor. "Harry, you're older than I."

"A little, yes."

"You're an honorable fellow, and you know the world. Now, I don't like William . . . if he really *is* William. Not that he's cut me off from the fortune. I don't think that's what counts with me. But my heart doesn't warm to him. Never has. Harry, tell me on your solemn and holy word of honor: what would you do if you were in my place?"

"I'll tell you," said Traynor. "I'd ride with the boys and I'd tell them that you wanted them to do William no harm. That would gloss over your reputation. But in the meantime, if I got a fair chance, I would say that I wanted a shot at the damned Indians who were running off with your brother and carrying him away to the prairies. I'd pretend to take a shot at them, if the chance came, but by heaven I'd see that my bullet found the heart of the impostor and murderer who is masquerading in the name of your house."

Jack Sutton gasped. Then: "I'll do it!" he cried. "I want to do it. And you know what's wisest and most right. I'll do it, Harry."

"Good, Jack. Then ride with me. For if anyone finds him tonight, I've an idea that I'll be the man. Do you hear? I have a premonition that I or Thunder Moon will die tonight."

They swung into their saddles, and now it could be seen that Traynor had not wasted his life in that part of the world. When he was seen mounting, half a dozen who were in the same act called to him that they would go with him. For whether at the dinner table or in the hunting field, no man had a better reputation than Harrison Traynor for surety and keen wit. These others wanted a leader, and they turned readily to him in the emergency.

He ran them over with his eye. They were what he wanted. Not so many as to make a clumsy crowd, but enough to push that fighting devil, Thunder Moon, to the wall. Every man of them was armed to the teeth, and every man of them knew how to use his weapons. Whether from the back of a galloping horse or shooting at a mark, there was not one of them but had put in long years of training. Moreover, they looked as thoroughbred as the horses upon which they were mounted and, Traynor knew, as he glanced at their faces, that he could count upon them in the fight which he hoped would end up that ride. For, he told himself, with a swelling heart and with set teeth, that life would not be worthwhile for him if he lost Charlie Keene. And lose her he would, he knew, so long as William Sutton lived. Death alone could end that affair perhaps, and the touch of the great healer, Time.

Traynor had in view a maneuver both simple and practical. Three roads pointed toward the west. West toward the distant prairies he felt sure the fugitives would press. If he could occupy those roads, he would be apt to bag the four. People more familiar with the lay of the land might have been apt to take secret ways and passes among the marshes and through the woods, but the Indians were comparative strangers—even Standing Antelope—and therefore Traynor was fairly sure that the band would take to the highways.

In the meantime, he had only this handful of men. The others from the ball had scattered here and there, each party with some idea of its own. Not far away, there was a low, rolling ridge which crossed the three roads, and ran on beyond them. Traynor put one man to watch each of the side roads and he, with young Jack Sutton and seven others, took cover in the trees looking down on the middle way. They dismounted and Jack Sutton made a speech to the little group.

He told them, with apparent earnestness, that he must beg them not to fire a shot at his brother, William. Let them try to take him alive. As for the Indians who were with him, of course they should be shot down as quickly as possible. It was for that purpose, he said, that he had joined their number. His speech was received with respect, and Traynor tapped him lightly on the shoulder.

"But suppose, Jack," broke in one of the party, "that your brother opens fire on us. He's not the sort of man who misses a target twice. Are we simply to stand up under his fire?"

"My friends," said Jack with dignity, "I only can ask you to show some restraint and try to give my brother some favor."

"Aye, Jack," said Traynor, "that's spoken like a man, and of course we'll do what we can for him." A moment later, he found occasion to whisper in the ear of Jack: "Let the rest mark down the other Indians, if we have a chance to fire, but you and I'll train our guns on Thunder Moon. Agreed?"

"Yes," said Jack through his teeth.

After that, silence fell over the party. Out of the west a wind was coming; the boughs above their heads began to sway. Somewhere nearby two branches were rubbing together with a dolorous mournful sound. Across the stars vague shapes of clouds began to sweep. The moon had risen now, and its light gave more surety and sense of power to the ambushers. Nothing happened until one of the older members of the group declared he thought that he heard the sound of distant baying like the voices of bloodhounds. The whole group listened intently, but they did not make out the sound again. In due time, they saw four shadows moving down the road just before them, not with a rush and sweep as they had imagined that the four would come, but merely trotting their horses.

"Cool heads, all of 'em," said Traynor. "They're saving their horseflesh for a brush. Now, boys, there they come. Mark down your men, except for William Sutton. No one aim at him."

The wind suddenly dropped. Jack Sutton, as he lay beside Traynor, could hear the hard breathing of his companion, and over a fallen log as a rest he drew his bead with a steady hand upon the body of his brother. He changed from the body to the head, for Thunder Moon looked so utterly formidable as he came down the road upon his horse it seemed impossible that one bullet could take his life.

The four riders drifted closer and closer. They were speaking, and the faint sound of the deep voice of William came across to Jack. It touched him as the sight of the man had failed to stir his heart and, putting his rifle down, he murmured to Traynor: "I can't do it, Harry. My God, how could I ever have dreamed of trying to shoot such a man . . . and my own brother. You were a devil to tempt me to it, Harry Traynor."

"You fool!" said Traynor. "Don't let your heart run away with your head entirely. There is a. . . ." His voice stopped with a gasp, for suddenly the four riders swept away from one another like dead leaves picked up by a whirlpool of wind. Traynor caught his mark again with a deft shift of his rifle, but as he closed his finger on the trigger a hand struck his arm and made his shot fly wild. It was young Jack beside him.

"I couldn't let you, Harry!" he said. "I know you mean the best for me. There's nothing for you to gain by his death. You're only thinking of me . . . but I couldn't let you."

"Damnation!" snarled Traynor. "You young fool, do you know that you nudged yourself out of Sutton House that moment?" Springing to his feet, he called on his companions: "We've turned them back. We'll go after them, boys, and ride 'em down or else turn 'em straight back into the hands of the fellows that must be following from behind. We've lost the first trick, but we'll take the trick that wins the game."

They mounted instantly and, flying across the open meadow, they drove on into the trees among which the four were now out of sight.

Chapter Thirty-seven

Courage of a Woman

Such was the cause of the ambush which would have stopped the flight of the four before it had well begun had it not been for the hawk-like eye of Standing Antelope, which detected the shadow of danger that lay before them. Sweeping back toward the trees at one side, they spurred for safety. Bullets still whistled around them, for the posse was firing as it came hot foot after them. Thunder Moon, ranging beside his old foster father, was suddenly aware that the noise of the pursuit had stopped and that the firing had redoubled but drew no closer.

"They are shooting at shadows!" laughed Big Hard Face. "Come, my son. The white men are fools. We shall slip through the hands of a hundred of them."

"Where is Red Wind?" asked Standing Antelope, pressing closer to them.

"Red Wind!" exclaimed Thunder Moon. "She has gone back to make a sacrifice of herself and let us escape. Listen! She is firing on them and drawing their fire. Ah hai! Who would have thought there was such courage in any woman! It is she! It must be she!"

With that, he whirled his horse about.

"Let her be," said Big Hard Face. "Is the life of a woman worth the life of a man? Let her be, I say. She is making a sacrifice that will be accepted. Her spirit will find happiness forever and in our safe lodge among the Suhtai, we will make her to be remembered."

So said Big Hard Face, with a logic as stern as his name, but Thunder Moon did not stop to listen. He lunged back through the woods toward the center of the noise of the firing, and so under the bright moon he saw what he had expected and yet could not believe. There was a thick natural hedge of compact bushes, with a little strip of cleared ground in a semicircle behind it. Up and down that hedge rode Red Wind, weaving back and forth on her horse, and reloading and firing her rifle with such wonderful rapidity that, taking into account the different points from which she was constantly firing, it might well have seemed that the entire party of four had taken cover there. The assailants had not yet worked around to the rear of the position. When that happened, Red Wind would die. She must have known, but she did not falter in her work.

Thunder Moon, looking at her, felt his heart swell and then almost stop with wonder at the sight. He had looked upon her as a mysterious combination of woman and devil, but he never had dreamed that anything could have controlled her other than purest selfishness. And here she was offering her life for the safety of the party—offering it without braggadocio, but simply. He heard the crashing of the guns of the posse. He heard the whistling of the balls. By miracle—or by dint of her constant shifting position—she had escaped injury. As she rode she fired, loaded, and fired again.

For a half second Thunder Moon endured the wonder of this spectacle and then he swept down to her. She turned with a faint cry as she felt the rush of something from behind and, as she had fired her rifle that instant, she grasped it by the barrel and swung it like a club above her head as she turned her horse around. Then she saw who was coming and let him take the bridle of her horse and sweep away, leading her beside him.

"Who gave you authority," Thunder Moon said, "to come back here and fight like a mad woman. Listen! They still are firing into the covert. You have baffled them more than all the rest of us had managed to do. But who bade you come here? Red Wind, am I mistaken about you? Are you a great-hearted woman, after all? Ah hai! What is a greater heart than that . . . to die for the safety of one's friends?"

He praised her as they rode. She looked neither to the right nor to the left, but kept her face straight forward and gave no sign that she heard a word he uttered. Thunder Moon was enormously excited. Before there had

223

seemed in this girl nothing but evil under well-controlled guises. Now there appeared to be something more—a self-sacrificing nobility. Courage he never had doubted that she possessed. But courage as a gentle and pure-souled power was the last quality which he would have attributed to her.

What shall man say of Thunder Moon and his fickleness? That very evening he had looked into the eyes of the white girl and told her that he loved her, but now in one instant Charlotte Keene's memory was dimmed as by the passing of a whole year. His heart began to leap and thunder as he saw the moonlight gleam on the red-metal braids of Red Wind's hair, brushed out the next instant as they swept on into the shadow.

Suddenly he said to her: "Somehow I knew at once what had happened and what you had done. Well, I certainly must have thought better of you than I guessed."

This was not a polite speech, but it did not disturb the girl. She looked more statue-like than ever. They rushed up to Big Hard Face and Standing Antelope, who were working their horses to and fro.

"It was as I guessed," said Thunder Moon, and he took the hand of the girl and laid it in the hand of his foster father. "Look, Big Hard Face, what she has done. They still are back there firing at the shadows. They are afraid to come closer. I shall be surprised if she did not kill one or two of them. Ha, my Father, what will you say of warriors who are killed by women? There is more danger in Red Wind than there is in three war chiefs. I always knew that. Take her. She is my sister. Twice she has saved us on this one night."

"Keep the rear, Thunder Moon," said the chief. "Keep the rear with Standing Antelope, while I make the trail with the girl in front. Shall we point quartering across that ridge?"

"Yes," answered Standing Antelope, "because I know that there is another road to the west running beyond that low hill."

So Big Hard Face turned the head of his horse and rode without haste. For though the men of Harrison Traynor had discovered that they had been firing for some time at an empty covert, still it would take them much time indeed to follow the trail by moonlight. The great opportunity of Traynor seemed to have come and gone again when he saw big Thunder Moon before him—and had his arm nudged as he drew the trigger.

Calmly, mildly, the chief spoke to the girl: "Tell me, Red Wind, if you hate us so much, why have you done such things for us as you have done this night? I cannot understand, and my head spins as I try to make out your reasons. Have you a reason, girl?"

She looked sidewise at him. "I have a reason. It is no reason that I can tell to you."

"Is it a noble or a selfish reason?"

She hesitated, smiling at the naïveté which asked such a question. At length she said: "It is not noble. It is not selfish. It is surely something else."

"But what else can there be?" asked Big Hard Face. "Everything in the world must be done for one reason or for the other."

"There are some things," said the girl, "that even a wise chief does not know about. Or if he has known them, he forgets afterward."

"Ha? Well," said Big Hard Face, "no matter what you may say, you have earned the right of talking freely with me and with all the tribe of the Suhtai. I shall not ask you questions which you do not wish to answer. When we come safely back to the Suhtai, you will be admitted to the council and allowed to sit with the chiefs and the wise men because of what you have done tonight, Red

Wind. Some old and wise chief will take you for a squaw."

"Peace!" said the girl sharply. "Listen! They are coming fast."

Through the night the booming, chiming voices of the bloodhounds swept rapidly toward them.

Chapter Thirty-eight

Brave Fight

Very deliberately, as men long used to peril in a thousand forms, the party determined how they would baffle the dogs. So much time had been lost when Thunder Moon went to say farewell to his mother that the whole countryside was thoroughly alarmed, and men were willing to risk their lives to arrest the flight of the little band. Nothing remained, therefore, except to cut across country as fast as they could. This they did, riding steadily, but never pushing their horses in spite of the cry of the hounds behind them. No horse in the world could have lived with dogs over such running as this, one moment through tangled woods, and the next struggling across marsh, and then fording a river and staggering up the farther slope of the stream. The hounds were sure to gain, unless the wits of the fugitives could turn them.

Presently they had an excellent chance. They came to a broad-faced little river, so shallow that they could ride their horses into it. On its verge they looked up and down and finally decided that here they must make their attempt at a trail which would throw the dogs adrift. Upstream, therefore, they went for well over a quarter of a mile, and by that time the voices of the hunt were breaking through the trees and finally went echoing up the river after them. Immediately afterward, they heard the sounds dying out, sure sign that the pack was in the water. Then deadly silence as every dog was swimming.

When the dogs recovered the trail, they would give tongue, of course. If the wisdom of Kingston turned them up the stream, then a crisis would come at once. In the meantime, the fugitives came to a spot where a shelf of rock stepped with comfortable ease from the waters, and there they climbed out. From the rock, a great trunk of a tree extended to the ground beyond and over that natural bridge they led their horses, one by one, without mishap. That this bridge might not be suspected, after they were across, Big Hard Face directed that they should turn the trunk from its place. That was done and the trunk struck the ground with a heavy impact. They stood listening, fearing lest the cry of the hunt would be attracted by the noise. Then, indeed, the cry of the pack did sound, but far, far down the stream.

"It is ended!" said Big Hard Face, in great relief. "One of the dogs has happened upon a false scent."

They remounted and pushed ahead through the woods, always aiming west but taking what advantage they could of the terrain. The cold morning was beginning when they entered a little natural pasture. All the world was silent. The fugitives were overcome with fatigue. Here they determined to make a temporary camp, rest the horses, and then move cautiously forward once more.

Big Hard Face set the example and, having loosed the girths of his horse, he stretched himself on the damp grass. They set no watch. All about them were the deep woods. There was no noise except the sound of the horses tearing at the grass, and not even a ghost could have come upon them without making a sufficient disturbance to put them on their guard.

It was not the noise of anyone passing through the woods, however, that wakened them before half an hour. It was a deep, rich burst of music as a dozen hounds gave tongue. Their trail had been recovered. They mounted once more. There was no sign of fatigue as yet from Sailing Hawk, and the three horses which had been taken from the colonel were Thoroughbreds. Thunder Moon made trail; the rest followed in single file. Ever the clamor of the dogs grew. They could distinguish the separate voices as every hound gave tongue, and now they knew that they had come to the end of their tether.

They found a natural tunnel through the woods. By the morning light they entered the path, and now they could make fair headway, letting the horses go at a trot. Even such a speed would not do, as they could tell in a few moments. Right behind them sounded the thunder of the pack, and the noise, caught as in a funnel, confused their minds. Even Big Hard Face nervously pushed his horse ahead, and Thunder Moon looked around and saw Red Wind watching him with acute, expectant terror in her eyes. It pleased him oddly, that sign of fear from her. It showed that she was not above human weakness, no matter how mysterious her strength.

He managed to fall behind with Standing Antelope and, the instant they were well to the rear, Thunder Moon flung himself from his horse and motioned to the boy to do the same. Clear-eyed, grim of mouth, the youngster waited for his orders. In either hand, Thunder Moon held a revolver and, where the tunnel turned sharply to the side and made a distinct angle, he placed himself and made the lad kneel before him, a knife gripped in his hand.

"They are not like other dogs," said the boy, taking up his position. "Remember, I have seen them. They come to kill, and kill they will."

"What pass my guns, your knife must count for," said Thunder Moon loudly, for the noise of the dogs was swelling. "Never slash at the throat. Give them the point, always the point."

As he spoke a great, reddish-brown beast turned the corner of the path and his bay turned to a snarl as he flung himself forward. He was the tried and tested leader who never had failed in a score of battles. In mid-air the bullet found him but he had sprung so far and boldly that, though he landed dead, with a brief howl of agony, his weight struck full on Standing Antelope and knocked him sprawling headlong to the ground. Two more, straining abreast, lurched bravely at Thunder Moon. He gave them a bullet from either gun. One shot smashed through the brain and one beast fell; the second was no more than a glancing wound and, like a fury, the great beast charged.

It would surely have gone ill with Thunder Moon then, but the Suhtai boy, lying on his back, stabbed upward as the bloodhound passed over him, and the poor brute writhed in convulsions of pain, dying slowly.

Still that charge came on as though the dogs were gallant cavalry. The horn of Kingston was frantically blowing a recall, but they gave no heed. They had heard the death cries of their leaders, and they went on for their vengeance. A double stream of lead met them. Never had Thunder Moon made better target practice. Twice a wounded dog managed to stagger on after being struck, but on each occasion the cunning knife of Standing Antelope finished the work.

The place became a shambles. Nine bodies lay there dead or dying, and the remaining dogs held back, at last thoroughly daunted. They were the weakest spirits of the pack. Now they shrank, turned, and fled yelping. Voices of men were sounding down the green tunnel now, and particularly the high-pitched yell of Kingston, demanding vengeance for his loss; but here, Big Hard Face and Red Wind came back, guns in hand, thoroughly alarmed.

"They are coming fast," said the chief. "They will charge against us. Reload. Reload, Thunder Moon."

He laughed, pointing to the bodies before him. "They have lost these lives already," he said. "Do you think they will come on for more? No, no. They never will follow us here. They will strive to block us at the farther end of the path. Go with me, Father. Hurry! Or they will take us like snakes in a hole."

Chapter Thirty-nine

No Way Out

They came from the tunnel that passed through that jungle-smothered marshland none too soon, for on their right they could hear horsemen working through a thicket. Before them now stretched a long sheet of firm ground and their horses swung away at a long gallop. As they started, they heard a wild yelping well to the rear.

"It is the hounds!" said Standing Antelope, wiping his hands and knife on the mane of his horse. "They are trying to whip the dogs onto the trail, but they will never take to this line again."

He laughed cheerfully as he spoke, adding: "Tell me, Big Hard Face, were you ever on a better war trail than this? Were there ever such great odds against you? Did you ever before make such fools of so many men?"

The old chief smiled at the boy. "We may talk afterward, perhaps. Let us think only of what our enemies are doing with their wits and with their horses. They are following fast, my friends."

For at that moment nearly a score of riders came out from the marsh and, seeing the distant fugitives, swung into a gallop in pursuit. Their mounts seemed to have neither spirit nor strength left to them. They had been floundering for too many hours through the steaming bogs of the marshland, pushing aimlessly here and there, rushing to meet every alarm, swarming out on many a false trail, and now the keenness was as great as ever in the riders, but the horses could not answer. Whereas the fugitives had gone steadily, without undue haste, conserving their horses at every turn of the way. They reaped a harvest now for that forbearance. Without effort, without a single whipstroke, they left the whole body of the hunt laboring far behind them, and soon lost to view. Only, from time to time, they had a glimpse of a few hardy riders who were able to keep their horses at a great effort by dint of whip and spur.

In that body of skillful riders went Harrison Traynor, and at his side was the constable. Never two finer riders had dashed across the country after fox or chasing pure sport. They lacked that instinctive skill which comes to men who have lived in the saddle, and all the four fugitives had spent almost as many hours on horseback as they had on foot. They knew how to rate their mounts at a slope; when it was wisest to dismount and lead the horse; when a downpitch was too sharp to be negotiated with speed without taking too great a toll of their animals. In addition, when the final test came, and the run for life or death had to be made, they knew how to wring from their tired horses the last bit of speed, strength, and service. For all these reasons, the four drew easily farther and farther away.

The country was changing, now. The flat land, steaming marshes, the straight, well-made roads gave way to rolling country, sometimes with hills the size of mountains, and the roads were either bridle paths, or else the roughest sort of wagon ways laid down with no pretense at engineering, but simply going where streams of wandering cattle first had marked out a course.

It had an advantage and it had a great drawback, this country. In the first place, it gave them a chance to work freely ahead. In the second place it was sure to place them under observation more easily, for they had only an occasional grove of trees to shelter them.

Until noon, they kept steadily to the hollows, pressing on without remorse for their flagging steeds; but, shortly after the middle of the day, they saw before them a small house and Thunder Moon declared that there they would take rest, find food for themselves, and grain for their horses. Better rest now, when there was no enemy in sight, than wait for the night. Because night was apt to bring them as much danger as it did security.

As they came up toward the house, they saw a man, a woman, and a child break for the place and rush away toward the corral where, hastily, each threw himself on a horse and plunged away down the valley.

"They arc going to spread trouble ahead of us!" said Big Hard Face and he unslung his rifle. "They must be brought back."

"They shall be," answered Thunder Moon and, beckoning to Standing Antelope, they swept in pursuit. Tired as their horses were, like all Thoroughbreds they were able to raise a racing gallop. Swiftly they came up with the trio, and a shot fired over their heads by Thunder Moon made them draw rein. They faced about in a panic of terror. The man had an old horse pistol in his hand and a set expression on his face.

"You murderin' devils," he said, "you keep your distance, or I'll count for one of you."

Thunder Moon rode in on him, his rifle under his arm. "Put up that pistol," he said. "If we wanted to do murder, we needn't have stopped to talk to you. You'll have no harm from us. We simply want you to come back to the house so that we'll be able to leave this place before you go to spread the alarm. We want food, too, for ourselves and these nags. If you're there, we'll be able to pay you for what we have to take."

The man hesitated, but the woman broke in: "We might as well die there, as here, and besides maybe he means to do what he says. It's William Sutton, Ben."

"I know who it is, well enough," replied the man. "Sutton, we got your word for this?"

"Yes."

Standing Antelope had remained just beyond hearing distance during this colloquy, ready at any moment to shoot but, as the three turned back toward the house, the man and women pale and sick of face and the little boy whimpering, the young Suhtai hurried to the side of his leader.

"There are three scalps and three coups for me," he said. "You don't want me to go back to my people with empty hands?"

Thunder Moon raised a sternly admonitory forefinger. "Don't touch them," he said, "with gun, knife, or hand.

233

These people have done us no harm, and they may do us much good."

"No harm," echoed the boy. "Are not the whites our enemies just as the Comanches are? If you saw three Comanches, would you let them live?"

"Be still," said William Sutton gruffly. "You speak of this which you do not yet understand."

Standing Antelope, however, was not appeased by this rebuke and, so long as they were in the shanty, his wistful gaze was turned upon one or another of his involuntary hosts, much like a dog eyeing a flitch of bacon hung just above his reach. By the time they reached the house, they found Red Wind already in possession of the kitchen, while Big Hard Face, in the adjoining barn, was finding ample rations of oats for the horses. From the moment the farmer's wife saw Red Wind, her attitude changed.

"My sakes!" she cried. "Why, this ain't no wild Indian. She knows cooking. Here, honey, gimme that bacon and I'll slice it. Willie, slap on some water to heat. Ben, you hand me that coffee can. I dunno what these folks have done but, now that they're here, they might as well have a chance to eat. They got their belts three notches deeper'n normal."

Thunder Moon and Standing Antelope worked strongly and steadily over the horses, rubbing them down, giving them from time to time a swallow of water, and tending them with the most precise care. Then, as they permitted the horses to bury their noses in the finest oats, they stood back to watch, well contented. Indian ponies needed no such care as this. A chance to roll after a long, heartbreaking ride, a little sun-withered prairie grass to graze on, and a few hours of rest enabled them to take the trail again with hardly diminished spirit. These long-legged, deer-like creatures were different.

Only Sailing Hawk seemed to combine the qualities of the desert pony and the racer.

No matter what happened, they could be sure now that they would have remade horses for the rest of their day's flight. They were in no haste to leave the shanty. They ate and paid for a hearty meal, and then they lay down on the floor of the cabin, with Red Wind to keep guard because, she said, she had no need of sleep.

She sat beside Big Hard Face, her eyes looking continually through the open door and down the valley, but no sign of a pursuer troubled her vision. Perhaps the trail had been lost by those who followed. Indeed, they had come across enough stretches of gravel and rock to have discouraged even the most expert Indian trailer.

The white family gathered to watch, big-eyed, enormously curious. They had changed their opinion of these visitors a great deal. In the first place, they had suffered from no violence. In the second place, they had been handsomely paid for all that had been eaten by horse and man. And in the third place, they were beginning to see that this was a distinguished adventure that would make them talked about by all the neighborhood, and envied wherever women or men met to gossip.

The three men lay in a row. They were asleep the instant that they closed their eyes.

"How did you hear of us?" asked Red Wind, looking at the housewife.

"From the telegraph office at Stanley. Messengers were sent over the whole country around here to get folks out to watch the trails."

"What did they say?"

"That you've murdered about a dozen people up the way. There must be near onto a thousand folks out looking for you right now."

"But not in this direction?"

"No?"

"At least they haven't looked for us here," said Red Wind.

"Ah," said the woman, "why should they have to do that? Because they know that once in the valley here, there ain't no chance that you'll get out."

Chapter Forty

There Will Be a Way

No chance for them to get out. Red Wind said not a word to alarm the three sleepers.

"Show me!" she said.

Straightaway the farmer and his wife and son took her outside of the shanty and to the hillcrest which overshadowed the house. From that point of vantage she could sweep the horizon and now she saw what was meant. All to the west and the north, beyond the hills, rushed a river of impassable white water, and to the south lay marshes from whose boggy face a mist exhaled visibly at that distance. From the east they had come, and that way was still open but, if they returned, they would find the gathered forces of their enemies ready to block the way.

Such was the prospect that she looked out upon. When she had seen it, she asked anxiously: "There must be some way across that river. It is not very wide."

"Swifter than an arrow," was the reply. "You couldn't never cross it, lady. Never in this here world, I'm tellin' you; never at all. There has been some that tried. Jake Mulvaney tried last year on a bet. Poor Jake, he didn't get half way across."

"The marsh, then!" said the girl. "Surely someone could get across that."

"With a boat, perhaps," answered the farmer's wife. "If you was to take a boat and drag it across the mud, and then float it off again, why, you might get across that way. I don't know. There's the Baynes gang. They live in there . . . a curse on 'em . . . and they manage to get across from side to side. But who's gunna be able to get that secret out of 'em?"

Red Wind seized upon that clue but, when she made anxious inquiries, she achieved nothing. The Baynes gang of ruffians lived in the marshes, to be sure, but how they managed it was a mystery by means of which they had baffled all pursuit. Many a time strong expeditions had pushed out against them, but in every instance the expeditions had failed. They were bogged down and eluded and the robbers still issued time and again to commit their depredations on the lands of their honest neighbors.

Red Wind, without another word, went back to the shanty and there she sat down in the doorway. She turned again toward the east and looked out at the horizon to see even a trace of dust that might announce the approach of horsemen, but there was no sign of a disturbance. They were gathering there, doubtless. They were gathering and making ready to stop the entrance to the valley with a perfect security.

"An' what are you gunna do?" asked the farmer of the girl, big-eyed with fear and curiosity.

"There will be a way," said the Omissis girl quietly.

"But what way, would you tell us? You ain't got wings, I suppose?"

237

"Do you see the big man? The young one? Do you know who he is?"

"He's William Sutton."

"His name is Thunder Moon. The Sky People will not let him die. He has many days before him."

"Maybe he's a kind of witch." The wife grinned.

"You will see," said the girl calmly. "He has been in the camp of the Comanches. He has gone alone into the warrior camp of the Pawnees and come out carrying their medicine bags and leaving their dead behind him. You see that I am not troubled now. All is in the hands of the Sky People. Now he sleeps. When he wakens, I shall tell him."

Again and again they tried to shake her calm conviction by pointing out the terrible imminence of the danger, but she merely smiled, faintly, in the same way which had baffled and disturbed Thunder Moon in the old days, in the teepee of White Crow. Fatigue kept the three soundly asleep until deep in the afternoon, when Standing Antelope wakened, rose softly, and came out to the girl. To him, in her soft voice, she related what she had heard and observed. He in turn climbed to the crest of the hill and looked over the countryside before he came back to her. He walked slowly, a sure sign that his thoughts were profoundly occupied. Then he sat down cross-legged beside the girl.

"We shall wait?" he asked at length.

"What else is there to do? What could we manage in the day? We must have the darkness. In the meantime, our horses are growing strong. So is Thunder Moon. The rest is in the hands of the Sky People."

Standing Antelope made no answer, but he withdrew a little and began to make medicine, picking up handfuls of dust and blowing gently upon it until there remained a few pebbles or shining bits of rock. According to their nature, size, and number he was receiving answers from the spirits; and the answers seemed to trouble him gravely.

"There are four of us, are there not?" he said, coming back.

"There are four," she agreed.

"One must be sacrificed," said the boy with great seriousness. "I see by the signs that have been given to me that only three of us can go free, perhaps. Tell me, Red Wind . . . if a life were given freely to the Sky People, would they let the other three go through to safety tonight?"

She understood his meaning instantly and caught her breath a little. However, she answered with an air of surety: "One must be lost. But who can tell which one of the four it will be? Who can tell which one the Sky People have chosen for death? And what a fool one of us would be to lay down a life which is not wanted?"

The boy considered this with a knotted brow. Nevertheless, he seemed relieved by this reasoning, relaxed and began to nod his head a little. "You are right," he answered. "They do not wish to have us presume to read their minds and understand their purposes. They are great spirits and jealous of their secrets. However, the medicine that I have made is very sure. One of us at least must die."

Red Wind fell into a gloomy study and remained lost in it when Thunder Moon and Big Hard Face came out of the shanty. With faces like masks they heard the story, looking sternly to the east where the danger lay. Then Thunder Moon looked to the westering sun and saw that the evening was not far away.

He said to Standing Antelope: "Saddle the horses; look to the guns, and see that they are clean. Tonight we shall have fighting."

With that, he walked off by himself and was soon lost in a little copse not far from the house. He was no sooner hidden there, than he sat down cross-legged near a tiny spring of water and, taking out the ingredients of his paints, he mixed them and began to daub his face. He took off his deerskin jacket next, and his painting was continued upon his body to the waist until Thunder Moon looked more like a devil than like William Sutton, heir of Sutton House.

When he had completed his ceremonies, he stepped into a clearing in the center of the trees and, taking his dream shield upon one arm, and his rifle in the other, he extended both toward the sky, where the pink of the sunset was beginning to gather in richer and darker tones. There he prayed as he had prayed before in the critical moments of his life.

"Sky People, all that was dim to me before I now understand. When I asked you what I should do for my foster father, you sent me with weapons in my hands to take him from the jail. You promised me safety. So I went, and it all happened as you said. There was danger, but you saved me from it. Now I have come away with Big Hard Face, but still there is a part of my heart that remains behind with my mother and the lodge of my father. I think, too, of the white girl. For this reason you are punishing me. You have drawn great dangers around me. You are catching me like a fish in the net. I understand. I do not reproach you for having saved me once and threatening me later. It is because you do not want to take me back to the Suhtai when my heart is still with the whites. But now I see the truth. I must go back to the Cheyennes and be one of them. Behold me. I have put on the sacred paint for the warpath. I denounce the God of the white man and accept you only. I give myself away from my father's lodge forever and take the teepee among the Suhtai. Let their way be my way. Let me be a weapon in their hands in the time of trouble, and let all my friends have red skin. Hear me Sky People, and if you accept my prayer, give me a sign."

He remained for a long moment, his shield and his gun extended in arms that began to tremble with fatigue, and great beads of perspiration formed upon his forehead and rolled swiftly down across his face. He said again: "All that is good has come to me from your hands. All that is evil has come out of my folly. Do not ask any wisdom of me except the wisdom which you have given me. Hear me, Sky People, while I make you this pledge and promise. When I come safely back to the tents of the Suhtai, where their enemies oppress them, I shall gather the warriors and go out and cover the plains with blood of the Pawnees. I shall make them howl like wolves, and then I shall take three living prisoners and sacrifice them to you to make you happy. All this I shall do for your glory, that men may recognize your power. But now give me life. Give life to the old man, and to the young warrior who rides with me, because he came into trouble through his love for me, following me from his distant country. Save the girl, too. But all that I have been among the white men I give away. Let whoever will pick it up."

He ended. His shoulders ached and his whole body began to shudder with exhaustion, and darkness swam before his eyes. It seemed to him that the darkening sky lighted a little and turned to a deeper rose and now, by degrees, the edge of a cloud pushed above the edges of the dark-pointed trees, a great cloud in which red fire was living, flooding the world with terrible light.

"Oh, Sky People! Oh, my Fathers!" cried Thunder Moon. "I accept the sign, and I shall drench the world with blood for your sake!" He fell forward and lay upon his face in the cool of the grass.

Chapter Forty-one

A Vow

Now it was while Thunder Moon lay there, semiconscious, overwhelmed by what he felt to be the direct manifestation of the will of the spiritual world and, while the evening rapidly darkened toward night after this final burst of crimson light that the watchers from the shanty looked anxiously at a small dust cloud coming up the valley trail. It seemed, at first, large enough to be the sign of a great body of people, but as it drew nearer and nearer it seemed more and more insignificant and Ben, the farmer, in a reassuring voice vowed that it could not be any large section of the posse. More likely, it was some emissary come to offer terms. For the farmer and his family had grown quite out of their first opinion, and now they looked upon the fugitives with the keenest interest. Only, at times, the keen, roving eye of Standing Antelope touched upon one of them and made them thrill with dread. The others were filled with dignity, and their soft, quiet voices enchanted the good wife, above all.

Now that cloud of dust drew nearer, and presently the farmer, with his glass, was able to assure them that only two forms were revealed beneath the mist. Standing Antelope was in a fury of excitement and eagerness.

"I understand!" he said. "That is the sort of thing that Thunder Moon always does. And now two great warriors have come to fight against the three of us. It would be good if Thunder Moon were with us now."

He glanced anxiously toward the trees in which the hero was still concealed.

"No," answered Red Wind, with the faint smile of assured conviction. "They haven't come to fight. If it were Thunder Moon alone that they expected to find here, no two men would dare to come against him."

The boy breathed a little easier. Yet there was a shade of disappointment in his eye—like a bull terrier glad to be freed from hopeless odds, and yet sorry to have missed a fight. In the meantime, the riders came on with a sort of fearless directness that made Red Wind, in spite of her prophecy, stand up to look again. Now they could see that the two were magnificently mounted upon long-striding horses.

Big Hard Face had picked up his rifle and risen to his feet when Red Wind called suddenly: "One of them is a woman. Look!"

A moment later it was clear to everyone. They came up the final slope side by side—Jack Sutton and Charlotte Keene. How different was she from the county beauty, now. Her hair straggled from beneath her riding hat and blew in wisps and tangles; her wrinkled habit was gray with dust; her eyes were hollow with fatigue, and a remorseless sun had burned the tip of her nose to a sharp red.

She came boldly on beside Jack Sutton, and the pair halted at a little distance.

"Are you there, William?" called his younger brother.

"Let us go out to talk with them," said Red Wind to the boy.

They went together and raised their hands in Indian greeting.

"Thunder Moon is not with us," said the boy gloomily. "He is near but he is not with us."

"Call him," said Jack Sutton. "Call my brother at once. I have important news for him."

"News that will take him back to your father's lodge?" asked Standing Antelope cunningly.

"No, no! God knows how he could return at once with three dead men behind him in the jail. But news as to how he can get out of this trap."

"He is away," said Red Wind, breaking in, "asking the will of the Sky People, and we dare not disturb him."

"Good gad," exclaimed Jack, "what utter nonsense."

"It's late," broke in Charlotte. "We may be followed. In any case, let's tell them what we've learned." She went on hastily: "We've found the leader of the brigands who lives in the marsh and we've bought his help. If you go down to the edge of the marshes a little after dark, he'll be waiting for you on this side of the bogs. He swears that he'll show you safely through to the other side, horse and man. But keep good watch on yourself. The man is a villain, and he wouldn't scruple to murder you all if he thought it worthwhile. Do you understand what I've said?"

"I understand," said Standing Antelope.

"You must go quickly," said the girl, "because we're afraid that another man guesses what we have done."

"Tell William," broke in Jack, "that Harrison Traynor may have guessed what we're up to, and in that case he'll try desperately to block you."

"We shall tell him everything," said Standing Antelope.

"And now," said Jack, "can't you call him in? I want to shake hands with him, at least."

"No, no!" exclaimed Charlotte Keene.

"What's the matter, Charlie?"

"I'd rather not. What I mean to say is that . . . we mustn't be here to worry him. You," she added, letting her horse make a step closer to Red Wind, "you came with Big Hard Face from the Suhtai, did you not?"

"I came from the Suhtai," replied the girl.

"You . . . you have been living with the chief?"

"I was given by my father into the lodge of Thunder Moon," answered Red Wind.

Charlotte gripped the pommel of her saddle. "You are his wife then, his Indian wife, I mean to say."

"I am only his slave," replied Red Wind.

Steadily for a moment, they stared at one another, and there was fire in the eyes of each.

"I've heard enough," said the white girl, her voice breaking. "Let's go back quickly, Jack."

"But you can't believe that he has a wife, really?" said the youngster. "You understand, Charlie, that William doesn't lie about things. And he never said a word about having a . . . a family among the Suhtai, you know."

"It isn't lying to be silent," she replied.

"I know you're wrong, Charlie."

"Jack, Jack," she said in a trembling voice, "you're a child and you're blind. Look at her."

Indeed at that moment, with the dim sunset light upon her, the massive double braids of hair glimmering in the shadow, and the brilliantly beaded dress flickering about her like a ghost of fire, it seemed that nothing in the world could be half so beautiful as Red Wind. Charlotte gazed for one more heartbroken moment, then turned her horse and fled down the valley as if she were being hunted by armed men, while Jack followed in the rear, vainly calling to her to ride slower, or to turn back.

The boy and the girl remained for a time, looking after them, and neither spoke until the pair had become once more a dwindling cloud of dust, barely distinguishable through the twilight. Then Standing Antelope said sternly: "Red Wind you have said the thing that is not."

She replied with sudden meekness: "You have heard me lie, Standing Antelope. But be a friend to me. Keep what you have heard from the ears of Thunder Moon. He would be angry. He would beat me. He would cast me out from his lodge. Besides, do you want the white woman to draw him away from us again?"

Standing Antelope looked fixedly at her, but finally he said: "I have thought that Thunder Moon was right and that you were filled with evil. Well, now I begin to remember what my father said: that many women are wicked merely because they are women. Pah! For my part, I never shall take a squaw. There never is any trouble except what you creatures make."

He turned to stride away, but she followed him with the softest of voices: "Standing Antelope, do you hate me, also?"

He wheeled sharply about and glowered down at her. "Should I not hate you?"

"I am a wicked woman," she said, "but I am very sad. Will you have pity on me, Standing Antelope?" She stood close to him, and looked up to his fiery young eyes until suddenly they softened and he began to blink as though a strong light had been flashed in his face. "Will you promise me to speak nothing of this to Thunder Moon?"

"Well, I shall promise!" he said. "Red Wind," he continued, "I shall be your friend. Because I see that you are strong, and that you can make people do what you want. You came out of the plains and made Thunder Moon go back with you. You do everything that you want to do. It is a strong medicine that you make. Hai! My heart is still beating because of it. As if I had seen a grizzly bear. Or something even worse than that."

He walked away from her and Red Wind, facing toward the shanty at that moment, saw a lofty form stepping from the cover of the trees not far away. Upon his arm was a shield, and in his right hand the rifle glimmered through the dusk. It was Thunder Moon, coming back from his time of solitary prayer. He came swiftly and proudly to them.

"I have talked with the Sky People!" he said to Big Hard Face. "And they have promised me freedom from this danger. They sent me a red sign, which means that blood must be shed. But in the end we shall have the victory. They are angry with me because I have been living among the whites. But I have given them up. I have turned my face forever back to the plains, Father. And so we shall be happy together, once more."

Big Hard Face said nothing, but looked quickly upward and presently he murmured: "I shall not forget." Plainly he had made a vow.

Chapter Forty-two

Through the Marsh

It was Red Wind who told Thunder Moon of the message which had just been brought, promising a chance of release. She forgot to mention that Charlotte Keene had been there, and merely said that Jack Sutton had come to say that he had probably been able to buy his brother from danger.

"Listen!" said Thunder Moon, greatly moved, "I thought that I left only a mother behind me. Now you see that I have a brother, also."

"It was the work of the Sky People," broke in Big Hard Face eagerly. "They put the spirit into your brother. Now let us start. It is deep dusk. There are the camp fires where they watch for us in the throat of the valley. Mount, Thunder Moon. Let us go."

They took to the saddle immediately and, saying good bye to the farmer and his wife and son, headed straight across the valley toward the marsh.

"How great are the Sky People!" said Thunder Moon, looking toward the twinkling lights of the distant fires. "Look! with what care they regard me. They hear my words. They are kind to me. I make a prayer, and first they answer me with a sign and, after that, they make this to happen naturally by sending me my brother. The miracles that they perform are all made to appear easy and simple things. What sacrifices we shall offer when we come back to the Suhtai." He laughed aloud, filled with the sense of his own great power on earth and upon the spirits of the air.

They came to the edge of the marsh. They had to go carefully along its verge, for one false step might plunge a horse up to the knees in muck, but presently out of the gloom a figure appeared before them.

"Where's William Sutton?" asked the voice. "Now, the rest of you keep back and don't try no rush, because I got more men behind me, and we're ready to shoot if this turns out a fancy trick. Is William Sutton one of you?"

"I am William Sutton."

"Step out here for a minute by yourself," said the rough voice.

Thunder Moon willingly advanced alone, his fingers

kept continually near the handles of a revolver. When he was very close, he could make out a low wide-built man, who held a double-barreled rifle of an old make under his arm with a careless ease which denoted that he knew all about the uses of the weapon.

He said, now: "That's close enough. If you're what they say you are, then you know all about crooked work and dirty games, and you can cut a throat as well as the next one. Are you the Cheyenne?"

"I am."

"I had a cousin was murdered by one of them red devils. Some day I'll have it out with 'em for that, too."

There was nothing but sheer brute in this fellow, it was patent. Still Thunder Moon was patient, merely saying: "My brother paid you a sum of money to see me safely across the marsh with my friends. . . ."

"Your friends? The talk was about you, and not about the rest. What I have undertook to show the whole mob of you through to. . . ."

"The price was paid for me and all my party," said William Sutton.

"I'll see you damned first!" answered the ruffian. "I ain't had more'n enough money to sort of get me interested in this job. But if the whole party is to come across with me, I'm gunna see another thousand in cold cash."

Thunder Moon was silent.

"What's a little bit of money to a rich man like you?" quickly asked the swamp pirate.

Thunder Moon stepped a little closer during this speech.

"If I paid you what you ask, you'd call for more," he said. "You'll take us across for the money you've already had."

"Why should I?" asked the pirate sharply. "I've had the money paid down to me. What for should I pay any more attention to you folks unless you'll pay again?"

He finished on a note of triumph, and from the shadowy bushes near by there was a burst of brawling, mocking laughter. "Well said, Stevie. Well talked up, boy."

"You leave it to Stevie," said that ruffian. "He can talk for himself and for all of the rest of you, too."

"Your name is Stevie," said Thunder Moon gently, stepping still closer toward him.

"Yes, it is."

"Stevie, there are two things for me to do. One is to tell you that if you see us through this trouble we'll be friends to you later on. The other is to cover you with a revolver and shoot the matter out."

"What good would you gain by shooting? Would it get you through the marsh, man?"

"It would be a comfort to finish off a robber like you, Stevie, and here you are." He snapped his revolver into his hand as he spoke, but Stevie merely laughed through the semi-darkness.

"You ain't gunna bluff me, Sutton. You need me too bad to shoot. Now, I'm gunna treat you real fair and square. You pay me only a measly little five hundred dollars more, and I'll take you across the marsh, horse and man, all of you."

"You'll take me anyway, Stevie . . . no, don't try to step back. Stay where you are. You've had your money. Father! Come up! Come up, Standing Antelope!"

The party advanced behind him, and the marsh pirate, not knowing exactly what he had better do, presently found himself closely confronted by the old chief, young Standing Antelope, Red Wind, and above all by the fame and the mighty hand of Thunder Moon. He had not had the courage to retreat, for fear lest Thunder Moon should send a fatal bullet after him.

Now he said loudly: "Mind what you do, Sutton. I

got friends watchin' all this and only askin' a word from me to fire on you and sweep you all into hell. I guess you realize that."

"Lead on, Stevie," said Thunder Moon gravely. "There's no danger from us. Lead on and take us across the marsh."

"May you like what you'll find on the far side of it!" said the brigand bitterly. "Come on, then, if you're gunna drive a bargain as hard as this, and may you get much good from it, all of ye, and be damned to ye!"

So, pleasantly, Steve Baynes led them toward the marsh and there followed an hour of close and bitter work. Yet, by miracle, they were actually working their way across the marsh. Often their horses were almost belly-deep in water, but there were places where there was firm sandy or rocky bottom underneath. Often again, they were pushing through thin slush. Most of all they found themselves traveling upon firm land which was scattered in bits here and there throughout the drowned marshes, and so they crept on toward the farther shore. It could not have been more than a brief half mile that separated one side of the marsh from the other, but during the entire hour they were weaving back and forth and slowly making headway through the swamp.

"And don't think that you'll be able ever to come back and cross without me," declared their unamiable leader. "Little Dan Sargent, he was a wise one and he said that he could do it. Well, the bog ate him up, horse and all."

"If it was the bog that ate him, Stevie," broke in a voice from the nearby darkness, "how come it that you had the pickin' of the bones?"

"I found the stuff! I found the stuff!" snarled Stevie. "That's what I said to you Chip Tucker."

Chip laughed, with a noise more like the melancholy wailing of a wolf than the laughter of a normal man.

"I've found stuff the same way," said Chip Tucker. "It takes eyes to find such things in the swamp. Oh, it takes eyes, and it takes guns too. Grand guns!"

"You're a fool!" answered Stevie.

They went on through the darkness, the brigands pushing in as closely as they dared until Thunder Moon and Standing Antelope warned them back again and again. Plainly these lawless ruffians envied the purses and the good horses which belonged to the people they were guiding. They were not a hundred yards from a rising slope that promised to be good, sound land, and the end of the bog, when someone came hurrying toward them, his feet sucking noisily out of the mud.

"Stevie! Stevie!" he called. "Are you there?"

"Here, Dick!"

"I've finished off the other bargain and. . . ."

"Shut up, you fool!" exclaimed Stevie angrily. "Have you got no wits?"

He began to confer closely with this messenger.

"There's treachery in this talking," said Red Wind decisively to Thunder Moon. "Push straight on, oh, Thunder Moon. These men will sell you for the value of a single hunting knife or a handful of beads. They are greedier than Comanches."

"There is no one so quick as Red Wind," said Thunder Moon, "to see evil in anything and in everything. However, you may be right. Push on, Standing Antelope. No, I shall go first, and find the right way. The rest of you follow me in single file, and keep close behind me."

So said Thunder Moon, and rode to the head of the procession at once. The rest pressed close. "Here, you," said Stevie anxiously. "You can't go on that way. You'll wind up in a hundred feet of muck and bog unless. . . ."

"Then come and show me the proper way through."

"Not until I see more color of your money."

"Keep close behind me," said Thunder Moon to his companions. "There's no trusting these devils and I think we can get through this way." He drove steadily ahead.

"Will you come back?" screamed Stevie in a great fury.

"No."

"Then take this and be damned to you."

He fired both barrels of his rifle in rapid succession.

Chapter Forty-three

Hear, Oh Tarawa

The horses floundering more than knee-deep in sticky mud and slime, William Sutton and his little single file of followers were suddenly made a focus upon which a dozen weapons began to play. Sheltered behind the shrubs and the trees, or in hollows in the ground, the marsh rats fired rapidly. Straight ahead, from the rising slope, two or three other rifles were playing upon the shadowy little procession.

The night light, and the twisting and bobbing and heaving of the Thoroughbreds as they struggled through the ooze spoiled the aim of the ambushers until Standing Antelope heard something strike Big Hard Face with a noise like a fist pounded home. He knew suddenly that a bullet had hit the chief.

"You are wounded!" said the boy, pressing up beside

the old chief. "Tell me how I can help you, oh, Big Hard Face!"

The heavy arm of the warrior was raised and brushed his offer away.

Now they heard the voice of Stevie shouting behind them: "There's double money for us if ye bring down the big man. Hit William Sutton, boys. He's our meat!"

There was a loud exclamation of surprise rather than pain from Standing Antelope at that moment to show that he, also, had been struck by a bullet, but he did not on that account hold back. Now Thunder Moon felt the hoofs of his stallion bite home through the mud against firm footing, growing steadily shallower with every inch that they advanced. Just before him he saw the loom of starlit grass on the shelving bank, and this, he knew, was the end of their journey, hardly two bounds away from Sailing Hawk.

He turned to regard his party. Standing Antelope properly brought up the rear, twisting in the saddle and firing again and again. Red Wind was next, and just behind Thunder Moon rode his foster father. "Now, Father!" said Thunder Moon. "One moment more and we are free."

"How many rifles are there before you?"

"We'll know when we reach the place," said Thunder Moon.

"Wait!" cried the old hero. "Keep where you are one minute. I have an idea, Thunder Moon."

Striking his horse a terrific blow with his whip, he sent it bounding right past his foster son and up the slope beyond. As he went, his voice roared above the cursing, the grunting of the horses, the sound of the guns, the calling of the bandits, one to another: "Hear me, Tarawa! I offer myself a free sacrifice for my son. Let all the rifles be emptied into me."

Bursting past Thunder Moon before the latter realized what was happening, the big chief reached the dry, firm footing of the bank and drove his horse straight up it at a fence of brush beyond. There was no doubt of the prescience of the old warrior then, for instantly from that close ambush half a dozen rifles flashed at such a range that hardly a single ball could have missed its target. Still, as though no single blow could down his great spirit, Big Hard Face rode gloriously ahead and straight into the little thicket, firing his rifle as he went and then swinging it like a club above his head. There was no doubt, now, that this ambush was well prepared with extra rifles and pistols, for as the old man rode on to his doom, a second and a third volley went crashing against him. On the very verge of the thicket he fell from his horse with a battle cry cut short on his lips.

Past him, as he fell, like a furious lion and a wild young panther went Standing Antelope and Thunder Moon, charging to avenge the fall of their chief. What a vengeance they had. The guns of these enemies had been emptied into the body of one hero. Here was the rifle and then the knife of Standing Antelope at their throats. And here, worst of all, was the double revolver play of Thunder Moon. Six chosen rascals of the marsh pirates stood in that covert, and only three of them dragged themselves away, badly hurt, going like snakes or beaten dogs, close to the ground, leaving a crimson trail behind them. The seventh man was no marsh rat. Tall and straight, yielding not an inch to his danger, this apparent leader of the ambush saw Thunder Moon and Standing Antelope drive through the gunmen before him without flinching. His own rifle he had reserved for the last moment, and now he pitched it up and drew a bead on Thunder Moon. At that instant the latter fired and saw the tall fellow sway. The rifle exploded aimlessly and Thunder Moon swept his victim from the ground and caught him by the throat.

"Traynor!" he exclaimed. "Harrison Traynor!"

The voice of that gentleman answered him: "You've killed me, Sutton. But even after I'm dead, you still can't have her. I've put up a wall between you that will last forever. I'm only half a loser, you see."

He tried to laugh, but that instant he turned limp in the arms of his destroyer; Thunder Moon felt for the heart. It beat no longer.

There was no difficulty in making on with their journey. Now the marsh which had been so difficult for them lay between them and the pursuit. Traveling by night and resting by day, the three made swift progress. Their fourth companion lay far behind them. Thunder Moon had written back to his brother and mailed the letter at the first little town they reached:

Bury Big Hard Face like an Indian, on a platform raised toward the sky with his weapons around him, and kill a good horse beneath the platform. So his spirit will be able to hunt through the hereafter when he wants to ride across the sky!

All that was demanded in that letter was done with scrupulous care, and Big Hard Face was properly interred after the manner of his ancestors.

In the meantime, leaving the white settlements behind them, the little party struck out across the plains. They were making good time. Their horses were inured to the work by this time. Standing Antelope's wound in the thigh had healed, as well as two or three scratches which Thunder Moon had received during the course of the conflict. So for several weeks they beat toward the north and the west, striking out for traces that would tell them how the Cheyennes had been marching. They found them at last among the hills and, halting on the brow of an eminence, the three riders looked fondly down on the glimmer of the fires in all the lodges of the Suhtai.

"Look!" said Thunder Moon, "I have had double sorrows. I have lost two fathers and I have lost two mothers. The lodge which is to receive me there is now empty. You shall be my brother, Standing Antelope, and you shall be my sister, Red Wind . . . and we shall have happiness together."

The girl rode on past him, as though she did not hear, her head inclined.

"What is wrong?" asked Thunder Moon of his companion. "Is she angry again? Has the mysterious spirit come over her once more?"

"Oh, Thunder Moon," said the boy, "the Sky People have made you very great but very blind. Do you think that you can make Red Wind happy by calling her your sister?"

"I shall call her my daughter, then," said Thunder Moon.

"You are a fool!" said the boy.

"Do you think that she wants to be my squaw?" asked the great warrior. "How can you speak such nonsense? From the first day when she came to the Suhtai, she showed that she hated me."

"She tried to run away because she knew that if she stayed she would want to belong to you. She did not want to be your squaw, because you are a white man, and sooner or later she was afraid that you would leave us and go away to your people. She sent you away. It was by her managing that you went away. But afterward she was sick at heart and had to follow you."

"Standing Antelope, you say the thing that is not true."

257

"I cannot give you wits if you will not have them!" said the youth.

"Wait here, Standing Antelope. I am going to speak to her."

Thunder Moon rode rapidly ahead, and presently Red Wind came drifting back to him. At the edge of a stream she stopped her horse, and he knew that it was not from fear of the ford but because she waited for him that she had paused there. For that reason he rode more slowly. There was no moon. Even by the starlight he saw the curve of her throat, and the dull, copper glimmer of her braided hair.

FAREWELL, THUNDER MOON

Chapter One

The Pawnees Are Out

Out of the hills came a red rider. He went like the wind, his long, heavy hair streaming across his shoulders. He was a big man. All the Cheyennes were big.

The pony beneath him seemed absurdly inadequate to carry such a bulk, and yet it continued to run. It was polished with sweat which ran down to the middle of its belly and, at the parting of the hair, dripped off in a steady shower. Where the stirrup leathers or the knees of the rider touched, the horse was rubbed to lather. Lather formed, too, behind the elbows of the running pony and before the stifle. Foam from its gaping mouth blew back and flecked its shoulders, its breast. Its ears were flattened with labor and with agony for the Cheyenne in the saddle punished it forward with the most determined cruelty. He worked over the struggling animal, appearing to pay little attention to the direction in which it ran, but exerting all his ingenuity to torment additional speed out of it.

It was far spent. It went down a slope with a vain effort to lengthen its stride sufficiently. It struck the following rise with a drunken stagger, and the Cheyenne snarled brutally at it, and struck it with his club.

Torment or not, it was going only at a hard gallop when the Indian topped the rise and saw before him another warrior in the hollow beneath, a man who had heard that violent approach, the hoofs of the tired pony beating and scattering the rocks. He of the hollow had halted his horse—a lofty and noble-appearing chestnut—and had swung into the crook of his left arm a long-barreled rifle. At wait, he regarded the other.

From a distance seeing the rider of the chestnut, the speeding warrior began to make frantic signs, and drove straight down on the other. As he came by, still he kept his animal at a gallop. The big chestnut was turned then and galloped easily at his side.

"You are one of Thunder Moon's men!" exclaimed the rider of the pony. "I tell you by your horse and by your rifle. Tarawa has put you here to relay the warning to our people. Ride on! Do not spare the tall horse this day. Use whip and club on him. Make him fly, because fly he must. The Pawnees are out! Spotted Bull is leading them. I myself have lain for two hours and watched them, and counted them. They are a host. They are well armed. Their horses are good. They travel slowly, like men wishing to keep their horses and themselves fresh for a battle. Even now perhaps they have picked up my trail and are rushing behind me like wolves, but now you carry on the warning."

The second warrior said not a word in reply. He took his rifle and handed it to the other, who carried a war bow alone. He gave him also a pouch of ammunition, so that if the brave were indeed overtaken by the flying Pawnees, he might give a good account of himself until help arrived from the Cheyenne camp.

After that, he sent the chestnut flying. No Indian pony could have matched the speed of that Thoroughbred. It devoured the ground with mighty bounds, and the rider urged it neither with hand nor heel. Only with his voice he talked to it, and the big horse smoked on over the ground like a red mist caught on a storm wind. It was not for lack of will that the rider failed to strike the mare, for again and again his hand rose and hung suspended, as one who well knew that if there were a mark or blemish upon the beautiful coat of the mare, he would be called to a strict accounting when he entered the camp.

Presently he broke out of the hills into a stretch of gently rolling ground. A river angled sharply out of the highlands, and then rolled smoothly away along the undulations of this fatherland of the prairies which, further eastward, drew off as level as a gigantic playing field. Where the river swung in a wide bend through this pleasant country—treeless, but spotted with drifting lines of shrubs here and there and rich with tall grass that swished about the legs of the running chestnut there was an Indian village placed at a suitable distance from the water's edge. One could tell that the tribe prospered by the whiteness of the teepees and by the numbers of horses which moved in herds nearby, under the care of many keen-eyed boys. A thin stream of people went from the village to the water and back—women to wash, or girls to carry in water or wood, or boys to frolic and play and make themselves strong. Oh, glorious youth of the red man, too proud to labor!

The warrior on the red mare, taking note of all of this, smiled a little in pride, and rode on at a greater pace than ever, for the mare was keen at the sight of her home. Like a flung lance, horse and man darted into the circles of the teepees and, in the innermost circle, the rider flung himself to the ground. The mare, sliding to a halt on braced legs pony fashion, cast up a billow of dust before her, for here the grass had long been worn away and the surface of the ground had not been scoured recently by a heavy wind.

There were three teepees close together in this innermost circle and into the nearest of them—a noble, gaudily painted lodge—the warrior turned. He first struck against the board which was posted near the entrance. A voice spoke within. He lifted the flap and entered.

Inside, squatted at the back of the lodge upon a folded buffalo robe, was a chief who wore a hideous mask of a face. In close fight with the enemy he had lost one eye, his right cheek had been slashed across three separate times, and the flesh had gathered above the ghastly pallid furrows of the wounds. A side stroke with a battle axe, glancing off the top of his head, had laid one whole side of it bare and, though around this bare spot the hair grew luxuriously, still at the best it was only a partial scalp which he would offer the hand of a victorious enemy. Nevertheless, to his people he was a handsome object. His wounds were proofs of his dauntless valor, and he was in fact the war chief of this detachment of the great Cheyenne nation. He was now smoking a long pipe whose bowl was of the true pipe rock, and he rose and greeted the other with a resounding: "How!"

"You have brought news, Young Snake," he said. "Will you eat first and then smoke, or first will you speak?"

"The Pawnee wolves will not let us smoke or speak," said Young Snake. "Word was brought to us out of the hills. The Pawnees are on the warpath. Spotted Bull moves at their head. They are very many. Their horses are good and they count many rifles. They come straight toward our camp."

The chief smiled, and the expression was a dreadful grimace.

"When they come to us with guns and scalp knives," he said, "they are not coming against a squaw. Our men are not children, and our boys are not girls. But these Pawnees are fools. I have heard that Spotted Bull is a wise chief. But does he think that the medicine of Thunder Moon has grown weak?"

"A hungry wolf," said Young Snake, "will try to pull down a bull moose. The Pawnees are hungry. Their scalps have been drying long over our fires. They have lost their honor and their name on the prairies. Men smile at the Pawnee nation. They are very hungry and they forget the medicine of Thunder Moon."

"Go to Thunder Moon, my friend," said the war chief. "Ask him if we shall draw out our fighting men. Perhaps he will take down fire from the Sky People and fling it in the faces of these fools, and then send them wandering and blind."

This pleasant thought made the eyes of Young Snake flash, as though in foretaste he already was ripping away the scalps of helpless men. There he left the teepee at once and crossed to an even larger one, whose skins were as white as snow and which had recently been painted with all of the skill that an Indian can show. Close beside it was another, much smaller lodge. At the entrance to the larger one he struck the board. A woman's shrill voice, quavering with age, bade him enter, and he stood just inside the threshold and looked about him with a good deal of awe.

To one side an ancient crone was rising. Her back was bowed with many years, but her long arms were still sinewy and strong. From beneath the folds of her eyelids bright, bird-like eyes peered at the stranger as she rose to greet a brave of her tribe.

"Thunder Moon is not here, White Crow?" he asked with a good deal of respect in his voice and in his manner. Indeed, he was like one treading upon sacred ground.

"You come here with sweat on your face," said White Crow. "There is trouble for the Cheyennes again, and so they remember that I have a son in my lodge. Hungry dogs always have soft eyes when they smell food."

This bitter speech did not abash the warrior. He merely asked her if she could tell him where he could find her foster son.

"How should I tell you?" asked White Crow. "He sits by the river in a dream. The white devils have stolen his heart. Only a part of him is with the Cheyennes. Shall I tell you where to find him? Perhaps Red Wind will know."

He left the lodge and stood at the entrance of the smaller teepee, after casting one rather anxious glance through a gap among the tents and toward the open prairie in the direction from which the Pawnees might be expected. He dared not question the wisdom of the war leader, no matter how indifferent that hero might seem to be.

In answer to the blow of his hand on the entrance board, the flap of the teepee was pushed aside and, carrying in her hand the half-completed moccasin which she had been beading, Red Wind stood before the brave. Over one shoulder a great braid of copper-colored hair, looking as smooth and heavy as that metal in fact, dropped down even below her waist. But she had the dark skin and the dark eyes of an Indian. In twenty cities of white men, one might have hunted vainly to find another woman half so beautiful.

Farewell, Thunder Moon

"Red Wind," said the warrior, "I have come to ask where I may find Thunder Moon. Where has he gone?"

Her face clouded at once. "How should I know?" she asked with some bitterness. "Does he live in my teepee? Is he my husband? I am only a stranger who lives on his kindness. Why should he open his mind to me and tell me where he moves?"

She stepped back as though about to drop the flap of the teepee, then added coldly: "Go to Standing Antelope. He is more to Thunder Moon than all the other men among the Cheyennes. Go to him and ask him. He cannot fail to know the mind of the great warrior, by night or by day."

The flap of the teepee straightway fell and the brave remained for a moment, scowling, as though he was minded to call the girl back and teach her better manners. But he altered his mind and, turning, he strode rapidly through the village until he came to a much smaller lodge, in front of which sat a handsome young brave with such feathers in his hair as denoted feats done in battle in spite of his youth.

"Thunder Moon! Where is he?"

Standing Antelope frowned. "I do not carry him in my hand," he said. "How shall I tell? I only know where his mind is. In the land of his white fathers."

Chapter Two

The Wisdom of Thunder Moon

To the blunt answer of the youth, Young Snake, a hardened and seasoned brave, returned a baleful stare in which he surveyed the youngster from head to foot. Standing Antelope did not shrink from the survey, repaying it with a calmly insolent glance. Correction hesitated in the mind of the older man. It was true that Standing Antelope was young, but he was swift as the wind. He was not vastly experienced in life. On the other hand he had ridden on long forays at the side of Thunder Moon, and from that strange and terrible man he had learned gunplay with such skill that few among the Cheyennes would have been willing to stand against him.

Young Snake contained himself with saying: "A true friend should be as one's shadow."

With that he walked haughtily away, and plied his query again of a boy at the outskirts of the town, having remounted the chestnut mare in the first place. The boy had no hesitation at all. He pointed toward a clump of trees on the bank of the river, and toward this Young Snake galloped at full speed. He was growing nervous. It seemed to him, as he cast a glance over his shoulder at the wind-ruffled grass of the prairie, that the whole fate of the Cheyennes rested upon his activity. For what if the Pawnees should suddenly appear in a rushing charge?

He made the mare travel at high speed toward the designated clump of trees and, dismounting, he pressed through them and found Thunder Moon reclining at ease. Young Snake gazed upon that mighty form with awe. No tribe on all the plains possessed such power of hand as the Cheyennes and among all the Cheyennes there was no one to match the resistless force of Thunder Moon. Now, as he lay at ease, his strength appeared more formidable than in action. Hercules's striking is less suggestive of might than Hercules's leaning upon his club. In the hand of Thunder Moon lay a book, partly shaded by the down showering of his hair, cut short when he had lived among the whites, but now grown very long again. He brushed back this hair so that it fell more in order across his shoulders and nodded to Young Snake. Only at that hint did the messenger dare to speak.

"Thunder Moon," he said, "the Pawnees have been seen in force among the hills. They are going fast, and straight toward this camp it seems. Spotted Bull leads them"

"I am not the leader of the Cheyennes," said Thunder Moon. "This is a message for Bald Eagle."

"I have spoken to Bald Eagle. He told me to ask you if he should lead out the braves, or if you instead will go out and throw the fires of the Sky People in the faces of the Pawnees."

Thunder Moon thrust himself up on one arm. So doing, the buffalo robe which covered his shoulders dropped off and showed him, Indian fashion, naked to the waist and otherwise clad in trousers of the finest deerskin, heavily beaded in an intricate fashion.

"Am I," he said, "to be called upon every time the Pawnee dogs howl on the plains?"

269

Young Snake said diplomatically: "Battle is a small thing to Thunder Moon. He rides along through the country of the enemy. He sees them in crowds, their wise warriors and their brave young men, and he laughs. If he has need and so wishes, he calls upon the Sky People, and they send him help. They guide his bullets. They speak wisdom in his ear. We are not like you. It is true that we call the Pawnees wolves and dogs, but they are wolves and dogs that may bite!"

Thunder Moon closed his book with a reluctant sigh. He stood gathering into his hand a heavy cartridge belt which also supported at either side a long holster out of which the handles of revolvers appeared. This he buckled about his waist. From the tree beside him he took the long rifle which was leaning against it. Young Snake, his dignity not impaired by waiting upon so eminent a warrior, picked up the fallen robe and threw it over the wide shoulders of Thunder Moon. Sun browned as they were, the naked flesh of the shoulders of Thunder Moon had showed clearly his white blood. Now that his body was covered he looked almost perfectly the part of an Indian for his hair was black and coarse, his eyes dark, and his face and throat were so bronzed that there were actually in the tribe paler complexions than his own. He had the face of an Indian, also—the wide, powerful jaw and the high cheekbones and the look of cruelty and decision, but perhaps there was more sensitive molding in his mouth and in the chiseling of his aquiline nose.

The rifle he carried in his left hand. In his right, he walked with a staff and so left the woods. Young Snake pointed to the mare.

"Will you ride?" he asked.

"While you walk?" asked Thunder Moon kindly. "No, brother. I have not loaned the mare to you in order to

270

take her back the first time there is weariness in my feet."

They crossed the level stretch between the river and the village, Young Snake leading the mare behind him. As they went, a little crowd of boys swept down and swirled around them, like so many agile young birds on the wing. A boy of thirteen leaped before them, dancing backwards to keep out of their way.

"Is there war, Thunder Moon?" he asked cheerfully. "Is it true that the Pawnees are riding? If that is so, take me with you! I shall guard your back. No one shall come at you from behind. Take me with you, and I shall count one coup, or else may I die, and my scalp dry over a Pawnee fire."

"Boy," said Young Snake as reply, "have you learned the ways of men? Do you speak to a chief before he has spoken to you?"

He made a threatening gesture as he said this, but Thunder Moon merely smiled.

"What is your name?" he asked.

"I have no name!" cried the child. "I have sworn that I never shall take a name. I am nothing . . . until Thunder Moon sees me fighting, and then calls me what he pleases. He may call me anything, but he never shall have to say: 'Coward!' "

"Young fools boast and wise men smile," said Young Snake. "You raise a dust before us. Go away!"

"Go to my teepee," said Thunder Moon, still gently. "I shall give you an old rifle. Swear that you will not try to join a war party for a whole year. Go to Standing Antelope and he will teach you how to shoot. At the end of a year from this day . . . then we shall see how straight you can hold the rifle in your hands."

There was a wild yell of joy from the youngster. He leaped high into the air as though from a springboard, and then whirled and darted for the river to tell the swimming, wrestling, running boys there of the great prize which he had been promised.

Young Snake muttered: "You will turn all of our boys into beggars, Thunder Moon. Out of your hands good things flow faster than words out of the lips of other medicine men."

They entered the village. A young brave stepped suddenly beside them and raised a hand in greeting.

"Young man," said Thunder Moon's companion, "the chief is busy. He has no time for words with you."

"Are you in trouble?" asked Thunder Moon.

"I have a sore heart," said the other.

"Tell me, then, as we walk on."

"I am the unlucky man who married the daughter of Crooked Horn. I paid six good horses for her. She came to my lodge in the afternoon. She was gone by the night with another man. Now Crooked Horn refuses to give back my horses."

"He gave you his daughter," said Thunder Moon, "but he could not promise you the power to keep her. A thing that is done is ended. Where is the girl now?"

"They have gone back, I think, to the rest of the Suhtai. I only wait to settle my dispute with Crooked Horn before I follow them."

His face set; his nostrils expanded with savage resolution.

"Let them go," said Thunder Moon. "A woman who leaves one man will always leave two. She will cost her new lover horses, perhaps more than six, before he sees her for the last time."

"My empty lodge makes my heart very sick," said the brave.

"Then give away your lodge and all that is in it, except the weapons. Give the rest to the poor, and go to live with the other young men. Tell me . . . are you not the man who counted the coup on High Buffalo?"

"I am that man," said the youth. "Thunder Moon's eyes see all things, and in his mind he never forgets."

"When you ride on the war trail again," said Thunder Moon, "you shall ride at the side of Young Snake, here, upon one of my horses, if that will make you happier."

The youth could not speak. Joy choked him.

"Happy!" he cried at last, in a ringing voice. "This day I am born again! Thunder Moon, I shall give everything away. Since you have made me one of your men, I have better than a teepee of buffalo cowhide because I have the whole sky for a lodge."

"As for the woman," said Thunder Moon, "it is best for you to think no more of her. If she had been a good woman, she would not have left you so soon after going to your teepee. Since she has proved herself to be a bad woman, why should you yearn for her? Does a man hunger for the thing that makes him sick?"

The young man went on, fairly reeling with joy.

"Once more! Once more!" said Young Snake. "The riches of the lodge of Thunder Moon are very great, but the riches of his wisdom are still greater."

Thunder Moon shook his head, with a faint smile.

"Ride through the camp and gather my men," he said. "We are going out to find those Pawnee wolves who dare to come so close to our city. That is to say, we shall ride out if Bald Eagle gives us his permission."

Young Snake whirled without a word, bounded upon the back of his horse, and hastily rode off through the camp. His face was illuminated with a confident joy, for the Cheyennes never took the dread of defeat with them when they rode out behind Thunder Moon. The latter had gone on into the teepee of Bald Eagle and briefly stated his purpose.

"Brother," said the war chief, "whatever your mind tells you to do is good. Shall I ride with you?"

"Only those who ride my horses are going," said Thunder Moon. "But you shall ride if you will."

"I stay here, then," said the chief. "Let the young men go out and gather the scalps of the dead men whom Thunder Moon leaves on the ground." He looked down as he spoke, for fear that the other would see the poisonous envy and hatred which at that moment was overflooding his soul.

Chapter Three

Treachery

All musters were quickly made in the Indian village. The followers of Thunder Moon rapidly assembled. He himself was cantering a horse among the teepees and encouraging his braves to hurry, until he came to the lodge of Standing Antelope. Here he called and, after a moment, the youth appeared at the entrance. A buffalo robe was gathered close about him. He appeared bowed, as if in pain or in weariness.

"The Pawnees!" called Thunder Moon. "Are you riding? Have they failed to bring you word?"

"Oh, my Father," said the young warrior, "there is hot pain in my heart. I don't think I could sit on the back of a horse. Besides, you do not need me. The finest braves follow you. Even without them, you could not fail. The Sky People ride at your side."

"When I come back," said Thunder Moon, "I shall see you again and then we shall talk about your sickness. Rest quietly and keep your mind cheerful. A sad mind makes a weak body, Standing Antelope."

He rode on. Standing Antelope stared gloomily after him. Then he retired to the quiet of his teepee. There he sat with the robe gathered around his head, trying to shut out the noises of celebration, the shouts of farewell and encouragement, as the braves gathered and departed on the war trail. His whole soul was on fire to join those riders who went out to hunt glory and to count coups, and he trembled with the passion for war. Yet he controlled himself and, for a long hour after the riders were gone, he waited. At last he got up and put on a suit of beaded deerskin.

He picked up a revolver but, remembering that this was a gift from Thunder Moon, he promptly laid it aside again. With only a knife at his belt and a staff in his hand, he walked out and went with dignity through the village. As the passage of a whirlwind leaves behind it circling little towers of dust, so the Cheyennes were gathered here and there in excited groups, discussing the war alarm. One seasoned brave, carried beyond himself, was prancing around and around in front of his lodge, like a rooster courting a hen and chanting a hideous war song. Standing Antelope went past this celebrant and came to the teepee of Red Wind. He spoke. She came to the entrance and smiled cheerfully on him.

He went close to her and said in a quiet voice: "He is gone, Red Wind. Let us go also. I have horses ready. Once we are away, he never will be able to find our trail."

She looked narrowly at him.

"Are you asking me to run away with you?" she asked bluntly.

275

He drew himself up.

"I am," he said.

"And why should I go?" asked Red Wind.

"My teepee is filled with wealth," he said. "I have fine backrests and many painted robes, and good pipes, and also pots and everything that a woman could wish, such as beads."

"Who gave you your wealth?" she asked.

"I fought for it," he said.

"You fought under the shield of Thunder Moon," said the girl.

"I have taken wounds in battle," he said. He pointed to a scar that seared his shoulder.

"Scratches," she said, "but Thunder Moon, with his medicine, has turned the bullets of the enemy away from you."

"Thunder Moon himself never will say so," he insisted.

"Because he is modest and he does not boast about the friendship of the Sky People."

"I have not only wealth," he said, "but I have wonderful swift horses."

"They are the red horses of Thunder Moon," she answered, "which he gave to you."

Standing Antelope struck the ground with his staff. "I have counted seven coups in battle!" he declared.

She answered: "You have counted your coups with Thunder Moon riding beside you, striking down every danger that came at you."

"You talk like a woman blind with love," replied Standing Antelope.

"Who, then, is greater than Thunder Moon?"

"Bah!" said the youth. "He never has passed the test. His heart was broken. It is said that he cried like a girl when his foster father would have tied the thongs in his flesh when he was a boy."

"It is very well for the Cheyennes to remember that day," murmured the girl. "He has saved them a thousand times in battle. Now they sneer at him."

"He never is brave, except when he knows that the Sky People are with him."

"Who rode into the land of the Comanches and took away their god, their Yellow Man . . . took it away from their own medicine lodge? The Comanches have had no good fortune since that day."

"A woman only looks with one eye and therefore how can she see the truth?" he replied. "Thunder Moon never has taken a scalp."

"But he has counted more than thirty scalps . . . and in battle."

This testimony caused Standing Antelope to pause for a moment. Then he muttered: "It is true that the Sky People give him power. They make his heart bold, too. But why do you care so much for him?"

"Because he is the greatest and the bravest and the richest and the strongest chief among the Cheyennes!"

"He is not a chief," replied Standing Antelope. "Neither is he a medicine man."

"Whatever he is, he is himself," she said. "Who do the Pawnees fear? Who makes the Blackfoot tremble? Why do the Sioux leave the Cheyennes in peace?"

Standing Antelope bit his lip. Then he replied: "Of what use is a fine horse to the man who cannot sit on its back?"

"What do you mean by that?"

"You love Thunder Moon. Yet what are you to him?"

"Do you think," she answered angrily, "that I shall like you better because he likes me less?"

He said with emotion: "You do not know me, Red

Wind. I am not old. But I am a man. Already I may speak in the council. The old men listen. Why will you not listen to me, Red Wind? You are nothing to Thunder Moon. He keeps you here out of his kindness. He is no Cheyenne. There is not a drop of Indian blood in his veins. I say that. You know it also. You have seen his father and his mother in the land of the white men. They despise us because of our red skins. So does he despise us!"

"He left his people and came back to us," she retorted.

"Because his people drove him out. He never has smiled since that day. His heart is full of the memory of the white girl whom he left behind him."

It was the girl's turn to grow excited. She gripped both her hands hard and her breast heaved. "Thunder Moon takes what he wants, even out of the camp of the enemy," she said. "If he wanted the white girl, he would have taken her. You should know this."

"Among Indians, he is an Indian," answered Standing Antelope. "Among white men, he is a white. Among the whites, the word of a girl unstrings the arms of the strongest warriors. This I have seen, and you have seen it and know it also. You talk to make your own heart strong, but there is no strength and there is no truth in your words."

She stared at him, as though what he said had entered her heart deeply, and he went on: "Now you are sad and angry, because I have told you the truth. See what I offer to you in exchange. I am not a magician. I cannot call down the Sky People. I am not as rich as he. I have not a whole herd of such matchless horses as he inherited from Big Hard Face, who stole them from the whites . . . from Thunder Moon's own father. But I am a Cheyenne, and I am a man. I have passed the tests. I have had the thongs fastened deeply in my flesh, and I have dragged the buffalo skull until the thongs tore through the flesh and set me free to become a warrior. I have counted seven coups. I have taken five scalps. My gun shoots straight. I can strike hard with a lance. My knife is not dull. In the council I am not a fool. Also, I am young. If I have done something before, I shall do more hereafter. Besides, I love you. I have gone among the young women of the Cheyennes. They are no more to me than stars when the full moon is in the sky. I have ridden out on the war trail and fought hard, and gone hungry, and welcomed every pain because I hoped in that way I could drive away the thought of you."

"Standing Antelope," she said sternly, "how do you think that I may trust you? If you could betray a friend, would you be true to a woman?"

"I give up a friend whom I love for a woman whom I love still more," he said. "Besides, I have shown you that he will never make you his squaw. He has learned among the whites their ways of marriage. His wife would have to be a real wife, and one only, according to the ways of the whites. For the one woman, he already has made his choice."

Suddenly she drew her robe about her head. "Ah," she said, "you can break my heart, but you cannot take me away from him." She turned suddenly back into her lodge.

Standing Antelope went away with a pausing step. Bald Eagle, from before his own lodge, watched him going and motioned to him. The youth, half reluctantly, went to his chief.

"You have a sore heart?" said Bald Eagle.

"I am not happy," answered the brave.

"Patience, patience," said the war leader. "Patience will win the longest battle. Brave men know that the last blow is what decides the fighting."

The two looked fixedly upon one another with understanding, and then Standing Antelope resumed his way to his own lodge. It was a bitter day to him. Besides, it placed him in a quandary. He hardly could trust that Red Wind would not tell Thunder Moon of that conversation. If this were done, how could Standing Antelope remain in the camp without fighting against Thunder Moon? No matter how boldly he had spoken in the presence of the girl, he well knew in his heart of hearts that he could not stand for an instant before the strength and the skill of the white man.

So he sat in his teepee and thought long thoughts. Twice he was on the verge of mounting his best horse and deserting the tribe, but always he resisted that temptation. He was so sick with love that he hardly cared how soon death came to him.

Chapter Four

Two Braves Meet

Armed to the teeth, Thunder Moon's band of chosen braves voyaged across the prairie. It was a sort of honorary troop which he had formed. He saw that every man was as perfectly armed as possible. Each carried a rifle of the best quality. Revolvers were of no use in their unfamiliar and inaccurate hands. But they had good knives, axes to fling at a short distance or use in hand-to-hand fighting, and long, slender lances, topped with the finest steel. Each, too, carried a shield of the toughest hide of the back of the buffalo bull—a substance so stout that often it stopped a spent bullet and still more often deflected a glancing one though, of course, it was of little use against rifle fire well aimed and at a reasonable range. It would, however, serve as a defence against hand-flung missiles, and against axe stroke or lance thrust. All of the score of warriors who followed Thunder Moon were armed in this fashion. They set off their weapons and their defensive arms with a fluttering host of feathers and many a pound of bright beads, so that the party flashed and glistened almost like ancient knights in armor, crossing the plains.

Though they had been carefully trained by Thunder Moon in the proper and accurate use of the rifle, their chief strength lay in their horses. First stolen from the herd of Sutton on that distant day by Big Hard Face, the foster father of Thunder Moon, the original nucleus had increased to two score animals, old and young, and nothing that trod the plains could be compared with them. It gave them over other warriors on the prairies the same advantage that fast ships had over less weatherly enemies—that is to say, they could stand down for battle when they chose, weaker parties could not escape from them, and overwhelming numbers they always could flee. Many a time the force of these advantages had been proved. With a keen and restless confidence the warriors now followed their leader. They looked upon him almost as a god, convinced of his invincibility in war.

In two hours they put the camp well behind them and they had broken into the region of higher hills when the advance guard whirled and raced back. He had seen the Pawnees. They were coming straight up the valley— nearly five score warriors, well armed and mounted as the first report had accurately stated.

Thunder Moon ordered his men to dismount. He con-

281

cealed them in the long grass of a hilltop, leaving three
men in the rear to handle the horses and keep them in
readiness for a retreat. When this was done, he rode
boldly out into the valley in full view of the advancing
Pawnees. It was his hope to draw them straight past his
concealed force which then could pour in a searching
fire and make away to their horses and escape before
the pursuit became effective.

Upon a little swell of ground in the midst of the valley
he took his post and watched the irregular body of the
Pawnees jogging toward him. Nearly every warrior appeared to carry a rifle. In the rear a large herd of horses
was being brought on by several Pawnee boys.

Coming still closer, the Pawnees suddenly seemed to
recognize an enemy. They flogged their horses into a
gallop and bore down upon the lone horseman at a terrific speed. Still he did not move from his position,
though some of the enemy already had unlimbered their
rifles and were firing. The distance was still too great
for any sort of accuracy.

The bullets, in fact, were fired by those who realized
that they were mounted on slow horses and, therefore,
could not get up to the battle in time to do execution on
the stranger, except with a chance, long-range shot.
Thunder Moon watched that charge with a grim satisfaction. He was just about to twitch his stallion around
and send him flying to the rear when he saw a chief
break forward through the mass of the Pawnees and begin to make many violent gestures, shouting.

A great war chief of the Pawnees, perhaps, encouraging his men to the charge! He saw that the warriors
were restrained on either hand. Their pace became
slower. Suddenly the whole body halted at the front,
those in the rear bringing up their ponies and then stop-
ping so as to form a fairly dense line.

The leader, in the meantime, advanced by himself and signaled with sign language from a distance that he wished to converse with the solitary rider. Thunder Moon, nothing loathe, advanced in turn. They met in the midst of the valley. Thunder Moon saw before him a stocky, powerful man of middle age or a little less, with a particularly gross and brutal face.

It was Spotted Bull, a famous and lucky hero among the Pawnees, particularly distinguished for raids in which he had driven off horses from the Cheyennes, the Blackfoot, and even from the Sioux themselves—a tribe which, on account of its great numbers, most of the other plains warriors were glad to leave alone.

This chief came straight up to Thunder Moon, his rifle in its case, his shield slung over his shoulder, and only his long, light lance in his hand. Even this he did not carry on clear to the point of meeting, but jabbed the butt of it into the ground and rode on empty-handed to the meeting. He raised a hand in greeting.

He said to Thunder Moon with much complacency: "Now that two such famous chiefs have met, Thunder Moon, let me know why we should not part as friends?"

"What friendship has there ever been between the Cheyennes and the Pawnees?" asked Thunder Moon sternly.

The other was undisturbed. "No doubt," he said, "we are generally at war with one another, but that is no reason why there should not be peace, now and again. What are you to gain today from me? No doubt you have some of your men hidden nearby, watching with their rifles. Probably you have not so many as I. Even suppose that the Sky People guide your bullets and kill some of us from a distance, still you are not apt to do us much harm. If you take any of our blood, then we must try to have vengeance, and that would mean for many days your village would be very uncomfortable. Men are not happy when they are surrounded with stinging bees, and the Cheyennes do not sleep soundly when they hear the wolves howling in the night."

At the aptness of this remark, Thunder Moon could not help smiling a little.

"On the other hand," went on Spotted Bull, "it is very hard to find any honor from Thunder Moon. All the nations of the plains know that very well. Now I wish to say to you that we have not ridden out to do any harm to the Cheyennes. We do not wish to strike at your young men. We have enough horses to carry us very well without trying to steal some of yours. . . ."

Here his eye could not help glistening with hunger as he looked at the mighty stallion which Thunder Moon bestrode.

"We have another goal, brother," concluded Spotted Bull. "That is why I offer that we should all be friends for a few days. My brother is wise. He knows that it is easy to snuff out the flame of life in a brave warrior. Yet it is not easy to raise another in his place."

The leader of the Cheyennes nodded. "Everything that you say is true," he said. "If we have not had peace in the past, it is no very good reason why we should not have peace for a time now. I am not the war chief of the Cheyennes in this village. A great warrior, Bald Eagle, leads us."

"Bald Eagle has that honor of being war chief but," said the Pawnee, with a flattering frankness, "if it were only for Bald Eagle, perhaps we should not be so anxious to have peace with the Cheyennes just now. It is Thunder Moon whom we know very well. We have seen his hand striking. Also, I know that when he speaks, all of the Cheyennes listen. Let me have your promise to speak for us. After that I shall care nothing."

This flattery touched Thunder Moon sufficiently to make him answer: "Spotted Bull, you speak very kindly. Kindness from a stranger makes the brain sleep. I shall try to do what you want. If you are not riding into our country in order to make war on us, what is it that you wish to do, and where are you going?"

"A good rifle is best kept in one holster," said the cunning Pawnee, "and a secret is safest when it is lying in one mind. But to a famous man I must give an answer. Is it not true, Thunder Moon, that not very long ago you went to live among the whites for a time?"

"That is true."

"And that you left them?"

"Yes."

"That in fact they hunted you out?"

The frown of Thunder Moon was a sufficient answer.

"These things are talked of among all the tribes on the plains," said Spotted Bull. "The Pawnees," he added with additional flattery, "were not unhappy when they heard that Thunder Moon had gone. They were not very glad when they learned that he had come back again to the Cheyennes. But I know that after such a thing has happened, you have no great love in your heart for the whites?"

"If a dog is kicked," said Thunder Moon, in oblique answer, "he licks the hand of his master who beat him. If a wolf is struck, he leaps at the throat."

"So!" said the Pawnee chief, "Thunder Moon will teach the white men that they were fools to throw him out. This I can understand. It could not be any other way that a man would act. Then I freely tell you that I was riding against the whites."

"That will be a great war," answered Thunder Moon. "I have been in their country, brother. I know the numbers of their warriors. Since we are speaking as friends, I tell you the truth."

"I am not riding against their towns," answered the Pawnee. "But they have sent out a party into the plains. That party has killed a Pawnee. It is right that they all should die like dogs and that we should take their scalps, their horses, and their weapons!" He added: "It is said that they have very fleet horses, but I think that they cannot run as fast as the Pawnee bullets."

"You have told me the truth," said Thunder Moon. "I have nothing to say except to give you peace."

Chapter Five

Gray Bear

Out of the grass arose the twenty Cheyennes, took their twenty horses, and sat in the wind, their feathers blown sheer back upon their heads, watching the Pawnees—those ancient, traditional enemies—ride slowly past them into the heart of the valley. They looked down to the unharmed Pawnees; they looked without regarding the greater numbers. For they were invincible, they felt. They were the men of Thunder Moon, who would not know defeat. They looked to the foe, and then they looked to their leader and their faces grew darker.

All the Pawnees went past. They went in a silence, like the silence of guilty apprehension, until the Cheyennes ground their teeth. The longer the Pawnees marched upon their small ponies, quietly past, the more powerful and secure they felt themselves. They saw beneath them four score honorable scalps growing upon Pawnee heads, and their hands clasped the handles of their knives and they rolled eyes of agony upon one another.

Then the enemy departed through the hills, rising and dipping like a ship through green seas, streaming soon out of sight.

"Suppose that they turn and ride for the village?" asked one gloomy warrior. "Suppose that they are riding now with all their might, now that we cannot see them any longer?"

Thunder Moon said: "If we had fought, we would have killed some of them. They would have killed some of us. The speed of our horses would not have saved us altogether. Horses cannot run faster than bullets. I never have heard a truer thing said than that. I would not kill twenty Pawnees at the cost of five Cheyennes!"

So he spoke, but one of the younger braves muttered, no louder than a whisper: "That is what he says to us now, when his blood is cool. But let his blood get hot and he would throw us all away for the sake of fight. Thunder Moon perhaps has lost the support of the Sky People. Perhaps they no longer hear him speak."

So they said. Eyes widened with fear at the mere thought. There was malice, too, in their faces. Thunder Moon, though he did not hear that malicious voice, plainly understood the meaning of those expressions. But he did not heed them. He had known for years the quality of having divine or semi-divine powers attributed to him. Impossibilities were asked of him. If he did not undertake them with a smile, then it was because he was lazy and cruel, or else because he had lost his powers. Or again, if the slightest thing turned out well, it was not because of his own brain and the strength of his own mind, as it was because of the Sky People.

He hardly knew what he felt about them now—those dim beings of the upper world. There had been a day when he would have shuddered at the mere thought of doubting their existence, but now he had altered somewhat, having lived for long, long months among the white men of his own kin. He could not help remembering the books which invaded the marvels of the sky and made the rain and the blowing of the winds all seem normal and natural things, not attributable to the wrath or the pleasure of the spirits, but entirely to the physical powers of the sun which lifts the waters from the ocean and causes all the weight of the winds to blow.

Yonder, over the mountains, where the rivers run down to the eastern sea, it was easy enough to give credence to the spirit of science. Not so easy upon the broad breast of the prairie which, with mysterious curve, presses man up closer to the wild bosom of the sky. Though his mind would often say no, yet in great moments his instinct and all his heart made him look upwards for help as he had done so many times, all his life. He had not actually prayed to the Sky People for these many, many months. For this, even, he felt more and more guilty. Perhaps they had turned their backs upon him. So he understood perfectly the shadow that ran over the faces of his men, like a cloud shadow running over a group of hills.

His thought turned back to the last thing which had disturbed him. The Pawnees rode to attack the whites. Somewhere they would strike the wanderers and wipe them out perhaps. He was amazed and troubled by the thought. Amazed to know that it could pain him so deeply, when he remembered how those of his own color, his own blood, had driven him out with bullets!

Then he called forth Young Snake. There was hardly

a better or a more seasoned warrior in his entire band.

He said: "Go back with the other men to the village of the Cheyennes. I am riding alone."

Young Snake looked upon his master with a burning and a hungry eye.

"Oh, Thunder Moon," he said at last, in a voice that actually quivered, "I hear you and I understand. There is no longer glory for Thunder Moon in striking the enemy with so many followers. He wants to go alone, his guns speaking, and the Pawnees falling. He wants to count twenty coups in a single battle. But think of us. We follow you for the sake of glory!"

Thunder Moon could not help smiling a little as he answered: "Do you think that I would attack them single handed, one man against eighty? Is that a wise man's thought, Young Snake?"

Young Snake answered with a perfect devotion: "What are many enemies to you, oh, Thunder Moon?" He explained himself with the most cheerful of smiles: "When the Sky People ride with you, do they count the number of the faces of the Pawnees before them?"

The big man answered briefly: "The Sky People bid me to ride alone, and not for the sake of a battle. I have told you what to do. Ride back to the village. I will not change my mind."

At this direct command, Young Snake obediently drew off. The other warriors sulkily heard his voice, and suddenly they fled across the hills on the homeward trail, like so many shadows mounted upon red streaks, so rapidly did the big chestnuts run.

Thunder Moon rode on alone, and with the greatest caution, upon the trail of the Pawnees. He knew that there was need of every care. No matter how friendly Spotted Bull might be when Thunder Moon appeared with a band of practiced warriors at his back, all mounted upon those most dreaded, those most desired coursers, nothing was clearer than that the Pawnee chief would break ten thousand promises, would break them in a very ecstasy of delight, so that he could have the joy of taking or slaying Thunder Moon, that fire-brand, that bolt from heaven, lodged in the hands of the lucky Cheyennes.

So Thunder Moon went on cautiously, his care redoubled because he knew his own deficiencies upon the trail. It was well enough when he voyaged across the plains with some of the most expert trailers of the Cheyenne nation to guide him aright, to spread out before and behind to catch the very first signals of danger. It was another matter when he had to make such a journey alone.

Even an Indian woman, even an Indian child, had sharper eyes than his, had quicker senses to note the changes upon the grass, the leaves, the ground, which indicated that other life stirred nearby. By the flight of the very birds, they could read what was passing along the surface of the earth, many miles away, and yet all of these abilities were quite beyond the talents of Thunder Moon.

Certainly though he went, he knew that he was overtaking the Indian column. The walk of the big stallion was equal to the jog of the Indian ponies, and the trot of the chestnut was the equivalent of a mustang's canter; whereas the long-striding gallop had no counterpart among the hobbling, broken gaits of the prairie horses.

There was no dust cloud ahead to show him the nearness of the Pawnees. He could tell, in a way, by the manner in which the bent and trampled grasses were coiling upwards again, the heads still moving. Twice, therefore, he halted. Twice he started onward with the keenest caution, knowing that such a wise chief as Spotted Bull was not apt to trust to an informal treaty of peace such as had just been completed, but would surely throw out rear guards to spy against any possible surprise attack.

He came to a narrow little gorge where a stream wound back and forth through the flat, pebbly bottom. He went down this, where the grass grew so tall that it brushed against the feet of Thunder Moon. The sun glittered like the flashing of steel blades on the polished surface of the grass, like the flashing of steel blades but not quite like the dull sheen of a rifle-barrel.

Thunder Moon whirled in the saddle as the rifle jumped to the shoulder of the Pawnee. He saw a hideous face, streaked with war paint, and he flung the heavy bull-hide shield from his left arm straight at the Indian.

The rifle spoke. The shield staggered to its course and fell to the ground as the bullet ripped sidewise through it. It would have been easy to finish off the man with a bullet from his revolver, but Thunder Moon was full of the white man's fighting madness such as never comes over a savage brain. The Indian fights as coolly as a wild beast—he always avoids risks if he can. Twenty men will not press home a charge against three, if the rifles of the three are loaded. But the white man rejoices in a sort of drunken, berserk lust of battle for battle's sake. He marches willingly behind the banner of a lost cause; and with a cheerful mind he volunteers for the most desperate hazard. So Thunder Moon followed his flung shield with a leap like a catamount that drove him from the back of his horse and straight upon the Pawnee.

It was a practiced and wide-shouldered warrior, bull-necked, cunning of hand, with an arm of iron. But he could not stand against the charge of Thunder Moon. He had dropped his rifle and caught out his knife just as the

291

weight of the white man smashed into him and bore him heavily to the ground.

Kneeling beside him, Thunder Moon watched the stunned victim gradually open his eyes. He made no further attempt at resistance. Blankly he gazed up at the leader of the Cheyennes, and waited for death. Thunder Moon gathered to his hand the knife, the hatchet, the rifle of the Pawnee.

"The Pawnees keep good treaties and their word is sacred," said Thunder Moon bitterly. "Hardly two hours have passed since I made friendship gifts to your chief and received the same from him. Here is a wolf in my path, jumping at my throat."

The warrior did not attempt an answer.

"Rise!" said Thunder Moon.

The Pawnee rose to his feet.

"Is there any reason why I should not send a bullet through your brain?"

"Dog of a Cheyenne!" answered the Pawnee with a dauntless heart. "The Sky People turned my bullet aside from your heart. Or else you would lie dead here, and tonight I should be a great man among my people. Kill me as you please. I am not sorry that I tried to end your days."

"What is your name?"

"It is known to my people."

"I can tell you," said Thunder Moon, "by the scars across your shoulder. You are Gray Bear, are you not?"

At this the discretion of the Pawnee could not prevent a flash of pleasure from appearing in his eyes.

"A man will be known even in the lodges of his enemies," he said. "A great warrior is named in the camps of the foemen! I am Gray Bear."

"You have taken Cheyenne scalps, Gray Bear."

"I have taken three Cheyenne scalps. One from a man,

one from a woman, one from a child. Even you, Thunder Moon, cannot kill me three times. Not even all the skill of the Sky People could teach you how to do that!"

"Where is your horse?"

"He is near."

"Show him to me."

The Pawnee whistled. A pony sprang up from the grass and came forward.

"Your horse knows you," said Thunder Moon. "Get on his back. Ride on with me."

The Pawnee obeyed without a word, but a settled sternness of gloom appeared on his face, as though he were seeing, long beforehand, the burning fire in the Cheyenne camp where the women would torment him to death.

They journeyed on to the brow of the rising land. As their heads came up across the top of the grass, they could see in the distance the moving line of the Pawnees, with the sun winking upon the bright tips of their spears.

The prisoner sighed, ever so slightly, and Thunder Moon said to him: "Keep close to my side. Ride slowly. All may be better for you than you imagine."

Chapter Six

Attack

The problem of Thunder Moon was now considerably complicated. He had to watch a strong and capable warrior at his side—even if that man were disarmed—quite likely to undertake any desperate and sudden attack upon him. In addition, he had to look out for other rear guards who might have been thrown out to watch.

For some time they journeyed on, having cautious sight now and again of the Pawnees who traveled before them over the top of some grass-grown hummock upon the prairie. There were no further encounters with subtle watchers who lay in the grass.

While they rode on, the mind of Thunder Moon turned somewhat between the dangers which beset him and the glory which he already had won upon this expedition. To take a scalp was most brave and admirable—but not a scalp had he ever taken. Inward repugnance could not be overcome in that direction. To slay in battle was a great deed. To count a coup was yet more worthy. But best of all was it to carry into the village of the Cheyennes a prisoner and, of all prisoners, who so welcome as a grown and famous warrior? The women had a thousand wrongs and remembered deaths to avenge. They would expiate them upon the person of this brave. The grim face of Gray Bear already acknowledged his approaching fate.

Another thought, too, interfered with the mind of Thunder Moon. He could not help remembering that the whites among whom his kin lived would never have acted thus toward a prisoner. A defenseless man was not to be harmed physically. He might be imposed upon, but his life was sacred.

This new standard troubled Thunder Moon and made him scowl askance at the Pawnee. Then, almost against his will, he looked up and was aware of a small white cloud sailing across the upper heavens, filled with radiance, as though the sun were seated in its center.

"The Sky People," he thought inwardly. No matter how little he consciously believed in that old superstition, in spite of himself he was comforted and reassured.

They came up behind another hummock and Thunder Moon suddenly reined back his horse, for he had had a view of the line of the Pawnees crouched behind a low ridge just before him, their horses held further down the slope. Beyond, across the prairie, came a stream of wagons. More than a score, he guessed them to be, plodding one behind the other through the rich sea of grass.

Sheltered from view once more, he said to Gray Bear: "Spotted Bull rides to attack those wagons?"

The answer of the Pawnee was indirect, but from the heart: "May he take many scalps! May he cover the wagons with blood! May he take some of them to kill afterwards, little by little!"

"Why do you hate the whites?" asked Thunder Moon. "Have they killed a son or a brother of yours?"

"No."

"Have they carried off any of your horses or a squaw?"

"What are women and horses?" said the Pawnee with contempt. "They may be taken again from enemies. The Blackfoot, the Sioux, and the Cheyennes," he declared with a glance of defiance at Thunder Moon, "raise the horses which the Pawnee wolves will ride! It is not for that that I hate them."

"For what reason, then?"

"Because they do not believe in our spirits, they do not fight in our ways, and they do not live by our customs. Why should you ask reasons for hating the white man, have they not driven you out? Yet your skin is white, also."

This answer effectively silenced Thunder Moon and made him look bitterly on his captive. He could understand the taunts, open or implied, of the Pawnee. They were aimed at rousing in him such a furious and headstrong anger that a bullet or a knife stroke would quietly

295

and more fully end the life of Gray Bear and thereby save him from the hands of the Cheyenne women.

He did not answer, but now, by degrees, they both worked up again to the edge of the ridge and looked over on the scene which was developing. The Pawnees kept the same position, except that a band of a dozen, to the right, were moving down the hollow on their horses as though to be prepared to make a flank attack.

In the meantime the wagon train came closer and closer, moving with a sort of assured slowness, like a force conscious of its own strength and calmly despising all danger.

There were fully twenty of the big canvas-covered schooners, drawn by teams of oxen, a little gap between the rear of one wagon, and the horns of the following cattle. With their clumsy but powerful steps they pushed on through the prairie. Around the train rode horsemen, three or four in front, and others to either side. It seemed that they rode for pleasure and comfort rather than to keep guard, for otherwise they should have been pushed out to ten times such a distance, so as to act as spies in the treacherous Indian country.

The leading wagons had begun to mount a slight rise. The wind was dead. In the mortal stillness, Thunder Moon could hear the creaking of the great wheels upon their axles and, dimly, the shouts of the ox drivers as they used their goads freely. For this train was long out from the settlements, and the cattle were weary—soft with such lush green fodder and weak with the long days of labor.

Those dim voices, like thoughts rather than physical facts, haunted Thunder Moon with a strange sadness. He suddenly saw the house of his father, and the big white walls flooded with sunshine and with showers of green climbing vines. He heard the Negroes singing in the fields. He looked through a window of his heart and saw his mother in the stately library, her needlework in her lap.

What thoughts had she of him since they had driven him back to the wilderness and the wild people?

A rifle shot cracked from the hollow before him. He saw the long line of the Pawnees break over the crest of the low ridge and pour with the most fearful yells across the level, brandishing their spears, shaking their rifles above their heads.

"Ha," grunted Gray Bear. "They will swallow those white men. They will take the cattle, and the horses, and the guns, and the whiskey, too. There will be much firewater among so many wagons. All is ours!"

For the moment he had forgotten that he was himself a wretched captive, that the most unlucky white man in that train was hardly to be pitied more than himself.

The wagon train, threatened so suddenly on the plains, instantly began to act. The leading wagons turned sharply around and began to move toward the rear, while the frantic, yelling drivers goaded the oxen to a trot, then to an inconceivably heavy, lumbering gallop.

While the head of the train turned back in this fashion, the rear likewise curled about to join the front. The purpose, of course, was to form the wagons into some sort of a rough circle, from which, as from the walls of a fort, the riflemen could keep up a steady fire and drive the enemy away.

Slowly, slowly moved the wagons. The Pawnees rode on wings to strike. Gray Bear groaned with eagerness and with joy as he saw the probable success of the charge.

There were brave and ready men in that caravan, and the rifles worked steadily. Three of the red riders were knocked out of their saddles, but the rest rode on, lying flat along the backs of their ponies, and screeching like so many devils.

The head and tail of the caravan, gradually nearing, now seemed to have an equal chance of actually locking, when a bullet fired by one of the Pawnees struck a bullock which was struggling forward in the lead team from the rear. The animal dropped, dragged in the yoke, and then the wagon slewed around to the side.

It was only possible to close the gap at this point by having the wagon next following veer outside the one which had been checked. But the driver of the second wagon, utterly confused, merely halted when the one before him was checked. It was the old habit of following the leader which all the drivers soon learned upon the prairie.

In this case it proved fatal. The progress from the rear being stopped, the whole caravan looked a helpless thing, like a hedgehog which quite fails to curl up before the reaching paw of the lynx rips up its belly. But he who drove the lead wagon was a man of sense. Seeing that he could not join the rearmost ox team, he turned in almost at right angles to the left, and the other wagons streamed after him, thus striving to close up a smaller circle which would protect at least a portion of the entire line.

Now into the open gap the Pawnees streamed, screeching like mountain lions over a kill. They rode erect, firing to either side. But they had divided their attention; some turned on the nearly defenseless wagons to the rear. Some raced on to try to prevent the front half of the train from closing up. The latter were foiled, and Thunder Moon saw them recoil as the circle was completed.

Chapter Seven

Who Are You?

Well sheltered behind the wagons, the men of the circle maintained a steady fire against the Pawnees, but the latter now had a similar shelter. They swept in a single rapid wave over the remainder of the wagons. Wild cries of agony and wilder cries of triumph went up to heaven, and then the Indians threw themselves into position behind the captured wagons to open fire upon those which remained. After the first few moments, seeing that they were making only a small impression upon the remainder of the white fighters, they gave the greater part of their attention to the looting of the train in their hands.

The wind was dead. A thin smoke cloud from the firing of many rifles began to sway out and envelop the battle. Thunder Moon turned to his captive.

He had come with a bland satisfaction to see the wiping out of the whites. He found in his heart an increasing rage. Under his glare, the Pawnee chief winced, but Thunder Moon merely said to him: "You are free. Go back to Spotted Bull. Tell him that our truce is ended. He has counted many coups and taken many scalps. His hands are heavy with plunder. Tell him to guard himself: the Cheyennes are on his trail."

The Pawnee did not wait to be reassured. He gave merely one incredulous glance to his captor, then he sent his pony off at a jog trot. When he was a hundred yards away, as though suddenly mastered by fear, he put the whip to his horse and shot off in rapid zigzags across the grass, like a snipe flying upwind. Thunder Moon grimly watched him go. Bitterly he wished for those chosen warriors whom he had sent back under Young Snake.

He turned the tall stallion and drove at full speed back toward the Cheyenne village. In less than an hour, he sighted the smoke above the teepees, then the village itself. His horse was tramping through the water of the little river. He sent his shout before him and the whole town roused itself in answer. As he came up, Young Snake was the first to gallop out to greet him, armed at all points. Behind him streamed the rest of Thunder Moon's own private band of adherents. Other volunteers young and old, eager to take the warpath behind so famous and lucky a leader, galloped in pursuit. Thunder Moon waited for no more. With that advance guard of proved and well-equipped warriors, he headed across the prairie. He did not follow the straight line toward the scene of the recent battle and slaughter of the whites. Instead, he cut off at right angles to that line of march. He reasoned that it would be very strange if Spotted Bull should remain to exult on the field of the battle after the warning that he had received through the liberated captive. He was more apt to take the first and the quickest trail toward his homeland.

If he moved to the left, it was very likely that Thunder Moon would cross that line of march. If he moved to the right, he would be free. With one chance in two to gamble for, Thunder Moon drove his men remorselessly. Even those fine horses on which he had mounted his chosen men—the wealth of his dead foster father and his own glory—were now punished relentlessly forward while the others, mounted on the Indian ponies, lagged to the rear in spite of all that whip and club could do to punish them forward.

Ten miles of prairie rolled behind them, and then a youth scouting ahead whirled back to announce that there was visible in the distance a column of riders, coming straight toward them at a round pace. Thunder Moon himself pushed forward and swung to his eyes the glass which he always carried. Instantly he recognized the Pawnees by their cropped heads. Behind the file of warriors came the herd of horses, mixed with the cattle recently taken from the wagons of the whites. A foolish move for Spotted Bull to have taken such slow moving animals if he wished to move with celerity.

There was no doubt about his haste. He had pushed out to either side two or three scouts to ride in advance. The line came on with gaps in it, showing that some of the horses were being distanced by the rest.

Not Indians alone rode in that procession. The very first thing that Thunder Moon saw—more moving to him than the flashing of a sword—was the long waving of a woman's hair. Then he made out the bundle of an infant in her arms, two children riding one behind another on another horse and, upon a third a man evidently wounded or broken hearted, for his head was sunk upon his breast.

Thunder Moon smiled, and the smile was not good to see. His own dispositions were easily made. The horses were swept back into a sunlit hollow. The riders were thrown forward into the high grass along the ridge of a knoll which was rather a small wave of green than a hill. In a moment the Cheyennes were out of view, peering out through the grass blades at the procession of the Pawnees.

In a murmur Thunder Moon passed his word among

301

his warriors—to everyone who recaptured alive one of the white captives of the Pawnees there would go in full and free possession one of the chestnut horses. It was a gift worth the risking of life!

In the meantime it appeared as though this stratagem would be wasted. Far distanced by the ride of Thunder Moon's band across the prairie, a score of Cheyennes on their war ponies had clung to the trail and now these were in plain sight, coming rapidly on.

Spotted Bull must have sighted them at the same time. Some thirty of his own warriors were dispatched to the side to confront this strange menace but, though he deployed across the line of the Cheyenne approach, still the out-numbered Cheyennes came on. They well knew that somewhere in the sea of the tall grass, Thunder Moon and his chosen warriors were placed.

The Pawnees on the other hand, as though amazed by this resolute advance, wavered a little, uncertain. Spotted Bull himself, with half a dozen of his best warriors, rode out to reinforce his advance guard while his main body, now reduced by half, came slowly on with the captives.

All was working out for the best interests of the Cheyennes. The late comers from the village bore straight on against Spotted Bull. Just behind that chief lay Thunder Moon and his chosen fighters in the grass; and straight toward the concealed line came on the rest of the Pawnees. One Pawnee division was already tacitly taken from the rear; the others would be swept with surprise.

To the left, from Spotted Bull's immediate adherents, a rifle cracked and then another, but Thunder Moon, half rising to his knees, saw with joy that the Cheyennes kept on their rapid advance, merely fanning out their line so as to offer poorer targets. The head of the Pawnee main body was jogging close and closer. A dozen yards from Thunder Moon's concealed warriors—and then, silently—the Cheyennes rose to their knees in the grass and, with a deliberate aim, they blew the head of the column to bits.

The sudden blast of more than twenty well-aimed rifles took the Pawnees so completely by surprise that it was as though the ground before them had opened and spat forth fire and destruction into their defenses. They rolled back in utter confusion. The Cheyennes leaped in among them with clubbed rifles, with knives, and with thrusting narrow-headed lances.

Thunder Moon, his rifle cast aside, a revolver in either hand, made at the woman and saw her Pawnee guard whirl on her with lifted hatchet. Two quick shots dropped the guard. Thunder Moon stood at the head of the horse and looked up into a white, drawn, bewildered face, and saw trembling hands that clutched the infant closer.

"Have courage," he said rapidly to her. "You are safe. No one will harm you."

He turned back to the battle; but it was ended already. The men with Spotted Bull, amazed and unnerved by the eruption of rifleshots immediately behind them and with a rush of Cheyennes pouring toward them, did not even pause to discharge their rifles, but turned and fled. As they turned, the riders on the Cheyenne ponies whipped vigorously in pursuit. Woe to the Pawnee whose horse stumbled or proved a laggard!

The tall chestnuts, rushed up from their hiding place in the hollow, were hastily mounted. They darted away to join the pursuit, their long strides rapidly overtaking the fugitives. In another instant the sounds of battle were scattered far across the prairie and in all directions. Here was a Cheyenne group busy taking scalps. Others rounded up the herd of cattle and horses. Others took the fallen plunder. Still the greater part were scouring the plains east and north and south and west to count fresh coups and hunt down the traditional enemy.

It was as great a stroke as Thunder Moon himself ever had delivered. Yet he felt no keen pleasure as he looked on the work which was still under way. It seemed to him, with a stabbing suddenness of truth, that the death of one white, even woman or child, was more than enough to counterbalance all the vengeance which he could execute upon the entire Pawnee nation.

Bitterly he realized this. He had been cast out from among his people. He knew in full what they meant to him and that an Indian name and an Indian life never could give him an Indian's heart.

The white fugitives were gathered in a close cluster, surrounded by half a dozen braves who were disputing as to which actually had rescued them—a problem which Thunder Moon himself had to solve. The two children and the woman who carried the infant were half hysterical with joy and with relief. He had them placed on the ground to rest and steady their nerves. He turned to the white man and found, as he had expected, that the latter had been wounded, a rifle ball having passed through his left thigh so that it had been a constant agony for him to remain in the saddle.

With all the skill which he had learned from whites and Indians, Thunder Moon cut open the trouser leg and cleansed and dressed the wound. A swallow of whiskey out of a flask restored the color to the face of the sufferer and he said quietly: "God knows what luck sent you here at the right moment. But if you had come a few hours before, you would have saved a horrible massacre."

"I saw the attack," said Thunder Moon. "Tell me. Did the last circle of the wagons hold? Or did the damned Pawnees break through and slaughter them, too?"

"No, they beat the Pawnees off. You. . . ." He paused,

looking earnestly at Thunder Moon. "Do you know me?" he asked.

"I?" said Thunder Moon. "Certainly not."

"Will you tell me who you are?"

"I am a Cheyenne. They call me Thunder Moon."

"By heaven," said the other, "I thought so! Your hair was shorter when I last saw you, and you were not so sun browned, but you are William Sutton."

Chapter Eight

What the Sky People Did

To this recognition Thunder Moon replied in the uttermost astonishment: "Who are you? Where have you seen me?"

"I'm Charles Siegler," said the other, "and I used to see you near your father's place. I had the small farm down the road with the row of poplars in front of it and the pool beside the trees. Do you remember me, sir?"

Thunder Moon closed his eyes. He remembered very well the tall, slender, graceful trees, and their images ever afloat on the surface of the little lake.

"I remember you, Siegler. I remember you very well," he said. "No doubt you were one of the men who hounded me out of the country with guns and dogs? Were you one of those?"

"No, sir, I thank God!" said the other with violence. "I had nothing to do with that bad day's work."

"Bad day?" said Thunder Moon darkly. "Was it a bad day's work to hunt down a murderer?"

"Murderer?"

"There were dead men in the jail behind me."

"Ah, and was that it?" asked Siegler. "As a matter of fact there were no dead men at all, and he who hounded the others after you knew it very well. No, sir, since your leaving there was never a time when a great many people did not make a stir about bringing you back. Your father and mother have gone to the expense of fitting up the wagons and the cattle to go across the prairies and find you."

"To find me!" cried Thunder Moon. "How many died when the Pawnees rushed the train?"

"I saw five men down, and three women, and three children," said Charles Siegler.

"Eleven dead," muttered Thunder Moon. "But why in the name of my father's God did he send out women and children to help hunt for me?"

"Those were not all his men," answered Siegler. "We fell in with another small train. We made one party, to travel together as far as we could into the country of the Cheyennes. After that, they were to go on alone. They were mostly in the tail of the wagon train. They went down with a crash when the Pawnees charged. God help them!"

"Who went out commanding my father's men?"

"Your brother, sir."

"Jack?"

"Yes."

"Is he . . . hurt?"

"No, sir."

"Jack is commanding them," muttered Thunder Moon, turning the words over and over in his mind, with a total bewilderment.

"No man is keener to find gold than he is to find you, sir."

"Is that likely?" broke out Thunder Moon suddenly. Then he added: "Jack's come with the rest . . . to find me. It's got to be believed! Is there anyone else in the party that I know?"

"I think there are and particularly there is. . . ." Siegler checked himself.

"Go on, man."

"There is one you'd better see with your own eyes before you're told about, Mister Sutton."

Thunder Moon rubbed his chin with his hard knuckles. He looked away across the prairie and he saw the men of his war party coming gradually back, some from such a great distance that they were mere specks. Others were disappearing in the hollows in part and growing big against the sky again, as they climbed the slight knolls.

It had been a great victory. The scattering drew back. In that sudden assault, not a single Cheyenne had been killed or seriously injured. Not a horse had been lost. Mortal fire having blazed suddenly in the faces of the Pawnees, they had fled without attempting more than a random and half accidental shot, here and there. A few grazes from bullets, a few shallow wounds caused by random lance thrusts or by knife cuts were all. Just enough had been done to raise the spirits of the warriors.

The pony-mounted volunteers from the village had not done such great execution upon their enemies, but even they had their scalps to show and their coups counted. Altogether seventeen Pawnees were dead and seventeen scalps were hanging from the bridles of the Cheyennes. There was not a man of the entire party who had not counted at least a single coup. It was a glorious victory. There was loot besides, in abundance, not only

307

from the Pawnees but from the whites who had first been plundered by the Pawnees.

Young Snake, splashed with blood from head to foot—part of it running from a shallow, unregarded wound in his own broad right shoulder—came up to his leader with a face convulsed with joy.

"Take all the men and go back to the village," said Thunder Moon. "My band is tired. They have fought hard and ridden as only Cheyennes can ride. Go to Bald Eagle and ask him to send out some new men. The Pawnees are men. Spotted Bull is not among the dead, and he may attempt to come back and fight once more."

"Spotted Bull," answered Young Snake, "is a brave man, for a Pawnee. But he has this day seen the fire of the Sky People flung in his face. He will not come again this day or this year within a week's ride of Thunder Moon and his men. I, Young Snake, saw him ride from the battle and never look back, but I shall do everything as you wish."

"Listen to me sharply," said Thunder Moon. "In the wagon train there are many white people who are my friends. They are to be treated as friends. They have come a great distance to find me. Let the young warriors come out and be a guard between the white men and the roaming Pawnees. Do you hear?"

"I hear and I shall tell Bald Eagle."

"Go to the teepee of White Crow, my foster mother. Give her the rifle and the clothes and all the weapons of this dead Pawnee. Load them upon his pony. Tell her that I killed him and two more with my own hand. She is an old woman and she needs to hear pleasant news to make her heart light and young again."

"Oh, my Father," said Young Snake—though Thunder Moon was much his junior, "it is no wonder that the Sky People love you. Your thought is always for others.

This I shall do. White Crow shall sing louder than all the women of the Cheyennes. Also, they shall be silent while they hear her singing because of her son. Shall I go?"

"Go at once."

The other was off at once, gathering his men about him with shouts. Off went the warriors across the plain. There remained behind the dead, stripped bodies of the Pawnees, the whites, and Thunder Moon.

The whites gathered close around him, looking fearfully across the plain, as though they expected terrible danger to flow in upon them from its vastness at any moment.

He reassured them gravely: "The Pawnees have lost heart. The Indians are not like the white men. When they are beaten, they go off to make new medicine. The white man stands up and fights again. Every kind follow their own ways. Tarawa sees it all. God, you call him, but he is one spirit."

Several horses had been left to them by the express command of Thunder Moon. The woman and the two children were mounted. The wounded Charles Siegler was slung in a rude litter between two ponies. So they started back across the prairie, Thunder Moon riding his great red stallion and leading the litter horses behind him.

The woman pressed eagerly forward. She was half weeping and half laughing. Her husband had been with her in the wagon which the Pawnees attacked. He had attempted to fight but, when the Indians surrounded him, he had tried to get through to the safe circle of the wagons before them. What had become of him she did not know.

She did not have to wait until they completed the entire journey to the wagon camp. A solitary rider loomed out of the grass before them, swept closer—and presently her high, tingling cry rang before her. The rider swept closer and embraced her. It was her man who had flung himself on a horse after the battle and determined to follow blindly on the trail of the Pawnees who had his wife and his child captive. Doubtless he would have died when the rear guard sighted him, but Providence had intervened on his behalf in the form of Thunder Moon and his band.

He came to that leader, when he had heard the story from his wife, and took the hand of the pseudo-Cheyenne in both of his. He could not speak. His face worked like the face of a child. Thunder Moon looked upon him with a strange happiness and sadness at once.

If he had not followed the first cruel working of his fancy, not a one of all the white men, his countrymen, would have fallen.

They journeyed on at a slow pace, controlled by the necessity of keeping to a gentle rate on account of the wounded man who, nevertheless, laughed at his own plight.

"They would have ridden us back to the Pawnee camp," he declared. "There the devil-women of the tribe would have buried splinters in me, and set 'em on fire. I know their little ways. May they all be damned!"

At last, far off, they saw the wagons, all exactly as Thunder Moon had seen them, the small, cramped circle at the head of the line and the rest of the wagons scattered in a broken line just as they had stood when the Pawnee charge broke into their midst.

He said to the happy husband: "John Sutton is in that train?"

"Him? Without him, we'd all be dead. He was drivin' the lead wagon . . . it was him that had the sense to turn in short and make the small circle . . . God bless him!

He done a day's work that would've lasted him for the rest of his life." He added: "And the girl, too. I seen her handling her rifle like a man."

Thunder Moon asked no questions. An odd, stinging hope was awakening in his breast, and he looked with a scowl at the slow pace with which the litter bearers kept up the line.

In profound wonder he looked up to the broad surface of the sky, now gathering color for the sunset time was upon them, and he saw one golden cloud high above the rest, with a bosom filled with rich fire. The Sky People! thought Thunder Moon. They have brought my brother out to find me.

Chapter Nine

"Can I Do That?"

When they came still closer, they saw that all the people of the caravan, more than a score, were gathered around a mound of newly turned earth—the common grave in which the dead had been placed. Thunder Moon could see afar the man who was reading the service for the burial. Three women were in the listening group—one of them had fallen to her knees in grief.

A little nearer, and now they could see faces. Yonder he knew the tall form of his handsome brother, Jack Sutton. Hardly a brother he had seemed in the old days. How different to find him here on the prairie.

A queer thrust of joy passed through the heart of

Thunder Moon and his closed soul opened. He hurried on ahead of the others, scanning the group which had now turned away from the grave and toward him.

They began to shout. One of the women ran out with a wild cry that passed into the mind of Thunder Moon, never to leave him again.

She passed him and reached the litter and cried out again. There was as much agony of joy now in her voice as there had been agony of sorrow and pain and hope before.

Yonder man who had been reading from the Bible was now revealed as no less a person than Colonel Keene, looking no less courtly on the wide floor of the prairie than he had been in his own house.

Thunder Moon brushed straight on. His brother was hurrying toward him, calling out with honest joy in his voice—that same brother who once had so bitterly envied the man who had returned from the wilderness. Colonel Keene also moved forward, waving his hand in wonder and delight. Yet these people were hardly in the eye of Thunder Moon. He looked beyond them to the third woman—younger than the others, more slender—beautiful Charlotte Keene!

She did not advance with her father to greet Thunder Moon; rather she shrank back into the crowd. The more she shrank, the more savagely and well he knew that she loved him as much as ever he had loved her during the long and lonely months since he left her and rode westward toward the prairies.

The instant that he felt that hot wave of confidence in her, he could turn his attention to his brother and the colonel. They greeted him with the purest amazement, as well as joy. His hands were wrung. Big Jack Sutton danced like another Indian himself, and a thousand questions poured out.

How had he known that they were there? How had he chanced to come that way? He told them he had met Spotted Bull, trailed him, watched the attack on the wagons, sent in his challenge—which had the effect of drawing the cautious Pawnees hastily away from the rest of the wagons—intercepted him, sent back his men, and so here he was. After all, there was less of a miracle in this coincidence than had seemed, for had not the caravan been voyaging west these many weeks, striving to find the section of the Cheyenne tribe to which Thunder Moon, alias William Sutton, was attached?

"Where's Charlotte?" asked the colonel. "She wouldn't let us go off without her when we started on this expedition. She wanted a taste of frontier life. God knows we've had too much of it today . . . the Pawnee devils."

Charlotte was with them at last, shaking hands and gravely telling William Sutton that she was glad they had found him. To Thunder Moon she looked almost childishly small, compared with the tall Cheyenne women. Even compared with Red Wind. All the other people of the tribe had to be met, and there was a glad hubbub of voices except from those who had lost friends or family in the battle.

To escape from that spot, Thunder Moon urged them to march straight on because they would find water within two miles. So the cattle, recaptured from the Pawnees, were put to the wagons, and the train forged ahead until the darkness came. Camp was made at the edge of a small stream. Men and animals drank. Three fires were lighted, for brush was plentiful. Dinner was cooked. All this while Thunder Moon had little opportunity for conversation because his presence was required here and there, directing the way, helping to picket the horses and oxen, and taking command in general.

313

Later he would have a chance to talk with Charlotte Keene. There was in him an infinite tide of things to say to her. When he came back to the fires after all of this work, he found that Charlotte had gone to the wagon to sleep. The other women and children, equally exhausted, disappeared under the canvas.

All the camp grew quiet. With low voices Colonel Keene, Jack Sutton, and Thunder Moon talked together. They watched the head of the fire rise and snap off in the blackness, under the chin of the stars.

"One of you has done most of this," said Thunder Moon. "Which one is it?"

"We pulled together," answered the colonel gravely. "We did everything together. We each had our motives."

"And what was yours?" asked Thunder Moon of his brother.

Jack Sutton grew red, but his glance would not waver from the face of the other. "I had to find you," he said, "in order to let you know that I understood at last what an infernal puppy I'd been. I had to find you and tell you that I'd been a greedy fool . . . that I'd wanted to rob you of your rights . . . that I'd envied you the estate . . . great God, Will, I never could have called myself a man if I hadn't made some effort to find you. I'd even plotted against you . . . that last night . . . I'd betrayed you . . . or tried to. . . ."

Thunder Moon glanced at the colonel.

"He knows all about it," said Jack Sutton. "I told him and I told Charlotte. I'm clear with them at least. Perhaps some day I can be square with my own conscience."

"It was Harrison Traynor that put the killing into your mind," said Thunder Moon.

"It was," admitted the younger man.

Now across the firelight reached the great hand of

Thunder Moon, so famous across the breadth of the prairies for its power. It was laid upon the shoulder of Jack Sutton.

"Brother," he said.

They looked full at one another with a world of understanding and affection.

"We made up our minds to come after you. It was a long pull, we thought at the time. We joined with the caravan ten days ago. The length of the train was what nearly finished us off, as you had a chance to see. God knows that the rest of us were lucky to have you look on just then."

"Now that we've fairly met," said the colonel, "we must put the question which we've come to ask. Do you come back to your father's home with us?"

Thunder Moon frowned. Then he gathered the robe around his broad shoulders. He lighted his pipe and blew a puff toward the ground, and a puff into the air, and another cloud of smoke he struck with his hand and made it scatter into nothingness toward the horizon stars. In this Indian fashion he continued his smoking unconsciously, frowning in thought.

"I came back to my father's house," he said, "and I tried to live like a white man."

"A good job you made of it, almost from the first," said his brother.

"The first whites whom I saw hunted me like a fox. I settled down in the house and in the end, after a great deal of hard work with the brain and reading of books and sweating and grubbing and wearing stiff clothes that grip the shoulder muscles, in the end of all of this, when I had learned to love my father and mother and the old white house, I was driven away because I would not let my foster father lie in a jail."

"It was Traynor who did that," said the colonel. "God

rest the dead, and Traynor is among them. I cannot help saying that I never heard of any more treacherous and devilish action than that of Traynor's against you, and the raising of the crowd to hunt you . . . when Traynor knew very well indeed that there were not three dead men left behind you in the jail. You'll find no more Traynors when you go back with us, my lad."

"There are other things," said Thunder Moon. "It is true that very often my heart is sick to go back among my own kind. Still here on the plains, a man is a man. There is freedom. There is no one to say to me: "Go."' Or, "Come."' Or, "Stand."'"

"Who is there to say that to you in your own home, Will?" asked his brother.

"There are a good many things to stop me . . . pity for my mother . . . respect for my father . . . and always the hard fist of convention beating into a natural man's face . . . to say nothing of the law which keeps its rope around every neck."

The colonel at this smiled, and nodded. "Of course it's true," he said. "But, after all, there is something gained . . . polite conversation . . . culture. . . ."

"Have you ever listened to Indians telling stories?" asked Thunder Moon.

"No," admitted the colonel. He added: "With us, you would at once be a distinguished member of society. Your father is very old. Frankly, he is not very well. We don't expect him to live through the next winter. In case of his death, you would step up as the head of the family. The head of the whole estate."

"If I were head of the whole estate," said Thunder Moon, "could I then do as much as this?"

He whistled—a long, bird-like, mournful note—and then he raised a hand as a warning to listen. Almost at once, out of the darkness, they heard the rapid beating of the hoofs of a horse. Then into the firelight came a young Cheyenne. He brought the mustang to a halt close to the fire and raised long, slender lance and shield in salutation to Thunder Moon. That posture he maintained for a moment, unstirring, except as his lithe, muscular legs gave with the heaving ribs of the pony.

Thunder Moon spoke a few words in Cheyenne, and the warrior whirled the pony and was gone in a flash.

"Can I do that, when I am the head of the estate?" asked Thunder Moon.

Chapter Ten

For and Against

That wild vision out of the night was still in the minds of the listeners. They were still half dazzled by the wild light in the eyes of the mustang, in the eyes of the Cheyenne brave.

Then the colonel said slowly: "There are more than sixty slaves on your plantation, William."

"Here," replied the other, "I have more than twenty free men. If I go on the warpath, hundreds of others will follow me if I choose."

"To take scalps?" asked the colonel sharply.

Thunder Moon flushed. "I have never taken a scalp," he said.

"Come, come," said the colonel, "there is something to be said in favor of a comfortable house, contrasted with a shivering teepee in the winter snows."

"There is," admitted Thunder Moon, "but we have fire, food, and plenty of robes. The old men tell tales. There are always feasts, and the winters go away as fast as running water."

"That may be," replied the colonel, "but isn't it true, William, that you're held by something else more than anything that you've mentioned?"

"By what?"

"You have a pretty young wife among the Cheyennes, haven't you?"

"I?" exclaimed Thunder Moon.

"Let's be frank, my boy. The girl who speaks English. She herself told my girl that she was your wife."

"Red Wind?"

"Yes, that was her name."

"Said that she was my squaw?"

"That's right. What of it, William? That's not a disgrace. A man lives in Rome like the Romans. Besides, there are ways of arranging these matters. Only . . . I hope and trust that there are no children as yet William?"

"She told Charlotte that I am married to her?"

"No doubt she simply meant that she had been taken as a squaw, Indian fashion."

Thunder Moon set his jaw hard. "That explains a good many things," he said. "And your girl believed her!"

"I want to talk frankly," said the colonel. "You will imagine I had to have a pretty strong reason for making such a journey as this. A still stronger one for letting Charlotte go along with me. The fact is, William, that you were something more than a friend to her."

"I love her," said Thunder Moon quietly. "I told her so."

The colonel seemed to inhale this speech like incense. "If you care for her, that settles it," he said. "We'll arrange all of the minor difficulties. Then back you must come with us, my boy. Life has been a little drab and dark for poor Charlie since you left us."

"Suppose," said the pseudo-Cheyenne, "that I build a trading fort in the hills. The Cheyennes would still be around us. Would Charlotte be happy here in the open country?"

"She has a thousand friends," said the colonel. "You know that, William. It would be hard to ask her to come out here. But I think she would do whatever you asked . . . except that you could not very well ask her to share your life with the Indian wife."

The colonel had put this as gently as he could, but his old eyes glimmered with ire and contempt as he spoke.

Thunder Moon arose.

"I go back to the village," he said, "and there I shall see Red Wind and bring her back with me to tell your daughter the truth. I have had no wife among the Cheyennes. Old White Crow, my foster mother, is the squaw in my teepee. I have placed a lodge for Red Wind near us. She was left alone in the world. I was a friend to her, and she has hurt me when my back was turned. But you will hear the truth from her own lips!"

The colonel fairly groaned with pleasure. "My dear boy," he said. "My dear lad! Bring her as fast as you can. Start with the morning. We'll head on in this direction."

"There will be Indians in front of you and around you," said Thunder Moon. "They are my friends, the Cheyennes, and they will keep you from trouble. Go to sleep now. You are all tired. In the morning I start for the village."

They took his word for it and went to their blankets, but Thunder Moon sat by the fire, the blanket huddled closely around his shoulders. He knew that he had come to a parting of the ways where he must choose one of the roads that branched before him. Drawing him toward the house of his father was his love of his family and the passion he felt for Charlotte Keene, and there was the pull also of his own blood and kind. On the other hand among the Cheyennes he was a force. He was like a king of the body and the spirit. There were other chiefs who led them, nominally, in war. But to Thunder Moon they turned as to a prophet and a preserver in times of evil. In peace they surrounded him with their adulation and their homage. He could not walk abroad without having respectful way made for him. The children flocked around him, as though to touch his hand would be to insure strength and fortune to them. Though he half knew that his mysterious authority was based upon a sham, yet in a way he could not be sure. The Sky People were to him half a superstition and half a fact.

The night grew colder and more still. The fires died. Only a blur of red light now glistened in the eyes of the picketed animals, or gleamed on the iron rims of the tires of the tall-wheeled wagons. This was the land of his knowledge and he loved it because he was familiar with it. Far away was the realm of the white man, and dreaded because it was unfamiliar.

Here upon the prairie he was a name which rang through all the red nations—Thunder Moon! But far to the east where his father's house stood, he was simply William Sutton, vaguely known as a man raised among the Indians—a nonentity—a thing without being, so far as the minds of other men were concerned. He sighed as he thought of it.

Looking up from his thoughts, he saw that it was the first glimmering of the gray dawn. Now he rose and, mounting the red stallion, he started back across the prairie. The Cheyennes swung in like gray ghosts to meet him, but he waved them back to their watch and bade them bring on the whites in the morning. Thus he went on swiftly.

The sun was half up over the horizon when the stallion waded through the creek and went up the slope beyond toward the village which already was up, for the Indian begins his day with the sun. Young women were coming down to the river for water. Boys stood about, shivering with the early cold. Warriors began to appear, wrapped in their buffalo robes. When he was sighted on his familiar horse, what a shout went up in welcome!

It was to Thunder Moon more than wine to the connoisseur. It was more than music to the music lover. Dignity was cast to the winds by these proud red men. They swarmed out about him. He had led them to battle the day before. The young braves had come back enriched in scalps, counting their coups. Half the night the scalp dance had lasted, the recounting of facts. Here was the author of that triumph.

They brought him in a tangle of cheers and exulting shouts to his lodge. He went in and found White Crow busily laying out the trophies which he had sent to her. It was rather a grisly sight. Complete in shirt and leggings of deerskin, heavily beaded because the dead man had been a Pawnee of note, with a mass of feathers for the head dress and with rifle and lance and knife and hatchet, it seemed as though more than a thin ghost of the dead were there.

White Crow turned to her foster son with a toothless grin of joy that almost made nose and chin touch.

"Last night a woman sang in the scalp dance," she said. "I told of the coups you had counted, oh, my son. I told how you had laid your braves in the tall grass. I told how the Pawnees were like puffs of smoke. You struck them and they disappeared forever. Spotted Bull is a great chief. He is a lucky warrior also. But my son is Thunder Moon. Ha! My soul is hungry to see the spirit of Big Hard Face. He must have leaned low from the happy hunting grounds last night to listen. All the people shouted your name together. Thunder Moon!"

He listened, delighted. If there was something childish about this, there also was something magnificent. He passed the pleasant thought away.

"Where is Red Wind?" he asked.

The jealous old squaw exclaimed: "Asleep, perhaps . . . that lazy creature. Or whispering with Standing Antelope. Hark what I have said to you a hundred times. No good ever has come from her. No good ever will come! She was bane to her father, bane to her people. She is poison and famine in the lodge. Now she talks with Standing Antelope. She makes his eyes as bright as the eyes of a hungry wolf. Is that a good thing? Be wise, Thunder Moon. A young woman is worse than firewater. Send her away. Give her to Standing Antelope. Let him have her!"

"Does he want her?" asked Thunder Moon gloomily.

"All the young men are fools. They look at her and turn their heads away as though she were a full sun in the middle of the sky. Do you ask me if they want her?"

"He is my friend," said Thunder Moon more cheerfully. "If he wants her, then he shall have her. First I must talk to her."

"Give her away . . . and talk to her afterwards," insisted White Crow. "She will not want to leave you. Now she has a lodge to herself. She only has to work for herself. Why should a useless woman wish to keep a lodge and do all the work for a warrior?"

Thunder Moon stepped outside the lodge and saw just before him a tall, athletic youth agape with pleasure and sorrow. Turning to look in the same direction, he saw Red Wind coming up from the river, carrying water, and the great braid of her copper hair shone like golden fire as it slipped down over her shoulder.

Chapter Eleven

Happy?

She came to Thunder Moon with a smile and paused before him. He waved her on into her teepee and followed her in. She, putting down the skin of water, turned to him and offered him the place of honor on a folded robe, with a comfortable backrest behind it. He refused with a curt gesture.

"Red Wind," he told her with a dignity of anger, "you have made me not happy."

She clasped her hands loosely before her and looked at him with submission.

"I am not wise," she said meckly. "Tarawa has not given me a mind like the sun or the moon. All of my days here seem to have gone by me like the wind over the prairie grass. Surely I have done nothing to make the great chief angry. I have had a dark thought, perhaps, and he has made medicine and he has read my mind."

Thunder Moon scowled darkly upon her. "Are you talking to some other person?" he asked. "Are you talking to some foolish other person, Red Wind? Between you and me there is an understanding. You know that the medicine I make is only for the eyes of the Cheyennes. We have no real belief in the Sky People."

"Do you deny them?" she asked him quickly. "Would you stand under the open sky and tell them that you deny them?"

He sighed and shook his head. "There is no more strength in my mind than there is in a chain of grass," he admitted. "But that is not true of you. There is no foolishness in you, Red Wind. There is nothing in you except thought. You laugh at the Sky People and at all the Indian ways, and at all the Indian medicine. Tell me if that is true?"

"How should I say that," asked the girl quietly. "Who am I not to believe what my master believes?"

"I am not your master."

"What are you then?"

"I have only tried to be your friend."

"The lodge that I live in is yours," she said.

"I have given it to you," he answered.

"Gifts," she said, "are given to those who deserve them. What have I deserved from you? Nothing . . . nothing! I have brought you only trouble. But this lodge is yours, and the backrests, and the weapons, and the beads . . . those bags and bags of them. Here out of the yellow and the green and the red beads, I have made you these moccasins, my master. I hoped to give them to you at a great feast but, now that you are angry with me, I give them to you as a peace offering."

She brought them to him. Made of the softest and the finest leather, she had worked them over with a consummate skill in strange patterns, such as he never before had seen. He took them and thanked her.

"But still you are laughing at me, Red Wind," he said. "In your heart you are laughing."

"In my heart, I am afraid."

"Why do you act as though you were a slave?" he said.

"What else am I?" she demanded. "I am not your daughter or your sister. If I were, you would sell me for a few horses to one of the men in the village. Perhaps you could find one who wants me. I am not your squaw. What am I, then, Thunder Moon?"

"Whenever you choose to play the child and be helpless," he grumbled, "there is no way that I can talk with you. But that is not fair to me, and I think that you know it."

"Tell me how I must speak to you," she asked. "The will of Thunder Moon is my will."

He stamped upon the floor of the teepee. "Do you want a husband?" he asked. "Twenty times I have begged you to tell me which one of the young men among the Cheyennes pleases you. Young Snake I have seen looking at you."

"What pleases you is pleasing to me," she replied.

"Answer me!" he commanded. "Tell me what you think!"

"Do I dare?" she asked plaintively. "Young Snake is a great friend of yours. He is your bravest warrior, next to Standing Antelope. If I should speak a bad word against him, you would beat me and have me weeping."

Thunder Moon went closer to her. He towered above her darkly.

"I have never raised a finger against any woman or against any child," he said. "This you know. Why do you speak to me in this fashion?"

Her eyes closed. "Oh, Thunder Moon," she murmured, "whatever I say is wrong. Whatever I do cannot please you."

"Speak truth, and be yourself," he begged. "There are wise women and cunning men among the Cheyennes,

325

but there is none like you. I myself am only a child compared with you. Why do you act in this way? Is it because you are partly white and partly Indian?"

Her eyes remained closed. He saw the long dark lashes against her skin. He could not tell why she had closed those eyes, or what thought was in her mind, or weariness, or disgust. From the beginning he never had been able to deal with her openly and easily. She was a problem beyond his solving.

"How can I tell what is the evil in me?" she asked. "Thunder Moon sees me, and understands much better."

He drew back from her, shaking his head. "Is it true that you hate me?" he asked her suddenly.

At this she opened her eyes. They were dull and angry.

"Hate?" she said.

"You saw the white woman whom I loved. You told her that you were my wife among the Cheyennes! That was a lie, Red Wind. Why did you lie to her?"

For almost the first time in his knowledge of her, he saw that she was staggered. Her color altered. She rested a hand against the nearest lodge pole.

"There are many rich men and wise men who loved her," said Red Wind at last. "Why should she have had you too?"

There was no acting now. Manifest fear was in her face.

He said slowly: "In spite of that, she has found me again."

"She!" cried Red Wind, starting most violently.

"She is one of the women in the wagon train the Pawnees raided."

"They could not find her body with a bullet!" cried the girl, with a sudden outbreak of savagery and despair.

Something like fear stirred the heart of Thunder Moon. He looked at her in amazement.

"She is alive and well," he answered sternly. "You would gladly have seen her dead in the attack. Is that true?"

She did not answer but watched him with a sort of sullen defiance, as one who realized that she had said too much to retract.

"After this," went on Thunder Moon, "there is only one thing you can do to help me. You must come with me to the white camp. You must go before her and tell her that on that other day you lied to her and that you never have been my squaw."

Red Wind turned pale indeed. "When must I go?" she asked.

"At once."

"Thunder Moon," said the girl in a trembling voice, "do what you wish to me today. But let me stay here till tomorrow in quiet. The wagon train will come close. It will be easier then for me to speak to her. I need a little time to think of what I must say. It is not easy even for a woman to admit that she has lied."

The big man sighed with pity. "That is true," he said. "Because of your pride, Red Wind, there are times when I admire you as I admire strong men. Because of beauty also, sometimes my heart has been open like the sky to the south wind, when it comes at the end of winter and turns the prairies green again. We shall wait until tomorrow before you speak to her. In the meantime it is not right that you should remain any longer as a part of my family. I see that bad talk has started. Everyone must be made to know that you are not my squaw, and it will be better for you to pick out a husband from among the Cheyennes."

She listened with great dark eyes that suddenly narrowed in thought.

"Then I must choose a husband?" she asked.

"It is better. You see that. When you do not have me to take care of you, you must go into the teepee of some warrior of the tribe."

"Then let it be Standing Antelope, if he will have me."

"He is young," cautioned Thunder Moon.

"He is brave enough to ride at your side, Thunder Moon."

"Shall I send for him?"

"No. I shall ask a boy to go with a message to Standing Antelope. When he comes, then I shall talk with him and ask him if he would have me for a wife."

"There is little doubt of that!"

"I shall ask him how many horses he will pay you for me . . . how many would you demand, Thunder Moon?"

He flushed at this. "You think," he said, "that I have kept you in order to make myself richer by giving you to some chief for a wife? No, no! This lodge and everything in it is freely yours. All the beads, and the robes, and the dressed deerskins, and the knives and the saddles. Besides that, I shall give you one of my best horses . . . one of those tall red horses. Standing Antelope will be as rich as any man in the tribe when he takes you for a squaw."

She bowed her head. "My master is like one of the Sky People," she said. "Where he gives his kindness, he gives greatness and wealth also."

"You will be happy then, Red Wind?"

"Happy?" she exclaimed.

She threw up her head and broke into such a wild laughter that Thunder Moon backed out of the teepee with trouble in his heart and went slowly into his own lodge. There he found White Crow waiting for him, her brows quizzically raised and a smile of cruel satisfaction on her withered lips.

Chapter Twelve

Red Wind's Vengeance

Left now to herself, Red Wind saw clearly and calmly that her back was against the wall and she pushed back the grief and the rage which invaded her mind. There were two natures mingled in her—that of the white and that of the Indian. If she had the wild heart of an Indian, she had a white brain, calm and clear.

Since that old day when her father had brought her among these Cheyennes and palmed her off upon Thunder Moon, she had worked cleverly, insistently, in her own way to win the love of that hero of the ugly face and the wide shoulders. A dozen times she told herself that she was victorious but never with more certainty than when she had gone into the white man's land, to the very house of Thunder Moon, and there had managed to draw him away from the woman he loved. The triumph had seemed complete. She would have wagered her soul that before another moon passed she would be installed in the lodge of the hero. While many a moon came and went, she seemed as far from him as ever.

Now was the end. She knew it beyond doubt and beyond hope. He had learned of the artifice and the lie with which she had kept the white girl from him and there would be no forgiveness.

From the door of her lodge, she called a scampering boy and asked him to carry her message to Standing Antelope. The boy was off like an arrow. It is a privilege to carry messages to a warrior so young, so brilliant, so famous. The girl retired once more into the lodge and sat down with her thoughts. The extent of her failure was clearer and clearer, and a boundless malice rose in her. All that love she had felt for the big man turned swiftly to poisonous grief, and then anger, and then settled hatred. She had offered him her soul in the palm of her hand, and he had turned his back upon her.

A voice at her lodge entrance. She called. Standing Antelope was before her. He was as different from Thunder Moon as were their names. The one was like a lordly bison bull, able to make the earth tremble and overawe the hearts of the strongest warriors. The other was like a soaring flame, as swift, as light, as dangerous. Those young hands of his had been filled with weapons by Thunder Moon himself, and by that warrior instructed in their use.

A painted buffalo robe was now gathered about the youth, but in spite of the things she could see that, like flame again, his whole body was trembling. His black, eager eyes gleamed at her. Here was fire, and it would burn at her bidding.

She stood up to greet him, gravely and gently, as she well knew how to speak to men, and she said in the metaphorical speech into which an Indian could always drop in time of need: "A woman should be like a child and never speak to warriors until she is first noticed. A shield which is cast down cannot leap up into the hands which own it, and a lance cannot strike if it has fallen to the ground and lies there unregarded. But I have been bold, and I have sent for you, Standing Antelope. White Crow will scold me for this. She will beat me afterwards."

The warrior's hand made a convulsive movement. The robe parted and she saw that he instinctively had grasped the handle of a knife.

"The tongue of an old woman," he said, "is like the tail of a puppy. It cannot stop wagging. But there are ways to prevent the falling of blows, Red Wind."

"What could I do?" asked the girl, making her eyes large with helpless grief and fear. "What can all the Cheyennes do? Have they any strength to place against the strength of Thunder Moon?"

Standing Antelope jerked up his head and set his teeth hard. "There are more winds in the sky than one," he said darkly. "The rain does not come out of one cloud only."

She shook her head. "When Thunder Moon speaks, all the Cheyenne warriors tremble. When he lifts his hand, they all bow their heads. How should I dare to speak against White Crow, or stop her hand, if she raises an unstrung war bow to strike me?"

"To strike you!" said Standing Antelope, half choked with emotion.

She had slipped on the bank of the river and bruised her arm against a rock only the day before. Now, with a swift movement, she exposed her arm to the elbow and showed the discolored bruise.

"That was to keep the blow from my head," she said.

The young brave folded his arms across his breast, as though by the strength of his own hands he were striving to compress and control his excitement.

"There is a chief in this tribe," he said. "Bald Eagle is a chief."

331

"Shall I complain to him? He would laugh in my face and send me away, for fear lest Thunder Moon should send disease to kill all his horses, or give him bad luck on the warpath."

Standing Antelope drew softly a step nearer: "You speak as people speak who do not know the whole truth. It is true that many of the warriors fear Thunder Moon. Many of them ride behind him. So do coyotes follow the grizzly bear, for the sake of the leavings after the kill has been made and the killer has feasted. The warriors are glad to ride behind Thunder Moon because, after he has struck, the least of the young boys are able to count coups and to take scalps. It does not mean that they follow him because they love him."

She looked down to the ground, to hide the burning exultation which she knew was springing up into her eyes. Then she sighed and said slowly: "If you give a horse grass from your hand, he is grateful and, if you throw meat to a dog, he kisses your hand. Therefore, of course the Cheyennes are grateful to Thunder Moon, and love him for the good he has done for them."

"They are not horses," said the youth, "and some of them are not dogs! Some of them know that Thunder Moon despises them. He uses them as men use a dog . . . to carry a burden, to run on an errand. He uses them at best like children. The council is called and all the old men speak, and the chiefs, and all of the experienced warriors who have taken scalps and counted many coups. After they have ended, Thunder Moon speaks like a voice from a cloud. He tells them that they have talked very wisely and very well, but he himself has wisdom from the Sky People and therefore they must do only what he advises them."

"But is it not true that the Sky People protect him and guide him?"

"Have you forgotten," said Standing Antelope, "how he had to run for his life from the white people? They were his own kind and his own blood. But they kicked him out as one kicks out a mangy dog through the lodge entrance. If the Sky People work for him, why did Big Hard Face have to lay down his life to save that of Thunder Moon? Why did not Thunder Moon turn and take the lightnings out of the sky and throw them in a river of fire against his enemies? No, we have seen him hunted with horses and dogs and guns, like a wolf. We have seen him running. Therefore, I say that all his talk about the Sky People is a great lie."

Having said this, Standing Antelope turned suddenly a little more toward the entrance, and his body stiffened. His glance rolled anxiously upward, as though he half expected that, in reward for such a blasphemy, the thunders of the actual sky might at that moment descend upon his head.

The girl saw and a faint smile of understanding and contempt flashed upon her lips, glimmered in her cold eyes, and was gone again. This boy was a tool, and no more than a tool. With him she could strike a glorious blow of revenge, she felt. She summoned an expression of terror and wonder and ran to the youth.

"Standing Antelope," she whispered. "Beware! Pray quickly to Tarawa before you are stricken. Pray for protection."

His lips were pale purple with his fear, but presently he mastered himself again and said as stoutly as he could: "You see that nothing happens. I am safe. I am safe because I am not afraid of Thunder Moon."

She affected an air of intensest admiration: "Oh, Standing Antelope," she said. "Is it true then? Are you alone among the Cheyennes able to stand against Thunder Moon? Are you alone able to save me from him?"

333

"Are you in danger from him?" asked the brave. "Does *he* also strike you?"

"The heaviest blows are not given with the hand," she said.

He waited, keen as a knife, for more.

"See how he keeps me here," she said. "I am neither his slave nor his sister nor his squaw. I am nothing! I am like a dog on a chain. It can only be seen. So am I. Thunder Moon keeps me here. He keeps me here so that he can point me out to strangers and to the whole tribe. It is because I satisfy his pride. He shows them what I am. "She is not worthy to be my squaw"' is what he means to say to them."

Standing Antelope made a gesture in the sign language. For many a time the Indian, overcome with emotion, still will speak in the language of gesture which is known to the entire people of the plains. Unable to speak, he now expressed vastest wonder that what he heard should be true. She continued in haste, following up the effect which already had shocked him so:

"What life have I? Even a horse is at least allowed to walk out to the pastures and run with the wind. But I cannot do that. If he will not have me, why will he not let others have me? What am I to him that he should want to keep me here? If a warrior or a young brave so much as looks at me, Thunder Moon frowns terribly, and the warriors turn their heads away and pretend that they were not looking at me at all."

She allowed her voice to rise softly to a little breaking point of vexation and grief.

Then Standing Antelope, his voice as shaken now as his body had been before, exclaimed: "This is wonderful, Red Wind! We all have thought . . . all of the warriors and the young braves . . . that you cared for nothing except Thunder Moon. That you lived because he willed you to live, and breathed because he willed you to breathe. Have we all been wrong?"

"Look at his picture in your own mind!" she answered with a wild enthusiasm of anger, letting her hatred shine boldly from her eyes: "Is there an uglier face on all of the prairies?"

Chapter Thirteen

The Double Edge

Personal beauty did not, as a rule, greatly disturb the thoughts of young Indian girls. Instead, they were more apt to fill their minds with the number of horses their prospective husband might own, the quantity of beads or weapons in his possession. A fine headdress of nodding feathers was apt to be more to them than the features of an Apollo.

Standing Antelope looked deeply into his mind and did not see any corresponding image for a moment. Then he stared at Red Wind again. Even among the white women of Thunder Moon's true people, he had remembered no beauty like hers. Next he recalled the heavy brow and the great aquiline nose and the broad jaw of Thunder Moon.

For his own part, he always had admired those features and envied them for fierceness and strength. That face, with battle shining in the eyes, had more than once made Blackfoot and Pawnees and Sioux flinch from the charge. He could see that the girl might have another viewpoint.

Beauty then for the beautiful! As he thought of this, he could not help but remember his own image in polished metal, in the mirrors which had amazed him in the house of Thunder Moon's father, and in the standing water of a pool when he leaned to drink. A shock of hope and pleasure ran hotly through the veins of the young brave.

"Tell me then," he said suddenly, "you always have hated Thunder Moon?"

"Ah, Standing Antelope," she said, "you have drawn the truth out of my heart. I could conceal nothing from you. Now you will go to Thunder Moon. He will kill me for speaking as I have spoken."

The warrior answered with a strange quickness.

"What you have told me is as much a secret as though you had spoken it only to your own heart. Will you believe that?"

"If you have said it. There are no lies on your tongue, Standing Antelope. All the other Cheyennes might scorn a woman so much they would not tell her the truth. They laugh in my face perhaps. But you are too proud to lie even to a woman."

He said: "You want freedom, Red Wind?"

"Ah, yes! I die for the lack of it, friend."

"I have not," said the youth, "a herd of great horses like Thunder Moon. I have not many rifles. I am not followed by many braves. Yet if you will come with me, as I tried to say to you not many days ago. . . ."

"Would you take me?"

"I? Tarawa see my heart."

"In spite of all the Cheyennes? Thunder Moon would follow us."

"The prairie is broad."

"The Sky People would point out our trail to him."

"Listen to me," said the boy, "I have often been with him on the trail and, once away from the camp, Thunder Moon is glad to let the other braves lead. He will not ride out from the camp unless he has in his party a good trailer, one who knows by a glance at the trampled grass how long before a horse had stepped upon it. No matter how the Sky People befriend him, they leave him blind upon the plains. This I know. I, as a young man, have shown that great chief the way, like a child led through the darkness."

"If he started to pursue us, he will have the finest trailers in the tribe to ride with him."

"Perhaps he will not pursue. There is a certain bigness in his heart. He might not pursue. He might simply let us ride away. I do not think that he would beg a woman to return to him after she once wanted to go away."

"Then why has he kept me here, like a wretched slave?"

He was silent, brooding upon this point. Remembering in a flood his old affection for Thunder Moon and all of the courage and the strength and the kindness which he had found in that famous man, his heart failed him a little. He looked at the girl with a keen thrust of suspicion.

She met that glance with a steady boldness of eye. He sighed. Her beauty was a solvent which loosened all of his thoughts. He could not face her and remain true to himself and the better heart which was in him.

"If we fled away together," said the girl, "he would not long remain behind us. He would soon pursue with others."

"Let them find our trail. We shall outride them if we cannot outwit them!"

"Who can outride the red horses?"

He struck his hands together.

"It is true," he admitted in despair. "It is very true that no one could ride away from the twenty men on his great horses." Then he added: "You are wise. Even Thunder Moon has asked for your advice and followed your counsel. Be wise now, Red Wind, and tell me what I can do. Look at me only as two hands which are willing to work for you."

It was exactly the point to which she had wished to bring him, but now she affected sorrow and despair in her turn again.

"There is only one way," she said.

"By which we could escape from him?"

"Yes."

"Then let me know."

She shook her head.

"You beg for your freedom. You will not open the door to it!" he exclaimed eagerly.

"It would be my freedom and your death," she said.

Sobered a little, he stared at her. With the slender staff which he carried in his hand, he struck upon the hard-packed earthen floor of the lodge.

"Who can tell when death will come?" he said. "I have done something in my life. I have counted coups. I have taken scalps. I have made myself known among the Cheyennes. The enemies of my people have heard my name. The chiefs come to me and speak kindly. When a party goes out upon the warpath, they ask me if I shall ride with them. I, like a fool, have refused to go, except when Thunder Moon was my leader. I have done something and, now, why should I be afraid to die? I am not afraid. Tell me in what way we can go free then?"

"I am his captive," she said slowly, "as long as he

338

lives. But a dead man has no hands to hold even a weak woman."

At this sudden suggestion, no matter how she had tried to lead up to it, the warrior shrank a little, and looked at her as though she had opened a pit that looked down to the bottom of the world.

He said at last, rather huskily: "To murder Thunder Moon?"

She did not answer. Passion, vengeance, envy, jealousy, dead love were all in her face. But no matter what feeds the fire, it casts a light. So her beauty, half Indian and half that of a white woman, flared before the eyes of Standing Antelope, and puzzled and bewildered him.

"Do you know," he said, "what comes to the man who murders in his own tribe?"

"He is outcast forever."

"That is true," said Standing Antelope. "I should be a man without a people."

"But Thunder Moon is no Cheyenne!"

"He is more than that. He is a stranger who has been trained among us. He has left us, and still he has come back. At this moment the warriors are speaking of him. His name is filling up their mouths since he drove Spotted Bull like a dog across the prairies."

"Let that be true," she said. "Ah, Standing Antelope, you do not know me. My heart has been full for many years. I have had no way to give out what is in it. If you were with me, I think that I could make you happy, even as a man without a people."

He did not touch her. A dazed look came in his eyes merely.

"It is time," said Standing Antelope simply. "When shall I kill him?"

"This night, this night!" said the girl with a wild eagerness. "Kill him this night, and then we shall ride under the cover of the darkness."

Amazed, he stared at her.

"Will you love as you hate?" he asked her.

"You will see," said the girl. "There is no flesh in me. There is nothing but fire, Standing Antelope. Kill this man, and then we may be happy together. If he lives, I shall burn up like a leaf in the autumn sun."

He hesitated, his eyes wandering swiftly from side to side.

"The best of all that is in the lodge I shall pack," she assured him.

She had mistaken his meaning. He answered hotly: "This was the gift of Thunder Moon. There is nothing here that is really yours. Take nothing. Strip off your rich clothes and the beadwork. If you have some old, tattered dress, take that."

"At least, we shall ride off on two of the red horses."

"Not for a single stride!"

"But he has given two of them to you."

"They are his gift," said the other sullenly and sadly. "I want nothing that is his. I shall not take the rifles he has given to me. Look. Nearly everything that I have is his gift. But I shall throw everything away except the little that is my own. I wish that Tarawa would give to me the power to strip off from my mind the things which Thunder Moon has taught me. That I cannot do. But if he has made my hand skillful, he has only given it the skill which will take his own life."

At this, as though the saying of the word brought up the vision of the dead brightly before him, he straightened himself with a swelling breast before her. And great, desperate eyes. Then he turned, and went hastily out of the lodge without speaking another word.

She, following to the flap of the teepee, looked after

him and saw him going off with a rapid but uncertain step. She gripped her right hand hard. Standing Antelope was a keen knife, to be sure, but the metal was apt to snap under a strain, she felt.

Chapter Fourteen

Brothers

In the heart of the afternoon, the wagon train came up. It did not cross the river, but remained upon the farther side of it, at the express suggestion of Thunder Moon. He too often had seen that white men and red cannot agree very long together, and the first gladness of meeting rapidly turns to trouble. He decided that he would keep the current of the river between the two camps.

Almost immediately, however, there was a flood of the red men among the wagons, their eyes and then their hands prying everywhere. Thunder Moon stood in the center of the camp and raised his great voice. Great as thunder it boomed and rolled among the scattered wagons of the circle. When he had finished his brief admonition in the Cheyenne tongue, the Indians gathered together and slunk off toward the river. Only their chiefs remained.

Bald Eagle had come bearing a present of beaded moccasins and three Indian ponies, the fattest and therefore the best of his herd.

Colonel Keene received him, with Thunder Moon acting as the interpreter, received the presents, made others in return, chiefly of good knives of which the tribe at this moment was in great need. For working on hides of tough buffalo bulls and cows for teepees wears out knives faster than anything in the world.

The exchanges being made, the colonel showed himself astonishingly liberal to other chiefs who had accompanied Bald Eagle, until that dignitary, his arms literally filled with what to him were magnificent treasures— strings of beads hanging from his arms and half a dozen hickory hafts for axes thrusting out like pins from a pin cushion—at last said to Colonel Keene:

"In the land of the white man, there is a great medicine. It turns thoughts into knives and bullets, and wishes into beads and bright cloth. We only can give you meat and robes of buffalo hides. But our hearts are very warm. We thank you and we thank Thunder Moon who has drawn so many good things to the Cheyennes."

The chiefs departed. Colonel Keene set about looking for William Sutton in person, but that unreclaimed white man was seated in a corner of the wagon circle lost in conversation with Charlotte Keene. The colonel, after one long look, turned elsewhere.

Thunder Moon had said to the girl: "The Cheyennes do not tell lies except to public enemies. I am going to call the biggest of the chiefs. You shall hear him say whether or not I have a wife among his people."

But she answered frankly: "Do you think that I've come all these hundreds and hundreds of miles to argue with you, or to take testimony? I don't care! There's only one important thing . . . which is that you and I are sitting on the double trees of this particular wagon in this particular place. I know that and I don't care about the rest."

He watched her with a content too deep for speech.

All that existed on the prairies seemed, at that moment, little enough compared with her.

"If you've come here," he said suddenly, "would you stay here, Charlotte?" She looked down to the ground. He could feel that she had been struck a blow, but she glanced up to him again almost immediately, and said: "I can stay here."

"It would be a wilder and a harder life than you've been accustomed to," he assured her.

"Not so hard as my life since you left me, William."

He was silent for a moment, listening to an echo of her voice, as it were, pronouncing his Christian name— so long unfamiliar in his ears.

"I could build a house for us. Do you see where the hills begin to go up there?"

"It looks like blue, rolling smoke."

"Yes."

"I see them more clearly now."

He smiled at her.

"You will learn to use your eyes in this country. If you look still harder, you'll see the mountains beyond the hills."

"They're almost lost against the sky," she said.

"The fleck of white. . . . more blue than white, but with a shine in them . . . those are the snow caps of the mountains."

"Ah!"

"There where the hills and the mountains divide?"

"Yes, I see the gap, I think."

"A great river comes down from the highlands there. I've chosen the valley. We could build there."

"Yes," she said.

"Does the thought of it make you sad?"

"Nothing really makes me sad today," she answered obliquely.

This humility in her disturbed him more than any prayers that he should go back with her to the whites of her home. He remembered her in other days, imperially ruling among the youth of the countryside and the old white houses. Now she submitted, swallowed all argument.

He, watching her more closely, saw the stain of blue beneath her eyes which made them seem larger and deeper. Grief had placed that stain there, he knew well enough. A great tenderness came upon Thunder Moon. He scanned her more and more closely, like a book—a book whose mere title he had seen and loved before, but this was all the closely compacted print, filled with infinite meaning he had not known. Her very face was half strange to him. The longer he gazed, the more deeply he was staring.

"You think of your friends," he said.

"Yes, I think of them."

"If you think of them a little today, you will think of them a great deal later on."

"Perhaps. But that will not keep me away, William. I'm not a weak thing, to sit and mourn and complain. You must trust me in saying that."

"I do trust you. Out of this thing we're going to find happiness, Charlotte."

She turned her head and smiled at him and, by that single glance, he knew truly the depth of her love which had brought her here to him. Facts could not have demonstrated it, any more than words can illustrate music.

He went to the colonel and told him the conclusion briefly. "Charlotte agrees that she'll try to live out here with me."

The colonel sighed. "Charlotte would agree to anything," he said. Then he added: "Now, my lad, I won't begin with giving you advice. Your lives are your own.

Only permit me to say: no one gets something for nothing in this world of ours. We pay as we go. A bad investment leaves you bankrupt in the end."

"I don't quite understand that."

"I mean that the sorrow you cause is the sorrow that you will eventually have to feel."

Thunder Moon, turning this thought in his head, went back toward the village. There was to be a feast at which all the chief men would appear. The colonel and Jack Sutton would be there.

Indeed, he found Jack Sutton already in the village, having broken through the express orders that no one was to leave the wagon circle. Jack was surrounded by a large and curious throng. Men and women pressed about him. Children dived reckless among the edge of their elders, and so strove to creep through the forest and come to the sight of the white man. As Thunder Moon came up, he heard over and over again the simple phrase:

"It is the brother of Thunder Moon! It is the blood brother! It is the brother of our medicine man!"

He smiled a little, with a lifted heart. Standing Antelope at that moment went by hastily, with his light, noiseless step, and Thunder Moon reached out to him and caught him by the shoulder.

The boy winced away from the grip and turned for an instant a dangerously darkened face. Every Indian is the master of some degree of dissimulation and, almost instantly, he made his face clear again.

"You still are a sick man," said Thunder Moon gently. "I shall have to take care of you. You must come to my lodge and eat what White Crow cooks for you. She is a wise old woman. She knows the herbs."

"My brother is kind," said the youth, his voice extraordinarily faint.

"Look," said the big man, "you are pale. Your very voice is weak. You no longer are always dancing on the tips of your toes, trying to make yourself taller. Ha? Standing Antelope, I shall have to pay more attention to you. If you had been with me yesterday, you would have taken three scalps and counted half a dozen coups, and that without the slightest danger. I must have you closer beside me from this time forward."

Standing Antelope said not a word.

"Have you seen my brother Jack?"

"No."

"What? Not seen him yet? See how they crowd around him. But we'll break through, I think."

He laughed with pleasure at the thought of his power over these wild people. Jack Sutton was calling: "They have me half choked with dust already, Will!"

At a single word from Thunder Moon, the crowd opened and gave back rapidly. They smiled and chattered gaily at the sight of the two brothers, standing side by side, and exclaimed hastily: "But he is not so tall! Nor so wide! Nor so big in the feet and the hands! He is hardly a brother to Thunder Moon!"

Thunder Moon strode on, dragging Standing Antelope with him, and exclaimed at last: "Here's my brother among the Cheyennes, Jack! You've not forgotten Standing Antelope?"

Standing Antelope, who understood the words perfectly, closed his teeth hard to keep back a groan.

Chapter Fifteen

With Steel in Their Hands

It was Bald Eagle in person who noted the wild and unhappy look of Standing Antelope and took occasion to stop him a little apart from the crowd.

"Brother," said the war chief, "your friend has become greater than ever on this day. Therefore, you are greater also, and yet I see a shadow on your forehead. How can this be?"

The boy answered nothing for a moment but considered the older man. At length he said grimly: "Your arms have been filled with presents. Another such a day and you will have to live in two lodges. One for yourself and one for your wealth. Still you do not seem happy, Bald Eagle."

That battered chieftain frowned at this readiness of tongue in so young a warrior, and he said sternly: "A youth listens. An older man speaks!"

"To what do *you* listen, then?" asked Standing Antelope. "To your own heart, do you not?"

"All men listen to their voice of the spirit," said the chieftain.

"Let me tell you, then," said the boy, "that your heart has been beating so loudly that even I heard it."

Bald Eagle could not make a reply, but it was plain that he was startled.

"I have heard your heart say," went on Standing Antelope, "that although your arms have been filled with gifts . . . beads and guns and powder and lead and knives . . . and everything that the heart of a great warrior could wish, yet you had rather that this day and those presents never had come to you."

The chieftain pulled his robe about his shoulders with a convulsively impatient gesture.

"What do you wish to say to me, Standing Antelope?" he asked. "Have you been drinking the white man's firewater and grown dim in the brain, like a mountain wrapped in a mist?"

"I have not been drinking firewater," said the boy, "but I have been looking at the heart of the great chief and war leader, Bald Eagle, and I see fire in it . . . smoke and fire about to break out. The heart of Bald Eagle is very hot. Of what use is his name as war chief? The young men follow Thunder Moon on the warpath. How do they regard Bald Eagle? He is only a name and no more to them."

The chief was thrown into such a frenzy of anger by this speech that, for a moment, he seemed about to fling himself at the throat of the youngster, but he controlled himself long enough to say in a voice like distant thunder: "Has he sent you to me to give me these taunts?"

Standing Antelope answered quickly: "Look at me, Bald Eagle! It is not as a stranger or a spy that I have understood what is within you."

Bald Eagle's wrath was quite dissipated by astonishment as he listened to this speech, and he answered: "Young man, do I understand that you are telling me that Thunder Moon no longer is your friend?"

"How can he be my friend?" answered the boy. "He keeps in a lodge beside him a woman, like a dog on a chain. He would not give her to me for the price of a hundred good horses."

"Red Wind . . . Red Wind!" exclaimed the chief softly. "I know that friendship is more powerful than rawhide ropes, well twisted. But a woman is stronger still. With a touch of her hand she snaps stronger ropes of kindness than these. The Sioux give us war outside the camp. Our women give us battles inside our lodges. That is what has happened to you, Standing Antelope."

The boy, somewhat heated by the implied reproach or contempt in the words of the other, said hastily: "When a man is sick of a great fever, does he laugh at the doctor who can cure him?"

Bald Eagle's eyes narrowed to squints.

"One says to the doctor, how will the cure be made? With prayer and medicine . . . or how?"

Standing Antelope looked swiftly about him, and then stepped closer.

"With the knife," he whispered.

The nostrils of Bald Eagle expanded.

"Come with me," he said. "It is plain that we have much to say to one another."

Never in the history of the tribe had there been a greater feast. An Indian feast is not made with food but with conversation and here, present among them, were the kin of that man of mystery, Thunder Moon. They looked at the thoughtful face of the colonel, and upon the handsome, pale features of Jack Sutton. They said among themselves: "Truly, Thunder Moon has something more than an Indian name and a Cheyenne tongue. He has also no little part of the blood of a Cheyenne by sympathy. See his face! It is almost as dark as ours! His features are those of an Indian. His hair and his eyes are as dark as ours. His way is our way and he is one of us!"

While Jack Sutton was saying to his brother: "You are a great man to these people, Will."

"Do you wonder," said Thunder Moon, "that I can't leave them forever?"

"You could come out to see them every year or so," suggested Jack Sutton.

"Perhaps I could. But the tribe would be wandering. They might be scattered to the four winds before I came back again. As a matter of fact, I think that I have had some share in holding them together."

"They admire you. They know that you're useful," said Jack Sutton, "but how many friends have you really among them?"

"There is Standing Antelope," answered the big man. "He's young, but he's a man. I've seen him tested in fire."

"Where is he tonight?"

"Sick, in his lodge. I've been to see him. He has a fever. Hands dry and forehead hot. Tomorrow I begin a course of medicine for him."

"He has a dark look, that youngster," said Jack Sutton. "Who is that about to speak?"

"They are passing the coup stick," said Thunder Moon, smiling faintly. "Do you hear?"

"I hear, but I don't understand. What does the hard-faced old chap say?"

"That he who has counted five and thirty coups in battle shall be permitted to hold the stick and count three coups which he has struck. This is a compliment to me, Jack. You see, none of the rest has counted so many.

"I shall count one coup," Thunder Moon said in Cheyenne, the coup stick now in his hand. "The Comanches sleep in a great tent. The Yellow Man is among them, a great medicine. Among all the Comanches there is no medicine half so strong as this."

A murmur went through the circle. A hundred times they had heard the story, and a hundred times their eyes had gleamed exactly as they gleamed now.

"The circles of the warriors sleep with bows and rifles at their sides," continued the narrator. "But one man comes among them. He is a Cheyenne. He goes from tent to tent like a shadow. The Sky People breathe in the faces of the sleepers. They are like the dead. The stranger passes . . . one man rises, half awake. The Cheyenne strikes, and the man is still. His medicine bag is in the hands of the Cheyenne. His soul is lost forever. The warrior goes on. His heart is not afraid. He comes to a greater tent. It is the medicine lodge. Within it sleeps one man, or hardly sleeps. He rises. He prays. He prays to the Yellow Man. The shadow of Thunder Moon soon falls upon him. He feels the cold hand of death. The hand reaches forth and is laid upon him. He is dead. The Yellow Man is taken. Upon him Thunder Moon counted a great coup! He struck the face of the Comanche medicine. He waited, ready for thunder and lightning. But nothing followed. The Yellow Man did not stir. Thunder Moon picked him up and fled with him through the camp. He was followed, but he escaped. Comanches lay dead behind him. There was blood on his hands. He came again to his friends. The Comanches had lost their strong medicine. This coup that I counted was a true coup. It was struck on the body of the Yellow Man."

He passed the coup stick from him.

"Let he who has counted fifteen coups receive this stick!"

Thunder Moon translated to his brother softly, and added: "Bald Eagle can speak of this coup. He's a great warrior."

Bald Eagle spoke. Others followed. Briefly, and in murmurs, Thunder Moon translated the sum of the tales

which were narrated, and the other two white men beside
him listened, fascinated, to bloody and wild deeds done
in the midst of fierce battles, or in the camp of the enemy
in the dead of the night.

The night grew old. The colonel himself was asked to
narrate one deed he had done. He told, briefly—while
Thunder Moon translated—of an adventure with Gulf
pirates while on a pleasure cruise—and Jack Sutton con-
tributed a narrative of the hunting of the marsh brigands
through their lairs. There was much applause and, at
length, with a prodigious handshaking all around, the
feast ended. Thunder Moon accompanied his brother and
the colonel out of the tent.

A crowd followed but left them at the edge of the
village.

"As odd and interesting an evening as I ever passed
through," said the colonel. "But why are you down-
hearted, Thunder Moon?"

"Because," said the other, "I cannot understand this.
They should have sent out twenty young men . . . with
torches, perhaps . . . to show us the way to the wagons.
I don't understand it. What's in the mind of Bald Eagle?"

"He's forgotten, of course."

"Indians never forget their manners until they are
about to run amok," replied Thunder Moon and, still
gloomily thoughtful, he went with the others down the
slope toward the bank of the river.

"I go first," he said. "Watch the rocks that I step on.
At this height of the water, there's no need for you so
much as to wet the soles of your boots. Watch me cross,
and then follow."

He went lightly, jumping from rock to rock, across

the river. As he reached the farther shore and turned toward his two companions who were about to follow, silent, shadowy forms arose from the brush behind him, with the gleam of steel in their hands.

Chapter Sixteen

On the River

The quick old eye of the colonel saw the danger first. His shout of horror was not a word—simply a vague, piercing cry—and it turned Thunder Moon about to find bright-edged steel gleaming in his very eyes and the voice of Standing Antelope exclaiming: "No bullets! No bullets! Bullets never can kill him! Only the edge of the knife! Only the edge of the knife!"

But if bullets could not kill Thunder Moon, knives surely were at his throat. He leaped far back from the rush, his revolver coming into his hand as he sprang, and he made out, with horror and bewilderment, that one of those close assailants was no less a person than that trusted lieutenant, Young Snake. Two more came behind the first pair, with Standing Antelope rushing into the lead, swift as a panther.

A gun boomed heavily from across the river. It was Jack Sutton's rifle, for he had carried the gun with him and, with a shot which was partly quick skill and partly luck, he sent a bullet through the head of Thunder Moon's right hand man. The fellow toppled without a sound, his loose shoulder striking literally across Thunder Moon's knees. A shot from the Colt doubled up the second of the leaders, and there was Standing Antelope, coming in with the screech of a wildcat. There was time for a bullet, but in the last instant Thunder Moon could not draw the trigger. Instead, he swayed aside from the flash of steel, and struck at the lithe body with his fist. Hard upon the ribs the blow struck home. Standing Antelope, stunned, bruised, breathless, dropped writhing upon the river bank.

The fourth man had swerved like a football player as he saw the mischief into which his companions had fallen and was merely a crackle of faint sound as he shot off through the brush.

Thunder Moon did not follow. Heartsick and bewildered, he leaned over the fallen. Young Snake was gasping out his last breath. Over him Thunder Moon leaned as his brother and the colonel came floundering through the water to get to his side, quite missing the way across the dry rocks.

As he leaned over Young Snake, Thunder Moon saw plain recognition and plain hatred in the face of the wounded brave.

"Young Snake," he said, "I have mounted you with one of my best horses. I have led you on to much honor. Never before had you counted a coup or taken a scalp until you came among my followers. Why have you tried to murder me like a wolf of a Pawnee?"

"Because I am not your dog, to come and go when you whistle. And because . . . I hated your pale face."

So spoke Young Snake, and snapped at the air over his shoulder with a last convulsion of savagery and fury, and died.

Thunder Moon leaned above Standing Antelope, who

was raising himself to his hands and knees. He stood upright and folded his hands across his breast. He was naked to the waist. He was painted as for war. Two eagle feathers were thrust into the long black masses of his hair, which glimmered in the starlight. He waited in silence for the falling of the blow as the colonel and Jack Sutton came breathlessly ashore.

"Standing Antelope!" cried Jack in horror.

Thunder Moon waved the two aside and drew the boy aside.

"I am sick with sorrow and trouble," said Thunder Moon bitterly. "You too, like Young Snake, always have hated me?"

The boy tried to answer, and at length he forced from his lips a gasping: "The Sky People still watch over you. Strike me now to the heart. I shall not speak again."

"Lad," answered the older man gently, "we have traveled too many trails together. You are as free as though you still were my best of friends among the Cheyennes. Tarawa forgive you and purify your mind. Will you not tell me what made you come at me . . . in the night . . . with three fighters to help you? Murder, Standing Antelope! Thank the spirits who have saved you from it!"

Standing Antelope, trembling like a leaf, answered: "I did not hate you always, as the rest have done. It was because you would not take Red Wind for yourself, nor give her to anyone else."

Thunder Moon exclaimed in bewilderment: "This very day I told her that she should take you for a husband. This very day, Standing Antelope! Are you mad?"

"You?" cried the boy. "You told her that?"

"Yes, yes. This morning. When I came to speak to her, because she had said among the whites a thing about me that was not true."

"Ha!" breathed Standing Antelope, and reeled heavily.

355

The arm of Thunder Moon supported him. "My young brother," he said, "she has lied to you also. Is it truth?"

"Why?" groaned Standing Antelope. "What devils could be in her?"

"I shall find her for you, if you want her, and give her to you, for that is my right," said Thunder Moon.

"Shall I make a liar into my squaw who keeps my lodge and raises my children?" asked the boy fiercely. "But now I see more things, and more clearly. It is the white squaw, oh, Thunder Moon! It is the white squaw that has driven Red Wind mad with jealousy. On account of her she has tried to bring about your murder and she has simply used my knife! She said that she would wait for me up the river at the three trees. But now I know that she will not be there. She has betrayed you. She has betrayed me. Why was I ever born?"

He turned from Thunder Moon and ran off through the brush, heading swiftly up the river.

Thunder Moon turned back to his two white companions. Down from the village, on the farther side of the river, came dancing lights, as men and boys ran to learn what had caused the wild shouts and the explosions of guns. The light of the torches fell like the tresses of gleaming red hair spread over the surface of the water.

"See," said the big man slowly. "The river was between me and my life as a Cheyenne. The river is between us, and I never can cross it again. There is blood upon the water. This night my friends have gone from me. I was a Cheyenne. My name was Thunder Moon. All the prairies knew me. But Thunder Moon is dead. Do you hear? The knife of Standing Antelope found the heart of that chief. He is dead. He will return no more."

He started resolutely ahead, drawing the two with him.

"I was two people in one," he said, with a sudden

calmness, "but now one half of me is dead. I am going home to my own people. I am William Sutton at last."

Farther up the river the Cheyenne boy, Standing Antelope, leaped breathlessly out from the covert and ran beneath the three trees where Red Wind should have been waiting for him.

She was not there. There was no sight of her. There was no sound. Only the wind hushed through the leaves of the trees with a hissing sound.

About the Author

Max Brand™ is the best-known pen name of Frederick Faust, creator of Dr. Kildare, Destry, and many other fictional characters popular with readers and viewers worldwide. Faust wrote for a variety of audiences in many genres. His enormous output, totaling approximately thirty million words or the equivalent of 530 ordinary books, covered nearly every field: crime, fantasy, historical romance, espionage, Westerns, science fiction, adventure, animal stories, love, war, and fashionable society, big business and big medicine. Eighty motion pictures have been based on his work along with many radio and television programs. For good measure he also published four volumes of poetry. Perhaps no other author has reached more people in more different ways.

Born in Seattle in 1892, orphaned early, Faust grew up in the rural San Joaquin Valley of California. At Berkeley he became a student rebel and one-man literary movement, contributing prodigiously to all campus publications. Denied a degree because of unconventional conduct, he embarked on a series of adventures culminating in New York City where, after a period of near starvation, he received simultaneous recognition as a serious poet and successful popular-prose writer. Later, he traveled widely, making his home in New York, then in Florence, and finally in Los Angeles.

Once the United States entered the Second World War, Faust abandoned his lucrative writing career and his work as a screenwriter to serve as a war correspondent with the infantry in Italy, despite his fifty-one years and a bad heart. He was killed during a night attack on a hilltop village held by the German army. New books based on magazine serials or unpublished manuscripts or restored versions continue to appear so that, alive or dead, he has averaged a new book every four months for seventy-five years. In the United States alone nine publishers now issue his work. Beyond this, some work by him is newly reprinted every week of every year in one or another format somewhere in the world. Yet, only recently have the full dimensions of this extraordinarily versatile and prolific writer come to be recognized and his stature as a protean literary figure in the 20th century acknowledged. His popularity continues to grow throughout the world.

MAX BRAND
TWO SIXES

To read the work of Max Brand is to experience the Old West in all of its glory, energy, and humanity. And here, all restored to their original length, and collected in paperback for the first time, are three of Max Brand's greatest short novels. In "Winking Lights," a chance encounter and burning curiosity lead a rider to an ancient hacienda and a trapped young woman. A tenderfoot in a Mexican border town learns hard lessons about trusting gunfighters in "The Best Bandit." And in the title novel, a frontier gambler is given a rare second chance in life . . . if he's willing to take it.

___4508-7 $4.99 US/$5.99 CAN

Dorchester Publishing Co., Inc.
P.O. Box 6640
Wayne, PA 19087-8640

Please add $1.75 for shipping and handling for the first book and $.50 for each book thereafter. NY, NYC, and PA residents, please add appropriate sales tax. No cash, stamps, or C.O.D.s. All orders shipped within 6 weeks via postal service book rate. Canadian orders require $2.00 extra postage and must be paid in U.S. dollars through a U.S. banking facility.

Name_____
Address_____
City_____State_____Zip_____
I have enclosed $_____ in payment for the checked book(s).
Payment <u>must</u> accompany all orders. ❑ Please send a free catalog.
CHECK OUT OUR WEBSITE! www.dorchesterpub.com

MAX BRAND
SIXTEEN IN NOME

Joe May, an overgrown youth with a skinny neck and a large Adam's apple, has eaten only once in the last thirty-six hours and is feeling desperate. When he provides a small service for Hugh Massey, owner of the most famous husky in Alaska, all Joe has in mind is a possible reward. He heard that Massey's life revolves around that dog . . . and a chance to murder the man he hates with an undying rage. But he never thinks he will become the bait Massey needs to lure his enemy into a deadly trap—a trap that will set off an epic trek across hundreds of miles of frozen country, to a river of ice known as the Yukon.

___4486-2 $4.50 US/$5.50 CAN

MAX BRAND

THE ABANDONED OUTLAW

No writer captures the American West better than Max Brand. And nowhere is Brand's talent more evident than in these three classic short novels, all restored to their original length, and collected in paperback for the first time. In "The Gold King Turns His Back," young Miriam Standard is more than capable of running her father's ranch, but finds she has much to learn about the Westerners' meaning of honor. In "The Three Crosses," an ominous prediction leads a cowpuncher to a showdown with a notorious gunfighter. And the title novel finds a young woman caught in the middle of a lifelong rivalry between two men, one of whom is an outlaw. Experience the West as only Max Brand could write it!

___4465-X $4.50 US/$5.50 CAN

Dorchester Publishing Co., Inc.
P.O. Box 6640
Wayne, PA 19087-8640

Please add $1.75 for shipping and handling for the first book and $.50 for each book thereafter. NY, NYC, and PA residents, please add appropriate sales tax. No cash, stamps, or C.O.D.s. All orders shipped within 6 weeks via postal service book rate. Canadian orders require $2.00 extra postage and must be paid in U.S. dollars through a U.S. banking facility.

Name_____
Address_____
City_____State_____Zip_____
I have enclosed $_____ in payment for the checked book(s).
Payment <u>must</u> accompany all orders. ❏ Please send a free catalog.

MAX BRAND

SLUMBER MOUNTAIN

Here, for the first time in paperback, are three of Max Brand's best short novels, all restored to their original glory from Brand's own typescripts and presented just as he intended. "Outland Crew" is an exciting tale of gold fever and survival in a frontier mining town. In "The Coward," a man humiliated in a gunfight finds a fiendishly clever way of exacting revenge. And in "Slumber Mountain," Brand presents a harrowing story of man versus the wilderness as a trapper fights for his life against the mighty wolf known as Silver King.

___4442-0 $4.99 US/$5.99 CAN

The Lightning Warrior

The Indians call the great white wolf the Lightning Warrior because of the swiftness of his attack. But even the giant Colbolt isn't interested in the massive wolf until Sylvia Baird makes the beast's pelt the one condition for her hand in marriage. She thinks she is safe, but when he returns with not only the pelt, but the wolf itself, and demands his prize, Sylvia's only hope is a desperate flight for freedom. Colbolt sets out in determined pursuit, but he's forgotten Sylvia's newest ally. . .the Lightning Warrior.

___4420-X $4.50 US/$5.50 CAN

Dorchester Publishing Co., Inc.
P.O. Box 6640
Wayne, PA 19087-8640

Please add $1.75 for shipping and handling for the first book and $.50 for each book thereafter. NY, NYC, and PA residents, please add appropriate sales tax. No cash, stamps, or C.O.D.s. All orders shipped within 6 weeks via postal service book rate. Canadian orders require $2.00 extra postage and must be paid in U.S. dollars through a U.S. banking facility.

Name_____
Address_____
City_____State_____Zip_____
I have enclosed $_____ in payment for the checked book(s).
Payment <u>must</u> accompany all orders. ❑ Please send a free catalog.
CHECK OUT OUR WEBSITE! www.dorchesterpub.com

OUTLAWS ALL

From Alaska to the Southwest, Max Brand, the master of the Western tale, brings the excitement of the frontier to life like no one else. His characters live, breathe, struggle and triumph in a world so real you can hear the creaking of the saddle leather. Gathered in this collection are three classic short novels by Brand, all filled with the adventure and heroism, the guts and the gunsmoke, that made the West what it was.

___4398-X $4.50 US/$5.50 CAN